The
LAST DAYS *of*
NEWGATE

ANDREW PEPPER

PHOENIX

A PHOENIX PAPERBACK

First published in Great Britain in 2006
by Weidenfeld & Nicolson
This paperback edition published in 2007
by Phoenix,
an imprint of Orion Books Ltd,
Orion House, 5 Upper St Martin's Lane,
London WC2H 9EA

An Hachette Livre UK company

9 10

Reissued 2011

A CIP catalogue record for this book
is available from the British Library.

ISBN 978-0-7538-2168-8

Typeset at the Spartan Press Ltd,
Lymington, Hants

Printed and bound in Great Britain by
Clays Ltd, St Ives plc

The Orion Publishing Group's policy is to use papers that
are natural, renewable and recyclable products and
made from wood grown in sustainable forests. The logging
and manufacturing processes are expected to conform to
the environmental regulations of the country of origin.

www.orionbooks.co.uk

Andrew Pepper lives in Belfast, where he is a lecturer in English at Queen's University. His first novel, *The Last Days of Newgate*, was shortlisted for the CWA New Blood Dagger.

By Andrew Pepper

The Last Days of Newgate
The Revenge of Captain Paine
Kill-Devil and Water
The Detective Branch

For Debbie

[T]he gulf between how one should live and how one does live is so wide that a man who neglects what is actually done for what should be done learns the way to self-destruction rather than self-preservation.

NICCOLÒ MACHIAVELLI, *The Prince*

PART I

*

London, England

FEBRUARY 1829

ONE

A metallic glint preceded the thrust of a knife blade, as a voice, a female voice, shouted his name.

'*Pyke.*'

It may have saved his life.

The blade drew blood on his neck, a nick rather than a wound, and, turning like a whip, he stared into the hate-filled eyes of his attacker. Michael Flynn lunged at him again but this time he swayed backwards and avoided the blade's arching loop, steadying himself before taking a grip of the Irishman's wrist and snapping it sideways in a clean jerk that may well have broken bone. Flynn's shriek confirmed his pain and, more importantly for Pyke, the knife clattered harmlessly on to the taproom's sawdusted floor. Pyke released his assailant's limp wrist and surveyed the mass of hostile faces assembled in the taproom of the Blue Dog tavern. He saw the back of her bonnet, bobbing as she hurried for the door, but she was too far away to be stopped. Later, he could not be sure he had not seen her face as well, but no clear image lodged in his mind. Momentarily he considered going after her, but he had more pressing issues to address. Though wounded, Flynn remained a dangerous adversary and Pyke wasted no time in retrieving the knife from the floor and pressing the blade against the receiver's throat. His fee for sending his former associate to certain death on the gallows would be a mere ten guineas. It would have made practical sense to slit the man's throat in the alley outside the tavern and leave him for the resurrectionists but, whatever else he was, Pyke was not an assassin.

Instead he delivered the papist thief to his Bow Street offices and roughly pushed him into the felons' room, ignoring the man's threats to expose him.

It may have seemed incongruous, to some, that, only a few hours later, Pyke was being transported in an open carriage through the manicured grounds of an English aristocrat whose wife had claimed ancestry with the first earl of Essex, but he was neither amused nor unsettled by having to move between different worlds. Nor was he concerned by the inequalities such a difference drew attention to. He would leave such thoughts to the politicians: the blustering Whig aristocrats who spoke about freedom and responsibility in public and abused their servants in private, and Tory landowners who cared nothing about the hardships their wealth and privilege created for others.

Pyke had no time for radical sentiment, nor was he what one might call a monarchist. But he managed to amuse himself, if only for a moment, with the agreeable thought of a mob from the Blue Dog overrunning Lord Edmonton's country home and hunting him with scythes and axes.

The carriage, a new, lighter two-wheeled cabriolet, had covered the treacherous terrain from Bow Street and north through Hackney and Homerton in less time than a short-stop stagecoach. Yet it had left him exposed to the elements and Pyke cursed Edmonton for insisting they meet at Hambledon Hall rather than at one of his town houses. That, and the inclement weather, redoubled Pyke's determination to charge Edmonton at least twice the figure the old man intended to offer him.

As the afternoon rain began to clear, the old Elizabethan

hall became visible, its crenellated stone walls and Gothic, semi-fortified tower reminders of an era long gone. Still, Pyke was disappointed by the distinctly shabby interior. There were none of the excesses that he had been expecting. Lit dimly by gas lamps and candles, the entrance hall had the feel of an empty tomb. Pyke reluctantly allowed one of the servants to take his heavy coat and was informed that Edmonton would be down to greet him in due course. Etiquette demanded that Pyke remain where he was, and so he unhesitatingly made his way through large doors into the Great Hall, an unappealing room cluttered with dark furniture and adorned with a gallery of grim-faced ancestral portraits. Ornately carved wooden brackets held up the heraldic panels of the ceiling. In the distance Pyke heard the soft notes of a piano and followed the sounds through another smaller set of doors, along a corridor and to the threshold of a lounge room warmed by a fire.

From the doorway, and without drawing attention to his presence, he watched Emily Blackwood, Lord Edmonton's only progeny. Pyke followed her fingers as they stroked the piano's keys and noted a contradiction between her expression, fixed in concentration, and her body, which moved in time with the rhythm of what she was playing.

She wore an embroidered muslin dress that enhanced her delicate frame. Her dark hair was gathered in a simple comb and offset her pale skin. He admired her fine looks as someone might appreciate a painting by Turner, an object that was pleasing to the eye but ultimately bland. Far better than Turner, for Pyke, was Hogarth, with his scenes of despair and violence. Better still was Hieronymus Bosch; those phantasmagoric images of human suffering made him feel, at once violated and aroused. In short, there was something too virtuous about Emily Blackwood, an element that shone from within her and made her not just unobtainable but somehow too perfect. He wondered whether she might crumble or snap into pieces, should anyone try to fuck her.

Though reluctant to spoil the moment, he feigned a cough. She stopped playing and looked up at him, startled and then angry. They had met once before when he had last performed a service for her father; however, he could not tell whether she recognised him or not. She worked for the philanthropist Elizabeth Fry, a woman of some public esteem, who had long campaigned for improved conditions in Newgate prison.

'I would tell you to make yourself at home, but clearly you have already followed such advice,' she said, without moving from behind the piano.

'You are a very fine pianist.' Pyke stepped into the room and ignored her indignation.

'You fancy yourself as an expert?' she asked, sceptically.

'At first, I thought you were playing a piece by Mozart, one of his piano concertos perhaps. But then I considered the way you carried yourself, as though you were trying to hold something back against your will, and it made me revise my opinion.'

Her anger abated and a curious expression spread across her face. 'You presume to know me, and what I played, perhaps a little too well.'

'Last month, I saw this German fellow, Felix Mendelssohn, give a fine rendition of Beethoven's Emperor Concerto in town. What you were playing reminded me a little of him.'

'Mr Pyke, you are clearly more cultured than your reputation suggests.'

'Oh? And what does my reputation suggest?' He tried to hide his satisfaction that she had remembered his name.

'When people talk of you, they do so with a reverence that borders, I would say, on fear.'

'And you imagine that I seek to encourage such a reputation? Or deserve it?' He was wearing a shirt with a collar to hide the cut he had received from Flynn's blade.

This time she smiled a little. 'I would imagine it serves your own interests quite well.'

'My interests as a thief-taker?'

'I have heard that only one of those words describes what you are, Mr Pyke. Or what you do.'

He couldn't stop himself laughing. He looked at her again, approvingly this time. 'You seem to know an awful lot about me, Miss Blackwood.'

'I know you're a Bow Street Runner but I have little idea of what Bow Street Runners are meant to do. I can see you're confident to the point of vulgarity. I would guess your age to be a little over thirty. I have heard other less agreeable rumours about your profession in general which I do not wish to dwell on. Beyond that, I have been blissfully unaware of your existence and intend to remain that way.'

Emily Blackwood was, indeed, very pretty, but not as pretty as she might have been had her dress been tattier, or her hair not so immaculately pinned up, or had she not worn her breeding so aggressively in the company of others.

Pyke had been told he was handsome, although not in the suave if effete manner of an English gentleman. His thick black hair, curled in places, mutton-chop sideburns and swarthy olive skin suggested someone coarser, more readily associated with Continental peasants and bandits. A former lover, after she had been discarded, had described his lips as cruel and his pale grey eyes as lacking in sentiment. Another, while running the tips of her fingers suggestively across his bare chest, had commented that there was not an ounce of fat on him, although she too had delivered more disparaging remarks about his appearance after he had admitted growing bored of their affair.

'I have heard something about your own good work, Miss Blackwood. Since Mrs Fry first visited Newgate there have been some important changes.'

'It's a shame that our interests largely concern the female prison, for otherwise you yourself might benefit from the reforms at some future point.'

Pyke allowed her remark to pass. 'Your fine looks belie a sharp intellect,' he said, amiably. 'But then your piano playing already revealed that fact.' He was interrupted by the sound of raised voices and the urgent clip of heeled shoes striding across a wooden floor. Edmonton himself entered the room, wheezing like a wounded animal, followed by someone Pyke knew only by reputation; in the flesh, Edmonton's brother William seemed frightened of his own shadow.

'Dammit, Pyke, were you not told to wait in the entrance hall? Do you imagine I care to walk through my own home searching for hired help?'

Pyke bowed his head. 'Please accept my apologies. It was selfish of me to forget that such strenuous exercise might cause you discomfort.' He detected a smile on Emily's face.

Edmonton's bloodshot eyes narrowed. 'As I am reminded that conversing in a manner above one's station does not make one a gentleman.'

Pyke let the insult pass. It was true he had worked hard to erase any lingering trace of the rookeries from his speech and was as comfortable holding forth with aristocrats as with the working poor of St Giles.

'You seem agitated, Father.' Emily's demeanour belied her apparently sympathetic words. 'What vexes you so?'

'What vexes me?' Edmonton, who was carrying a newspaper, glanced down at the front page. ' "The particular case of Catholic Emancipation will not be stated in detail . . ." *Pah*. The cowards are afraid to, that's why.' He crumpled the newspaper and threw it into the fire. 'It's the consequence of handing over power to a military man and a turncoat industrialist with liberal blood running through his veins.'

'Except liberal blood doesn't extend to easing the hardships most ordinary people have to endure,' Pyke said, looking across at Emily. 'And the idle rich remain idly rich.'

'What poppycock,' Edmonton said, wiping spit from his chin. 'You sound like a damn Jacobin.'

'Or worse still, a reformer,' Emily said, playfully. 'Excuse me for being presumptuous, Mr Pyke, but perhaps you might enlighten us as to your own political convictions.'

'The word "conviction" implies I have a firm opinion on such matters, one way or the other.'

'You would like us to believe you are entirely without conviction?' Her eyebrows were raised.

Pyke smiled as best he could. 'I think tradition should be upheld only when under attack from reformers, and reform should be upheld only when under attack from traditionalists. Apart from that, the business of politics is best undertaken by those of us who seem to believe our goal as human beings is a selfless one, rather than to serve our own ambitions.'

'How delightfully cynical.'

'What I mean is I have no politics myself and am happy to leave such business to men of your father's . . . *abilities*.'

Edmonton accepted the compliment without apparently detecting its irony. 'That's enough of such pleasantries. Make yourself scarce, girl. The menfolk have some important matters to discuss.' He rearranged his white waistcoat, revealing buckskin breeches that were stretched so tightly

9

over his belly it seemed as though they might split at any moment.

'Please excuse me, Mr Pyke, I have some flowers to press,' Emily said, smiling mischievously. 'But I have no doubt our paths will cross again.' She collected herself to depart. 'Until they do, I bid you farewell and hope you have a pleasant trip back to the city.' She glanced out of the window. 'It is such a ghastly day.' Turning to Edmonton, Emily added, '*Father.*'

Edmonton muttered something inaudible and shook his head.

As a Bow Street Runner, Pyke worked for two magistrates, Sir Richard Fox and his second-in-command Brownlow Vines, who both presided over the courtroom at Bow Street and oversaw the operations of the Runners. The Runners were the capital's de facto police force; foot patrols roamed the city streets as far east as the Ratcliffe highway, while the horse patrols covered an even wider area stretching as far north as Enfield. In his ten years as a Runner, Pyke had served on both patrols, though he had more quickly taken to the latter, in spite of the showy uniform – a blue greatcoat over a red waistcoat and spurred Wellington boots. Chasing highwaymen and livestock thieves on horseback, armed with pistols and truncheons, across rugged country terrain had been eminently preferable to patrolling the city's back alleys on foot. Now, however, Pyke was employed almost exclusively as a thief-taker and as a recoverer of stolen goods. Under Sir Richard's instructions, his job was to arrest those malefactors accused of crimes as various as murder on the one hand and embezzlement on the other, and deliver them to Bow Street. But part of his job was also to provide a service to well-heeled clients who had been victims of crime, usually robberies. If he successfully recovered what had been stolen, Pyke would be paid a finder's fee. Two years earlier, Pyke had performed such a service for Edmonton, whose Belgravia town house had been relieved of six thousand pounds' worth of jewellery and bonds. On that occasion, Pyke had orchestrated the return of all the stolen articles, and had earned a fee of three hundred guineas.

What Edmonton did not know was that, in collaboration with another Runner who had a personal score to settle with the aristocrat, he had executed the robbery.

Edmonton introduced his brother, and Pyke remembered he was a banker. His double-breasted jacket and trousers were cut from cheap cloth and made him look more like a Puritan minister than a successful businessman. He was frail in comparison with his brother, and seemed to occupy the background, as if it were his natural place in the order of things.

'I don't know how much you know about banking, Pyke, but suffice to say, my brother owns and manages a collection of small country banks . . .'

'We have branches in Norwich, Ely, Colchester and King's Lynn.' William spoke in a soft, almost effeminate voice.

'Yes, quite.' The lord turned a hard stare on his brother. 'A small business, then, but not an insignificant one, you'll understand. I take an interest only when scandal or ill fortune threaten to impugn the family's good name. I fancy my brother will not mind if I let it be known that my judicious intervention helped save the business from ruin during the last banking crisis a little over three years ago.'

'Well, that's not entirely the case . . .' Beads of sweat had gathered on the brother's forehead.

'For heaven's sake. If I wanted your opinion on the matter, I would have asked for it. Can I speak without being interrupted?'

'I just didn't want Mr Pyke to think the banks were managed recklessly. A well-regulated country bank only issues notes in fair demand . . .'

'What Pyke thinks of your rather modest acumen as a businessman is quite beside the point,' Edmonton said, 'but then again we would not be in this mess if it were not for your childlike sense of what constitutes appropriate security and your wholly predictable lack of judgement.'

William glared but refrained from starting an argument.

'Now, would you permit me to speak without interruption?'

William mumbled something weakly in response.

The function of a country bank, Edmonton went on to explain, was to oversee the circulation of banknotes in a particular area, and exchange banknotes belonging to the Bank of England and other smaller banks for their own. It was also to facilitate the transfer of funds from cities to towns and vice versa.

'Usually there is no need to transfer hard currency between banks, unless one is embroiled in a banking crisis, in which case it might be necessary or prudent to bolster one's cash reserves.'

William stood in silence next to the fire.

'Presently, however, the opposite is the case. All our banks are performing admirably and it is incumbent on us to transfer the surplus capital to where the demand is greatest. For our bank, that is London. Now, we keep all our surplus currency and a great proportion of our general circulation in government security inside the Bank of England itself but, and this is the vexed issue, on occasion we have to take it there ourselves. We currently lease an office close to the Bank of England on Cornhill in which we have installed a vault. The funds from our various country banks are transferred there for safe keeping, and when it is deemed appropriate, are taken under heavy guard to the Bank of England.'

Pyke forgot about the icy temperature. Large sums of money were being discussed.

'Until now everything has worked perfectly well.' Edmonton drank liberally from a glass of claret. As he did so, his Adam's apple swelled to the size of a small plum. 'But, I am afraid to say, the last two deliveries, one from the bank in King's Lynn and the other from the Colchester branch, have been . . . how can I put it without sounding *vulgar*? Well, suffice to say, two thousand pounds has gone missing. Not enough to break us, you will be relieved to hear, but banking is a business built on trust, and if our investors discovered that such a sum had been stolen from under our noses, well, you can understand the awkward position it would put us in.'

He made a point of glaring at his brother. William kept his eyes on the floor. His face, however, was crimson.

On each occasion, Pyke was told, the carriage transporting the money had been held up by a team of four masked riders, once near Waltham Abbey and once just outside Chelmsford. On both occasions, the guards riding with the carriage, who were also employed as parish watchmen, had been beaten unconscious. Although the men had been armed, they had not managed to let off a single shot. Pyke did not bother to tell Edmonton that, as someone who had served on Bow Street's horse and foot patrols, he considered watchmen to be wholly ineffectual. Edmonton explained that he did not imagine for a moment the attacks had been random. Rather he believed information regarding the transfer of money had been leaked by someone within the bank to his associates. Edmonton also claimed he knew who was responsible and berated his brother for employing this man in the first place.

William continued to stare in silence at the floor but his hands were clenched so tightly the whites of his knuckles were shining.

'Would you care to share that information with me?' Pyke asked.

'That would depend on whether I can count on your services regarding this matter or not.'

'Since we are what one might call old acquaintances, how would you feel if I proposed a modest fee of, say, five hundred guineas?'

Edmonton's face puffed up like a bullfrog's throat until it was so blotchy he could no longer hold in his indignation.

'*Modest!*' He made to loosen his collar. 'My God, you are an impudent sort. It's almost *half* of what was stolen.'

'I see your mathematics is as well developed as your generosity as a host.' The brother, Pyke noticed, was also without a drink.

'Or my sense of righteous outrage is as well developed as my prudence.' Edmonton's neck wobbled as he spluttered.

'In which case, I would be prepared to accept as little as four hundred.'

'You're a man to be reckoned with, aren't you?' Edmonton's laugh was without warmth. 'Perhaps you could furnish me with the name of any true-born Englishman of good stock who might agree to such an offensive fee?'

'I could intimate there are no such persons, but my final offer would still be four hundred.'

'A thoroughgoing cad as well as a rascal.' Edmonton addressed his brother in a manner that suggested he was almost enjoying himself. 'Can you believe I am being spoken to in such a manner?'

'I'd wager you make more than double that figure in the rents you collect every week of the year.'

'You see what I mean?' Edmonton slapped his brother

heartily on the back and turned to face Pyke. 'Since I'll admit you have amused me with your show of youthful temerity, I will offer two hundred.'

'Three hundred or you can find yourself another man.' This time Pyke folded his arms. He sensed Edmonton's resolve weakening, which surprised him. Pyke had planned to settle for as little as a hundred.

'You know how long it would take a skilled worker or a manservant to earn that kind of money?' Edmonton said, not quite mollified.

'Perhaps three years. In the case of your staff, nearer to six, I would fancy. You could get a man for less money, but not one who might be able to recover what was stolen.'

'Of course, I forget that recovering stolen items is a particular skill of yours.' Any trace of amusement disappeared from his expression. Pyke wondered how much he knew about their previous business arrangement.

'Are we agreed upon two and a half?'

Edmonton stared at him for a while without saying a word.

'Then if we've nothing left to talk about, perhaps you would have one of your servants inform my driver that I intend to leave at once.'

'By God, man, will you stop being so damn hasty?' Edmonton took out a handkerchief and wiped his mouth. 'I'm persuaded that a fee in the order of two hundred and fifty guineas might be appropriate in these very exceptional circumstances. Of course, it goes without saying such a fee would only be paid on successful completion of the task. Should you fail, you would receive nothing.'

'Naturally.'

'Good,' Edmonton said, shaking his hand. 'Now, perhaps, I can tell you about this rascal Swift. My brother, I am afraid to say, made the mistake of hiring this man six months ago and put him in charge of security for the Cornhill office. I am told he served with the duke in Spain. He is the only man apart from my brother and the branch managers who knows where and when any monies are to be transported. Since the managers only have knowledge of their own affairs, and the two carriages robbed thus far hailed from different banks, we can safely rule them out. That's why I suspect this Swift fellow. He's your man, I would lay my life on it.' Edmonton spoke as if his life was worth a great deal. 'Follow him from the bank's Cornhill offices. My brother can furnish you with the address. That scoundrel will lead you to the money or at least to the brigands who took it. It will be the easiest fee you've ever earned.'

In the entrance hall, while Pyke waited for his coat, he witnessed an encounter between Edmonton and his daughter that made him reassess his first impression of her. In fact, he heard as much as he saw; raised voices swelled into full-blown shouts, Emily's as well as her father's. Pyke was sufficiently intrigued by their argument to approach the half-closed doors behind which their altercation was taking place, but before he could determine what was being argued about, Emily flew through the doors and almost knocked him down. He had no choice but to fend her off with his hands, but his touch seemed to provoke her to further outrage. Brusquely she pushed him away and, gathering up her skirt, ran past him without uttering a word.

TWO

After an hour spent trawling the numerous taverns and alehouses surrounding St Paul's Cathedral, Pyke found his uncle, Godfrey Bond, in the Boar tavern on Fleet Street across the road from Middle Temple Gate. The old man was slumped back in his seat in the corner of the taproom. Since there was no natural light and the room was illuminated only by candles and the reddish flame of occasional grease lamps, it was difficult, if not impossible, to tell who anyone was. This suited most of the customers, who appeared less interested in social activities than in pouring gin down their throats.

The exposed brick walls and the low ceiling, covered with begrimed, grey-patterned wallpaper, augmented Pyke's fear of confined spaces. He had suffered from the condition for as long as he could remember. Or rather ever since, as a ten-year-old boy, he had watched his father lose his footing in a stampeding crowd and disappear under their feet. Forty thousand people had been gathered outside Newgate prison to witness the execution of Holloway and Haggerty, two robbers who had been convicted of stabbing a London botanist and leaving him to die at the side of a turnpike in Hounslow. The crowd had been too great for the space they had been herded into and chaos had ensued. Pyke had seen women and children suffocating to death as they were pressed against walls and barricades. Later, once the crowd had finally dispersed, he had found his father lying battered and not breathing in a ditch. His face had been crushed and his clothes were dirty with other people's shoe and boot prints.

Pyke pushed his way through the mass of bodies gathered in the tiny room and chose to ignore the stares of ill-concealed antipathy from those who either recognised him or simply disliked being watched by a stranger.

Collapsed between empty pewter ale pots and gnawed pork chops was the unconscious frame of his uncle's drinking companion. Pyke recognised the Reverend Foote, Ordinary at Newgate prison. Godfrey often plied Foote with drink in exchange for stories of woe and despair that Foote collected or overheard from the prison's condemned men and women. It was Foote's task to compile an account of their lives. For a small fee, he would pass these details to Godfrey, who would then print and sell them for a penny to the assembled crowd on the day of the execution.

As far as Pyke could tell, these stories carried several contradictory messages: on the one hand they suggested crime did not pay, that it was a sin against God, and that the most heinous crimes were still punishable by death; and on the other hand they made it clear that crime was exciting and heroic, and that criminals acted as they did because society left them no other option. Pyke thought all these explanations were too simple. For him, crime was simply a means to an end. If stealing was the only *available* means to achieving one's freedom and well-being, then it made sense to steal.

In his earlier life, Pyke's uncle had been a respectable publisher of radical political pamphlets and as a much younger man had counted figures such as Paine, Wollstonecraft and Godwin as his friends. He had long since abandoned such lofty inclinations, and for the last twenty years had scraped a living publishing sensational tales of criminal wrongdoing which he cobbled together from the annals of old Newgate calendars and from confessions sold to him by Foote. His editorial policy was to concentrate on tales that were especially gruesome and dwell upon specific instances of deviance. In each case, he would try to remove attempts by previous writers to impose moral judgements on the stories. The published sheets were cheaply reproduced and sold for a penny, mostly to the working poor. Godfrey would often tell Pyke that his readers found more of their own lives reflected in his stories than in tales penned by Jane Austen.

Godfrey was the closest thing Pyke had to a father. But theirs had always been an ambivalent relationship that reflected their shared desire both to remain independent and to cultivate familial support and companionship. It was a bond that had finally found its own equilibrium. While they no longer shared the same living space or felt any compunction to intervene in one another's lives, a certain degree of warmth had begun to emerge in their dealings.

As a surrogate parent, Godfrey had never imposed even a modicum of discipline on him. Rather, he had provided Pyke with a small room in the attic of his Camden Town apartment and allowed him to come and go as he pleased. It was an arrangement that had suited Pyke, and one that permitted him to gain his education in the ways of the street, in such a manner that if things ever got too dangerous or intimidating, then the door of his uncle's home was always open.

'Oh, it's you, dear boy. You know Arthur, don't you?' At the mention of his name, Foote did not actually move but, for a moment, stopped snoring. 'All he can offer me these days, it seems, are dreary tales of common thievery and domestic woe. Think about it. Who wants to read about real life? If I published the stuff he's giving me, I'd bore my readers half to death. They want piracy and mass murder, not stories about the grinding effects of poverty.' He shook his head, wistfully. 'Where, I ask you, are the Jack Sheppards and Jonathan Wilds? *Outlaws* who defined an age. Who do we get instead? Who are our heroes? Bentham? Peel? That oaf Bulwer? Where's the unpleasantness or the proper violence in his stories? Believe me, dear boy, I feel like a vulture gnawing on a stripped carcass.' Godfrey rubbed his eyes and yawned. 'So tell me, what brings you down to this gutter to see me?'

Godfrey had a mane of unkempt white hair and was not preoccupied by how he looked. He cared little for contemporary fashion and, aside from his small publishing business, he took an interest only in what he could eat and imbibe. Though his sexual proclivities were a mystery to Pyke, he'd warmed to abstinence in recent years with a dedication that surprised those who knew him.

Pyke told Godfrey about his visit to Edmonton's country home and asked what he knew about the man's business.

'Edmonton, you say? *Hmmm.*' He closed his eyes. 'His wife's a descendant of the earl of Essex, if he's the one I'm thinking about. You say his brother owns a bank?' He frowned. 'I've heard Edmonton's tight with the Tory Ultras but that's hardly news. I'm afraid that's it, but if you give me a couple of days, I can ask around, see what else I can dig up.'

'There's a daughter, too. Emily Blackwood. She's part of Elizabeth Fry's circle.'

'A daughter, eh?' Godfrey's grin widened so that Pyke could see his blackened teeth. 'That sounds intriguing.' His grin evaporated. 'And dangerous.'

'Anything you can find out for me would be much appreciated.'

'Acquaintances, business associates . . . corset sizes?'

'I'm reliably informed that Edmonton doesn't wear corsets,' Pyke said, smiling at last.

'What a pity. I do so like a man who's concerned about his figure.' Godfrey patted his own girth but his expression became serious. 'They're an abominable lot, the Ultras. Edmonton, Eldon, Newcastle, Cumberland. All of 'em would shit in their own food and eat it if it would hold up reform,' Godfrey said, working his way around the various ale pots, looking for dregs.

Still drunk, Foote heaved his head off the table and stared at Pyke, confused. Saliva hung from his mouth. 'That's right, an abomination. We're an abomination to them, you know. A veritable abomination. Mark my words, times are changing, boy. We'll be for the rope. Our faces don't fit. They won't tolerate us for much longer. The whole thing's a disgrace.' Foote looked up at him, expectant of an answer, but since Pyke didn't know what was a disgrace and who 'we' or 'they' referred to, he said nothing.

But Godfrey nodded solemnly in agreement. 'We're a dying breed, that's for certain. A dying breed.' He reached for an empty ale pot. 'Hail to the new captains of industry, the bureaucrats, the politicians. The future is yours.'

It saddened Pyke to see Godfrey so old and out of sorts. As someone who had witnessed his uncle hold his own against Godwin, discussing the relative merits of polite anarchy, or Paine, arguing about the evils of organised religion, Pyke felt angrier than he had expected that Arthur Foote now constituted his uncle's preferred drinking companion. As he left, Pyke kicked the chair away from under Foote's hulking frame and watched him tumble on to the floor.

From the position Pyke had taken up in Batson's, the coffee

house across the road from William Blackwood's Cornhill office, there was plenty of time, over the following two days, to assess his subject. Swift, if that was the man's name (for Pyke took nothing Edmonton told him at face value), was punctual, arriving at the office on the dot of nine and leaving at five. He appeared to live an orderly life. On both days, Swift took the same route from work to his moderate apartment on Finsbury Square, and on both occasions it had taken him exactly twelve and a half minutes, walking at a brisk pace.

Swift was moderately built, with sandy hair and bushy eyebrows. He had a large brown mole on his chin. If Pyke had to make a snap judgement, he would say that he didn't care for the man. Like many ex-military sorts, Swift had a mincing, almost arrogant gait that suggested that the folk who traversed the pavements in his immediate vicinity were necessarily of a lower order.

On the third afternoon Pyke had taken up his usual position in the window of the coffee house when he spotted a carriage rattle past him carrying Emily Blackwood and a female companion. On impulse, he picked up his coat and set off after the carriage, which had slowed to allow a procession of sheep and their drover to pass by, heading north to Smithfield market. It took him a few moments to catch his breath, and while he did so, Pyke peered into the well-appointed interior of the carriage.

Emily did not seem to recognise Pyke or did so only reluctantly, once he had made his introductions. He made an inconsequential remark about the cold weather.

Her companion, Jane Norman, was introduced as a member of Emily's committee of female prison visitors. She couldn't contain her excitement. 'But has Miss Black-wood told you our wonderful news? It seems an anonymous benefactor has bequeathed a not insignificant sum of money to us and we will be moving to more respectable offices on the Strand, no less, within the month.' As she spoke, she pulled her shawl tighter around her shoulders.

Pyke said it was good news and, with a broad grin, added he'd always felt it was easier to spend other people's money on frivolities than his own.

This drew an amused look from Emily. 'Mr Pyke is, indeed, a dour, puritanical soul who does not believe in frivolities of any kind.' She was wearing a heavy overcoat, a printed wool dress and a matching wide-brimmed bonnet. She wore no gloves and her slim fingers had turned blue in the icy temperature.

Mrs Norman screwed up her face. 'Really? What does he do for amusement?'

Emily turned to face him. 'What *do* you do for amusement, Mr Pyke?' she asked, her eyebrows arched.

'You mean when I'm not robbing from the undeserving rich?'

That seemed to upset Mrs Norman but Emily just laughed. 'And oppressing or locking up the deserving poor?'

Mrs Norman asked, 'Is this man really a thief?'

'He's a Bow Street Runner,' Emily explained, looking at Pyke. 'I'm told it's the next best thing.'

'Except when you come face to face with a real villain and you holler for someone to keep you safe.' He held her stare and whispered, so that her companion could not hear, 'Tuck you up in bed.'

She proffered a throaty laugh. 'Somehow I can't see you as my nursemaid.'

'You don't think the outfit would suit me?' he whispered, again so Mrs Norman couldn't hear.

Emily seemed to be enjoying herself. 'I'm not sure you'd have the stamina for it.' She lowered her voice to a whisper. 'Or the figure.'

'And if I told you I shaved liberally . . .'

The procession of sheep had passed by and Emily's carriage was now blocking traffic behind them. Pyke smiled, said he hoped their work continued to save souls and dug his hands into his pockets.

As the carriage pulled off, he looked back along Cornhill and saw Swift emerge from the bank's office and hurry down the crowded street in the direction of Wren's great cathedral.

Swift pursued his usual path to the bottom of Cornhill, but instead of rounding the Bank of England and turning northwards for home, he continued across the road until it turned into Cheapside. The dominating presence of St Paul's loomed. Pyke followed him at a discreet distance and was actively intrigued by Swift's urgency and the apparent change in his manner. On other occasions, Swift had seemed utterly at ease, taking no notice of his surroundings, but this time he was much less certain of himself and constantly looked behind him. Even his irritating gait was notable by its absence.

After the cathedral, they headed down Ludgate Hill, where the street became narrower and the surroundings less salubrious. The buildings were shabbier and the road filled with potholes and horse dung. On Cornhill, most of the premises had been banks, offices and coffee houses. Here they were taverns, pawnshops and tobacconists, and the cobbled streets they spilled out on to were choked with people of every class and hue. Pushing his way through a throng of unfamiliar faces, Pyke struggled to keep his prey in view and willed himself to shut out the unmelodious din of iron-clad hoofs clattering against the stone cobbles and market traders pushing their barrows loaded with stale vegetables.

On the far side of the street, Pyke was suddenly

distracted by four boys closing in on a well-dressed man. Two stalked him from behind, two from the side. One of the boys from behind tipped the man's hat and, as his hands left his pocket to catch it, Pyke saw his watch being removed and his vest pocket being emptied by the boy next to him. Only when the boys had parted ways and disappeared into the adjacent back alleys did the man realise what had happened, by which time it was too late. No one came to his rescue when he cried for help.

On Fleet Street there was a noisy procession involving a ragtag bunch of poorly dressed whiskered men; some were banging tins, others shouted anti-papist abuse. They were heading for Hyde Park, where one of Daniel O'Connell's supporters was organising a rally in favour of Catholic emancipation. Pyke knew this because all the Bow Street foot patrols had been summoned by Sir Richard Fox to police the situation and keep the two warring sides apart. They had been told to act as peacemakers, but Pyke knew as well as anyone else that, should there be trouble, many of the assembled Runners would join forces with the Protestant mob and turn on the papist rabble-rousers. Pyke had no special affinity with the Protestant religion, which he saw as joyless and disciplinary. But he would not lose sleep over the spilling of Catholic blood. In the end, Catholics and Protestants could kill themselves and others to earn glory from a God who didn't care about them, but Pyke would not be fooled into such pointless sacrifice.

But he was grateful for the distraction of the march, because it meant he could conceal himself in the crowds. As he walked, Pyke occupied his mind by trying to guess where Swift might be heading and, for no other reason than the habit of adjusting himself to the worst outcome, he opted for the rookeries of St Giles. A man could instantly lose himself in the warren of blind alleys, passages and yards that made up London's most overcrowded slum.

Nowadays Pyke rarely ventured into the rookeries, both because of the physical danger and because the chances of catching someone were remote. Bow Street Runners were usually well known and often found their paths barred by hostile onlookers. Furthermore, the dense network of inter-linked yards and passages meant that thieves could escape pursuers without too much exertion.

Yet when Swift crossed over on to Drury Lane and darted into a side passage adjoining one of the street's many theatres, Pyke decided not to give up his pursuit, even though the alley led into the heart of the rookery. He was now excited by Swift's presence in such a place. Who did he know here? And what was the purpose of his visit?

Pyke had grown up in this neighbourhood but still didn't know all its nooks and crannies. Nor did it ever feel like home, whatever that term might mean. He had never tried to romanticise its narrow streets and ripe smells, either to himself or to others. It was a brutal place where desperate men and women lived desperate lives. He knew the buildings all too well, just as he knew what might be inside them, together with plagues of rats. Cobblers and gin distillers trying to put together a living in rotten hovels that stank of human faeces; broken-down forgers oxidising coins in substances that would eventually kill them; prosti-tutes fucking against alley walls while pimps waited in the shadows to mug the customer of whatever money was left; tricksters on the lookout for their next mark; scavengers trawling the slum's black holes for signs of food and life; travellers crammed ten to a room swapping germs and tales of other places; men and women living in near-constant darkness who shouted and fought and drank and swore and fucked until their despair no longer seemed to matter.

But of all the rookeries Pyke knew and feared – feared because in his world you were only ever one step away from poverty – the bleakest was the Holy Land, an area that housed most of the city's transplanted Irish population. It was there, in 'Little Dublin' as some liked to call it, that Swift ended up. Antiquated hovels backed on to narrow streets. In windows filled only with tattered paper, grim stares met his wary gaze. Livestock roamed freely in and out of open doors and the smell of burned animal fat wafted from rooms that housed as many as could lie top to toe on bare floors. These people didn't care about political emancipation, he thought grimly, only about where their next meal was coming from.

Halfway along a typically windy street, Pyke was close enough behind to see Swift disappear, without warning, into a run-down building. A small sign on the door indicated it was a lodging house for dock workers and their families.

Pyke waited for as much as a minute and followed Swift into the building. Without natural light, the candle-blackened entrance hall was gloomy and the room smelt of wax and cooked food. The walls and ceilings seemed to press in on him. Hearing a noise from somewhere above, he started to ascend the rickety, corkscrewed staircase; on the next floor, he inspected the various closed doors but, on hearing the sound above him once more, he opted to continue his ascent of the staircase and found himself on the upper-floor landing. Everything was quiet. In all probability he had lost Swift downstairs or out of the back of the building. Looking around him, he counted five doors, all of which were closed.

Pyke tried one of the doors and found it was locked. Turning to the adjacent room, he eased the handle and applied pressure to the door. As it swung open, the rusted hinges groaned audibly.

The stench hit Pyke with an explosive force. It seemed to invade his nostrils and peel off the skin from the inside. Pyke did not think of himself as delicate and, in his work as a Runner, he had been confronted by rotting animal carcasses and the occasional dead body, perhaps even of his own doing. Still, he had to check himself as he entered that room, and take his time to adjust to a smell that was so visceral it made him want to be sick.

It was a bleaker room than many prison cells and it had neither heating nor natural light. A torn mattress filled almost a quarter of the floor space. The rest of the room was occupied by two motionless figures pressed against the wall farthest from the door. Taking a candle lantern from the landing, Pyke set it down on the wooden floor in the middle of the room. He called out but did not get an answer. Nor did the occupants move or even flinch. At first he fancied they might have been high on laudanum, but almost at once a squelchy feeling underfoot put paid to such a notion. Pyke had known even before he'd stepped into the room that the smell was that of putrid flesh and fresh blood, and it took less than a few seconds of rational thought for the two figures to become corpses. Still, it wasn't until others arrived with gas lamps and replacement candles that the full horror of the scene would reveal itself. Then he would see for himself what had happened. He would see that a man and a woman no older than twenty had been bound and gagged. He would see that their throats had been cut from ear to bloody ear, and that the cuts themselves went so deep their heads had almost been severed from their bodies.

If that had been the extent of the horror, then, gruesome as it was, Pyke might have been able to walk away from what he had witnessed there, with his fortitude and resolution intact, for he had long adjusted himself to the fact that human beings were capable of committing acts of unfathomable cruelty.

In those first moments, he did not see the bloodied sheets tossed on to the floor nor the metal pail beside them until his eyes had fully adjusted to the darkness. While both corpses had been propped against the wall like rag dolls, the metal pail was right in the centre of the room. Pyke kicked it and felt something move inside. Gingerly, he edged the lantern into the middle of the room with his foot and bent over, peering into the pail.

Pyke spotted a tuft of hair. It looked like a small animal.

He brought the lantern closer.

What he saw, then, was a collapsed jumble of tiny, delicate limbs and soft, pinky flesh. He saw a head, then two legs, two arms, a body, some feet and fingers. He strained for a better look, not able to trust his eyesight, and saw that the head, tiny as it was, had been squeezed out of shape, as though someone had taken it between their thumbs and pressed as hard as they could until it split apart like a piece of overripe fruit.

There was a faint whiff of urine but no liquid in the pail, just a dead baby. Pyke prodded it with his finger and instinctively pulled back. It did not move. The bruised flesh resembled melted wax. Pyke looked into its staring eyes, like small chunks of freshly mined coal, and felt unsteady on his legs. Supporting himself against the wall, he tasted bile in the back of his throat and barely had the chance to open his lips before a hot spike of vomit exploded from his mouth.

THREE

Once reinforcements from Bow Street arrived, it took them a further two hours to clear the upper floors of the lodging house and herd the curious residents downstairs into the apartment and back yard of the landlady, a plump spinster called Dulcibella Clamp. She, of course, objected vociferously to her home being overrun, as she put it, by foreign hordes, but only, Pyke fancied, because it gave her lodgers the chance to see how comfortably she lived, in comparison with the squalor of their own quarters. Pyke, whose task it had been to take her statement, dismissed her objections and went to rejoin Sir Richard Fox and Brownlow Vines, who were waiting for him on the second-floor landing. Having summoned as many gas lamps as they could solicit in such a short space of time, Fox and Vines were surveying the upper floors of the lodging house, now flooded in brilliant light.

Pyke was not surprised by the enthusiasm with which they had responded to his discovery, for they had dispatched all available men under their authority to the scene. He knew they were not necessarily moved by the incomprehensible horror of the murders. Rather, as politically minded bureaucrats, they intended to use this opportunity to stake their claim on the events of the day.

Fox and Vines had come from separate dinner appointments and looked utterly out of place, dressed in formal attire and standing in a dismal building in one of the worst slums of the city.

'There will have to be a proper investigation, of course,' Fox said, as though the matter had already been agreed upon. 'The sooner whoever did this is behind bars the better it will be for everyone.'

'I can't imagine Peel would want it otherwise.' Vines nodded.

'Perhaps, but then again, I wouldn't want to speculate on what our venerable Home Secretary might have in mind.'

'Given Peel's propensity for changing his mind, who would?' Vines glanced disparagingly at Pyke. 'But he'll use this as an opportunity to limit your authority.' He disliked Pyke's closeness to Fox and as a result took every opportunity to make his life as uncomfortable as possible.

'Peel might want to,' Fox said, absent-mindedly rubbing his chin, 'but does he yet have the power? I am still the most senior police officer in the city.'

'For the time being anyway,' Vines muttered, with dejection.

As all runners were, Pyke was aware that Peel was shortly going to introduce the Metropolitan Police Bill to the Commons with the expectation of winning the House's approval.

'Peel can do what he likes. I have the law on my side. So until I am informed otherwise, this investigation will be run from Bow Street.'

But Pyke noted wryly that Fox had still been sufficiently worried about Peel's plans to arrange a dinner with Sir Henry Hobhouse, a retired Tory who continued to enjoy a close relationship with Peel.

Vines also seemed to detect Fox's anxiety and said, 'Except that the law is only what the law-makers say it is.'

He was meticulous about his appearance, and was

rumoured to be the favourite of more than one lady of good standing. His fashionably cut jacket evoked the spirit, if not the style, of Brummel. Pyke often caught Vines staring at his thinning hair and truncated sideburns in the mirror. Vines made no secret of the fact that he wanted to succeed Fox when he retired, and was no doubt distressed by Peel's proposals for a new police force because they threatened his own plans for advancement.

'Have you any thoughts in these matters, Pyke?' Fox said, turning to him.

It might have seemed strange to outsiders that Fox would value and solicit his opinions, but in the light of their long-standing association, this was neither unusual nor revealing.

'You know what I think, Sir Richard. When Peel wins the vote, which he will, the first thing he'll do is try and incorporate all policing activities under the direct control of the Home Office.'

For weeks, the ranks of the Runners had been buzzing with rumours about the planned reforms and the sense of unease this news created was not helped by the fact that Fox himself believed that Peel might prevail. In the past, Peel had overstepped the mark by unfairly castigating the existing system for being corrupt and inefficient, but this time he had sensibly opted to stress the positive aspects of the proposed reforms: that everyone in London would have the same access to the same force, regardless of rank, situation or address.

When Fox had solicited his opinion, what Pyke did not say, because it would have implicated himself, was that Peel disliked the Runners not just because they received incentives and rewards for work successfully undertaken but rather because, in order to do so, they had to mix freely with criminals. In other words, Peel did not understand that they could not do their job without information provided by criminal informers. And while Pyke took it upon himself to personally benefit from these illicit associations, he had also made more arrests and gained more convictions than any other Runner attached to the office.

But unlike Fox, who believed in the Bow Street Runners so completely that it blinded him to the political realities of the situation, or Vines, whose main concern was to haul himself up the career ladder, he had no love for the organisation he worked for, and no special feelings for its leaders.

For him, being a Runner was simply a means to an end. It enabled him to travel to all parts of the city under the protective cloak of Fox's authority.

Fox told them that he had briefed Sir Henry about the situation during dinner. This news would be passed on to the Home Secretary. Vines seemed disturbed by this information.

'Was that wise, telling Hobhouse so quickly?' he said, unable to conceal his frown.

'Perhaps not wise but necessary,' Fox said, firmly.

'But surely it might have been prudent to take stock of the situation ourselves before asking for outside assistance.'

'Even if you don't, I have to consider the wider implications of all this. A young couple and their newborn baby, slaughtered in their own lodgings? My God, it's the Ratcliffe highway all over again.'

Though Pyke had been only thirteen at the time, he still remembered the froth of panic and moral outrage that had been whipped up when a man called Williams had murdered two families in their homes on the Ratcliffe highway.

'And look what that did,' Vines said, shaking his head. 'It placed police reform right back at the top of the political agenda. You can guarantee Peel will use this situation to push the police bill forward. It's like a gift, fallen into his lap. If there are any waverers left in the House, it'll drive 'em running into Peel's grateful arms. And we will have a new police force before the month's out.'

Pyke allowed Vines's words to settle before he said, 'Even a man of Peel's undoubted ambition would not consider a mutilated newborn to be some kind of political gift.'

Vines reddened. 'Yes, well, I'm sure you know what I meant.'

'Pyke's right,' Fox said. 'Whether Peel will exploit the situation for his own purposes is not for us to speculate. For now, I fear we have more pressing issues of public order to deal with.' He looked up at Vines. 'I take it the building and its perimeter have been secured and the mob outside placated?'

Sullenly, Vines said it had been taken care of. He explained that two of *his* men, Goddard and Townsend, were questioning the residents, particularly those who roomed on the upper floor, and any pertinent information would be relayed back to him. Pyke was tempted to ask how Goddard and Townsend would know what information was pertinent or otherwise but he kept his silence. He also knew for a fact that Goddard and Townsend were, by no means, Vines's men.

'Good, well, perhaps we should start by paying some attention to the three victims. That would seem to me to be a matter of enormous sensitivity.' Fox turned to Pyke. 'Have you managed to identify them yet?'

Pyke realised Vines had not yet grasped the significance of Fox's concerns and he was not about to make it easy for him.

'The landlady, Miss Clamp, told me that the building has five rooms on the top floor she rents out to lodgers. All of them are a good deal larger than the one hired by the victims. Most have seven or eight people sharing, each person paying two shillings a week. This room, on account of its size, went for four shillings in total. The two victims shared it with another girl. Young and pretty, according to Miss Clamp. She didn't know the girl's name but had overheard rumours to the effect that she might be the dead woman's cousin. Miss Clamp gave us a good description, though, and the men downstairs are looking for her as we speak.'

'There was a *girl* who shared the room with them,' Fox said, sounding aggrieved. 'You say a cousin?' He rubbed the ends of his moustache, as though deep in thought.

'According to the landlady.'

'And she's *downstairs*, as we speak?'

'Townsend and Goddard are looking for her downstairs, as we speak,' Pyke corrected him.

'Well, for heaven's sake, let's find her and talk to her, see what she knows.' Fox seemed irritated, to the point of distraction.

'I'll talk to Townsend and Goddard once we've concluded our business here.'

'Do that, man.'

Dressed in a wool coat and plaited undershirt, with a waistcoat, cravat, pantaloons and boots, Fox looked and sounded more like a military general than a magistrate.

Pyke remained silent.

'And what about their *names*?' Fox demanded, impatiently.

'Stephen and Clare.' Pyke waited for a moment. 'I don't know if they were married or not.'

'Did you get a *surname*, dammit?'

Pyke nodded. 'His name's Magennis. One "g" and two "n"s.'

35

Fox took a moment to digest this news. 'If I'm not mistaken, that's an Irish name.'

Vines, who came from an Anglo-Irish background, said, 'Indeed it is.'

'I know these things are, how should I put it, rather *complicated*, Vines, but do we know whether Magennis is a Protestant or Roman Catholic name?'

Vines finally seemed to grasp the problem. 'I believe it's a name that can be associated with both traditions.'

'I see.'

Pyke waited for a moment. 'Stephen Magennis kept an informal diary. I read what little I could understand. It seems the two of them arrived in London together during the middle of last year. From Ulster. They took the boat from Belfast to Liverpool and travelled to London by coach from there. The landlady informed me he worked at the docks, as do most of her lodgers. There was a brief mention in the diary of his father. It seems he's part of the Orange Order.'

Into the silence, Vines muttered, 'God.'

Fox nodded. 'And news of the murders has already spread far beyond these walls.'

'Just take a look outside,' Pyke said, digging his hands into his pockets to keep warm. 'The lynch mob is beginning to gather.'

'Yes, quite,' Fox said.

'Right now there are forty or fifty people downstairs. Any or all of them might know of the identity of the victims. No doubt there are others in the neighbourhood who also know, or soon will. Very shortly, I have no doubt, the street below us will be swarming with journalists from *The Times*, the *Chronicle*, the *Post*, the *Herald*, the *Advertiser*, the *Public Ledger* – need I go on? They will be gleaning this information from whoever will talk to them, and tomorrow we will all be reading about how two honest, upstanding Protestants and their newborn baby were slaughtered in their beds by a papist assassin dispatched by Satan himself.'

Fox stared at him, aghast. 'Very imaginative, I'm sure, Pyke, but I don't see how that helps us.'

Pyke shrugged. 'I'm just trying to outline the seriousness of the situation to *everyone* in the room.'

'I think we're aware of the seriousness, without your vulgar theatrics,' Vines said, hotly.

'Are you? Then how might news of these murders affect the mood of the Protestant mob I saw earlier today heading for Hyde Park and a showdown with O'Connell's supporters?'

Vines did not have an answer.

Fox looked at Vines. 'On this occasion, the confrontation in Hyde Park passed off without incident but only, I have to concede, owing to the fine work of my men.' He paused for a moment, to smooth out the tips of his moustache. 'But the whole business of Catholic emancipation has poisoned the atmosphere. Pyke's right. This could not have happened at a more inopportune moment.'

Having read the newspapers, Pyke knew that Catholic emancipation had become a hot political issue because O'Connell had recently thrashed the duke of Wellington's candidate in a County Clare by-election and demanded to be allowed to take up his seat in Westminster. As Roman Catholics were barred from serving in high public office, O'Connell's demands could only be fulfilled by changing the existing legislation. Pyke had also read that, as a blue-blooded military man, the duke was instinctively against granting relief to Catholics but, in his capacity as Prime Minister, he also understood that compromise was inevitable. Pyke appreciated that Peel, risking the ire of his Tory peers, was preparing to change sides and throw his support behind Catholic emancipation.

'I, for one, am greatly perturbed by the prospect of a Protestant mob, swarming through the city attacking anyone who crosses their path,' Fox said. 'And until any changes to police affairs are sanctioned by the House, we are expected to enforce civil obedience and the rule of the law.'

Vines nodded glumly in agreement.

'Sir Henry insisted that I go to Whitehall tonight and report directly to Peel.' Fox looked at Vines, then at Pyke. 'Perhaps I could call upon one of you for some assistance in this matter.'

Vines said, quickly, 'I would be more than happy to accompany you, Sir Richard.'

Fox rubbed his chin. 'In part, it is my responsibility to present our initial findings to the Home Secretary. In such a role, perhaps you could outline what you might say at the meeting.'

Vines glanced nervously at Pyke. 'Well, I shall report exactly what has happened and what steps we've taken to secure the area and find the man, or the men, who did this wicked thing.'

'Yes, quite so. But we will be addressing intelligent men, and therefore cannot offer them flimflam. How would you describe what *might* have taken place in that room?'

'I would say that it was the work of a maniac, a madman,' Vines said, pacing around the landing.

'Is that it?'

'You don't think it was the work of a sane, reasonable man, do you?'

'Perhaps not.'

'Well, I don't see how one can draw a more definitive conclusion at this early stage in the investigation.'

Fox nodded briskly. 'Perhaps you might share your thoughts on this subject with us, Pyke. After all, you were the one who found the bodies.'

'What does Pyke know?' Vines asked, glaring at him. 'And reason would suggest that we can't parade a man of Pyke's dubious standing in front of the Home Secretary. His type are the very reason Peel's got it in for the Runners.'

Vines had long suspected some of Pyke's actions erred on the side of illegality but had been consistently unable to prove his complicity in any wrongdoing.

'You mean the type whose physical exertions involve inevitable risks and whose intimate knowledge of the city's less salubrious environs garners results?'

'What rot,' Vines said, turning away. 'You should hear what this Flynn character has been saying about Pyke. We can't shut the Paddy up. The man's clearly—'

'A stinking liar,' Pyke interrupted.

'He's a receiver. Swears Pyke here paid him a fee for looking after items that had been stolen . . .'

'Enough,' Fox barked. 'For the time being we have more pressing matters.' He glared at Pyke and then at Vines from under his greying eyebrows. 'Tell us what you saw in that room and speculate on what it might mean.'

Pyke told Fox he would try but was not sure that he had very much more to offer. Vines snorted. Pyke held in the urge to strike him and took a deep breath.

He described how he had discovered the bodies and briefly sketched out the circumstances that had led him to the building in the first place. He did not mention Lord Edmonton's name or anything about the robberies he'd agreed to investigate. Fox chose not to push for the information but Pyke knew he would want to know about such things eventually. He explained that once reinforcements had arrived, he'd taken their lamps and re-entered the room in order to see what he might have missed. He had also given the victims' possessions a cursory examination and found little of note: a necklace and ring, a pocket handkerchief, some letters and two Bibles.

As for the adult victims, their hands had been tied behind their backs with strips torn from their bed sheets. Although he could not be certain, it seemed probable that whoever had killed them had also bound them up. Both victims had suffered heavy blows to their heads and Pyke speculated that their attacker might have entered the room, knocked them unconscious and then tied them up; in that order. He did not know why this had happened. The door had a basic locking device but it had not been forced, which suggested either that the lock had not been used or that one or both of the victims had invited their attacker into the room. This did not prove that they knew him but it didn't disprove it, either.

Describing how the strips of material had also been used as gags, Pyke noted that the two adults had not been blindfolded. He said he didn't know what this meant. He had inspected the mouth and hand bindings and detected on them the unmistakable scent of urine. He had detected the same scent in the metal pail where the dead baby had been discarded but on closer inspection had found no urine in it. It was pure speculation, he went on, but what if the murderer had beaten the victims unconscious and, for some reason, had wanted to bring them around? Might he have looked around for water and, if no water was immediately at hand, might he have not used what *was* immediately at hand to do so? Might he have not taken the pail filled with urine and thrown it into their faces?

Pyke underlined the fact that this was only a guess and heard Vines mutter something under his breath.

The extent and depth of the cuts indicated that whoever had administered them was a powerful man. A razor blade had probably been used, and since no such weapon had been found in the room, it seemed likely that the killer had taken it with him. Indeed, on reflection, the scene itself seemed quite orderly. Whoever had done this was *not* a madman. The neatness of the scene suggested the murderer's actions were premeditated.

Both victims had bled to death; Pyke explained that he had found two pools of fresh blood surrounding both corpses. In addition, their bodies had begun to stiffen. Therefore, he proposed that the killings had taken place during the previous night. Other residents had heard screams coming from the room and had assumed that the woman, who'd been heavily pregnant, was in the process of giving birth. He had found another set of sheets, this time stained with dry blood, stuffed under the mattress. It seemed likely these had been used during childbirth. Clearly, he added, the killings had taken place *after* the baby had been born, but perhaps only by a few hours. The birth and the killings had taken place on the same day. Pyke did not know how or whether the two incidents were connected, and said he could not think of anything that might link them.

Pyke left the hardest part until the end.

The baby, he said, dry-mouthed, had died when its skull had been crushed between the killer's thumbs. Because he *did* actually see thumb prints gouged into the baby's temples, and around its throat. He hadn't been able to summon up the strength of mind to lift the baby out of the pail, in order to determine its sex, but when he had done so, he would pass on that information.

Once he had finished, Fox offered him a generous smile. 'I think, Brownlow, your skills might be better used here tonight, keeping up the men's spirits.'

Vines looked away without speaking.

'I think that settles it, doesn't it?' Fox nodded his head vigorously, apparently pleased with himself.

FOUR

Outside, the temperature had plummeted and the cobbles of Drury Lane were as slippery as sheets of ice. The footman who had pulled down the steps from Fox's carriage said, 'Watch how you go, sir,' but something about the way he'd said 'sir' suggested he did not believe the word applied to Pyke. The street was still thronging with carts and wagons, in spite of the late hour, and the yard in front of a nearby hotel was a hive of activity in the wake of a coach that had just come to halt. It was a murky night and the air tasted of dirt. Pyke had never ridden in Fox's carriage before and was surprised at its luxuriousness. The seats were cushioned and the curtains made of lace. Fox pulled them closed in order to block out the sea of faces outside on the street and tapped on the ceiling of the carriage, to indicate that they were ready to depart.

As Fox pushed backwards in his seat and exhaled, Pyke took a moment to consider the man he had always thought of not exactly as a friend but certainly as a mentor. The lines etched on to his forehead indicated fatigue as well as worry. Perhaps the strain of having to safeguard Sir Henry Fielding's vision for the Bow Street Runners was beginning to take its toll. Certainly he had been more irritable than Pyke had seen him for a long time. Neither of them spoke for a while. Fox's mood was funereal; Pyke suspected he was less affected by the deaths than he was concerned about the likely implications for the future of the Bow Street operation.

'Did you find the girl?' Fox asked, eventually. He had a habit of peering down his nose at people as he spoke to them. He pulled his woollen muffler tight around his neck and blew into his hands.

Pyke said he'd talked to Goddard and Townsend but they hadn't managed to locate her yet. He assured him that they would continue to look for her. Fox shook his head, as if the blow were a personal one, and told Pyke that locating the girl was their top priority.

'I hope you don't think I was too harsh with Brownlow earlier,' Fox said, with studied casualness.

Pyke had enjoyed Vines's humiliation but said nothing.

'I fear he might have already struck a deal with Peel, or at least with someone involved in the process of setting up this new police force.'

'What kind of a deal?'

'Brownlow is not an idiot. He senses that the writing is on the wall for us, so to speak, and he's been making contingency plans to safeguard his own future. Exactly what has already been agreed upon, I'm afraid I don't know.' Fox seemed disappointed, above all. 'When things are changing so quickly, it's difficult to know who one can trust.' He waited for Pyke to look at him. 'We trust one another, don't we, Pyke?'

Pyke nodded in a non-committal way. He didn't think Fox wanted a firmer response.

Shortly after he had joined the Runners – he had been recommended by George Morgan, the now bedridden father of Pyke's mistress Lizzie – Pyke had been compelled to come to Fox's rescue; and his actions had forever affected the way in which Fox dealt with him. At the time, Jim Salter, a blackguard who had been arrested by a team of

Runners and was awaiting trial on multiple charges of theft with violence, grand larceny, embezzlement and house-breaking, had arranged for members of his gang to break into Fox's office and hold him at knife-point until Salter had been released. Pyke had inadvertently interrupted their efforts to subdue Sir Richard and, by chance, had had on his person a Long Sea Service flintlock pistol that had just been requisitioned from another villain. While Salter was a truly formidable character, his gang lacked his fortitude in the face of adversity. One of them had attempted to hold a knife to Sir Richard's throat but seeing the man's shaking hand and sensing his lack of resolve, Pyke had produced the pistol and raised his arm, as if to take aim. He still remembered how calm and in control of himself he had felt. When the man had refused to release Sir Richard, Pyke had simply fired the pistol, narrowly missing his head. The loud blast of the exploding weapon was sufficient to ensure his capitulation. The rest of the gang had surrendered and were later tried and hung. Fox himself had been impressed and even a little awed by Pyke's performance and, afterwards, told Pyke he had made a friend for life. At the time, Pyke had simply been grateful for Fox's gratitude but, as the years had passed, he had come to rely upon, and exploit, the protective cloak that the man's continuing support afforded him.

'I want you to be my eyes and ears on this investigation. I am not privy to Peel's intentions in this unfortunate business, whether he will want to be involved in an official capacity or not. But whatever Peel decides, and whatever he says, I want you to look into this matter on behalf of Bow Street, and I want you to find the man who did those things.' In an unusual display of emotion, he grabbed Pyke's arm and stared with watery eyes. 'Do you understand?'

Fox's sudden outburst, whether it was provoked by passion or outrage, took Pyke by surprise.

He nodded and assured Fox that he would do as the old man asked. In fact, he had already made up his mind to conduct his own investigation, whether Fox sanctioned it or not.

A little later, Fox wanted to know whether Pyke had any business that might distract him from the matter in hand. 'If you have to share out some of your work, I'll see that you're properly remunerated.'

Pyke assured him he had no such business.

'Even what took you to that lodging house in the first place?' When Pyke said nothing, Fox continued, 'In the past, I have been aware of instances in which the activities of persons under my authority have transgressed the official sanction of the law. Perhaps I should have taken a firmer stance against such practices. Perhaps this laxness on my part is one of the reasons why the Home Secretary does not seem favourably disposed towards us.' His stare intensified. 'I am well aware of the business Brownlow alluded to earlier, Pyke. A man by the name of Flynn, a known receiver of stolen goods who is currently being held in the felons' room, is making all kinds of scurrilous accusations against you. The man claims that you have been personally responsible for countless burglaries during a period extending as far back as the last days of our current monarch's much-lamented father. Am I to assume that his accusations are entirely false?'

Pyke appeared wounded by the slight and assured Fox he had never dealt with the man in any capacity.

'If I am prepared to draw a line under whatever you may have done in the past, I'd like to feel I had your unequivocal support on this matter.'

It was a strange request, one that bristled with repressed anger.

Still, Pyke said he would do whatever the old man asked him.

'Excellent.' Fox nodded, seemingly back to his old self. 'And you'll keep me informed with regular reports?'

Pyke promised he would.

'Well, that's settled, then.' Fox held out his hand and Pyke shook it without knowing *what* had been settled.

It struck him only later that, in agreeing to be Fox's eyes and ears, he had permitted himself to be used in a way that he couldn't quite fathom. But then again, he had no plans to disclose everything that he turned up. Fox would find out only what he wanted him to.

The fact that the private chambers of the Secretary of State for the Home Department were disappointingly spare was not a reflection on the rest of the building. Indeed, as they were led through a maze of interconnected rooms, it was hard not to be impressed by the ornate furnishings and gilt decorations, and, in one instance, a cantilevered staircase that extended through the full height of the building. But when they were finally ushered into Peel's private chambers, Pyke was surprised to discover that, with the exception of the vast library of books that lined every part of the wall, the man's office was small and functional. The impression of being cramped was augmented by the large number of people already in the room. This was not the informal meeting between themselves and the Home Secretary Fox had been expecting. Even to Pyke's untrained eye, it resembled a full-scale conference of war.

Peel was standing in front of a large mahogany desk. He was a tall, elegant man with a long distinguished face and a full head of curly, reddish hair. He was fashionably dressed and wore powder, though this was perhaps explained by the fact that he had come directly from an official function in order to convene the meeting. Excusing himself from another conversation, Peel came over to greet them. He seemed to know Fox well and referred to him amiably as 'Sir Richard', but there was no warmth in his voice, and he treated Pyke as he might have done a servant. He wasn't actively rude but simply seemed to look through Pyke as though he were not there.

'Right, gentlemen, if you could all take a seat, perhaps we could make a start.' He spoke with a faint Lancashire accent. 'First of all, I would like to thank you for coming here at such short notice. Your assistance at such a vexing time, I can assure you, is much appreciated. Most of you will already know one another but for those who are less familiar with the persons gathered in this room, perhaps you will permit me, for the sake of expediency, to go around and make your introductions.'

Their chairs were arranged in a semicircle arching around the desk that Peel now sat behind.

'To my right,' Peel began, 'is, of course, Sir Henry Hobhouse, the now retired Home Office under-secretary who, along with the gentleman next to him, William Gregson, a fine barrister in his own right, has been assisting me in drafting the new Metropolitan Police Bill. As I'm sure you all know, I will be presenting the bill to the House next month.' He glanced over at Sir Richard. 'I've asked them to sit in on this meeting because the terrible events of this evening, and my proposed response, have implications for our legislative programme. Next to them is James Hardwick, the esteemed criminologist who, I am reliably informed, studied under Becarria. Mr Hardwick will provide us with a preliminary report into the psychological background of the man who killed these people.'

Pyke looked at the bespectacled young man with his smug expression and oiled hair and wondered how he was able to comment on something he knew nothing about.

'To my left, we all know Sir Richard Fox, the chief

magistrate at Bow Street, and next to him is . . .' Peel looked at Fox rather than at Pyke. Fox said, 'Pyke,' and Peel nodded and said, 'This is Mr Pyke, who is a Bow Street Runner and had the misfortune of discovering the dead bodies. Mr Pyke will, I hope, report *precisely* what happened. And finally we have Charles Hume, who served under the duke at Waterloo.' Peel did not elaborate beyond this and left Pyke and others in the room wondering in what capacity Charles Hume had been invited to the meeting.

The only other person in the room was a large, bug-eyed man with black hair and coarse skin. Peel did not introduce him and he took a seat at the back of the room.

'I'm sure I don't need to underline the seriousness of the public-order situation we're now facing. Nor do I need to stress the significance of what's happened in relation to the Metropolitan Police and Catholic emancipation bills that I'm planning to present to the Commons in the next few months. You'll understand, of course, these events threaten both pieces of legislation, yet also underline their importance . . .'

As Peel spoke, Pyke studied the impassive faces of those gathered in the room and then the expensively bound editions mounted on the wall behind him. He wondered how many of them Peel had actually read. He seemed like an intelligent man but Pyke could not help but think that the quantity of books functioned, in the main, as a reminder to others of Peel's superior learning.

Peel asked Fox to explain what measures had already been undertaken to police the area and secure the scene of the murders, and Fox outlined what had already been done by the Bow Street magistrates and Runners. If nothing else, Fox's account served to reinforce Pyke's belief that he had authorised such an extensive deployment only in order to garner the political capital.

The more he was seen to be doing, and the more the Runners were seen to be involved with the investigation, the harder it would be for Peel to push them aside.

When he had finished, Peel thanked Fox for all the fine work that had been done, and in his forthright way said that, as someone who remained integral to the business of policing the city, Sir Richard, when it came to the preservation of public order, was still very much needed for his expertise.

No one in the room could have missed the implication behind what he was saying.

Fox seemed appalled. 'With all due respect, Home Secretary, as the events today in Hyde Park demonstrated, there is no other organisation or group of men *currently* available to perform such a task, except of course the armed forces.'

'At present, yes, you're quite right.' Peel regarded Fox with amusement.

'So it's not a gift you're bestowing on us, Home Secretary, this *burden* of policing the city.'

'It is a duty I'm asking you to perform.'

'Asking or commanding?' Fox said, like a bad-tempered card player, unable to see he was compelling Peel to show his hand.

Peel just smiled. 'This is the problem with having to make decisions within a system comprising different and sometimes competing authorities. As a military man, the duke would say the same thing. Can you imagine what would happen on a battlefield if there were two generals on the same side, each employing a different strategy? It's why I intend to bring all aspects of policing in London under one single authority, to be established under the direct control of *this* office.'

In that moment, whether Fox realised it or not, Peel

had driven a nail into the coffin of the Bow Street organisation.

Fox tried to gather his thoughts. 'But that still leaves the pressing question of *how* to proceed with this particular investigation.'

Peel regarded him with amusement. 'In what sense?'

'Well, as de facto head of policing in the capital . . .'

'*Nominal* head of policing,' Peel said, as though clearing up a minor quibble. 'As of tonight, the investigation into the St Giles murders will be handed over to a team assembled under the authority of this office, to be led by our friend Charles Hume. Charles distinguished himself serving under the duke at Waterloo and if, as expected, the new bill is passed, I intend to ask him to be one of two commissioners responsible for overseeing the new force. The investigation will be run from what I hope will become the headquarters of the new force at number four Whitehall Place. The adjoining watch house that backs on to Great Scotland Yard will house his team while number four is being prepared. Of course, Charles has my full authority in all matters regarding the investigation. I hope you will all work closely with him to ensure that we find whoever perpetrated this abominable act before the mob rears its ugly head and before a drop of Catholic blood is spilled.'

Pyke was impressed with the ruthlessness with which Peel had dealt with Fox.

But Sir Richard was not quite beaten. 'Pardon me, Home Secretary, for bringing up a matter so trifling as the law, but will the arrangements you propose earn the approval of the House?'

Peel wasn't even slightly thrown by the question. He explained that it was for precisely this reason that he'd invited Sir Henry and William Gregson to the meeting. Perhaps he might hand over to Gregson to explain where the government stood from a legal standpoint? Gregson ran through some preliminary details and stated that so long as any authority with a mandate relating to policing functioned under the guidance of a sitting magistrate appointed under the terms of the 1792 Middlesex Justices Act, it had the full sanction of the law.

Fox sank back into his chair, folded his arms and said nothing. Pyke made a guess that the 'sitting magistrate' selected by Peel and Gregson would be Brownlow Vines.

Behind them, Pyke could still feel the intimidating presence of the anonymous heavy-set man.

'Now that's been taken care of,' Peel said, moving swiftly on, 'and since all of us here share some kind of interest in these terrible murders, perhaps we can direct our attention to possible avenues of enquiry, so that Charles can properly proceed with the investigation.' He looked across at Hardwick and said, 'I believe Mr Hardwick here has some ideas he'd like to share with us.'

Whereas Peel had delivered his address from the comfort of his chair, Hardwick rose to his feet and turned to face the group, as though about to give a lecture. He was a weedy man, a bookish type who looked as though he had been bullied at school and had never recovered from the experience. In Pyke's view, although this type might be successful in their adult life, they always remembered their humiliation at the hands of others and, as a result, set out to wield their intellect like a weapon. His hair had been oiled and slicked back and his face, even without powder, was so wan that he seemed almost transparent. It took him five minutes to outline his own credentials.

Pyke yawned loudly and did not bother to cover his mouth.

'In recent years,' Hardwick explained, 'psychiatrists and criminologists have begun to devote their attention to a seemingly new phenomenon: examples of extreme violence usually enacted within domestic settings and displaying cruel and unusual properties that do not have a clear-cut explanation. We have called such a condition "homicidal monomania". Let me give you an example. A man, let's call him Edwards, without any record of violence or history of insanity, attacks a young child with a hammer for no ostensible reason. Why? Is this a passing outburst or a permanent state? And are both of these states mutually exclusive? At present the intervention of psychiatry into the realm of the law is only partial and questions such as these can only be answered provisionally, but having briefly looked over the details of this particular case, I believe it to be another example of homicidal monomania. As such, I would suggest that we are looking for a deeply disturbed man, not necessarily with a history of insanity in his family but one who displays, I am afraid to say, a pathology of the monstrous.'

Hardwick looked at his audience, expectant and pleased with himself.

Without raising his hand, Pyke said, 'I'd imagine that – how did you put it – "the intervention of psychiatry into the law" will be personally beneficial to you. It'll give you patients and, of course, status.'

Hardwick frowned, as though he had not understood the question. 'I'm sorry? You are . . . ?'

'I mean, I can see how you might personally benefit from inventing a condition such as – how did you phrase it? – "*homicidal monomania*". You say something exists, so it exists. And because it exists, it needs to be treated. And who can treat it but you? It's like finding or, in your case, *inventing* a disease that only you have the power to cure. I'm impressed by the effrontery of the scheme, if not by its scientific foundations.'

The murmurs around the room were, he suspected, of consternation at his impudence, and Pyke wondered whether he had overplayed his hand.

'And what do you know of science, Mr . . . ?' Hardwick's face was as black as thunder.

'Pyke will do.'

'What I am alluding to, and what a lesser mind such as your own might not have grasped, is that such ideas inevitably have much wider applications, *Mr* Pyke. At the heart of modern psychiatry and criminology is a belief that we have the power to treat and transform human behaviour. I'm sure if you had seen the fine work being undertaken by Philippe Pinel in France and Samuel Tuke in York in bringing to bear a moral regime on deviant behaviour, then you would not be so dismissive of the role psychiatry can play in bringing order to our world.' Peel nodded his head and Hardwick smiled.

'I have no personal experience of those places, but as is the case with all institutions, I'd wager that they are as oppressive in their own right as Newgate itself.'

That drew a thin smile from Hardwick. 'Except that the condemned man in Newgate prison would tear you apart, given half a chance, while those under Tuke's supervision would happily go on about their business. In whose company would you prefer to spend some time?'

'And let's say you were in physical danger from an invading army or were being bullied by someone stronger than yourself.' Pyke stared at Hardwick and smiled. 'Who would *you* turn to for help? A smiling lunatic or violent outlaw?'

'Good God, man, criminals of any denomination should not be lauded as *heroes*. They are but children who lack the necessary self-discipline to control their excessive passion.'

'Unlike you, Mr Hardwick, I grew up around such people

and there is nothing childish or ill-disciplined about most of them. They are just poor, desperate people doing what has to be done in order to survive.' Pyke decided it was time to move in for the kill. 'And is that who murdered our newborn baby just delivered from its mother's womb? A child?'

For the first time Hardwick's composure seemed to crack. He stammered something about the difference between conventional criminal behaviour and homicidal monomania.

'But practically speaking, *Mr* Hardwick, how does your diagnosis assist those of us actually involved in the process of trying to catch whoever murdered these people? Who, or what, are we supposed to be looking for? By the sounds of things, any of us here could be suffering from homicidal monomania, if the symptoms are undetectable under ordinary circumstances. Surely you don't suspect one of us?'

A laugh rippled around the room. An indignant Hardwick was about to respond but before he had a chance Peel intervened, to bring their discussion to an end. He thanked Hardwick for enlightening them with his *theories* and, addressing Pyke, said, 'If you find our friend's ideas to be less than useful in this particular instance, perhaps you could share with us your own thoughts regarding what you witnessed and how they might assist us with the investigation?'

Pyke made a point of addressing the room from where he was sitting. As he had done to Fox and Vines, he explained what had happened, what he had seen and what it might mean. When he had finished there was a sober hush in the room. Peel glanced nervously at Charles Hume. Hume merely nodded. Peel thanked Pyke for his illuminating thoughts, and said he was sure his discoveries would be of tremendous use to the investigative team.

Charles Hume agreed. Hardwick sat in silence, scowling. Beside him, Pyke heard Fox whisper, 'You stuck it to the bastards. Well done.'

As the gathering broke up, Peel came across to where he was sitting and asked Pyke whether he might be able to stay behind for a few minutes, so they could chat in private.

Fox answered him first. 'I think we'd be prepared to discuss relevant matters in a more *congenial* atmosphere.'

'I had rather hoped I might have a word with Mr Pyke on his own. I am assuming, of course, that such an arrangement might be acceptable to you, Sir Richard.'

'Why on earth should it not be acceptable?' Fox said huffily. 'I will wait for Pyke in my carriage.'

Peel put his hands into his pockets. 'You go on ahead, Sir Richard. It's late and I'm already concerned that I have taken up too much of your valuable time. I'll make my own carriage available to Mr Pyke.'

'Really, I don't mind waiting.'

'No, really, I insist that you are delayed no more.' His manner indicated that the subject was closed for discussion.

'Well, I've been told, haven't I?' Fox said under his breath. Peel either did not hear him or chose not to answer him.

'It perhaps does not need to be emphasised that any investigation, whether it's carried out by Hume or yourself, should be a discreet one. The public is fickle and their willingness to sanction a new police force is conditional on the belief that its role will be one of prevention and not detection. It's *one* of the areas where I disagree with Hardwick's assessment. He sees detection as one of the characteristics of preventive policing, whereas I believe prevention to be preferable to detection.' Peel had ushered Pyke into a chair just across from him. Up close, his skin was pockmarked and lumpy.

'I understand you're asking me to conduct some kind of unofficial or parallel investigation,' Pyke said, trying in vain to read Peel's expressionless face. 'I'm just not sure in what capacity that might be.'

That drew a shrill laugh. 'If you'll permit me to speak plainly, I would say that you're not a fellow who needs, or indeed cares for, official sanction.'

Pyke acknowledged the remark with a nod. 'And if you'll permit me to speak plainly, that is the kind of remark I would expect from someone who clearly enjoys such sanction as a matter of course.'

Peel's eyes narrowed. 'Allow me to further speculate, then. Perhaps Sir Richard has already asked you to continue with your investigation, regardless of the outcome of this meeting. For some reason, he has been quick to identify this incident as crucial to the continuing survival of Bow Street.' He looked at Pyke and smiled. 'You don't have to respond.'

Behind them, the brooding man entered the room and took up a chair. Peel did not acknowledge him.

'I didn't think it was a question.'

'I stand corrected.' The smile vanished from Peel's face. 'Correct me if I'm wrong, and forgive my crude attempts to read your mind, but when you were describing what you found in that room, I got the impression you have already developed a strong attachment to the investigation. Perhaps you will pursue this matter, irrespective of whether or not you are sanctioned to do so.'

'Perhaps I will.'

'Then all I am asking is that you keep me informed of your progress. In an unofficial capacity, of course.'

Usually Pyke did not have a problem reading the nuances and inflections of people's speech and actions. He could tell when someone was lying to him or trying to flatter him, even when those deceptions were dressed up in the most oblique disguises. In this instance, though, he could scarcely begin to decipher the various masks Peel had worn throughout the evening: cold, calculating pragmatist, political statesman, personal confidant. He had heard that Peel was quick-tempered, stubborn, oddly self-conscious and lacking in assurance, but he'd seen none of these characteristics on display. What he had seen was someone who could be a formidable opponent or a useful ally.

'You are perhaps wondering what advantage this type of arrangement might afford you?' Peel said, staring at Pyke with an unsettling intensity.

'It had crossed my mind.'

'It would not be possible to offer you any financial inducement.'

'Nor would I expect it.'

'But if, say, you *were* to continue with your own investigation, then perhaps as a courtesy to my office, you might share your findings with Charles Hume. Such an arrangement might be beneficial to our shared ambition of finding and being seen to find whoever carried out these abominable acts.'

Pyke digested this request. 'And if, for any reason, I needed to get in touch with you?'

'I would expect all of our correspondence to take place through Charles.'

Pyke decided to push the point. 'But say I had some cause to pass a message to you in person?'

For the first time, Pyke sensed Peel's unease. Taking his time, Peel motioned towards the dark-haired man who was sitting behind Pyke and said, 'Let me introduce Fitzroy

Tilling. He served under me while I was Chief Secretary in Ireland.' Pyke turned around to acknowledge Tilling.

'Let's just say, should the need arise and should Charles Hume be unable to assist you, you could contact me via Mr Tilling here.'

'It means you can have it both ways.' Pyke held Peel's formidable stare. 'Find out what I know and keep an eye on me at the same time.'

'You think me too devious.' Peel rested his large hands on his desk. 'I'm going to be blunt with you, Pyke, and you might think me hard for saying this. I am not particularly concerned about the deaths that you're investigating. I think them abhorrent, of course, but I am compelled to address my attention to a more general set of circumstances. If I am honest, I believe the Irish race to be an inferior one, at a lower stage of development than our own and, therefore, do not intend to alter any course of action already deemed by myself to be in the best interests of *this* country as a result of a few deaths, whether those who died were Catholics or Protestants. But I am, and have to be, concerned about the implications for public order, and the sooner this business is resolved the better it will be for everyone. I am not afraid to call in the armed forces because I am not afraid of being unpopular, but I see this course of action only as a last resort.'

When Pyke said, 'It is far better to be feared than loved if you cannot be both,' he saw the recognition register in Peel's eyes.

He was about to follow it up with another quote from the same source when the door to Peel's private office flew open and into the room strode a tall, muscular man, older than Peel by some years, dressed in a red riding coat, a silk cravat and buckskin breeches worn over stockings. He was striking rather than handsome, with grey hair, sideburns, a Roman nose and ear lobes that were as fat and long as half a pear. He limped ever so slightly. 'The King really is the worst man I have ever had to deal with, the most false and with no redeeming qualities.'

The man still hadn't noticed Pyke and continued, 'And have you heard the King's brother has recently returned from Hanover and is causing untold mischief?' As he slumped into a chair next to Pyke, the man finally realised Peel was not alone.

That was how Pyke found himself sitting next to the Prime Minister, the grand old duke himself, and he smiled inwardly at the thought of what he could do in that moment. Pyke was not enamoured of the aristocracy, nor did the duke's battlefield exploits impress him. He did not necessarily like or dislike the man, but simply because the opportunity had presented itself he imagined drawing out his pocket knife and driving it into the duke's heart.

'Arthur. Mr Pyke here and I were just discussing the relative merits of Machiavelli's account of statecraft.'

'*Who?*' The duke looked at Peel and frowned.

'Mr Pyke is a Bow Street Runner.

'Not him, dammit,' the duke muttered, ignoring Pyke. 'The other fellow.'

'A Florentine consort, I believe. He wrote a book called *The Prince.*'

'Oh.' The duke turned back to face Peel and shrugged. 'Why is *this* man relevant here?'

'Machiavelli lived in the early sixteenth century . . .'

'I'm not stupid, Robert. I meant this chap here,' the duke said, motioning without enthusiasm at Pyke.

'Mr Pyke was the man who discovered the bodies in St Giles.'

'What bodies?' The duke seemed both confused and annoyed. 'I'm the Prime Minister and no one tells me a bloody thing.'

Peel looked at Pyke and said, 'I think the Prime Minister and I need to have a talk . . .'

Pyke stood up and left.

FIVE

Lizzie's gin palace did not, as the name might suggest, belong to Lizzie Morgan, the woman who occasionally shared Pyke's bed. Nor did it belong to her father, George Morgan, who had once been a Bow Street Runner and had first initiated Pyke into the ways of earning additional income from the job. The establishment, which occupied a position at the north end of Duke Street, at the back of St Bartholomew's Hospital and adjoining the livestock market at Smithfield, was owned by Pyke himself – the happy by-product of a business arrangement that had also led to the capture and imprisonment of a notorious criminal. For a while, after this man's conviction, his base of operations had remained vacant. Pyke had bought the lease with reward money paid to him by the grateful owner of valuables Pyke had recovered. He had then transformed it into a drinking establishment replete with plate-glass windows and gilt cornices, ornamental parapets, spittoons, gas lights and illuminated advertisements announcing the 'medicinal' properties of the gin on sale. Initially George, who had just retired from the Runners, had assumed the day-to-day running of the bar, but a stroke had subsequently confined him to his bed and propelled Lizzie into the limelight.

Pyke had christened it the Smithfield gin palace, but ever since Lizzie had put on her apron and taken over the running of the bar, most folk simply referred to it as 'Lizzie's place'.

It was after three in the morning by the time Peel's carriage dropped Pyke outside the entrance. The main bar was deserted – the gas lamps had been switched off – and Pyke went straight up to his room, ignoring the powerful scent of human sweat, sawdust and alcohol. To his dismay, Lizzie was curled up in his bed, gently snoring. He envied her peace. Without waking her, he closed the door behind him and went back downstairs to the bar.

Pyke knew that sleep was beyond him, just as he also knew that he did not want to wake Lizzie and have to field well-meaning questions about where he had been and what he had been doing. But he could not settle in the empty bar and found himself yearning for someone to distract him from the unpleasantness of his own thoughts.

Even the laudanum, which he kept hidden away in a bottle behind the counter, did little to alleviate his anxiety.

A while later, still numb from the drug, he found himself walking, unaware of his surroundings or the biting wind, not knowing where he was going until he had reached the cobbled streets surrounding St Paul's. The giant cathedral stretched so far above him that he could hardly see the starless sky.

When he couldn't help himself, Pyke tended to prowl the streets around Wellington Barracks on Birdcage Walk, looking for 'dollymops': maids, shop girls and milliners who moonlighted as prostitutes to earn additional money and perhaps find someone to support them in a flat of their own. But given that he was half an hour's walk from the barracks, he didn't expect to find anyone except a street-hardened prostitute. Usually Pyke did not much care for their crude ways, preferring the faux innocence of girls who still believed in the possibilities of true love. This time he had no intention of being selective.

To his surprise, in a grubby all-night coffee house, he found a nervous red-headed girl, no more than sixteen years of age, wearing a loose coat over a tatty wool dress. Her nails had been chewed but were clean, and before she could tell him in a soft voice that she didn't do this sort of thing, he thrust a crown into her shaking palm. It was more than treble the going rate. He took her hand and led her, firmly rather than forcefully, outside. Her resistance crumbled when she saw the colour of the coin.

Outside, when she tried to speak, Pyke pressed his hand against her mouth, harder than he had intended, and saw the fright register in her dull eyes. In other circumstances, he might have stopped to say something to her, reassure her, but on this occasion he was too far gone to stop himself. As he pushed her against a wall in an alley adjoining the coffee shop and guided himself into her, he closed his eyes and tried to block the image of what lay inside that metal pail from his head. Moments later, as Pyke emptied himself into the nameless girl, rigid with terror, in a series of grim spasms, he felt as though he were standing over the metal pail peering down at his own corpse.

At one o'clock the following afternoon, Pyke was awoken by the unmistakable sound of cattle and sheep being driven along the narrow street below towards the vast market. On market days, the entire downstairs would be filled with traders, drovers, buyers and meat cutters standing three or four abreast along the entire length of the mahogany counter, smearing animal blood from freshly slaughtered carcasses on to cheap glasses from which they drank their gin. Even without the window open, Pyke could smell the filth and mire of the market and hear the screeching din of ten thousand frightened animals squealing, bleating, lowing and awaiting their demise. In spite of the rosemary and lavender sprigs thrown liberally on the floors throughout the building, the whole place would soon smell of offal, excrement and dead flesh.

Lizzie must have heard him splashing his face with water she had left in a bowl for him, because shortly afterwards she was in the room with him, wanting to know how he felt and where he had been until five in the morning, masking her suspicions with affection. She was an ungainly woman, sinewy and powerful despite her apparently slight frame, and easily capable of throwing a man twice her size out of the bar when it was called for. Up close, Pyke could smell the soap he had bought for her last birthday on her scrubbed skin and felt a pang of remorse: remorse that, despite her physical toughness, business acumen and loyalty to him, he was never more than ambivalent about the notion of sharing his bed and his life with her.

She had already lit his fire and piled it high with coal.

When he had finished telling her something about the previous day, downplaying the grimness of the murder scene and omitting his visit to Whitehall, her face was still creased with worry. According to rumours circulating in the bar, a Catholic family had been burned from its home in Saffron Hill and a man of Irish descent had been clubbed to death in Hoxton.

Pyke asked whether she had heard anything at all about the dead family. Lizzie shook her head.

'Should I be worried 'bout you?' she said, after a few moments of awkward silence.

Pyke reached for the trousers he had tossed on to the floor. 'I'll not be able to see you much in the next few weeks.'

'And you don't think I'm used to that by now?'

Pyke stared out of the window.

'That's all I'm owed, is it? A quick pat on the head and some words that don't mean a ha'penny.' Her skirt clung to her legs, emphasising the thickness of her calves.

'Lizzie?'

She looked up at him, surprised perhaps by the sudden tenderness of his tone.

He almost managed a smile. 'You know that you're a better woman than I deserve.'

Her expression filled with sadness and, as she turned to leave the room, her attempt to provoke a discussion dissolved into the space between them.

'Before his death, did your brother ever talk about his experiences serving Edmonton?'

Pyke turned from Townsend, with whom he had been talking, to a constable from the local watch who was blocking their path to the lodging house. He informed the affronted man he was there at the behest of Charles Hume. In the narrow street, there was none of the hysteria of the previous night: apart from a few curious onlookers, the place was almost entirely deserted. Certainly the residents, all potential witnesses or sources of information, had either been taken somewhere else or, worse still, dismissed. No doubt they had given false assurances and willingly taken the opportunity to disappear into the welcoming anonymity of the city.

Pyke wondered who had let them go. Did this mean Hume already knew something he did not? He dug his hands into his coat pocket and looked over at Townsend.

Townsend shrugged. 'He talked about lots of things, mostly what a ghastly, tyrannical creature the old man was.' Though a Bow Street Runner for longer than Pyke, Townsend had none of Pyke's ambition, and willingly permitted Pyke to act as he saw fit, so long as he was allowed to prosper from Pyke's enterprises. It had been entirely fitting that Townsend had come to Pyke three years earlier with news that his brother, a valet for Edmonton, had expired under mysterious circumstances and with a proposal to gain revenge on the man whom he suspected of arranging the death.

Townsend's brother had been accused of stealing from Edmonton. But before the charges had been laid out before the magistrates, his body was found floating in a lake in the grounds of Hambledon Hall. The coroner's jury had returned a verdict of suicide but Townsend had long suspected foul play. He had always believed his brother had discovered something about the aristocrat; something that had, in turn, hastened his demise.

Pyke had worked with Townsend to successfully realise a plan to defraud Edmonton, but Pyke knew the rancour his friend felt towards the man had not withered with time.

'Did he ever mention Edmonton's daughter?'

Standing at the bottom of the rickety staircase inside the lodging house, they looked up and saw two men struggling down the steps carrying a large crate. One of them said, 'Is that the last of it?' The other said, 'I don't reckon we need to bother with the mattress. If he wants it, we can always come back for it.' Upon seeing Pyke and Townsend, they lowered the crate to the floor. One of them, perhaps the foreman, who was a pugnacious man with a neck like a chimney stack, stared at Pyke as though there was some kind of bad blood between them.

When Pyke explained they were hoping to talk to Charles Hume, the man replied that Hume had returned to number four Whitehall Place, adding, 'You want him, you ask for him there.'

Pyke explained who he was and that he wanted to inspect the room where the killings had taken place.

The man said he didn't give a damn what Pyke did, but he wouldn't find anything in the room itself.

Once the two men were out of earshot, Townsend said, 'I remember him saying she was wilful. Wilful and able to turn heads, even as a girl. It goes without saying that the old man's genes can't have had much to do with her looks. I'm told the mother was a fair beauty.'

Pyke looked at Townsend, interested, 'What happened to her?'

They started to ascend the staircase. The whole building was eerily quiet.

'Apparently she went insane. This was well before my brother worked for Edmonton. But there were rumours that she'd been committed, against her will.' Though they were alone, he lowered his voice. 'The money was always on her side of the family, if you know what I'm saying.' Behind him, Townsend paused on the stairs. 'I heard that she died shortly afterwards. Convenient, don't you think? Just like my brother.'

Pyke digested the implications of this information for a few moments. 'Do you know anyone who works for Edmonton now?'

'Not any more,' Townsend said, breathing heavily from the exercise. He was a barrel-chested man with thick forearms. 'But I could ask some questions, see what I turn up.' At the top of the building, Pyke held up his lantern and motioned to the room.

Townsend looked at him. 'This is the place?'

Pyke wondered where the corpses had been taken and whether anyone had claimed them for burial.

At the threshold, Townsend hesitated for a moment and said, 'Why did you ask me about Edmonton?' His bloodshot eyes suggested his hate for the old man burned as brightly as ever. 'Has he got something to do with this business?'

Pyke thought about Swift but told Townsend that there wasn't a connection. He had other business with the old man. He did not mention the robberies. Townsend asked what he wanted to know about the lord's affairs and his family. Pyke shrugged and said he didn't know, but any information or gossip about the mother or indeed the daughter might be helpful. 'Family skeletons,' he said, half distracted by their proximity to the murder scene.

Townsend assured him he would do whatever he could. 'Shall we go in?'

Pyke did not want to, but since a further inspection of the room itself seemed necessary, he did not have a choice in the matter. He needed to know more about the victims and this was his last attachment to them, to their world. If, as he believed, the murders were not the work of a crazed madman, an escaped Bedlamite perhaps, then it followed that the victims had been selected and indeed killed *for a reason*. Find the reason and he would find the killer. Though he had said little to Fox on the subject, Pyke instinctively believed the victims had known their killer or killers.

They stepped into the room.

Apart from the mattress, it had been stripped bare. Even the floorboards had been scrubbed clean, and aside from the dark stains that remained, there was little or nothing to suggest what had taken place there.

Initially, when he had been told about the removal of all possessions to number four Whitehall, Pyke had been disappointed and angry because he had thought their usefulness as clues depended on their physical presence in the room. But as he waited for his eyes to adjust to the gloom, Pyke felt relieved by their absence and indeed by the

69

absence of the three bodies. The room seemed both larger and more peaceful. It afforded him the opportunity to *think*, to put himself in their places and try to imagine what they had gone through. Taking no notice of the dark stain, he sat down against the wall farthest from the door, in the position that he had found Stephen Magennis in, and put his hands behind his back, as though bound.

'Why did he tie them up?' Pyke said, half to himself and half to his companion.

He imagined his mouth was gagged, imagined the metal pail in front of him, and closed his eyes.

'You reckon he tied 'em up *before* he slit their throats?'

'Possibly.'

'Perhaps he tied 'em up in *order* to slit their throats. Keep 'em still.'

It made some kind of sense but Pyke was not quite convinced. Sitting in the darkness, he tried to imagine what had happened: in what order had the killings taken place? Had the murderer slit the throats of the parents and then throttled the baby? Or had it happened the other way around? What if the parents had witnessed the killing of their baby?

This thought struck him with the force of a lightning bolt. What might it have been like for them: having to watch as their own baby was strangled in front of their disbelieving eyes? To watch, bound and helpless, while someone squeezed the life out of the most precious thing in their life?

'What if they were tied up because the murderer actually wanted them to *witness* him killing their baby?'

Townsend was standing on the threshold. His figure was silhouetted in the door frame. 'Why would he want 'em to witness it?'

'What if he knew them?'

Townsend did not say anything.

'What if it was personal?' Pyke thought about it: what if they had been attacked and knocked unconscious initially, bound and gagged while unconscious, and brought round by having urine thrown into their faces? *What if they had been brought round because they were meant to see it happen?*

'That would be a brutal thing,' Townsend said, guardedly.

'The two of them were propped up against the wall, where I am. The metal pail was placed in the middle of the room. It resembled a stage. In which case, the parents might have been the audience.'

'You think someone would be capable of such . . .'

'Cruelty?' Pyke said, looking up at Townsend. It was almost impossible to imagine so, but instinct told him it was an idea worth pursuing. It didn't mean he was any closer to actually finding who had done these things, or why, but it did mean finding out more about the victims would perhaps lead Pyke one step closer to their killer. Or, indeed, their killers, because Pyke could not be sure that only one man was involved.

Townsend shrank back on to the landing. Pyke heard him mutter something under his breath.

Standing up, Pyke stretched his numbed legs. On the blackened wall he noticed a small crucifix. Nothing in the room indicated anything of the victims' personalities and, in order to find their killer, he needed to know something more about their lives. Therefore Pyke knew his first task was to do as Fox suggested: finding the missing cousin was now his main priority.

SIX

It had always amused Pyke that the view from Sir Richard Fox's walnut-panelled office at the front of number five Bow Street took in the Brown Bear tavern, where prostitutes as young as fourteen cavorted with thieves who used its upstairs rooms to plan robberies, exchange gossip and dispose of stolen goods. It amused him that the portrait of Sir Henry Fielding, the man who had founded the Bow Street Runners, which hung on the wall above a marble fireplace, stared down at Fox, who, in turn, stared out of his window at criminals going about their business. It seemed to make a mockery of Sir Henry's ambitions.

Fox did not appear to be suffering from any ill effects as a result of his humiliation at the hands of Peel. In fact, he seemed to be more enthusiastic than Pyke had seen him in a while – when Pyke stepped into his office he leapt up off his armchair, came over to greet him and launched into questions. What had Peel wanted and why had he insisted that Pyke stay behind?

Certainly Fox did not seem to be worried about the lynching of Catholics taking place across the city. All he said on the subject, with some satisfaction, was that Peel and the duke would have to postpone their plans to introduce the Catholic Emancipation Act. He didn't mention the Metropolitan Police Bill.

Pyke explained that Peel had merely wanted him to

elaborate on his speculations. Peel had seemed worried that, if there were parallel investigations into the St Giles murders, they might arrive at different conclusions and such a state of affairs could end up being politically embarrassing.

He said Peel had requested that he leave the investigative work to Hume's team, but he was to make himself available, to assist them if his help was needed. Pyke believed something of what he told Fox was true: Peel's desire to keep him close at hand *was* motivated by the fear that he might unearth something potentially threatening to the cause of police reform and Catholic emancipation.

Fox appeared to believe Pyke's account of his meeting without reservation. It was as he had expected.

But Fox was not about to relinquish his responsibility without a struggle and had already questioned Goddard and Townsend about what they had learned of the victims from any of the residents who lodged with Miss Clamp.

Pyke asked about the missing cousin.

Fox returned to his chair and sat down. 'A neighbour, Mrs Jackman, who shared one of the upper-floor rooms, was on speaking terms with the deceased. She informed Goddard that she didn't know whether the young girl who shared their room was Clare's cousin or not, but she provided him with a name and a description. Mary Johnson. No more than twenty years old, attractive but frail, with brown hair, a thin face and freckles. The neighbour chatted to her once. The girl had an Irish brogue. She told Mrs Jackman that she worked in a nearby factory as a seamstress, but Mrs Jackman said to Goddard that she often saw her dressed in expensive clothes, dresses made of satin and silk, and that she doubted Johnson would have been able to afford such items on what she earned as a seamstress.' He looked up at Pyke, pleased with himself.

'You're saying that she was not a seamstress at all,' Pyke said.

'Perhaps.'

'A pretty young girl with expensive clothes.'

'It means one of two things, doesn't it?'

Pyke nodded without much enthusiasm. 'That she had a suitor with money or she worked as a prostitute.'

'It's a start, isn't it?' Fox said, seeing his reaction. 'We have a name, a description and perhaps also know how she earned her money.'

Pyke gave him a hard stare. 'Even if that was the case, do you have *any* idea how many prostitutes there are in this city?'

The task of locating a young Irish girl who may have been whoring for money was not quite as daunting as it sounded, but it was not too far from finding the proverbial needle in the haystack. Pyke could rule out having to look too far from St Giles and the community in which she lived. Prostitution was rife across the entire city – from the taverns of the Ratcliffe highway to the fashionable assembly rooms of Haymarket – and theoretically Mary Johnson could have travelled to any part of it to ply her trade. But Pyke believed it was more likely she would have done so somewhere in or close to St Giles. This only helped slightly, for St Giles, since it bordered on the theatres of Drury Lane and taverns, hotels and private clubs of Covent Garden, contained the largest number of brothels and the highest concentration of prostitutes anywhere in the city.

Pyke knew that the image of a prostitute in respectable circles – a foul-mouthed tart with painted lips and false hair who called herself Sal the Siren or Anytime Annie – applied to just a fraction of them. Women from a variety of social backgrounds came to prostitution for a myriad of different reasons: to avoid destitution, to supplement a low income, to escape the shame of pregnancy or a broken engagement, to find a husband, to pay off a debt, or to run away from family.

Pyke was not looking for a type of woman. He was looking for a particular woman and it paid to know the difference.

As with all professions, there was an established hierarchy. At the top were the courtesans, who worked in the most fashionable areas and who solicited only wealthy gentlemen, and women who were kept in their own apartment by a single suitor. Below them were the board lodgers who worked and lived in brothels and paid a proportion of what they earned to a madam. Below them were those who hung about the lodging houses and taverns of the rookeries, and the dollymops who had other jobs as maids or cleaners and worked only to supplement their meagre income. At the bottom of the pile were the streetwalkers. Pyke doubted that Mary Johnson was anywhere near the top of that hierarchy. Nor did it seem likely that she worked full-time in a brothel or lodging house since she appeared to board with her cousin. This meant that either she worked on a casual basis, picking up men in taverns and coffee shops, or she walked the streets. And Pyke did not see her as a streetwalker; according to the neighbour, her clothes were too refined.

Though he had a full description and a name, his task remained a prodigious one: there were hundreds of young, pretty, dark-haired girls who picked up men in the taverns of the area.

But Pyke had two things going for him: first and most obviously it stood to reason that somebody knew Mary Johnson or knew of her and might know where he could hope to find her. More importantly, however, there was also the fact that Pyke had money and was prepared to pay generously for any information that might lead him to the girl.

Even though Pyke was aware of how badly he wanted to find and talk to Mary Johnson, it struck him as odd that he was willing to fund the exercise from his own pocket and had no chance of turning a profit on it. As he walked along Bow Street towards Long Acre and stared upwards at the vast canopy of frozen blue sky that stretched far beyond the limits of the city, he felt light-headed, as though the recklessness of his decision meant that he no longer understood himself as well as he once had.

After noon the temperature started to plummet, so that by the time dusk arrived the usually bustling streets of the capital were practically deserted. The conditions had driven even the hardy porters, cabmen and dung collectors indoors. It was so inhospitable that the river itself was in danger of freezing. Though it was only early afternoon, it also meant that the taverns and coffee houses were bursting with custom. In these establishments, Pyke found a cavorting mass of stinking bodies.

Even Pyke, who was used to the harshness of the city, was weary from his exertions, from walking its unforgiving streets and smelling its noxious smells: the grim odours of its wet pavements, the stench of the river at low tide, the tanneries where human excrement was used as an astringent, and the ubiquitous smells of horse dung, animal sweat, fried meat, rotten fruit and discarded herring bones.

Over lunch purchased from a street vendor, a hot meat pie dripping with warm gravy, he had watched as two men, one dressed as a Protestant minister, staged a 'conversion' play for the unwary crowd. The minister said a few prayers and sang a hymn and the other man rose up and started to spit on some rosary beads and an effigy of the Pope. Apart from Pyke, everyone in the crowd applauded wildly. The minister passed round a collection plate. Once the crowd had dispersed, the two men tipped the coins into one of their hats and disappeared into a nearby tavern.

During the day, Pyke visited countless taverns and brothels, asking for Mary Johnson and spreading the news about the reward money. He had narrowly avoided being attacked with a broken glass in the Black Horse on Tottenham Court Road and had come close to breaking the neck of a young thief who had tried to pick *his* pocket outside a brothel on the corner of Church Street and Lawrence Street in the heart of the rookery.

He had also suffered the stares of ordinary men and women in most of the taverns that he had visited. These were *his* people and yet they were as strange to him as a South Sea islander or an African pygmy.

The Rose tavern on Rose Street in Covent Garden had, during the last years of the previous century, hosted posture molls who stripped naked while standing on overturned crates. These activities still happened, though on a more informal basis, but the tavern's main business was straight-down-the-line prostitution. Upstairs, the madam, Polly Masters, an ugly woman with no front teeth and thick black hair sprouting from her bulbous nose, greeted Pyke with measured enthusiasm.

'The word's already got out that you're willing to pay twenty pounds to anyone who can deliver this Paddy lass, Mary Johnson.'

'Do you know her?'

As she shrugged, she afforded Pyke a glimpse of her cleavage. 'Maybe.'

Pyke paid no attention to it. 'Did she work here?'

'Might have done, I couldn't rightly say.'

'Twenty pounds is a lot of money, Polly.'

'Maybe, maybe not.' She adjusted her dress to conceal her bosoms. 'A few of my gals could earn as much in, say, a month.'

'Was Mary Johnson one of them?'

She met his stare. 'Could've been but she was a flighty one, that one. Her 'eart was never in it. Sweet lass, pretty, popular with the gen'lemen.'

Pyke asked Polly to describe Mary and she gave him a description that fitted with the one they had been given by Mary's neighbour. Polly shrugged. 'Haven't seen her for a while, I'm afraid.'

'Do you know where I might find her?'

'What's in it for you, Pyke? I mean, from what I can see, there're plenty of tarts in the city, more 'n enough to go round.'

'If you have anything worth telling me, you can leave a message at Lizzie's place, next to Smithfield.'

She gave him an amused look. 'Is it true love, then? You and Lizzie Morgan?'

He turned to leave.

'That lass, Mary, she came and went as she pleased. Not the kind of girl I much care for. Two days ago, when I weren't 'round, Mary crept in 'ere and cleared what little she had out of her room and scarpered. Vanished into thin air.'

This made Pyke turn around. 'You say this happened two days ago?'

'One of the gals might know where she went. And if I manage to dig it out of 'em, you'll be 'earing from me, Pyke. Keep that money for me. I'll want it paid in legal notes, too.'

Because it seemed to be a solid lead, Pyke said that if he managed to locate Mary Johnson as a result of her information, he would pay her fifty pounds.

Downstairs in the taproom, a man that Pyke recognised

but whose face he could not place lunged towards him through a crowd of drunken bodies. Pyke stepped to one side with ease and the knife that the man had been carrying sank deep into the flabby midriff of someone standing next to him. Pyke cocked his elbow back and punched it into the helpless face of his attacker, heard the bone in his nose crumple, and watched as the man careened sideways and sprawled on to the wet floor, taking down a dozen grown men as though they weren't any more substantial than a set of wooden skittles.

Godfrey Bond's publishing business, if it could be called that, was located in the basement of a building in St Paul's Yard, number seventy-two, which had once been home to the renowned publisher Joseph Johnson. Now, though, despite its proximity to Wren's great cathedral with its magnificent dome, the neighbourhood was an uninspiring one and, in recent years, had lost what little sheen remained, as pawnshops and lodging houses took over from more respectable businesses. Before long, his uncle often said, with amusement, the whole area would be awash with taverns, chop houses and slop shops.

Pyke found his uncle hunched over a manuscript in the back of the shop. Around him were piles upon piles of messily stacked books, pamphlets, papers and newspapers.

Godfrey looked up, saw it was Pyke and said he'd hoped it might have been a choirboy from the cathedral, lost and wanting his help. 'If it isn't enough I've got people sniping about the integrity of what I publish, I've also had word back from the pedlars who hawk my penny dreadfuls that readers think the stuff is boring and not nearly salacious enough. Meanwhile, I'm only too aware that what I've been putting out of late has been unoriginal, but there are quite simply no new stories, no one stimulating enough to write about. Defoe had Jonathan Wild and Jack Sheppard. Who have *I* got?' His uncle gave him a calculating look. 'Of course, if you were to agree to—'

Pyke cut him off. 'No, Godfrey. You know what I think about that.'

'Folk are bored with material like *Life in London*. They want the real thing. That's why Vidocq's memoirs are selling so well. They're calling him the first detective.'

'People like Vidocq because he's a rogue.'

'Exactly, dear boy.' Godfrey smiled. 'You wouldn't have to write it yourself. I'd get a proper writer, not one of those horrible balladeers. You wouldn't have to write the damn thing or even put your own name to it.'

'I value anonymity.'

'Ha, that's why you walk into any tavern in the city and people sink into their seats or crawl up the walls.'

'I don't want my life becoming public property.'

'It's not as if I'd expect you to tell me the truth, dear boy. My readers don't give a damn about the truth. They just want a good story with someone they can cheer for. We could even make you look good.' He glanced at Pyke and shrugged. 'Or bad, if you wanted to be bad. Good *or* bad. Just not both at the same time. It confuses people. They can't work out whether to shout for the man or rail against him.'

'You know what my answer's going to be. I don't know why you bother to ask . . .'

Godfrey nodded glumly. 'It gives you some indication of how bad things are.' He went to fill his glass from the jug but noticed it was empty. 'I assume you've read about the murders in St Giles? It's an awful business, I know, but if I could somehow get my hands on that story, well, it would sell like hot pies. Times like this, people need answers and explanations. You should've heard some of the preposterous tales that folk are spinning. One lad thought it was King Herod, returning to finish the job, another reckoned it was the vengeful ghost of Queen Caroline. These weren't the brightest minds, you'll understand.'

Pyke thought about *not* telling his uncle about his involvement in the events of the previous few days, beginning with the discovery of the bodies, fearing it might lead to a torrent of unwanted questions. But Godfrey would hear about it sooner or later and Pyke decided the news would be better coming from him.

To his surprise, though, the first thing that his uncle did, once he had been told the whole story, was to touch Pyke gently on the knee, look him in the eye and ask how he was bearing up.

Pyke had always felt it necessary to guard against his uncle's attempts to solicit favours from him. Yet as he looked into Godfrey's guileless eyes, he couldn't help but feel moved by the concern in them. Pyke started to open his mouth, but the extent to which recent events had unsettled him suddenly made him feel weak and the words wouldn't come. He thanked Godfrey for his concern and assured him everything would be fine.

Godfrey shrugged as though he did not believe Pyke. 'That other business you were asking about. You know. Lord Edmonton. I did a little digging.'

In the strains of the past few days, Pyke had almost forgotten about Edmonton and the robberies. He made a mental note not to overlook Swift and the question of what had taken him to the St Giles lodging house in the first place.

'It would appear that Edmonton's estate is in some trouble. The usual thing: the cost of maintenance outstripping the yield from rents. You mentioned his brother William, the banker. My source claimed that the brother's bank has been propping up Edmonton's estate for a while and keeping the lord himself in clover. He hadn't heard anything about the robberies, though. I'm afraid I can't help you there.'

Pyke thought about Hambledon Hall, Edmonton's shabby country estate, and about the strange act he'd witnessed, the two brothers openly bickering in front of him, Edmonton silencing his apparently weaker sibling.

'For what it's worth, I also heard that Edmonton is tight with the King's brother, the Duke of Cumberland. Damn nasty piece of work, that one. I'd be wary of anyone who claimed him as a friend.' Godfrey proceeded to regale Pyke with stories that he had already heard. Apparently Cumberland had once raped Lady Lyndhurst; he had also driven Lord Graves to suicide, possibly raped his own sister and, on one occasion, having received a blow on the head in the middle of the night from his valet in a botched assassination attempt, Cumberland had, according to some accounts, slit the man's throat and then convinced the authorities his valet had committed suicide. Godfrey also repeated rumours to the effect that Cumberland was engaged in a dastardly plot to poison the young Princess Victoria in order to steal the crown for himself and safeguard the Protestant ascendancy.

Godfrey pulled down his wine-stained shirt to cover his girth. 'You also asked about the mother.' He watched Pyke suspiciously. 'And the daughter.'

Pyke nodded but said nothing.

'The daughter, Emily, is an acquaintance of Elizabeth Fry. She's a committed reformer or an interfering do-gooder, depending on your point of view. They visit prisons, asylums and even factories, and write reports as a way of pressuring the authorities to improve conditions. Most of 'em are your wearisome God-bothering types, motivated by the usual nonsense about bringing the poor to the Lord, as though prayer and a few homilies about the Almighty will put food in their stomachs. Apparently this one doesn't do the work for the glory of God. I asked Reverend Foote about her. As the Ordinary, he knows her quite well. He doesn't much care for the reforming type but he told me something you might find interesting. Edmonton is not the kind of man who would readily allow his only unmarried daughter even the tiniest smidgen of freedom or the financial support to carry out work he, no doubt, regards as unbecoming.'

Pyke affected a frown. 'What are you telling me?'

'Well,' Godfrey said, enjoying himself, 'at the time of their marriage, control of the Hambledon estate, as the law demands, passed from wife to husband, but I'm told that the marriage settlement included a number of unusual provisions. A certain sum of money was settled on their future offspring *by trust*. I don't know if the wife had doubts about Edmonton's character even then but, at the time, he wasn't in any position to dictate terms. You see, *Lord* Edmonton was by no means a member of the landed gentry in those days. He was only titled as a result of his connections with Tories like Eldon and Winchelsea.' Godfrey tapped his nose. 'The old man, it would appear, has little power to prevent his daughter from doing what she damn well likes with her income and, I'm told, it's driven him nearly to the point of apoplexy she has chosen to use it in the manner she has.'

Pyke thought about Emily Blackwood and the violent argument with her father he had overheard. But he was also preoccupied by something else, something that had been on his mind for the entire day, something that related to the living arrangements of the deceased and their missing cousin.

First thing in the morning, he would pay a visit to number four Whitehall Place and examine what had been removed from the lodging house.

SEVEN

But the following morning, Pyke found himself standing outside the entrance to Newgate prison, waiting for Emily Blackwood to finish a conversation she was having with the Reverend Arthur Foote. Though he had walked past the prison, just a short distance from his gin palace, on numerous occasions since his visit to Hambledon Hall, this was the first time he had come across Emily. Pyke stared up at the building's blackened stone-clad exterior.

There were other prisons in London but Newgate remained the most notorious. In the past, Pyke had visited the interior of the prison, mostly in order to elicit information from convicts, and found it to be a depressing but unremarkable place. Others, however, did not share his ambivalence. To them, the prison would always represent a system of justice that was as brutal as it was unfair.

They were standing almost directly outside Debtors' Door, from where condemned men and women emerged on the day of their execution and began their last journey to the scaffold. Pyke watched Foote shuffle across the street in the direction of the King of Denmark pub, a cabman's watering hole that occupied a three-storey tenement building directly opposite the prison.

In the middle of the previous century, public hangings had been moved from the open spaces of Tyburn to the more confined areas surrounding Newgate and, indeed, other prisons in the city, in the hope that this might restrict crowd sizes and turn the events themselves into more sober occasions. This hope had not come to pass; what had happened instead was that the same multitude now thronged into the narrow streets surrounding Newgate on hanging days, at a risk to themselves and others. Pyke's own father had found this out, to his cost. Old Bailey was a street of ghosts. Pyke thought about the hundreds, perhaps thousands, who had died in these environs, either inside or outside the prison walls, and of the throng who went there to witness people hang. He did not believe such people did so either to be entertained or reminded that the justice system worked. Watching another man die was essentially a way of clinging on to what little humanity you had left that had not been taken away by the city.

As he approached her, Pyke waved to attract Emily's attention.

'This is a surprise, Mr Pyke, and a very pleasant one.' They shook hands as etiquette demanded and she smiled warmly, revealing dimples on either side of her mouth. Up close, her teeth were a brilliant white and in the weak morning sunlight her hair, which sat just above her shoulders, glistened. She made a comment about the weather, pointed out that it was cold enough for them to see their own breath, and said, 'Imagine how it must be for those inside the prison without access to heat.'

Though his grooming regime consisted only of shaving on every third day, changing his outfit weekly and his underwear twice weekly and bathing irregularly, he found himself self-consciously arranging his hair in some imaginary mirror.

'I am about to visit the quadrangle allocated to the female prisoners. Perhaps you would care to accompany me?'

The last thing Pyke wanted to do was witness the squalor

and misery endured by Newgate's unfortunates, but he found himself accepting her invitation. She seemed pleased by his decision and later, once the formalities had been taken care of and they were standing in a small courtyard inside the prison, she told him their society had been trying to impress upon the Ordinary and the gaoler the nature of *their* responsibilities to the prisoners. The gaoler should visit all parts of the prison and see every prisoner on a daily basis and the Ordinary should perform a daily religious service and visit the sick. Of course, this did not happen. She laughed bitterly.

Pyke said Foote was more famous for his powers of consumption than for his pulpit oratory. This time her laugh seemed almost flirtatious.

The prison was smaller than Pyke had remembered but its fortress-like buildings, cramped together in an almost piecemeal fashion owing to the lack of space, and the sheer granite walls that stood guard over the maze of concealed courtyards and passages inside the prison, revived his fear of confined spaces.

It was a crisp day but the washed-out blue sky was not visible, even from within the prison's open courtyards, so steep were the walls and so cramped were the buildings. From within the blocks and wards, Pyke could hear the shouts and wails of the prison's inhabitants.

He tried to imagine what it might be like, to be held in such a place, with no access to the outside world.

Emily seemed entirely at ease in their surroundings. She explained how the prison was laid out. She pointed to the north side where the debtors were housed and explained that they lived in relative comfort. They were visited by vendors who hawked newspapers and tobacco, potmen who sold pints of beer and local merchants who brought with them cold joints, fish and mince pies. The condemned, she explained, occupied the press-yard side of the prison. There were two dozen rooms and fifteen cells to accommodate eighty or ninety prisoners, many of whom were likely to be granted a reprieve or have their sentence commuted to transportation. Emily said children as young as twelve mixed freely with sodomists and murderers.

In the press yard in front of the condemned wing, she pointed to a large movable scaffold. Pyke had spotted it already. The condemned man stood on a false floor with a noose around his neck, she explained, and on the executioner's signal, it dropped, leaving him hanging in the air.

Pyke said he had seen many executions and that their pointless barbarity never failed to shock him.

'Really?' she said, squinting, even though the sun could not penetrate the interior of the prison. 'I would've imagined that their violence might have appealed to your baser instincts.'

'And what baser instincts might those be?'

This time Emily blushed. 'Perhaps the ones that endow you with such self-confidence.'

'You think my confidence to be unfounded?'

'Not unfounded,' she said, looking away, half-smiling. 'But I fancy you wield it as one might a weapon.'

'What sort of a weapon?'

'I don't know,' she said, still affecting a smile.

'A rapier, perhaps?'

'I was thinking more of a bludgeon.'

'Ah,' he said, shaking his head. 'Then perhaps you are mistaking confidence for heavy-handedness. For I would not consider myself to be confident.' He waited to catch her stare. 'Especially not around you.'

She looked away quickly. 'In any case, I would have imagined punishment better suits your world than reform.'

'Quite,' Pyke said, grinning now. 'Let's return to the safer subject of barbaric violence.' He made to wipe something from his eye. Above him, a crow was circling in the small patch of sky still visible from within the prison walls. 'Just because I believe the only way of subduing any power is through the exercise of a greater power doesn't necessarily mean I find such a state of affairs *appealing*.'

'That's quite a bleak view of human nature, isn't it? The weak being torn apart by the strong and the strong being torn apart by the stronger.'

Nodding, despite himself, he found her instinctive grasp of his position impressive. He had never tried to have a similar conversation with Lizzie.

'I would've thought that description perfectly fits what's happening inside this prison.' Pyke pointed towards the condemned block.

'But that's *exactly* it,' she said, excited. 'At present, that's how these unfortunates are treated and so they act as animals. Wouldn't you?' Her eyes glistened with enthusiasm. 'But what if they were treated differently? What if they lived in separate cells, had access to proper clothes, hot food, time to exercise and read, a routine, bedsteads provided for them? Might they act in a more humane way themselves?'

'You believe people are essentially altruistic?' Pyke tried to keep scepticism from his voice.

'Call me simple-minded but I believe that a tendency for goodness exists within all of us. Even you.' Then Emily did something that surprised him: she threaded her arm through his and said, 'Come with me. I'll show you the quadrangle allocated to women.'

All Pyke said was, 'I would not have called you simple-minded.'

She did not release his arm.

The space for female prisoners awaiting trial was limited to two cells and two large wards. Something like three hundred women and children were crowded into these rooms. The fact that the female prisoners were now overseen by a female gatekeeper was the result of pressure exerted by their committee, Emily explained, as the gatekeeper led them along a thick-walled passage to one of the two main wards. From the entrance, and protected from the ward by iron bars, Pyke watched the scene in front of him with fascination and horror. He counted ninety or a hundred people crammed into a room no larger than Sir Richard Fox's office. Some wore rags. Others were naked. The only warmth in the ward was provided by the inhabitants themselves. They huddled together in small groups. The smell of unwashed bodies and stale alcohol made him want to gag. A little girl, no more than ten, caught his eye. Her lackadaisical body and hollow stare spoke of a hopelessness that seemed so all-encompassing he had to look away. These were the human dregs, criminals perhaps but with their own explanatory tales of woe and despair, and Pyke didn't want to be among them – to have to see and smell them.

'Though it might seem hard to believe, considerable improvements have been made since Mrs Fry first visited here fifteen years ago. There's now better ventilation and lighting, fixed bed places, a new dining room and dining tables, an enlarged infirmary and a new wash house.'

Pyke said he had seen enough.

Outside in the yard, Emily said, 'When we talked at the hall, I got the impression you thought all reformers to be either petty meddlers or well-meaning tyrants wanting to transform the world in their own image. What we are trying to do here is rather *small*. Desks for the condemned, the removal of rubbish once a week.'

Pyke admired her forthright nose and hazel eyes. Emily did not seem out of place inside Newgate's walls. She was part of this world and, in a strange way, it suited her.

'Perhaps not you,' he said, choosing his words carefully, 'but others have grander visions.'

'And what's wrong with grand visions?' she asked, quickly. 'Even to me, Newgate isn't just a prison. It's a word that's become synonymous with a whole system of justice, a barbaric and arbitrary one in which the educated and privileged escape punishment because of who they are and who they know and the poor are killed regardless. You asked me why I did this. Let me ask you a question in return. Is it right or fair that one prisoner should have a good flock mattress, a double allowance of provisions, an endless supply of ale and prostitutes when required, while another, equally deserving prisoner is beaten, abused, starved and left to die?'

Pyke waited until he had her full attention. 'People who can't help themselves come from all ranks and stations. Even aristocratic families.'

Her surprise registered before her anger and she recoiled from him, as though he had slapped her. 'Men always imagine power is tied only to social class,' she said, recovering some of her composure.

'You mean, your father's power is more a product of his masculine position?'

'Is that such a surprise to you? That men like my father have been shaping the world to fit their needs for centuries?'

'Including who is defined as sane and insane?'

Emily's expression hardened. 'Don't presume to speculate about my family, Mr Pyke.'

'I was referring only to your *father*.'

'Your point is made,' she said, trying to appear unaffected.

'And I commend you on your skills as an investigator, though I was not in any doubt as to your . . . abilities.' She smiled coldly.

Outside the prison, on Old Bailey, Pyke said, 'If I said that's just the way of the world, the fact that some prosper, yes, because of their inheritance but also because they're ruthless or committed or just plain lucky, while others wither and die because they aren't, would you think me hard-hearted?'

She touched his forearm and pulled him into her stare. 'Is that you, Pyke? Are you ruthless and committed?'

'I would hope so.' He shrugged. 'But I also believe we live or die ultimately according to the whims of chance.'

'But what about those who aren't ruthless *or* lucky? What happens to them?' Her face was flushed with energy. 'When you see pain and injustice, can you really just walk away?'

What she said caught him by surprise and he pulled away because he didn't want her to see that he was capable of being moved.

Waiting for her footman to pull down the steps up to the carriage, Pyke asked her what she had been arguing about with her father during his visit to Hambledon. At first, she did not seem to know what he was talking about. Her eyes dulled a little and she seemed to withdraw into herself.

Emily shook his hand and while doing so pulled herself towards him and whispered, 'People aren't always who you imagine them to be.' Her breath felt hot and sticky against his ear. 'That applies to you and me as well.'

As she climbed up into her carriage, Emily was assisted by her servant, a young woman with a plump figure and a full, round face. Briefly, Pyke and the servant exchanged a glance, and in that moment Pyke was left with an uncomfortable sense they had met somewhere before, though he could not remember where or when this might have been.

Renovation work on number four Whitehall Place had already started, a sign perhaps that Peel was more than confident about his chances of forcing the police bill through Parliament. It was a sturdy, imposing three-storey red-brick building with ornately carved arched windows on the ground floor.

Pyke had perused the morning papers and all the editorials seemed to agree: the St Giles murders made the case for a centralised, uniformed police force even stronger. But the same editorials had not been so kind to the proposed Catholic Emancipation Bill. Only the *Chronicle* called for caution and circumspection and urged its readers to wait and see what the police investigation revealed. Others failed to denounce the wave of anti-Catholic violence that was sweeping the city and demanded, in varying tones of outrage, that the Catholic relief bill either be abandoned or put on hold until people had had the time to reflect on the situation. One had even called for Catholics to be forcibly converted to Protestantism or thrown out of the country. Pyke had read a letter in *The Times* written by Edmonton in which the old man had called upon his 'fellow countrymen' and 'brother Protestants' to 'stand forward and defend our Protestant religion and constitution' from 'disgraceful attacks' by 'Tory turncoats, papal agents and lovers of Rome'.

Pyke found himself wondering how such sentiments would affect his investigation.

Finding the main entrance boarded up, he wandered around the side of the building, along a narrow passage leading into Great Scotland Yard, and tried the door that led into the old watch house.

Almost at once, he found himself confronted by the same surly man whom he had encountered at the lodging house. Pyke said that he wanted to see Charles Hume and was told, curtly, that he would have to wait a long time. The man explained there had been an important development in the St Giles murder investigation but he did not reveal what it was and Pyke did not ask.

Pyke asked to see the possessions of the deceased. At first, the man informed him that such a request was out of the question. It was only when Pyke threatened to solicit the help of the Home Office that the man relented and directed him, reluctantly, into a small room that looked out over the side alley. He pointed at a cupboard and told Pyke that what little they had removed from the room had been placed on the top shelf. The dust already gathered on top of the cupboard indicated that the Magennises' possessions had not been regarded as important to Hume's investigation.

He removed the few possessions from the cupboard and arranged them carefully on a wooden table. One at a time, he picked up both the Bibles and opened them. The first was a King James edition. It was marked and dated: Edinburgh, 1792. He idly flicked through it but found nothing of interest. The other was a Douay Bible. It was marked and dated: Dublin, 1803. The fact that they had owned two Bibles intrigued him, as did the different editions and, indeed, the different places of publication. Edinburgh and Dublin. King James and Douay. Pyke paused, to consider the name. Douay. Wasn't that a place, too? He closed his eyes and racked his brain for an answer.

He heard Emily's voice: *People aren't always who you imagine them to be.* Who did he imagine Stephen and Clare to be?

What did he know about them? That they were

poor, working folk from Ulster, Ireland. They were Protestants . . .

Then it struck him: what had been bothering him all along. At first it was just the cousin's name. Mary. The mother of Christ. *The Virgin Mary.* There were plenty of girls called Mary who had nothing to do with the Catholic faith but, then again, how likely was it that Protestant parents from Ulster would call their little girl Mary? Pyke did not know, of course, whether Mary's parents were Protestants or not but the point was an intriguing one. What if Mary and indeed Clare were not, in fact, Protestant? What if Clare was Catholic and Stephen was Protestant? Douay, he now remembered, was a place in France. It was home to a Catholic monastery. *One of them was Roman Catholic.* That was what he had missed, what they had all missed.

Pyke sat at the table for a while and tried to consider how this new information altered the nature of his investigation. On its own, it did not explain or justify anything but it seemed to be a significant discovery, if only because of the ill-feeling that such a mixed attachment might have engendered in both families. Was that why they had fled Ulster in the first place? And had someone followed them to London and discovered that Clare was, in fact, expecting a baby? Was it possible that such news could have unbalanced a relation to such an extent that he had taken matters into his own hands? Did such hate exist, Pyke wondered, when directed at one's own kin?

One thing was for certain, Pyke decided as he stared down at the two Bibles on the table. It meant that finding Mary Johnson was more crucial than ever.

Later, when Pyke was finally shown into Charles Hume's office, the man did not want to hear about what he referred to as Pyke's 'fanciful notions' about Catholics and Protestants. Rather, he glowed with self-satisfaction.

'Listen, Pyke, I can tell you this much. We have now arrested someone and I'm almost certain he's our man. I cannot tell you his name but he's thirty years old, mentally ill, with a history of violence. He escaped from a nearby asylum two weeks ago. His sister lives in the street adjacent to the lodging house. We found a razor in his room and blood on his clothes. We're questioning him at the moment. It's only a matter of time before he cracks and when he does and we elicit a confession, that will be the end of it. The investigation will be closed.'

Pyke waited for a moment, allowing his anger at the man's complacency to pass. 'Tell me this, Hume, are you merely incompetent or is someone compelling you to arrive at a hasty and ill-judged conclusion?'

Hume put down his pen and stared at Pyke. 'You dare to presume that *I* am corrupt?'

'What motivation did this man have to kill these people? How do you explain that kind of hatred?'

'You can't apply rational logic to the deeds of the insane,' Hume said, as though the issue were beyond discussion.

'Except that this wasn't the work of a madman. A man blinded by hate, perhaps . . .'

'This city is about to tear itself apart and you're proposing that we further stoke the flames by making it public we're looking for some kind of religious bigot?'

'I'm not proposing to make anything public,' Pyke said. 'I just don't want to see a man go to the gallows simply to expedite the government's political ambitions.'

That pushed Hume too far. He was a military man and didn't understand the subtleties of political brinkmanship. He rounded his desk and stepped towards Pyke, as though preparing to strike him.

'Take that remark back, sir.' Hume's neck was corded with veins.

'When your man hangs and your puppet-masters pat you on the back, remember this conversation and think about how you feel.'

'If and when he hangs, it will be because a court of law and a jury of his peers have found him guilty.'

Pyke made to leave. 'Tell that to yourself when you are lying awake at night,' he said, hesitating at the door without turning around to face Hume.

Behind him, Hume was now shouting: 'This investigation is closed. Go back to Bow Street while you still have a position.'

EIGHT

The springs of the carriage groaned as the figure inside edged towards the window. The footman, an unsmiling man Pyke did not recognise, stood beside the carriage but made no attempt to pull down the steps, or open the door, either to permit the passenger to disembark or to invite Pyke into the carriage's interior. Nonetheless, it was clear from the manner in which the vehicle was parked outside the gin palace, and from the general demeanour of the footman, that Pyke's attention was being solicited. It was a windy night, and the visibility, impaired by swirling fog, was improved only slightly by a gas lamp that hissed noisily at one end of the narrow street. The unusual sight of a gentleman's carriage in the vicinity of Bartholomew's Field had already attracted the attentions of a gang of children who were prodding the unsettled horses, compelling the footman to round the vehicle and chase them away with an umbrella. Pyke took this opportunity to step forward and peer into the gloom of the carriage's interior. Edmonton's chalky face, slick with perspiration, stared back at him, like an apparition.

'It's always revealing and indeed gratifying to see creatures in their natural habitats,' Edmonton said, glancing contemptuously at the entrance to the gin palace. 'I thought the other day, when you visited Hambledon, that there is nothing more unpalatable than seeing vermin feast at the table of a gentleman.'

Pyke looked into the old man's arid eyes. 'Your servants seem to manage well enough.'

This drew a flinty smile. 'Part of me wants to admire you, for your spirit, pathetic and misguided as it is.'

'You'll forgive me if I don't feel able to reciprocate your generosity.'

They eyed one another warily, like two beasts circling in a cage.

'I presume you have followed Swift and that he has led you to my money,' Edmonton said, eventually, settling back into his cushioned seat.

'I have certainly followed him.'

'But not found my money?' It was Edmonton's money now, not the bank's.

Pyke heard a scream from one of the adjacent buildings and momentarily looked away.

Edmonton coughed up some phlegm into a large white handkerchief and then said, 'You will, of course, know that Swift has vacated his position in the bank and disappeared, then.'

Pyke didn't know but concealed his interest in this development. Again, he wondered what business Swift had in the lodging house.

Edmonton continued, 'But since you have been keeping a close eye on him, you will no doubt know whereabouts the brigand has fled to.'

'I have had other business to attend to.'

'What other *business*?' Edmonton's face glowered with indignation. 'Damnation, man, I'm paying you to work for *me*.' He spat these words out.

'You'll remember that you haven't as yet paid me a farthing.'

'You've an answer for everything, haven't you? Pray, tell me how you might yourself fare *inside* a prison.'

'Is that a threat?'

'It is, if you don't pull yourself together, find where this Swift fellow has gone and get my money.' Spittle flew from his mouth.

'And you're in a position to make such terms binding?' Pyke said, amused more than concerned.

'I heard there's a papist recidivist, Flynn, who's been making certain accusations about you. Claims you're no better than him: a dirty, dishonest thief.'

Now Edmonton had Pyke's attention. 'And?'

'What if Flynn's accusations could be substantiated? Corroborated, as they say.' The old man's grin revealed teeth as yellow as his skin.

'Evidence can always be fabricated. In any case, it would be a foolish man who did not take advantage of all available circumstances to further his own interests. These sentiments are as true for a poor man who steals an apple as for a rich man who steals a whole estate.'

Edmonton seemed taken aback but Pyke was more interested in searching his own brain for an explanation of how Edmonton might have found out about Flynn.

Pyke had used Flynn to store items that he had recovered from thieves but which he could not claim any ransom on. Flynn had tried to defraud him by selling on some of these items without consultation and would pay the ultimate price for his dishonesty on the scaffold.

With some effort Edmonton leaned forward, almost so that his head protruded from the carriage, and whispered, 'You know enough to make things awkward for yourself, boy, but not enough to make things awkward for me. Think on that before you do anything rash.'

Before Pyke could answer, Edmonton disappeared into the cab's interior and left Pyke to ponder his threats.

*

Lizzie was drunk and agitated. That was part of the problem. It made her combative, whereas he was just tired. The skin around her neck was flushed and blotchy.

'Thirty-seven messages, Pyke, and all from thieves and swindlers. You think I got the time to be your secret'ry?' Lizzie tucked her straw hair behind her ears. 'Why do you want to find this whore anyhow? Are you fucking her?'

Pyke could smell the bar on her clothes: the spiced gin and tobacco. He had once found her muscular forearms attractive but now they just seemed vulgar. He knew other men found her desirable, the kind who clung to the bar as though it were a lifeboat set adrift in the ocean. On occasions, the gin palace would attract doctors fresh from carving up human beings in St Bartholomew's Hospital, but mostly their customers were men who traded and slaughtered animals. In either case, they smelt of fresh blood. This was the kind of man who lusted after Lizzie, but Pyke was as certain as he could be that she had been faithful to him, even though he could not claim the same thing.

It was unfair, expecting something from Lizzie he was not prepared to reciprocate, but he did not lose any sleep over his own double standards.

His room was kept warm by a plentiful supply of coal. There were a few ostensible trappings of wealth – a large Turkish rug, a feather comforter on the bed – and one of the walls was adorned entirely with shelves of books. It was an unremarkable room, one that aptly suited Pyke's needs. Though he had in excess of three thousand pounds lodged in a City bank, Pyke did not like to draw attention to his modest wealth. Still, he sometimes enjoyed the envy money elicited in others and would show off his gold watch or a wad of banknotes simply in order to witness the stares of those less wealthy and fortunate than himself.

He asked whether Lizzie had heard anything from Polly Masters at the Rose tavern in Covent Garden.

'Whoever left you a message, they're all written out. I put the list on your desk.'

Later, in Lizzie's room, as Pyke guided his erection into her, his face pressed into her pillow, he tried to picture Emily Blackwood's expression, the way she would close her eyes whenever she laughed or the looks she gave him, with eyes that were inscrutable and alluring.

Pyke felt himself harden and used the jolt of excitement to finish, so he could return to the comforting silence of his own room. But as he lay there, staring up at the ceiling, Lizzie's sadness was tangible.

'What is it about me?' There was no anger in her voice. Only regret.

'What do you mean?'

'Sometimes I think you despise me.'

Sighing, Pyke shifted away from her. 'If I despised you, would I still be here?'

'But you're not *here*.' She looked at the empty space next to her. 'That's the problem.'

'Everyone has their problems.'

'Everyone has problems. Is that supposed to make me feel better?'

Earlier Pyke had read through the list of names that Lizzie had compiled, but found no message from Polly Masters.

'Am I just another woman to fuck?'

Pyke rolled over, out of the bed, and reached down to pick up his shirt, strewn across the floor. In the dimness of the candlelight he had to strain to see where he had left his shoes.

'You're right.' He was by the door, with his back facing her. His tone was as soft as he could manage.

'Right about what?' There was hope in her voice. He hated himself for it.

'I'm sorry.' He pulled the door open but still did not turn around to face her.

'Is that it? You're sorry?' She sounded angry. 'What the fuck are you sorry for?'

'You deserve better.' He made to leave.

Lizzie exhaled loudly. 'God, you're a cold bastard.'

Pyke guessed she probably had tears in her eyes but did not turn around to see whether he was right.

Much later, when he could not sleep, Pyke ascended the staircase up to the garret under the tiles where George Morgan's crippled form lay on the bed. Often, Pyke had wondered why Lizzie insisted upon tending her father, when he hardly seemed to know who or where he was, but equally he could not imagine casting the old man out on to the street or into an asylum.

Pyke stood by the window cut into the roof and looked out at the brick chimneys of the slumbering city.

In the darkness, George's chest expanded slightly as he slept, the only indication that he was alive. Until his stroke, he had been an impressive figure, but now he seemed as frail as a rose petal.

Under George's tutelage, Pyke had developed from ingénu into a hardened professional and he could still hear the man's raspy voice: *The law is what men want it to be. Only a fool or a coward fails to take advantage of the opportunities available to him.* Between them, they had once set up and arrested the capital's most notorious robber. As George put it, afterwards, that they had prospered from the spoils of this man's crimes was incidental to the fact that someone who had once bitten a prostitute's ear clean from her head, and pummelled an apprentice to death with his bare fists, had hung by the rope.

Stroking George's sweat-matted hair, he said, 'You were never concerned whether what you did was right or not, were you, old man?'

George, near comatose, had not spoken a word in two years.

'Do what you need to do and to hell with the consequence, that was always your motto.'

Outside, it had begun to rain and the drops of water fell on to the tiles of the roof like small pebbles.

'Take what you can but don't lose sight of who you are. And, above all, don't get caught.'

The darkness hid the fact that the stroke had immobilised one side of George's face. He seemed almost normal.

'So why am I bothered, old man?'

Pyke didn't know why Lizzie had never produced children, whether she was barren or not, but as he stood up beside the old man, he wondered whether he would ever be in a position to affect someone's life in the manner George had affected his.

Fox's cheeks were flushed and his moustache was ruffled and unkempt.

Newspapers were spread across the surface of his desk. He was reading a particular report. He ushered Pyke into the chair across from him and said that special police constables had arrested an escaped lunatic for the St Giles murders and would be charging him with these crimes. He read from the newspaper. The report made it appear that the man's guilt had already been proven beyond all doubt. This sense of certainty was matched only by the hyperbolic relief the newspaper's readers were no doubt supposed to feel at the prospect of this man being behind bars.

The journalist looked forward to the spectacle of the

hanging and wondered whether the seriousness of the crime merited some additional form of punishment.

Still, news of the man's arrest had done little to stem the growing wave of anti-papist violence. A Catholic church on the Whitechapel Road had been burned to the ground. Another had been ransacked and desecrated.

Fox, though, was not interested in stories about mob violence. His ire was directed at Charles Hume's 'botched' investigation.

Briefly Pyke told him about his own argument with Hume and about his hypothesis that the murdered couple were from different religious traditions. Fox muttered something about cover-ups and deception.

He was about to excuse himself when Gerrard, Fox's personal secretary, appeared in the room, closely followed by a young boy, dressed in rags, who explained he had been told by Miss Lizzie to pass a very 'hymn-portant' message to Mr Pyke and that he had been promised a shilling in return. He wanted the shilling before he gave Pyke the message. Pyke procured the money from Fox's indignant secretary. He glanced down at the note and saw Lizzie's scribbled writing. Gerrard chased the young boy out of the office and closed the door behind them.

'Anything important?' Fox said.

'I might've found the woman.' The note instructed him to contact Polly Masters at the Rose. Briefly he wondered how much longer Lizzie would continue to come to his assistance when he treated her so poorly.

'You mean Mary Johnson?'

Pyke just nodded. Fox had remembered her name.

'Then you must go at once to talk to her.' Fox's tone was insistent. 'Take my personal carriage. It will be quicker than flagging one down. Less costly, too. There's not a moment to lose.'

Pyke wondered how far he might push Fox's untypical generosity. 'I have promised a reward for information leading to Mary Johnson's whereabouts.'

'A fee?' Fox's expression darkened. 'What kind of a fee?'

'A hundred.'

'*Pounds?*'

'You told me finding the girl was our main priority. I took you at your word.'

'A hundred pounds?'

'It's a lot of money, I know,' Pyke shrugged. 'If you don't think it's wise to pay it, we can always wait.'

'*Wait?* Who said anything about waiting?' Fox winced, as though he were in pain. 'But you need to keep a check on your expenditure, Pyke.'

'I'll go and see Gerrard.'

'We're not awash with money.'

Pyke waited for a moment. 'Can I ask you a question, Sir Richard?'

'What is it?'

This time Pyke turned around to face his old mentor. 'Have you ever had any dealings with Lord Edmonton?'

Carefully Fox placed his pen down on his desk and looked up. 'Edmonton, you say?' He ran his finger over the tip of his moustache. 'He's one of the Tory Ultras, isn't he?'

'All day, I've been asking myself how Edmonton knows Flynn has been making certain false accusations against me.'

'I'm sorry, Pyke, but I fail to see how Lord Edmonton is relevant here.' But he would not meet Pyke's gaze.

'But you haven't had any communication with him?' Pyke folded his arms and tried to gauge Fox's reaction.

'Why on earth should I have had communications with that Tory bigot?' Fox was a well-known Whig. He sounded personally hurt by Pyke's question.

Pyke shrugged. 'If you hear that anyone has been passing information about me to other . . .'

'Then I will, of course, tell you about it.' Fox sighed. 'Flynn has already been before the grand jury. He'll stand trial within the week. The scoundrel is currently being held inside Newgate.' He hesitated. 'Listen to me, Pyke. I know that you've had dealings with this man in the past and I accept that such arrangements are . . . *necessary*. This is the issue that Peel utterly fails to grasp. Policing can never simply be about prevention. As I've tried to impress on Peel many times, prevention makes absolutely no sense without detection. And effective detection, I know, means rubbing shoulders with the likes of Flynn.' Pyke thought Fox was going to say something else but he picked up his pen and added, almost as an afterthought, 'Find the girl. That's the most important thing, Pyke.'

'Gimme the money and I'll tell you where you can find the Paddy girl. That's what we agreed.' Polly Masters crossed her forearms, as though to affirm the seriousness of her intent.

Pyke removed a ten-pound note from his pocket and held it out for her to see. 'For now. You'll get the rest if your information's good.'

Polly's frown deepened. 'If I tell you what I 'eard, I ain't gonna see you 'gain.'

'And if I just give you the money and I don't find this girl, I might not see you again.'

'I got me business to run. Where am I going?'

'What we have here is a failure of trust.' He let the note fall from his fingers and flutter to the floor. They were standing in her drab office. Even though it was only ten in the morning, he could hear a man's voice through the thin walls, grunting with desire.

As she bent over to retrieve the note, Pyke reached out and gathered up the skin around her neck and pulled her upright, ignoring her chokes and threats. Her plump fingers gripped the ten-pound note as though her life depended on it. He adjusted his one-handed grip around her neck and started to squeeze, and watched as her eyes filled with water and waited for her yells to subside to whimpers.

'Listen to me, you old hag. You know where the girl is. I want that information. I find the girl, I might contemplate giving you what I promised. You don't give me that information right now, then I'll kill you. Simple as that.' He squeezed her neck a little harder and kept his stare hard and dry, like a hangman's or one of the butchers' who frequented his gin palace and told stories of disembowelling terrified cattle with three swift moves of the cleaver. He felt her limbs loosen, life draining from her.

He slackened his grip, to allow her to speak. He heard her fart. The stink filled up the office.

'Jonathan Wild was strung up for less than what you do. And people spat on his dead body.' But there wasn't any fight left in her.

He let go of her neck and wiped his hand clean with a handkerchief.

Sullen and beaten, Polly told him that the girl was hiding out at a small lavender farm owned by James Wren on the river at Isleworth.

'Did you tell anyone else about this?' He slapped her hard around the face with his open palm. She bit her lip and licked off the blood.

'Answer me.'

'No.'

'You mention this to anyone and I'll kill you. Do you understand?'

She stared at him, humiliated, but as Pyke left she didn't once mention the forty pounds he owed her.

Sir Richard Fox's private carriage, an old-fashioned wooden cab adorned on the inside with silk window curtains and velvet cushions, was pulled by two horses and driven by Gaines, a sour-faced man who seemed to resent having to transport Pyke to his destination, as though the act were somehow beneath him. The carriage transported Pyke through the traffic along Oxford Street and past crowds of people milling around the huge plate-glass windows of new luxury stores. The recently macadamised surface afforded them a smoother passage, as they passed parkland adjoining the Uxbridge Road and Paddington's grand-looking ter-races, decorated with pilasters and ironwork balconies and finished with stucco.

Past Bayswater and Holland House, they rattled on new turnpikes into the countryside, with small farms replacing the West London mansions. The city, which always seemed endless when you were in it, now felt as insignificant as a twig dropping over the edge of a waterfall.

Out here, Pyke felt a sense of release that he had not experienced for a long time. He had once served for three years on the Bow Street horse patrol pursuing thieves and housebreakers along turnpikes and across open land and had, ever since, hankered for country air.

As a boy Pyke had witnessed the execution of two men who had murdered a man travelling to a lavender ware-house in Feltham. Now, many years later, he was journeying to meet a girl hiding out on a lavender farm in nearby Isleworth. Idly mulling over the web of connections that criss-crossed people's lives, Pyke found himself returning to the murdered baby and wondering what might have become of its life, had it lived.

As the frozen landscape flashed past him, he tried to remember what his own father looked like but could not summon forth a picture in his head. Often, he had watched as Lizzie tended to George, her bedridden father, and thought about his own father and mother and whether it mattered that he knew little or nothing about them, whether it hampered his progress through the world.

They found the entrance to Wren's farm with little difficulty and Pyke alighted from the carriage, instructing Gaines to wait in the same spot for his return. He decided to approach the farm itself on foot, not wanting to give away his position and frighten the runaway girl.

Keeping an eye out for man-traps – metallic contraptions that could snap one's arm or leg – Pyke undertook a preliminary tour of the farm, no more than a couple of acres in total. It was early March and there were no workers to be found anywhere. The ground was as unyielding as marble. There was smoke rising from the chimney of the main house, indicating that the owner and his family were perhaps still living there. If Mary Johnson was hiding on the farm without Wren's knowledge or consent, then it meant she had taken up a position in one of the two small green-houses situated on the river side of the farm. Pyke dug his hands deep into his pockets, to protect them from the cold, and hid himself in a large bush that offered him a vantage point to both greenhouses.

He did not have to wait for long.

NINE

Mary Johnson was too frightened to speak.

In a ramshackle building that was both a shed and a greenhouse, she cowered under her blanket like a whipped dog. There was no warmth in the building and Pyke wondered whether she had already contracted pneumonia. Her brown hair was straggly and wet, her freckled skin almost translucent, and her lips had turned an eerie shade of blue. Her frame shook underneath the blanket. Under different circumstances, she might have been attractive, but on this occasion Pyke felt only pity for the girl. The smell of stale cut lavender was as oppressive as the freezing temperature.

Pyke explained he just wanted to find out what had happened to Stephen, Clare and the baby.

'And who are ye?' A boy who had introduced himself as Gerry stood guard over the girl and stared angrily at Pyke. He was a lantern-jawed adolescent, with freckles and thick tufts of ginger hair. If sufficiently frightened or provoked he might have been a dangerous adversary, but after Pyke had explained who he was, and that he just wanted to talk with Mary, the lad stood aside and let Pyke have a proper look at her.

Pyke repeated that he had no intention of hurting either of them. He just wanted to ask a few questions. Mary didn't even have to answer him directly. She could just nod or shake her head, as appropriate. He asked whether she could manage to do that. She looked up at him and nodded once. Pyke removed his wool coat, bent down and placed it over her shoulders. He saw her smile.

'From time to time, you'd stay with Stephen and Clare in their room in Miss Clamp's lodging house.'

Mary nodded. Now, with his view of her unimpeded, she did not look any older than sixteen or seventeen.

'And Clare was your cousin.'

This time she spoke. 'She was older than me. My da and hers were brothers. After Mammy died, when I was just a girl, Clare would look out for me.' Her brogue was soft but distinctive.

Pyke waited for a moment. 'It can't have been easy for your family, her running away with a Protestant.'

The surprise registered in her eyes but his comments seemed to embolden her. 'I can't say any of us were too delighted by the idea but, then again, we weren't the problem.'

'You're saying it was his family who caused the difficulties?'

This time she held his gaze. 'You've not spent any time in Ireland, I'd wager.'

'Is it that obvious?'

That elicited a thin smile. 'I was going to say you wouldn't understand but I suppose that'd be stupid.'

'So when his family, Stephen's family, found out about their . . . attachment . . .'

'Stephen's not like them. Weren't like them, I guess.' She made no effort to conceal her pain. 'His da was a big Orangeman in this wee village in County Armagh. So was his uncle and so was one of his brothers. All Orangemen and all bristlin' with hate. Fact that Stephen turned out to be as normal as he was, that was a genuine, God-given miracle. They're mean people, Mr Pyke. Full of hate and resentment. Never accept our right to live in our own country. Myself, I don't much care for *any* religion.'

'But they cared, didn't they? And that's the reason that Stephen and Clare came to London, to get away.'

Mary nodded. 'No one would marry 'em in Ireland. For that matter, no one would marry 'em in England neither. Not 'less one of 'em converted.' She shook her head. 'Look, Mr Pyke. Even though Clare and Stephen mostly grew up in the country, they came to live in Belfast. It's a busy town, a port, in Ulster.'

Pyke just nodded.

'It's not a bad town, as towns go. Quite open-minded, compared to the country. But even in Belfast, they weren't far enough away . . .' Her eyes started to well up. 'I don't guess you can ever run far enough away from that kind of hate.'

'Only his family, the Magennises, they found out about Clare.'

'Moment that she and your man heard of it, they were on the next steamship bound for Liverpool.'

'And from there, they travelled south to London.'

Mary nodded. 'Didn't tell a soul where they were going. It was like the earth had swallowed 'em up. Then out of the blue, 'bout six months later, I got a letter from Clare, so I did. Tellin' me where they were and sayin' I could join up with them, if I wanted to. It weren't like I had anything in Belfast to give up, apart from a job in a mill . . .'

'So you left Belfast and travelled to London.' Pyke waited for a moment before he asked whether she had been followed. But it seemed to upset her, the notion that she might have been responsible for leading members of Stephen's family to London.

To fill the silence, Pyke asked her to tell him more about the family.

'So, 'bout a month ago, I saw him, Stephen's older brother, Davy, in London. In the name of almighty God, I almost died, almost keeled over there and then. Couldn't miss him. A burly, ugly fellow. Country stock, you know, Mr Pyke. Now you got to understand me. I ain't sayin' country folk are all like Davy Magennis. He weren't ever the brightest boy in the world but, see, he grew up around all these preachers, folks talkin' about this massacre and that one, Catholics killing Protestants, what happened a hundred years before, like it was yesterday. He didn't stand a chance, I suppose. He had hate beaten into him. That's why I said you wouldn't understand, Mr Pyke. This fear we have of the other lot. Now I'm from Belfast and I grew up around different people. Myself, I wouldn't want to marry an Orangeman but I wouldn't want to kill someone, if they felt different. But to Stephen's folk, papists weren't no better than whores and rapists.'

Pyke smiled at Mary. He decided she was older than he'd initially supposed. Older and more intelligent.

'Tell me what you know about Davy.'

'He was one of the first to join up to the new police force, the Irish Constabulary, when it was first set up in Ulster, 'bout seven years back. According to Stephen, your man was specially chosen. All it was, some fellow came visitin', said the new force needed good strong Orangemen like Davy. I guess his da pulled a few strings. Made Davy feel important. Way of getting the boy out of the house. Stephen didn't talk a whole lot 'bout his brother, Mr Pyke, but when he did, he spoke in a quiet voice, like he was terrified . . .'

'And this Davy fellow, he's been in the police ever since?'

Her expression darkened. 'For a while anyhow.'

'He's not any more?'

Mary shook her head. 'They had to discipline him. In the end, they threw him out just last year.'

Pyke asked what had happened.

'I don't guess you read about too much news from Ulster in your London newspapers, do you, Mr Pyke? This all happened last autumn. There's a fellow, Jack Lawless, a journalist in Belfast, one of O'Connell's lieutenants in Ulster. You heard of O'Connell?' Pyke nodded. Mary continued, 'And you probably know, us Catholics, we're in the minority in Ulster. Well, last autumn, Lawless announces he's going to raise a force in the south and enter Ulster, march from town to town holdin' meetings and the like, raisin' support for Catholic emancipation and collectin' Catholic funds. So Lawless gathers up maybe eighty thousand men and crosses from County Monaghan into Ballybay, which is nearly all Presbyterian and full of about ten thousand Orangemen with pitchforks and scythes ready to defend their town. All of the army and police in the whole area rush to the town. At first, they manage to get Lawless to avoid Ballybay and travel via another route. But then the two sides come face to face on the Rockcorry road and all hell breaks loose. There's a pitched battle and the police wade in, too. According to Stephen, in front of a thousand witnesses, Davy beats this Catholic fellow to within an inch of his life. Normally that kind of behaviour would go unpunished but there were witnesses. After that, there wasn't nothing that anyone could do for him, even if his da was a well-respected preacher. Stephen just said his brother had dropped out of sight. No one knew what happened to him.'

'He didn't go home?'

'Not as far as Stephen reckoned.' Mary sat up a little and stretched her arms. 'Though his family hold on to much hate, they still think of themselves as respectable folk, friends in the right places. Those friends like their violence to be carried out under the cover of darkness, not in full sight of a thousand other men.'

Pyke liked her analysis. 'And that's how you think Davy got the police job in the first place? Because his father had friends in high places?'

'That's what Stephen reckoned. Reckoned the da was friends with this fella, John Arnold, owns the biggest mill in Belfast, both of 'em up to their necks in Orange business.'

'I take it you can't remember any other names. Did Stephen ever mention specific names?'

Mary frowned. 'What kind of names?'

'For a start, the man who came calling to the home, recruited Davy into the police in the first place.'

'Not that I can remember.' She winced a little. 'I'm sorry . . .'

'I have to ask, Mary. Did you see any of what happened?'

'You mean to Stephen and Clare and the wee baby?' She was shaking, perhaps not just from the cold.

Pyke nodded.

A tear escaped from Mary's eye and rolled down her cheek. 'It was a small room. I didn't always stay there. I didn't like to get in their way and in the last month I had a room elsewhere . . .'

She did not want to elaborate and he decided not to push her. 'You didn't see anything, then?'

'No,' she whispered, staring down at the ground. 'I just heard about it later. I heard about it and panicked. I collected up a few things and hid out with Gerry in his room but even there I didn't feel too safe. I knew someone would want to talk to me but I didn't want him to find out. Davy. Gerry knows a man who works on this farm in the spring and summer. We've been here a few days now. It's brutal cold, too.' She wiped her eyes. 'In the name of Jesus, it was just a baby. Would you think it was even possible?' She was crying now. Gerry sat down next to her, trying to offer comfort.

Pyke wondered whether Mary was telling him the truth. There was no doubt she was terrified. But was she keeping something from him?

'Are you certain there's nothing else you can tell me?'

This time she looked away. Gerry put a protective arm around her shoulder and glared at him.

He waited for a while before saying, 'Do you think Davy killed them? Was he capable of doing something like that?'

'Do I think he was capable of it?' Mary said, wiping her eyes with the sleeve of Pyke's coat. 'I wouldn't imagine *anyone* was capable of doing something like that.'

'But you do believe he killed them?'

Mary shrugged. 'I don't know. Honestly I don't.'

'But it's possible that he did it?'

Her stare was devoid of emotion. 'I fancy it is. The longer you live, the more you realise that anything's possible. Even something as terrible as what happened.'

Once Pyke had deposited a bedraggled Mary Johnson and a grateful Gerry in a guest house in Isleworth, paid for a week's accommodation and warned them not to go anywhere or talk to anyone without his consent, he told Gaines to return him to Bow Street. As he sat in the carriage on the journey back to the city, Pyke considered what Mary had told him and thought about the implications for his own investigation.

He was close, now, to finding the real killer, not the unfortunate lunatic who was currently being held by Hume. For a lot of reasons, Davy Magennis seemed to be the likely candidate. From the start, Pyke had believed that whoever had murdered Stephen, Clare and the baby had known his victims. Nothing about the scene suggested a random attack. It had been premeditated and, Pyke had felt all along, motivated by hate. And now, according to Mary, Davy Magennis had been sighted in London: Davy Magennis, who was uneducated, physically strong and driven by hate; a man who had perhaps lost sight of familial links to his brother.

Mary Johnson was intelligent and credible. Pyke believed everything she had told him.

Pyke was now certain that Charles Hume and his investigative team had arrested and charged the wrong man. But he didn't necessarily believe that Hume was corrupt. Pressure for a quick arrest had, no doubt, been forthcoming from Peel and charging an escaped Bedlamite was politically expedient. So how might Hume, or for that matter Peel, react to Pyke's news? It was hard to judge. Or rather Peel was hard to judge. Hume would reject his claim outright and would threaten Pyke, should he continue with his own investigation. Peel, though, would have to be sensitive to the political implications associated with convicting and, doubtless, killing the wrong man. For Peel knew about Pyke's relationship with Fox and would be only too aware that Fox continued to wield enough political clout to cause him considerable embarrassment.

Peel could not afford to ignore his claims.

Pyke thought about taking his discoveries directly to Fox but he was concerned that Sir Richard simply wanted to use the investigation as a stick to beat the government with. Fox didn't care about the dead. Nor did Peel or Hume. But out of all of them, Peel was the one who could assist or damage Pyke's cause and, for this reason, Pyke made up his mind to present his findings, in the first instance, to the

Home Secretary, and give him the chance to pull Hume into line.

Pyke leaned out of the window of the carriage and shouted at Gaines, the driver, to take him directly to Whitehall. Outside, the branches of the trees were just beginning to thaw and the first signs of green were starting to show themselves. As he blew into his cupped hands to keep them warm, Pyke thought about the dead baby, more than anything irritated that it continued to unsettle him in a way he did not understand.

Pyke knew it would be hard to secure an audience with Peel himself, at least in the first instance. Peel, after all, had instructed him to deal either with Hume or Fitzroy Tilling.

Still, he did not imagine it would be quite so difficult to convince the guards outside the Home Office to even ask inside the building for Tilling. None of them seemed to know who Tilling was. Pyke explained that he was Peel's private secretary and offered them a brief description. He introduced himself as a Bow Street Runner working at the behest of the Home Secretary himself. He said he had urgent business to share with Peel. He said they would have to shoulder the responsibility, should his news fail to reach Peel, via Tilling. It was only when he made it clear that it was a matter of the utmost importance to the security of the state that they were provoked into action.

One of the guards said he would go and make some enquiries. The other, meanwhile, led Pyke into a dingy antechamber, set off the building's main entrance hall.

Pyke waited for almost two hours for Tilling to rescue him from the stares of the two guards. The burly man greeted Pyke without warmth and led him in silence through the main hall, past the same cantilevered staircase he had seen previously on his visit to Peel's offices and down a flight of stairs, to a room in the basement of the building. It was furnished with two chairs and a wooden table. A gas lamp hissed quietly in the corner of the room.

Tilling told Pyke he could spare him ten minutes. He wore a well-cut jacket over a silk neck stocking and styled dark trousers. Though he possessed neither beard nor moustache, his sideburns were thick and as dark as the hair on the top of his head. He seemed agitated and distant, as though the prospect of spending even a few minutes in Pyke's company was the last thing he wanted.

He listened, evidently bored, while Pyke explained what had happened and recounted, as briefly as he could, the course of his investigation.

While he spoke, Pyke wondered whether Tilling, as someone who knew Ireland well and had served under Peel while he had been under-secretary there, would be in a better position to comprehend the nuances of his account. He wondered, too, whether Tilling had Irish blood in him. He didn't speak with a brogue and if he was, in part, Irish, then it was almost certain that he belonged to the Anglo-Irish planter class. This would, of course, influence the way in which he made sense of Pyke's tale of Protestant bigotry and violence. Tilling might be hostile to the assumptions behind his claims. But in the end it was just a name that seemed to rouse the man from his indifference.

Pyke could not, of course, be *certain* that the name 'Davy Magennis' had registered as forcefully as he imagined, but it was also true that, as a rule, he rarely misread other people's reactions.

Afterwards, Tilling's demeanour *did* become more agitated and he stopped listening to Pyke's account and fidgeted in his chair. His manner did not become obviously aggressive but almost at once, and without warning, he stood up and told Pyke that he had important business to attend to. Assuring Pyke that his claims would be properly investigated, he thanked him for his efforts.

Tilling left him with the two guards and did not bother to issue any form of farewell.

TEN

It was a long time since Pyke had spent any real time in his gin palace and it struck him what an unpleasant place it had become. Perhaps he had deluded himself when he had first bought and transformed the building, hoping it would become a sophisticated drinking venue, with a better class of customer attracted by brilliant interior gas lights that shone through large plate-glass windows. Pyke's own reputation may have been successful in deterring society's dregs from regularly drinking there – the scavengers, petty thieves, coal-heavers and prostitutes who gravitated towards the neighbourhood's less salubrious alehouses and drunken ex-sailors who preferred the gin shops on the other side of the river. But offers of cheap gin were enough to lure all types of working men and women to the bar: porters from St Bartholomew's, animal drovers, stable boys and meat cutters from the market and traders who sold fruit and vegetables from their barrows, all of whom wanted to get fall-down drunk and didn't care about the ornamental parapets or the fact that the drinks were served in glasses rather than clay pots or pewter mugs.

Pyke had no affinity with his customers and showed little interest in the daily running of the place. It was an investment and it gave him a modest additional income. And if Pyke had no affinity with his paying customers, nor did he have anything in common with the people who worked for him. Aside from Lizzie, who was upstairs in the attic room tending to George, the faces were unfamiliar or hostile to him. But Pyke did not expect gratitude from his staff: those who worked behind the bar, the glass collectors, the cleaners, the ex-bare-knuckle boxer who policed the bar and the three kitchen hands who served up a simple menu of chops, baked eggs, hot eel and pea soup. The pay was low, the work hard and at times dangerous, and the hours were long. He exploited them but he felt no guilt for doing so. If they wanted to work elsewhere, he never tried to stop them.

Pyke sat on an overturned barrel at one end of the zinc-topped mahogany counter and looked at what his gin shop had become. Somehow the term 'palace' seemed too absurd for words. He looked at the painted barrels behind the bar, signs advertising 'The Real Knock-Me-Out Firewater' or 'The Devil's Own' and the wooden floor covered with sawdust and vomit.

There were two fights in the bar that night and Pyke wondered whether that was typical or not. One incident was relatively minor: a meat cutter, still wearing his blood-ied work apron, swung at and missed a younger man, who stepped inside the punch and landed one of his own on the meat cutter's jaw. The single blow sent the meat cutter sprawling on to the floor, and he was picked up and dumped outside by Billy, the ex-bare-knuckle fighter. The other fight was more serious. A ferret-faced man pulled out a pocket knife on a larger adversary and thrust the blade into the man's abdomen. He got away before Billy could apprehend him but Pyke watched as the ex-boxer picked up the bleeding man, dragged his limp body across the crowded room and tossed him out of the side door.

But Pyke's attention had been focused elsewhere. As he sat alone, amid the grim tumult of the place, a sea of unfamiliar faces quietly whispering to one another, just out of earshot, he could not get over the feeling that he was being watched; not simply by the drinkers lined up two or three deep along the entire length of the counter but maybe by an agent of the state who was masquerading as a market trader or a hospital porter. But he did not know whether his suspicions were genuine or had merely been fuelled by the laudanum he had ingested.

Pyke had other significant matters on his mind, too. He could not avoid the conclusion that he had somehow miscalculated or overplayed his hand with Tilling. Again and again, he tried and failed to make sense of the man's strange reaction to his findings. He'd certainly expected some kind of message from Peel or Tilling but so far nothing had come, and he was unable to determine what this silence indicated.

By the following evening, Pyke still had not received any message from Peel or Tilling and his feeling of anxiety had intensified: so much so that he had further increased his intake of laudanum. The drug numbed him a little but did nothing to lift his unease.

What had Tilling's changed demeanour signalled? That he knew Davy Magennis? Tilling had spent time in Ireland and Magennis lived there but the idea that they knew or had met one another seemed fanciful. But if Tilling *did* know or had met Davy Magennis and Magennis was responsible for the St Giles murders, did that, in turn, suggest that Tilling was somehow mixed up in them as well? The idea seemed too preposterous for words, not least because it implicated Peel himself. And whatever Peel was – cunning and ruthless – he didn't strike Pyke as an assassin, even if the assassination had been carried out by someone else.

Then there was the question of motive. Certainly the

murders had strengthened the case for a new consolidated police force, but as far as he could tell that particular argument had long since been won. The murders had also galvanised opposition to the Catholic Emancipation Bill; a bill which Peel supported and was about to present to the Commons. As such, the idea that Peel might be involved with the St Giles deaths did not make sense, but on the other hand Tilling's nervous reaction perhaps indicated otherwise.

Pyke watched Lizzie serving drinks and, for some reason, thought about the woman in the Blue Dog tavern who had called out his name, to warn him of Flynn's imminent attack. It bothered him that, although her voice had seemed familiar, he did not have an idea of who she was.

There was a time when he had thought Lizzie to be the most desirable woman in the whole of London. This sentiment was augmented by the fact that Lizzie had promised herself to a housebreaker whom George, her father, did not approve of. In order to break up this union, and to earn George's respect, Pyke had solicited the man's assistance, to steal jewels and bonds from a house on Great Russell Street, and arranged for four constables to make the arrest, while the robbery was taking place. During the trial the robber, who had a headstrong manner and a vicious disposition, had leapt from the dock, retrieved a knife from an associate who was seated in the public gallery and attacked Pyke. Now, a few years later, Pyke could not exactly recall how he had disarmed this man but he was struck by the gallantry of his own long-ago actions; the fact that he had been willing to risk life and limb for the woman whom he now took entirely for granted.

So engrossed was he in these thoughts that he did not notice Brownlow Vines until the man was practically breathing in his face. In his hat and gloves, Vines looked utterly out of place. It did not strike Pyke until later that Vines might be the emissary from Peel.

In an awkward gesture, Vines made to shake Pyke's hand, and when he saw that Pyke had no intention of doing likewise, he patted him on the arm. 'This is where you like to spend your time. How . . . *colourful*.'

Vines was dressed in a cream frock-coat, cravat, tight-fitting trousers and immaculately polished boots, and in the surroundings seemed even more foppish than usual.

'What do you want, Vines?'

Vines made a point of appearing to be hurt. 'May I suggest that I buy us both a drink?' He glanced over at the bar and tried to attract someone's attention. 'Miss. Miss?' It took Pyke a few moments to realise he was talking to either Lizzie or one of the barmaids.

It was a nauseating spectacle, Vines's attempt to flirt with Lizzie while one of the other barmaids poured two mugs of stout and placed them on the counter before him. Vines seemed pleased with himself, as though his efforts revealed his common touch. Lizzie had acted along, laughing at Vines's efforts at humour. She had even appeared to be flattered.

'Cheers,' Vines said, lifting up his mug.

'You're not from this world, are you, Vines?'

'Maybe not, but I can see its earthy appeals,' Vines said, making a point of winking at Pyke.

'In a place like this, you so much as look at someone else's woman, you're a dead man.'

The colour drained from Vines's face. He glanced across at Lizzie and then around the room, to see whether anyone had noticed.

'Lizzie,' Pyke called out.

After serving another customer, she came to join them. Pyke reached over the counter and kissed her on the mouth. It was an ugly, sloppy gesture, made worse by the fact that Lizzie bridled at his feigned attempt at intimacy, doubtless realising she was being used. Still, it elicited the reaction Pyke had wanted. Vines stared at them aghast, though Pyke didn't know whether he was appalled by the show of affection or by what it suggested about Pyke's choice of woman.

'Don't pretend this is a social visit, Vines,' Pyke said, once Lizzie had left them. 'What do you want?'

Vines was ambitious but stupid. Usually he had nothing but contempt for Pyke, but now he was pretending to be his friend. Pyke wondered whether Vines really believed he was taken in by his false show of bonhomie.

'Straight to the point, eh?' Vines looked at him with apprehension. 'I wanted to talk to you, away from the eyes and ears of Bow Street, about Sir Richard.'

'What about Sir Richard?'

They both took a long drink.

This time Vines whispered, 'I'm worried about him, Pyke. I think he's losing his mind.' He wiped froth from his mouth with his sleeve. 'Have you noticed the way he's been acting of late?'

'Acting?' Pyke raised his eyebrows. He'd noticed Fox's erratic behaviour but didn't say anything.

'The mood swings, the ecstatic highs, the lows.'

'It must be a hard business, watching everything that you've worked to build threatened by the people you most trust.'

Vines refused to meet his stare. 'Quite so, but he's blind to the realities of the situation, Pyke. This new police force is going to happen, whether he likes it or not. I know it. You know it. Why can't he see it? Sometimes progress is inevitable.'

'Depends what you mean by progress.'

'Many people would call a new, uniformed, city-wide police force progress.'

'And you?'

Vines smiled unconvincingly. 'My admittedly humble task is to serve, and not to make difficult decisions.'

Pyke rubbed his eyes and tried to focus. He felt light-headed, drunker than he should, even though he had imbibed only three gins and a mug of stout. Usually he could consume a bottle of gin and still shoot a man between the eyes at twenty paces.

Through blurry eyes, he stared at Vines and tried to work out what the man wanted. Vines had not, as yet, mentioned the murders, and did not seem to want to know about the investigation. All of which suggested that he had *not* been dispatched to Pyke's gin palace by Peel or Tilling.

Vines ordered another round of drinks and insisted on paying for them himself.

Emboldened by the alcohol, Pyke asked Vines whether he'd struck a deal with Peel or whether Peel had offered him a role in the new police force. They both took a drink.

'Is that what you think?' Vines looked at him, shaking his head.

Pyke didn't like being this drunk. He didn't feel particularly in control of the situation.

'Sir Richard thinks you're the magistrate that Peel is employing to preside over Hume's investigation.'

'Really?' Vines said, sounding more amused than perturbed. 'And that's why you think he's been acting strangely around me?'

Pyke felt his vision blur and closed his eyes, trying to revive himself. The room started to spin around him. He tried to respond but words failed him. Vines placed his hand on Pyke's shoulder and asked whether he was all right.

'I'm fine.' Pyke opened his eyes and smiled.

But Pyke was not fine. He was drunk: drunker than he had been in as long as he could remember. So drunk, all of a sudden, that he could barely sit up straight, let alone speak. The room became a jumble of noise and motion. He felt his mouth dry up, his head spin. He felt himself fall, and the next moment he was on the floor, lying in the sawdust, not knowing and caring how he had got there. It was a peculiar feeling, mellow and soothing in its own way, as though he had been deposited in his own soft cocoon. Hearing someone call Lizzie's name, he recognised her voice. '*Pyke, Pyke?*' He wanted to smile, and suddenly it felt as though he were afloat. Above all, he wanted to be left alone, but the voices persisted. Someone lifted him up, two people perhaps. He heard other voices. Vines, proposing, 'Take him to the bedroom.' They dragged him upstairs. His whole body felt limp. He did not put up a struggle but rather felt himself falling. Everything went black.

The first thing Pyke heard when he finally awoke from his feverish dreams was the squeals and grunts of petrified livestock being driven through the narrow streets outside the gin palace. Trying to open his eyes, he realised that the effort required to do so was beyond him. His mouth tasted stale and arid. He made another attempt to move but a sharp pain in his head wouldn't allow it. Remaining still, he took a deep breath and opened his eyes. Weak shafts of morning light pierced the thin muslin curtains. He stared up at the unfamiliar ceiling and soon realised he was not in his own bed. His eyes opened a little more and he fought the sudden pain that streaked across his forehead. Moving his head a fraction to the left, he recognised Lizzie's wallpaper, her dressing table.

Gently, Pyke turned a little farther to his side and saw Lizzie's sleeping form. Though Lizzie's back was turned to him, from where he was positioned her hair looked oddly dishevelled.

Pyke reached out and touched the back of her neck. As he did so, he tried to remember the last time they had woken up in the same bed.

Moving his body for the first time, something squelched beneath him. He lifted his head from the pillow, felt something damp against the back of his neck and had to fight off a wave of revulsion. His initial reaction was that he had pissed himself. His self-disgust was visceral. More awake now, though not yet clear-headed, it took him a moment to work out that his back, his arms, his legs and his head were all covered in something wet and sticky.

With a sudden movement, he sat upright, driven by a mixture of curiosity and unease. He was still fully clothed and his clothes were covered in the same moist liquid; the smell was sweet and yet overpowering.

Sitting upright and fighting off the dizziness, Pyke ignored the icy temperature, pulled back the blanket and almost fainted. The bed was awash with blood, as though someone had slaughtered a cow. At first, Pyke supposed that he must be cut; that he was delirious from the loss of blood. But he did not feel any pain, at least not apart from the pounding headache which was quickly ebbing away under the onslaught of panic. Rousing himself from the bed, he began to check himself, his back, his clothes, all of them dripping with fresh blood. And it was everywhere: on the bed, the sheets, the blanket, the floor, his clothes, his hands, his fingers, his toes, his genitals, and in his eyes, ears, nose, lips, hair and teeth.

Lizzie, though, was not moving, and it finally struck him what had happened, or at least that the blood was not his own.

Pyke stripped the blanket from her motionless body.

Wearing the dress he had bought her, she was lying half on her back, half on her side. There were two red-ringed stab wounds in the middle of her abdomen. Beneath her was a pool of her own blood. Quickly, he checked for a pulse but didn't find one. Her body was cold, indicating that she had been dead for a number of hours.

Lizzie had also taken a blow to her head. Pyke fought back the urge to gag.

He stripped naked, pulled down the muslin curtain and wiped off the blood. The cream material quickly turned crimson. Leaving his soiled clothes in a heap, he ignored the freezing temperature and went downstairs to the bar and opened a fresh bottle of gin.

Pyke put the bottle to his lips and did not stop imbibing the fiery liquid until he had to pause for breath.

Outside in the yard, he poured two buckets of icy water into a metal bath tub. As he submerged himself in the water, it felt as though his chest might collapse but, gasping for air, he took a bar of soap in one hand and, splashing icy water over himself with the other, he started to scrub himself: his face, his neck, his armpits, his torso, his hands, his groin, his legs, between his toes. He took another bucket of water and tipped it over himself, rinsing off the suds. He rubbed himself dry with a cloth and, picking up the bottle and putting it again to his lips, took another gulp of gin.

Upstairs he dressed in a dark jacket, plain shirt, trousers and boots and returned to the bedroom. He found the knife, a large hunting knife with a jagged blade, on the floor next to the bed. Having wiped it with the same muslin curtain he'd used to clean himself, he placed it carefully in his pocket.

Later, it struck Pyke that if it had not been market day and the street outside had been empty of livestock, they might have caught him. As it was, one of the constables dispatched to arrest him screamed at someone to clear a path through the street, and Pyke looked out of the upstairs window and saw them through the fog: ten or more men wearing tall hats, forcing their way through a stationary herd of cattle.

Even with these men bearing down on him, Pyke knew that he could not leave George to either perish in his bed or suffer some as yet unknown fate; perhaps a slow, painful death in a lunatic asylum. Ascending the stairs to the old man's garret three at a time, he could feel some of the horror of what had happened begin to hit home. Lizzie was dead. She had been slaughtered in her own bed, while he lay beside her. Briefly, as he knelt beside his old friend, he imagined trying to rouse him from his slumber to explain what had happened, the pain that news of his daughter's murder would cause, and he felt momentarily overcome by anger, bitterness and his own grief. But he could not afford to indulge these sentiments: men were coming to arrest *him* for the murder. He did not have time to wake George and talk to him and he did not need to do so. Pyke already knew what his old friend would ask him to do and without another thought he clamped George's jaw closed with one hand and pinched his nostrils with the other.

He had planned to count to twenty but did not need to go past ten.

Back in his own room, he collected what little money he could find, tumbled down the stairs, let himself out into the back yard and from there into the alley at the rear of the building. Finding an open cesspool, he wrapped up the knife in the muslin curtain and dropped the whole bundle into the dirty water. He heard shouting as the constables forced their way into the gin palace.

*

A freezing fog had enveloped the whole of Bartholomew's Field, the site of Smithfield market, making it all but impossible to tell which direction over the treacherous ground he was heading and, advantageously to him, all but impossible for the ten constables to pursue or even locate him. There were other constables attached to the market, appointed by the Corporation of London to regulate practices, but Pyke was not concerned about them; though it was only seven in the morning, they would be ensconced in one of the taverns that bordered the market enjoying their second or third 'rum hot' of the day.

Below him the ground was hard but slippery. The usual ankle-deep mulch of manure, rotten animal flesh and faeces had frozen solid, a boon as far as Pyke was concerned because it lessened the smell, but it meant the ground was not easy to walk across. In such conditions, he had seen people slip under the hoofs of frightened cattle and lose their lives. The slow-witted drovers did whatever they could, beat their animals with sticks and rods, gouged their eyes and squeezed their genitals, but they were rarely able to control beasts that were already well used to their cruel practices. When this happened, all one could do was look away and make out that the screams of terror were those of cattle rather than human beings. Afterwards, if the bodies were not at once attended to, they were snatched by the resurrectionists.

Around him through the fog, Pyke could see that cattle and sheep were pouring into the field from every direction. The bleating and lowing of terrified beasts were matched by the barks issuing from the frothing mouths of the drovers' dogs. Herds of long-horned cattle jostled for position among mounds of quivering animal flesh with Highland oxen. Visibility was less than ten yards and, perversely, was not helped by the drovers' hand-held lamps, which did little more than transform the fog into an impenetrable wall of white.

The cattle were arranged into smaller circles and between each circle was a pathway for pedestrians and a wooden handrail. Clutching the rail, Pyke followed the path until he was able to make out the faint silhouette of St Bartholomew's Hospital.

Surrounded by ramshackle buildings and the many narrow alleys and courtyards that made up the area to the east of the market, Pyke looked behind him to make sure no one had followed. He was still drowsy from the laudanum he had unknowingly imbibed and numb from the gin. Instinctively he knew he would need hard currency, but apart from this his mind was blank. Pyke knew, of course, that he was still in a state of shock, but he didn't have the time to indulge such feelings. He also knew, despite the fog and the early hour, that he was well known in these parts and if news of the murder spread he wouldn't last more than a few hours without being spotted and perhaps lynched.

In Field Lane, a steep, poorly ventilated street that backed on to the sewage-ridden Fleet Ditch, he bought a smock frock, some corduroy breeches and an old hat from a street trader for two shillings and changed into his new clothes in a narrow back alley behind the Old Red Lion tavern. Two young girls, carrying a pail of milk between them, hurried past him and giggled to one another.

In the Old Red Lion, he procured a pen and a scrap of paper from one of the pot boys and scribbled a note to Godfrey Bond, instructing his uncle to collect as much hard currency as he could manage, and meet him on the south side of London Bridge at midday.

He didn't want Godfrey arriving in a thieves' den like Smithfield or Field Lane carrying a large sum of money. He wanted their meeting place to be public, safe and identifiable, somewhere that even Godfrey would know how to find. And should Godfrey be followed, it was important that Pyke had his route of escape planned. In this scenario, Pyke would see anyone who was following his uncle and would be able to slip off into the labyrinthine streets that surrounded Southwark Cathedral.

Taking a half-crown from his pocket, he placed it into the pot boy's hand and explained that if he successfully delivered a note to a Mr Godfrey Bond in person, then Bond would give him a whole guinea for his efforts. The boy looked down at the coin in his hand and gave Pyke a toothy grin. Pyke told him Bond could be found at number seventy-two St Paul's Yard, and if he was not there the boy was to go to the George Inn on Camden Place. If not there, then the Castle in Saffron Hill, or the Blue Boar in Holborn, and if Godfrey was not in either of those places, the boy was to look for him in the New Wheatsheaf at the top of Ludgate Hill or the Privateer on Wellington Mews.

The boy squinted at him and grinned. 'I take it this friend of yours likes to take a drink.'

But stupidly, Pyke had not thought to take into account the fog, which had thickened throughout the rest of the morning, so that by the time he heard the Southwark bells, less than a few hundred yards away, chiming midday, he could barely see his own hands and feet, let alone the towering cathedral. The fog was thick but patchy, and as it swirled around him he caught glimpses of the new bridge, which was being built alongside the old one, wooden scaffolding supporting the giant granite arches, and beyond that, disembodied masks of tall ships bobbed up and down in the choppy waters like ghostly apparitions. It was bitterly cold, and his new clothes had left him desperately exposed to the elements. He dug his hands into his pockets and scanned the faces of those walking towards him across the old bridge for any sign of his uncle. The fog momentarily cleared and he saw Wren's mighty dome appear in the distance and then vanish, as though by a malevolent act of conjuring.

The bridge itself was, literally, falling down. There were no houses or shops on it, as there once had been – they had long since been demolished – and more recently the cobbled surface had been widened, to accommodate more traffic, but these changes had not made the bridge any more secure. The fact that a new bridge was being constructed was a testament to its decrepitude. The creaking arches, which housed waterwheels and supported the main crossing, had been badly damaged by the last big freeze, when the river had completely iced over.

Pyke could hear the giant waterwheels turning beneath him, sucking up the river's dirty water and pumping it across to both banks for human consumption. No wonder people existed on a diet of gin and beer and did not even think about drinking water they knew to be polluted.

Figures appeared ten or twenty yards ahead of him out of the fog. A city clerk hurried past him clutching a bundle of papers, already late for his appointment, followed by a Jewish pedlar whose feigned shuffle belied his hawk-like gaze and a respectably dressed woman who made a point of passing Pyke on the other side of the road. A few minutes later, a sweeper with an unsteady gait and a sweaty visage stopped for a while in the middle of the bridge and propped himself up with his broom. For the briefest of moments, Pyke thought he saw a woman with a plump face and a white bonnet appearing in the distance, but she turned out to be no more than an apparition. Was he just imagining the woman who had shouted his name in the Blue Dog tavern?

He blinked and rubbed his eyes, hoping they weren't deceiving him. Again, he wondered who she was and what she wanted from him.

At ten or fifteen minutes past the hour, Pyke was considering his options, wondering whether the boy had simply pocketed the half-crown and discarded the note, whether Godfrey had received the message at all, when out of the fog ahead of him appeared the portly frame of his uncle. Pyke recognised Godfrey by his shambling gait and the mane of white hair on top of his head.

He called out to him but Godfrey had stopped moving. He was doubled up and looked to be in discomfort.

'*Godfrey*,' Pyke shouted, louder this time. Still, though, the figure ahead of him did not look up.

Pyke moved quickly towards him, both concerned and irritated. As he did so, he did not think to look behind him. That was his second mistake. His first was to imagine that his uncle had not been followed. Still wheezing, Godfrey dismissed Pyke's attempts to help him but managed to utter, 'I'm sorry, I really am sorry.' Godfrey could have been sorry for a gamut of reasons but instinctively Pyke knew what he was referring to. Godfrey thrust a pile of banknotes into Pyke's outstretched hand but Pyke did not need his uncle to explain that 'they' had made him do it, in order to work out for himself what was happening. By this point, Pyke had already turned around and broken into a run, ignoring the shouts of the battalion of constables who had gathered to block his escape to the north side of the river. For ten or twenty yards, Pyke sprinted as a hunted fox would run, motivated only by fear and an instinct for self-preservation. But while he had expected, and even planned for, his route across the bridge to the north bank to be blocked, he had not for a moment imagined there might be constables amassed at its southern end.

Trying not to panic, he took a deep breath, while he considered his options. He looked at the massed ranks of constables, two or three thick across the bridge and gingerly closing in on him. Could he force his way through this human barricade? It did not appear likely. Nor did he think he would survive jumping from the bridge; if he did not drown, the icy waters of the Thames would kill him. Briefly, he cursed himself for not bringing some sort of weapon, a knife or a cudgel. Ahead and behind him, the two lines of constables edged warily towards him, as though they had cornered a wounded but dangerous animal. One of them yelled, 'Give yourself up, Pyke. There's no way through us.' The man sounded as nervous as Pyke felt. Dizziness swept over him. There was only one option left. Closing his eyes, he launched himself at one of the advancing lines; as he did so, he unleashed a blood-curdling scream. Pyke did not know what he screamed but it emanated from the bottom of his stomach and propelled him forwards into the startled constables at such a speed that, for an instant, he thought he might just break through their ranks and earn his freedom.

Then he took a heavy blow to his head, and another to his upper body, and felt his legs buckle, and the next thing he remembered was a bearded man with cheese-and-onion breath hunched over him, shouting that he was being arrested for the murder of Lizzie Morgan, while two other men applied leg-irons and handcuffs.

As he lay there on the bridge, panting, he didn't feel a thing: neither regret nor sadness nor loss, just a gaping emptiness that was one heartbeat away from death.

ELEVEN

The office at Great Marlborough Street magistrates' court, once the parlour of a private house, was too small for its current function: hosting an examination into the evidence against Pyke in order to determine whether there was a case to be answered in a higher court. Because he had been accused of a capital crime, the 'higher court' meant the Sessions House on Old Bailey. In normal circumstances, the room might still have been too small, but in the light of the feverish interest that Pyke's trial had generated, its size seemed even more diminished. It was not a grand room, by any stretch of the imagination: the blackened walls and ceilings and the oppressive smell made it seem more like a public house than a court of law. It was certainly shabbier than the corresponding office at Bow Street but the examination was being held at Great Marlborough Street on the insistence of the Home Office. Rightly, they felt that Pyke would receive a more favourable hearing from Sir Richard Fox than he would from any of the magistrates at Bow Street.

The office was choked with all manner of spectators. From the dock, an elevated platform fenced off by a wooden rail facing the magistrates' bench, Pyke watched as a line of eminent society figures took up their seats next to James Slingsby Bodkin, who was in charge of the hearing. He recognised Sir Henry Hobhouse, the retired Home

Office under-secretary and a friend of Peel, the radical writer John Wade, and someone who resembled Edmund Kean, the famous thespian. Beneath the bench, the room was thronging with less salubrious types: people who had queued through the night for the chance to see one of their own – one who had risen too far above his station – take a fall.

The fact that the working poor often sided with the pick of society never failed to surprise him.

But it was a spectacle, not a committal hearing.

Pyke did not have any doubt about the verdict or what would happen during the hearing itself: the coroner's report would be read out, witnesses would be allowed to give their evidence (especially ones whose words might incriminate him), expert testimony about Pyke's character would be aired, the prosecution counsel would lay out the evidence against him and Pyke would have a chance to refute the claims and challenge any of the prosecution's witnesses.

Bodkin would talk about the seriousness of the crime and the gravity of the evidence stacked against Pyke. He would ask Pyke whether he wished to say anything in his defence and when Pyke said nothing – as he planned to – the man would look around him at the packed office and then fix his gaze on Pyke and say in his small, affected voice, 'Accused, you will be committed to Newgate to take your trial at the ensuing sessions commencing on the twentieth day of March eighteen hundred and twenty-nine for the willing, cold-blooded murder of Elizabeth Morgan on the night of the fourth day of March eighteen hundred and twenty-nine in a drinking establishment on Duke Street in the Smithfield area of London.'

Pyke would say nothing in his defence, both in order to disappoint the expectant crowd and to rile Bodkin and the prosecution counsel, who, like all prosecution counsels, expected to use the committal hearings to elicit incriminating statements from the accused. He would also say nothing because it would hasten the court's proceedings.

If Pyke had no doubt he would be found guilty, however he conducted himself in court, what was the point of holding things up?

This way, he would be committed to a ward in Newgate prison by nightfall, from where he would be able to plan his next move, even as the forces of the criminal justice system were being marshalled against him. The grim irony of the gaoler being jailed was not lost on him, nor was he under any misapprehension about the real dangers he faced from elements within Newgate itself. If Pyke survived the first night, then perhaps he had a chance.

Chained by the hands and feet, Pyke was led by a turnkey through what seemed to be a never-ending maze of damp, narrow passages, illuminated only by occasional lanterns affixed to the walls. Periodically their progress was halted by heavy-set doors which were unbolted and opened in order to let them pass through. The sound of clanking iron drowned out the muffled shouts from the belly of the prison, but it was by no means a reassuring noise. As a Bow Street Runner, Pyke had heard numerous stories about Newgate. Sane men had become crazed within these walls; people had disappeared, never to be seen again; virile specimens had emerged from even short periods of incarceration as broken-down wrecks. Pyke, however, had more pressing concerns to address, and it did not surprise him that when he was led into the ward, his gaze fell upon Flynn, the receiver.

Evidently Flynn had been waiting for him, and the man's thin smile indicated that he had no intention of passing up this opportunity to exact his revenge, even if the man had tried to double-cross Pyke and therefore deserved his come-uppance.

He was a thin man with bushy whiskers and translucent skin that contrasted strangely with his thin lips. A depressive character with few friends and fewer social graces, his only joy in life, as far as Pyke had been able to tell, was inspecting his ledger books in order to determine his financial worth.

But Pyke was under no illusion about the threat that Flynn posed to him. He would slit Pyke's throat without giving it a moment's thought.

The ward itself was a narrow room, lit only by a fire that burned at one end; it housed twenty or thirty men, most of whom were huddled under blankets around the fireplace. Though the stone walls were thick, they appeared to keep in little of the heat. It was a sombre place, and as he was led across to the wardsman, Pyke felt the hard stares of his fellow prisoners. Three years earlier, another Bow Street Runner had been imprisoned for theft; during his first night on the ward, someone had stabbed him in the neck. No one had admitted to the attack. The Runner had died and, as his corpse was dragged away, other prisoners had clapped and cheered.

The wardsman introduced himself as Jack Cotton. Pyke ignored the scar that ran down one side of his face and offered him ten guineas as an act of good faith. Grinning, Cotton accepted the money without hesitation and led Pyke to a hemp-rope mat near the fire, gave him a horse blanket which he tugged away from another prisoner, put a platter of cold meat in front of him and produced a tankard of porter, which he thrust into Pyke's hand, along with a wad of tobacco.

Next to him, a toothless man with a boil on his forehead said, 'So you're the one they been talkin' about.' He broke into a chuckle and edged his own mat away from Pyke's. 'Sleep tight and don't let the bedbugs bite.' From the other side of the fireplace, a man stared at Pyke and spat snuff from his bruised lips. In one of the darkened corners, a half-naked man defecated and far away at the back of the ward, a young boy sobbed. Flynn watched the proceedings from a distance, his arms folded.

It was Pyke's plan to withdraw a little from the group huddled around the fire and try to remain awake during the night. It seemed inevitable that Flynn would make his move at some point, knowing as he would of Pyke's plans to be transferred, and Pyke wanted to be prepared for him. When the attack came, he had to act quickly; the last thing he wanted was a prolonged struggle, one that might encourage others to join in on the receiver's side.

From his position about ten or fifteen yards back from the fire, Pyke watched the men drink, gamble, laugh, swear and swap tall stories; soon they seemed to have forgotten his presence. Later, when the fire dwindled and the men passed into sleep, he listened for signs of his assailant but heard nothing. Eventually he feigned sleep in order to try to entice Flynn into action. A solitary rat scuttled past him, its claws scuffing against the wooden floorboards. Beside him the platter of meat and the tankard of porter remained untouched. He did not trust them not to have been tampered with.

When it came, Flynn was much stealthier and stronger than Pyke had imagined he would be. From nowhere, he pounced upon Pyke like a wild animal. At the same time Pyke felt something splash him in his face and sting his eyes. Later he realised that it was urine. The stinging sensation momentarily disabled him, and had Flynn been armed with a knife instead of a garrotting rope his attack might have been successful. Digging his knees into Pyke's arched back, the receiver tried to force the rope over his head, but Pyke was, in the end, the more powerful of the two, and he threw the older man in one jerk on to the hard floor, grabbing his throat with one hand, taking the rope with the other and threading it carefully around Flynn's own neck, before pulling it tight.

The older man spluttered and choked, but Pyke had neither the resolve to finish him off nor the desire to deal with another corpse. Releasing the rope, Pyke hauled the receiver up on to his shaking legs and pulled him close enough to be able to smell his breath. 'You made a bad decision and now you're paying the price.'

'Maybe they'll hang us together.' Flynn wiped spittle from his mouth.

'I'm a thief-taker, not a thief.'

'And now someone's taken you,' Flynn said, with a sneer.

'Maybe I'm not as corrupt as you think I am.'

'I don't *think* you're anything, Pyke.'

'If you come within a hundred yards of me again, I will kill you. Is that understood?'

Flynn looked down at the floor.

Pyke hit him in the mouth with such ferocity that one of the man's teeth lodged itself in his knuckles. Flynn collapsed in a heap. No one came to his assistance; in fact, no one seemed to be concerned by what had happened.

The following day Pyke paid ten guineas to the turnkey and a further thirty guineas was earmarked for the governor. He was transferred to a comfortable private room in the infirmary. If he had been a gentleman, the turnkey told him, then a little extra money might have secured him a place in the governor's own quarters, but as it was, the infirmary was the best that a man of his breeding could hope for. Once ensconced in his room, Pyke ordered a new set of clothes, a bedstead with a sound flock mattress, additional blankets, a choice of newspapers, a copy of Machiavelli's *The Prince*, writing paper, envelopes, a blotter and a pen, a chair for reading, a pint of gin, a pint of beer, a platter of cold joints and hams, two loaves of bread, a pipe and an ounce of tobacco.

It was a spartan room, warmed only by a small fire. Attached to the wall there was a crucifix, which he removed and threw under the bed.

As well as being private, the room was heavily fortified. It was locked from the outside by three solid bolts and guarded by two men; the only natural light came from a light-well built into the upper wall and fortified with iron bars.

Pyke persuaded the turnkey, with the governor's permission, to remove his handcuffs but the leg-irons remained. It was a condition of the agreement that saw him move from the ward to the infirmary.

The arbitrariness of the legal system did not surprise Pyke. He had witnessed sufficient abuses of power and privilege in his time as a Bow Street Runner to immunise him against any romantic notion that the English system of justice, unlike, say, its French counterpart, was fair-minded and all men were somehow equal under the law. The French had their Bastille; the English had Newgate. And while he had long since heard of plans to close and demolish the ancient prison, symbol of a regime that was as much feared as it was hated, Pyke was under no illusion that a necessarily fairer system of incarceration and punishment would take its place.

Pyke was personally distrustful of all legal and political institutions, and believed individuals prospered not by pursuing some 'worthy' vision of moral betterment through civic and legal reforms, but by showing superior cunning and ferocity in the face of opponents. Success, or in his case freedom, wouldn't come about through an appeal to the fairness of the law, but rather as a result of his own guile or through the discretionary authority exercised by Peel.

What bothered him most was his own impotence in the face of a system whose sole purpose seemed to be to destroy him. As a result of past successes, Pyke had naively come to believe in his own invincibility. Though he had never laid claim to radical sentiments, he had always felt able to tilt circumstances to his advantage. Now someone had decreed that he was to be sacrificed, and against this type of power his resourcefulness finally seemed a poor match.

But Pyke's righteous sense of injustice did not colour his every thought. Nor did he permit himself to indulge in fantasies of revenge. Nor even was he angered by the fact that he had been abandoned by his old acquaintances; he had heard nothing from Sir Richard Fox or indeed from Peel. Rather, his enforced solitude gave him the chance to sift through what had happened.

He knew he had not murdered Lizzie, which, in turn, meant someone else had killed her. The evidence also suggested that she had not been the victim of a random attack. Rather, her death had been planned in such a way as to implicate him; this much was clear from the arrival of the police constables, who, doubtless, had expected to find Lizzie's corpse and had been told to arrest him. The complicity of others was also indicated by the likelihood that Pyke had been drugged. Although he had taken a few drops of laudanum in his gin, the dose was nothing like what would have been needed to knock him out.

This suggested to Pyke that Brownlow Vines had been mixed up in the business of administering the laudanum or, at least, in distracting Pyke so he did not notice its aftertaste. But Vines had not acted alone. That night he had acknowledged someone behind the bar. At the time, Pyke had thought only of his pathetic attempts to flirt with Lizzie, but what if he had also signalled to one of the other servers? To Maggie perhaps, who had been called as a witness for the prosecution and who had perhaps administered the dose because she had been paid to do so?

But neither Vines nor Maggie had been acting on their own impulses. Neither had ever much cared for Pyke, but the idea they might seek to damage him and kill Lizzie for their own advancement seemed preposterous. Vines's involvement, in particular, implicated other parties. Sir Richard's long-time assistant was no killer. He did not have the stomach for it, and Pyke doubted it had been Vines who had delivered the fatal blows to Lizzie. None-theless, Vines was not the kind of man to offer his assistance unless there was some gain to be made. This meant Vines had cut some kind of deal with a figure who, in turn, had the power to mobilise a significant number of constables and watchmen. Only Peel himself seemed capable of such a task. And Peel could certainly offer Vines what he seemed to want.

This line of thought was bolstered by his instinctive belief that the decision to murder Lizzie and frame him had been taken as a result of his meeting with Tilling and his casual reference to the name Davy Magennis and his stated theory that Magennis, who until recently had served in the very Royal Irish Constabulary Peel had established, was the St Giles murderer. It was of course *possible* that he had misinterpreted Tilling's discomfort and that someone entirely different had been responsible for Lizzie's death but, instinctively, he felt this not to be the case. All of which posed a larger and much more serious question: if Fitzroy Tilling was somehow implicated in Lizzie's death, did it mean he had been acting on the orders of the Home Secretary?

Pyke had no answer to such a question, but still believed that Peel was his only chance of winning freedom.

Above all, Lizzie's brutal murder filled him with a sense of sadness, outrage and guilt. Pyke had known her for eight years, and she had lived with him in the gin palace for three. His ardour might have cooled in recent years but he had not stopped admiring her: her toughness, her honesty, her blunt manner. In his own time, he would try to come to terms with her murder, and when the shock had abated, and he had avenged her death, he would face up to his grief, but in the immediate moment he knew such sentiments were beyond him.

'Well, this isn't too bad. Not too bad at all. In fact, it's rather comfortable.' Godfrey's cheeks were the colour of ripe beetroots, perhaps because the prison infirmary was on the first floor and he had been forced to tackle the stairs. He walked with a limp, the product of a pain in his toe he always denied was gout. Dressed in a fustian jacket and moleskin breeches, he clutched a bottle of claret. Without being invited, he collapsed into the chair and picked up the copy of *The Prince*. 'It's a bit gloomy, isn't it?' Looking around the room, he said, 'You've done all right here, m'boy. I brought you some claret but I see that you're well stocked up.' He reached across, picked up the gin bottle and sniffed. 'Not the best, but I'm sure it helps. So how *are* you?'

Pyke said he was bearing up, under the circumstances. He could see that his uncle was keen to tell him something, so kept his response brief.

'You're the talk of the town, especially among the ladies. Seems opinion is divided as to whether you killed her, but even your perceived guilt isn't dampening people's enthusiasm. The papers, they made the most of your attempts to evade capture. Embellished things a little, as they're wont to do. Cruikshank did an illustration of you, appeared in the *Morning Post*. I should've brought it with me. It was rather flattering, actually. You're one of these brooding, intense types and, you'll like this, there's a queue outside your cell, society ladies, waiting for their personal consultation.' Godfrey chuckled. 'Of course, there are poor folk who just want to string you up, but that's just because they're afraid of you.' He picked up the claret and peered at the label. 'What does one do in here if one needs a corkscrew? I take it that there's no one to call.'

'You mean, like a butler?' Pyke raised his eyebrows.

'Quite,' Godfrey said, a little chastened, before carefully placing the bottle down on the table next to Pyke's bed. 'I have promising news. The other day I was taken to luncheon at the Athenaeum, no less. Delicious it was, too. Sweetbread *au jus* and the most tender lamb cutlets, with peas and asparagus, for the main course and an exquisite maraschino jelly with chocolate cream for dessert. All washed down with Madeira and champagne. Quite the banquet.' Godfrey wiped a spool of dribble from his mouth. 'My dining companion was a pleasant chap, too. Sharp as razors. Everybody says he's one of the top barristers in the city. Geoffrey Quince, QC. I didn't realise it, but he attended your committal hearing, out of interest, and he fancied he could drive a chariot through the Crown's case. He's even done a little preliminary digging and unearthed some promising material. Quince explained that the burden of proof always lies with the Crown and on the basis that all the evidence here is circumstantial, he

149

didn't think any jury in the land would convict, especially in a capital case.'

'What's in it for him?' Pyke asked, trying to conceal his scepticism.

'Your trial is a big draw, Pyke. Barristers like a challenge, you know that, putting one over on the Crown, but more than that, they like the spotlight. If he wins, the publicity could be advantageous.'

'I would imagine he's not cheap.'

'Quince would not be acting for you out of the goodness of his heart, if that's what you mean.' Godfrey sounded a little hurt.

'And I'm supposed to put my life in the hands of a man I don't know and who I've never met?'

'Here,' Godfrey said, pulling a crumpled piece of paper from his breeches. 'It's what they call a retainer. Quince drew it up on the spot. Sign it and I'm sure he will come and visit. You'd like him, my boy. He doesn't smile.' He put the document next to the claret bottle and smoothed it down with his hands.

'If I sign, I still want to pursue other options. And if I'm going to do this, I'll need your help.'

Godfrey held up his hands. 'My expertise is entirely at your disposal.' He paused for a moment and winced slightly. 'Of course, that's not to say that I wouldn't perhaps benefit from some small remuneration, a few scraps thrown my way, but you know I'd do anything for you.' This time he grinned. 'Within reason.'

Pyke nodded. 'I want you to contact Townsend. He's a Runner; ask for him at the Bow Street office. Offer him twenty guineas to look into the backgrounds of the turn-keys who work on the condemned ward. I also want to know who the judge at my trial is going to be. Ask Quince. He should be able to find out. I want a meeting with Foote, the Ordinary. You can arrange this. Foote won't bother to come if I say I need spiritual guidance, so tell him I'm ready to make my confession. He'll see the profit in it, for him. But the most important thing I want you to do is pass a note directly to Robert Peel. I don't know how you'll manage it, but it has to be given to Peel directly, not to one of his secretaries or servants. Like I said, it's important. My fate could rest on Peel getting the note.'

Godfrey stared at him, frowning. 'What note?'

Pyke produced a letter he had written earlier from under his pillow and handed it to his uncle. It read:

The prince will be hated if he is rapacious and aggressive with regard to property and the women of his subjects . . . He will be despised if he has a reputation for being fickle, frivolous, effeminate, cowardly, irresolute; a prince should avoid this like the plague and strive to demonstrate in his actions grandeur, courage, sobriety, strength.

Pyke had chosen not to sign it.

Scanning the note over Godfrey's shoulder, he noticed that his handwriting was more ragged than usual. 'You'll see it gets to Peel himself? It *has* to be delivered to Peel in person.'

Godfrey took the envelope and said he would do his best. 'I'm happy to do what I can to help, of course.'

Pyke eyed him carefully. 'But?'

'Oh, it's nothing, dear boy. I suppose I'm just worried about the usual. Money, the state of my business . . .'

'Your business has been suffering for the last twenty years.'

This seemed to pain Godfrey. 'Quite so. But you see, dear boy, I have just been reading Vidocq's memoirs. Now Vidocq is a quite reprehensible figure and, to my mind, all the better for it. I don't imagine, for a second, he actually wrote the book himself and, in my opinion, that's the problem. There's something missing. Don't get me wrong; the formula is the right one. Send a thief to catch a thief. But there's still too much moralising. If those elements could only be harnessed to writing that had the courage of its own base convictions it really would be something . . .'

'You know what I think about this, Godfrey.'

'At least think about it. Like you just said, I haven't published anything that's worth a damn in over twenty years. The penny stories about ravaged virgins and demented monks are good fun – don't get me wrong – but they won't be read in a year's time, let alone a hundred years' time. I just think your story's one that needs to be told. A simple man who's doing what has to be done in order to . . .'

Pyke smiled. 'Prosper?'

'I was going to say survive or get by, but prosper works just as well.'

'You think that I'm simple?'

'Did I say simple?' Godfrey feigned indignation.

'What about ingenious?' Pyke said, lightly.

Godfrey looked at him. 'You do understand I'm talking about a *creation*.'

'You don't think I am?'

Godfrey studied him for a while. 'You forget I know you as well as anyone, Pyke. I know for a fact that you can be a cold-hearted bastard . . .'

'Is there a but?'

'Would I be here if there wasn't?' He reached out and patted Pyke on the arm. 'This creation. He would just be a larger-than-life version of you.'

'A man without morals,' Pyke said, still trying to make sense of his uncle's comments.

'He would have morals. The story wouldn't. There's a

difference.' Godfrey hesitated. 'Will you at least think about it, dear boy?'

'I'll think about it.'

'Really?' Godfrey stared at him through bushy eyebrows. 'Actually, I met this chap the other day, a young shorthand reporter, rents an office close to mine, at number five Bell Yard. I happened to mention I was your uncle and he was keen to meet you; expressed a real interest in your case. I said I'd see what I could do. He's a novelist with big ideas.'

'Let's just deal with the matters at hand for the time being, shall we?' Pyke said, gently.

'Of course.' His uncle nodded vigorously. 'But you will give it some thought?'

'Yes, I'll give it some thought.'

'Splendid.' Godfrey slapped him on the back. 'Now perhaps we might pull the cork on this claret.' Then his mood seemed to darken and he looked up at Pyke and said, his eyes clear, 'I didn't say anything before but I just want you to know I'm sorry. Lizzie was a fine woman. As loyal and loving as they come.'

Pyke could not hold his stare and said nothing, as he felt guilt and sadness building within him in equal measures.

Two days before his trial was due to commence, Pyke was visited by Godfrey and the Reverend Arthur Foote. Both men reeked of gin, though Foote's stench was particularly noxious, an acrid mixture of fungi, rank breath, stale alcohol and soiled clothing. He stumbled into the room, took a moment to get his bearings, pushed his wire-rimmed spectacles right up against his bloodshot eyes, and farted loudly before falling into the room's only chair. Though Foote was maybe thirty years older than him and had a fuller girth, the two of them were of a similar height. Godfrey perched on the end of the bed, his chubby legs dangling over the edge. Pyke, meanwhile, stood by the door and listened while Foote waffled about his role in the case of prisoners awaiting execution.

'Well, boy, I suppose now's the time to unbosom yourself,' he said, finally.

Pyke did not respond.

'You see, as the Ordinary of this venerable establishment, it is incumbent on me – yes, it is my responsibility, nay prerogative – to elicit, at the behest of the condemned person, of course – elicit from him, at an appropriate time – yes, that would be right – elicit a confession in which the aforementioned unburdens himself to me of his sinful ways and waywardness.' His leer revealed a set of teeth that resembled decrepit gravestones in their unevenness. 'You're not a sodomite, by any chance?' He saw Pyke's expression and mumbled, 'Of course, I didn't imagine that you were.'

As Foote continued to ramble, Pyke studied him closely, making a mental note of the man's mottled, vein-ridden face, the stubble, the large wart on the end of his nose, the calluses on his hands, the hunched-up way he carried himself.

After Foote had departed, Godfrey stayed behind and Pyke asked whether he had heard from Townsend.

'Indeed I have, my boy. There are two turnkeys on the condemned ward who might be amenable to an approach.'

Pyke told Godfrey to instruct Townsend to make them an offer.

Godfrey nodded. 'Of course, if Quince were to win the trial, all these plans would be rendered null and void.'

Pyke said he had finally met Quince, and had been impressed with the man's capabilities. The lawyer had called at the prison that morning and Pyke's favourable reaction to the man had surprised him. His uncle nodded warmly. Pyke explained that the judge was to be the Recorder of London himself, Lord Chief Justice Marshall. Godfrey asked whether this was good news or not. Pyke just repeated what he had been told by Quince: Marshall was 'well liked' by the Duke of Wellington's administration.

'Let Quince earn his money, Pyke.' Godfrey didn't bother to hide his concern. 'He told me that we have a strong case.'

'Would he say anything different?'

Godfrey looked concerned. 'Promise me you won't try anything . . . *reckless* until after the trial?'

Pyke ignored the question. 'Did you manage to pass on the note to Peel in person?'

'Peel was in the Commons yesterday. There was a debate on the Catholic Emancipation Bill. Peel was presenting the case for the government. Knatchbull gave him a torrid time. They say the police bill will sail through next month but, as for Catholic emancipation, there's still a lot of opposition.'

'Did you give him the note?'

'A friend invited me to watch the proceedings. During lunch, I made a point of bumping into Peel. I handed him the note, yes, and he took it and glanced at it in front of me. Certainly it registered, but then again I couldn't exactly say *what* his reaction indicated. Peel's a hard one to read. I'd say he'd be a devil to play cards with.'

The tension drained from Pyke's body. All he could do was wait for a response.

The next morning Pyke awoke to find that an envelope had been slipped under his door. It was an unwelcoming day and a squally wind rattled the window frame. Pyke convinced himself he did not want to get out of his bed because of the icy temperature, but once he had retrieved the envelope from the floor he was still hesitant about opening it. Inspecting the envelope, he found that it did not appear to be a missive from Peel, at least not an official one. There was no name or seal attached to it. Upon smelling it he noticed a faint perfume. Eventually his curiosity overcame his anxiety and he tore the envelope open; the note was a short one. It simply said: *Keep your spirits up*. And it was signed with the letter 'E'.

It took Pyke a moment to work out who 'E' was and another moment to realise that he was not disappointed it was not from Peel.

The prison governor, Hunt, had a glistening, hairless head formed in the shape of a large egg. He was by no means an old man but was sufficiently aware of his own lack of follicles to want to wear a brimless hat, even indoors. In other ways, Hunt was a more old-fashioned dresser, preferring a short double-breasted jacket when the fashion was for longer and slimmer garments and trousers rather than breeches. Though they were alone and the door to Pyke's cell had been bolted from the outside, he seemed wary about moving any farther into the room than was necessary.

'I wanted to say I hope they find you guilty tomorrow and decide to string you up. I don't care for your type and I have to say it would be a pleasure to entertain you in our ward for the condemned, preferably just for a very short period of time.' His look was contemptuous but concealed something else.

'It didn't stop you taking my money, did it?' Without looking up, Pyke continued to read from *The Prince*.

'I agreed to your request because I felt it would be in the best interests of the prisoners if you billeted on your own.' Hunt smiled easily. 'Less chance of contaminating others.'

'How philanthropic of you.' Pyke yawned.

The governor waited for a few moments. 'A rather unusual letter arrived for you this evening.' He saw he had Pyke's attention and smiled. 'The book no longer interests you?'

Pyke said nothing and waited for the governor to continue.

'The letter was hand-delivered and sealed. It carried the personal seal of the Home Secretary, no less. It was delivered to me, with an attached note, from Robert Peel himself, instructing me to hand it to you without inspecting the contents. Which, I have to say, piqued my curiosity even more. I was concerned it might be a pardon, even though such matters are usually dealt with through official channels. Now I'm a respecter of authority and usually I would abide by the wishes of any Home Secretary without question. But this seemed to be such an unusual situation, and then I started to think about Peel and how the man has unfortunately disgraced himself in the eyes of his Protestant brethren, and I came to the conclusion that it was my duty, as a true believer, to open the letter and inspect its contents.'

'Very honourable of you,' Pyke said, half-raising his eyebrows. 'I'm sure that St Peter is busy preparing a place for you around God's dining table, even as we speak.'

'Are you mocking me, boy?'

'No, sir, but I am waiting to hear about the content of Peel's letter.' Pyke yawned again, in an effort to conceal his nerves. The letter would tell him much.

This seemed to placate the governor. 'Playing it calm, eh? Well, I have to say it's not good news for you.' He chortled, then his face turned serious. 'But it was a strange note, nonetheless; a quotation, though I couldn't tell from where or even what it indicates.'

'*The Prince*.' Pyke held up his book.

'Oh?' Hunt stared at Pyke keenly. 'How did you know?'

'Why don't you read me the quotation, and I'll tell you whether I was right or not.'

Hunt seemed confused and a little put out. 'You correspond with the Home Secretary, then?'

'So it would seem.'

Hunt stared down at the letter in his hand. 'It just says, "We can say cruelty is used well when it is employed once and for all, and one's safety depends on it, and then it is not persisted in but as far as possible turned to the good of one's subjects." That's all. Not even a signature.' He looked up at Pyke. 'It's some kind of private message, isn't it?'

Pyke thumbed through his copy of *The Prince*. Eventually he found the right passage. ' "Cruelty badly used is that which, although infrequent to start with, as time goes on, rather than disappearing, grows in intensity." ' Pyke looked up from the book. 'He's saying virtue is defined by its consequences, and politicians can be justified in sanctioning morally dubious acts as long as they result in the greater good.'

The governor looked at him, unable to comprehend how he might use this information for his own ends. 'It doesn't make much sense to me. But let's just say for the time being you were privy to truths about the Home Secretary that others might benefit from . . .'

'Such as yourself?'

Hunt scowled. 'I am thinking about the greater good of the Protestant brethren.'

'And you imagine I am concerned about such a sect?'

'You call the Protestant Church a *sect*?' He seemed appalled at Pyke's irreligiosity. 'Truly you are beyond redemption.'

'And we have nothing further to discuss.'

But Hunt was not quite ready to depart. 'I'm still

intrigued by your business with Peel. By this I mean, what business would the Prime Minister's right-hand man have with a common murderer?'

'We share an interest in Florentine philosophers.'

'Have it your way.' Hunt shrugged and held up Peel's note. 'This merely confirms that the trial goes ahead tomorrow as planned.'

'So it would seem.'

'Well, that's settled, then.' Hunt clapped his hands together and tapped lightly on the door, indicating that he was ready to leave. 'I almost forgot. I've heard troubling rumours about possible escape plans. I take such intimations seriously, even as I find them highly improbable. Newgate has changed since Wild's days and you, Pyke, are no Jack Sheppard. But just to make certain, I have taken the precaution of posting additional turnkeys outside your cell and you will be required to wear handcuffs and leg-irons at all times, even within your cell.' His chest swelled with self-importance. 'Your only escape will be when the hangman fits the noose around your neck. Still, I do not imagine Hades constitutes an especially pleasurable prospect.'

Reading *The Times* by candlelight, Pyke discovered a story on the second page in the 'Police' section which he scanned with mounting horror. The murders were attributed to a fresh wave of anti-Catholic violence that was sweeping the city. The bodies of a young man and woman had been found on Hounslow Heath. Both had been strangled. The report said the victims were Irish. The man, Gerald McKeown, was twenty-one and the woman, Mary Johnson, was seventeen.

Pyke distrusted anyone who openly expressed their emotions, but as he stared down at the words of the report he didn't in the first instance attempt to decode their meaning.

He just opened his lips, thought of not only Gerald and Mary but also Lizzie, and silently mouthed an impotent scream.

TWELVE

When Pyke emerged into the hushed courtroom from the subterranean passage that ran between the prison and the Sessions House on Old Bailey and took his place in the dock, he sensed the consternation of those gathered there to watch the trial. It had something to do with his choice of attire: a soiled smock-frock by no means conformed to the dashing image that had been circulating in fashionable society. It would be the first of many disappointments the spectators would have to bear, Pyke thought, as he scanned the packed courthouse for familiar faces. This was assuming, perhaps arrogantly, that some of the gathered audience wanted to see him walk free. Pyke understood that decadent ladies might find his unrefined charms alluring but was more concerned about reports of a mob assembling outside the building, demanding his head on a platter.

With this thought in mind, his gaze fell upon the portly figure of Lord Edmonton, who had taken up a seat on the bench opposite the dock and was talking amiably to his companion. Ernest Augustus – duke of Cumberland, earl of Armagh and the King's brother – was a tall man with a hideously scarred face, offset by a carefully manicured moustache and a pumpkin-shaped head. Though his wound had been honourably received during the Napoleonic wars, it transformed what would otherwise have been a merely overbearing face into something monstrous. He was slightly balding and prematurely grey, giving the impression that he was older than he perhaps was. The duke was dressed ostentatiously (and ridiculously in Pyke's view) in the uniform of a Hanoverian general. Edmonton saw that Pyke was looking at them and ran his index finger across his neck, to simulate the cutting of his throat.

A few places along from him, Sir Richard Fox was engrossed in a conversation with Viscount Lowther, an acquaintance of Peel. Fox looked old and worn, and though he had come to witness the trial he could not bring himself to look across the room and meet Pyke's stare. Pyke wondered what outcome Fox was hoping for, whether he wanted to see him walk free or not.

Pyke's gaze shifted to the public gallery and he saw Emily Blackwood. She was wearing an ivory dress and shawl, her hair pinned up and held in place by her bonnet. She seemed frailer than he remembered. For a moment their eyes met, and she smiled and mouthed a silent 'hello'. She seemed not to want to draw attention to herself. He wondered whether Edmonton knew that his daughter was present in the courtroom.

Pyke's attention was wrested away from Emily by the wheezing figure of his uncle, who had managed to persuade one of the court officials that he had urgent business with Pyke.

'Change of plan, I'm afraid,' he said, catching his breath. 'The Crown's case will now be presented by William Gregson. I've heard he's good.' Godfrey noticed what Pyke was wearing and frowned. 'What, in God's name, are you wearing that dreadful outfit for?'

Pyke ignored the question. 'Peel's lawyer. He helped to draft the Metropolitan Police Bill. I met him about a month ago.' It was depressing news but it confirmed what he already knew.

'Well, in that respect at least, we have got our own ace.' Godfrey looked around. 'I wonder where Quince has got to. He's cutting things a bit fine. Proceedings are due to start at any minute.'

'I told him I no longer required his services,' Pyke said, as though the matter was of no consequence. 'I said I wouldn't pay him for his time unless he agreed to relinquish his representation. That worked well enough.'

Godfrey stared at him, aghast. 'You did *what*?'

'It's a common enough occurrence. Defence attorneys withdrawing at the last minute to take up more lucrative work elsewhere.'

'*Why?*' Godfrey sounded angry as much as concerned. 'Who on earth is going to represent you now?'

'I don't need representation.'

Godfrey looked flummoxed. 'For God sake, boy, do you *want* them to hang you?'

Pyke didn't answer him.

Once the recorder, Lord Chief Justice Marshall, had read out the indictment, he turned his attention to Pyke, who was standing across the courtroom from him in the dock, and asked how he wished to plead.

'Not guilty,' Pyke said, loud enough for the whole courtroom to hear him.

Under his horsehair wig, Marshall frowned. 'I am led to believe that you are without legal representation. Is that correct?'

'It is, Your Honour.'

Marshall nodded gravely. 'I want to make it clear that this sorry state of affairs provides you with no legal grounds for arguing for a new trial at some later date.'

'I understand, Your Honour.'

'Very well. Let the trial begin.'

Once the jury was sworn in and two further judges had taken their place on the bench next to Marshall, beneath the sword of justice, the Crown's barrister, William Gregson, started to outline the case against Pyke. Emphasising certain elements of the Crown's case over others, he drew attention to the testimony they would hear from Maggie Smallman, the barmaid who worked at the accused's 'sordid' gin palace: she would tell the court that Pyke had threatened to kill Lizzie Morgan, his mistress, on numerous occasions. He drew attention to a neighbour's claim that he had heard the deceased call out to Pyke on the night she was murdered, begging for her life. He also told the court that Pyke's flight from the murder scene was undoubtedly a sign of his guilt. He acknowledged that the Crown's case relied on circumstantial evidence but pointed out that solid circumstantial evidence was often superior to eyewitness testimony. Pyke listened to his speech with interest but said nothing.

When Pyke offered no cross-examination of the first four prosecution witnesses, the recorder felt compelled to intervene. He asked Pyke whether he thought it aided his defence to allow the testimony of witnesses, even ones with questionable reputations and social standing, to go uncontested. He seemed puzzled. Pyke said he would try to play a more active role in the proceedings. Marshall replied it wasn't a question of what *he* wanted; rather, Pyke's liberty and indeed his life were being threatened by his indifference. Again, Pyke promised he would try to do better. Marshall shook his head, as though he were dealing with a simpleton.

So when the next witness, James Hardwick, was

introduced and outlined his own area of expertise – phrenology, or the relationship between the shape and size of a skull and the mind it contained – Pyke decided to involve himself in the proceedings.

He agreed to allow his own cranium to be measured and scribbled a few notes while Hardwick explained that Pyke's 'enlarged organ' revealed a propensity for 'recklessness, combativeness, destructiveness, self-esteem and secretiveness'.

When Hardwick had finished, Marshall asked whether Pyke cared to cross-examine the witness, and was about to move on when Pyke said, 'I do have one question, Your Honour.'

'Oh?' Marshall looked up at him, a little surprised. 'Go on, then.'

Pyke turned to the witness box and said he was very interested in Hardwick's claim about the relationship between 'anomalies' in the skull and 'enlarged cranial lobes' and an individual's propensity for recklessness and aggression.

'Am I correct in concluding that, according to your theory, such cranial features suggest a less developed mind?'

Hardwick nodded. 'Suggest is perhaps too modest a word.'

'Such features *demonstrate* a less developed mind, then.'

'Indeed,' Hardwick said, looking at Pyke warily. 'This was the thesis of Gall and Spurzheim and I see no reason to question it.'

'And this propensity for violence, even murder, *demonstrated* in one's skull shape and size, takes no account, you say, of social standing or class?'

'That is correct.'

Pyke smiled. 'Then since good science, as you well know, is based on the principles of scrutiny and observation, perhaps we might test this hypothesis, taking as our example the most esteemed of all men gathered here in this courtroom.'

Hardwick looked around him nervously. 'And who might that be, sir?'

'Why, of course, the King's much venerated brother, Ernest Augustus, duke of Cumberland and earl of Armagh.'

Hardwick stammered that such a request was both impertinent and counter-productive. Beads of sweat appeared on his brow. Attention in the courtroom shifted from the dock to the bench. The duke himself, who had been watching proceedings through a pocket telescope, did not seem to welcome the interest. He whispered something angrily in Edmonton's ear.

The recorder stepped in and scolded Pyke for his impudence. 'Either proceed with an alternative line of questioning or permit the witness to stand down.'

'But, Your Honour, this particular issue goes right to the heart of this man's credibility, and since the prosecution has chosen, perhaps unwisely, to build its case using what I can only describe as *pseudo*-scientific evidence, then I am surely within my rights, particularly given the gravity of the charges, to test this evidence using any appropriate means at my disposal.'

This time, the recorder looked baffled. Next to him on the bench, the duke and Edmonton conferred with one another in a manner that indicated their unease.

'Of course, I understand if the duke feels that participating in such an experiment is beneath him . . .'

This time Cumberland himself rose to speak. 'This is preposterous . . .' The way in which the light reflected on his facial scars made him seem demonic.

The recorder stepped in. 'I will not permit common prisoners to address esteemed members of this bench.'

'If he feels uneasy about availing himself . . .'

Cumberland, who had a reputation for impetuosity, interrupted. 'I have nothing to hide.' Then to Hardwick, he said, 'Go ahead, sir, do your tests on me.'

A ripple of approval spread through the courtroom and the duke seemed to warm to his new-found popularity. The recorder looked on, helpless, perhaps feeling unable or unwilling to overrule royalty. Dressed in military regalia, Cumberland stood up while Hardwick wrapped a measuring tape around his skull and peered closely at the point where the ends of the tape met. Hardwick was sweating profusely. Back in the witness box, he did not know where to look: at the recorder, Cumberland or Pyke.

Pyke decided to push things along. 'If I remember, the circumference of my own skull measured twenty-three and a half inches at its widest point. Is that correct?' Hardwick nodded blankly. 'Would you tell the court what the duke of Cumberland's skull measured?'

Hardwick stared at him, ashen-faced, then, with a pleading expression, turned to the bench. The recorder looked similarly perturbed but knew that, in the circumstances, Hardwick had to answer the question. Cumberland seemed oblivious to their concerns.

'Go ahead, sir,' Pyke said, calmly.

'One cannot judge character on the circumference of the skull alone. It is also a question of cranial shape . . .'

'The measurement, if you please, sir.'

'Your Honour?' Hardwick looked pleadingly at the recorder.

Marshall did not seem to know what to say.

'The measurement.'

Hardwick's voice fell to a whisper. 'Twenty-seven inches.'

'Could you repeat that figure, sir, and this time so that the whole court may benefit from your wisdom?'

Hardwick was crestfallen. 'Twenty-seven inches.'

Gasps of astonishment were accompanied by a ripple of nervous laughter emanating from the public gallery. Cumberland, who had finally grasped the implications of Hardwick's findings, turned crimson. The recorder did not appear to know what to do or say.

Pyke waited for a moment of quiet and said, very quickly, before he could be stopped, 'Given that the duke murdered his manservant in cold blood and raped his own sister, I am on reflection happy to concede the truthfulness of this witness's testimony.'

For a second, there was utter silence in the courtroom as people absorbed the shock of his remarks, and then pandemonium broke out. Gutsy cheers from the public gallery temporarily drowned out the groundswell of indignation from the bench. As the recorder attempted to reimpose order on the courtroom by repeatedly banging his gavel down on the bench, his wig slipped forward off the top of his head and fell six feet on to the table below, where clerks were administering the proceedings.

Two hours later, Lord Chief Justice Marshall began his summing up. He reminded the jury that they were to base their decision only on the evidence they had heard in court. He added that, scandalous and offensive as the accused's remarks had been during the cross-examination of one of the prosecution's witnesses, they were to disregard these comments in their deliberations. Bound and gagged, Pyke listened without interest from the dock. Looking across the room at the public gallery, he noticed that Emily had vacated her seat and wondered what this meant.

Marshall told the jury that, to return a guilty verdict, they had to be satisfied, beyond reasonable doubt, that on the night of the fourth day of March eighteen hundred and twenty-nine, in a gin palace on Duke Street in the Smithfield area of London, the accused had, with malice aforethought, murdered the deceased, Lizzie Morgan, by stabbing her twice in the stomach with a knife. Marshall then summarised all the evidence the court had heard, pausing to underscore those points that hinted at Pyke's guilt.

Once he had finished, he sent the jury away to reach a verdict. As they left, Pyke was removed from the dock.

It took the jury less than ten minutes. Back in the courtroom the foreman, when asked, said that they had unanimously reached a verdict. Enjoying the occasion, he paused, to clear his throat, and informed the court that the jury had found the accused guilty as charged.

The reaction inside the courtroom was a little muted. Outside, once news of the verdict spread, the cheers were louder. Those sitting on the bench nodded vigorously to one another in approval. Edmonton shook Cumberland's hand, as though he had been responsible for bringing about Pyke's demise. Farther along the bench, Sir Richard Fox stared down at his feet. None of the jury could bring themselves to look at Pyke. The recorder praised them for the verdict and added that it was unquestionably the right one given the damning nature of the evidence.

Finally he turned his attention to Pyke. In a suitably grave voice, Marshall said that he hoped Pyke had taken the time since his arrest to reflect on the heinousness of his crime, although this did not appear to be the case. He told Pyke it was his habit to encourage the condemned to make their peace with the Almighty, but since Pyke's behaviour suggested that he was beyond redemption, there was no reason to prolong his detention in Newgate.

Replacing his horsehair wig with a black cap, he banged

his gavel down on the bench and said, 'You will be hanged by the neck on Monday morning.'

This left Pyke only two days to plan his escape. It was less time than he had hoped for.

THIRTEEN

Separated from the rest of Newgate by the press yard, the prison's condemned block suffered from an austere appearance and a funereal atmosphere. In all, there were fifteen cells arranged over three floors, but it was rare that more than one or two of these was occupied at any time, especially, as a turnkey informed him, since in recent years the Bloody Code had been scaled back. This was a set of legal statutes which insisted upon capital punishment for crimes as trivial as forging coins. Pyke did not comment on the irony: he was being executed by an administration that wanted to introduce more humane forms of punishment. Nor did Pyke ask whether the man was one of the two guards who had been approached by Townsend and offered a hundred pound to assist him in his escape attempt.

Pyke had tried to make it clear that this aid would not involve them *physically* assisting his bid for freedom.

Rather, they were simply to turn a blind eye to particular occurrences, if and when they took place. As such, they might be dismissed from their posts for negligence but not prosecuted for aiding and abetting a crime. In which case, a hundred pounds would be more than enough to compensate them for the 'inconvenience' of having to find alternative employment.

When Godfrey visited him on the Friday evening, the

turnkeys were to make sure he was not searched, or rather, if he *was* searched, that their search did not reveal anything. Nor was Pyke's cell to be searched, after Godfrey's departure. He was starting to worry that the turnkeys would not honour their side of the bargain when Godfrey thrust a small key into his hand. He permitted himself a hushed sigh of relief.

This did not, however, mean that the condemned block's incarceration regime was a lax one. The governor's promise of additional security had been realised in the form of reinforced leg-irons and handcuffs. These devices, and the thickness of the stone walls, meant that Pyke's chances of escape would normally have been slim.

They still perhaps were, despite the arrangements that had been made, but he chose not to focus on such concerns.

Instead, after Godfrey had departed, Pyke rummaged through the items that his uncle had smuggled into the cell: the key, of course, but also charcoal, powder, soap, chalk, candles, rouge and a razor blade.

Sitting up against the cell door, in order that the turnkeys might not see him through the grated hole, Pyke worked through the night, using all his candles. By the time he heard the first cock crow, he had found a way of using the small key to unlock both the leg-irons and the handcuffs.

It rained for most of the day, the kind of relentless downpour that seemed to penetrate the tarred walls and dampen the inside of the cell and its few contents: a hemp mat and a horse rug. Pyke had wrapped himself up in the rug and settled himself on the mat, but had still been unable to sleep. Trying to ignore the cold and the stench of decaying animal matter, discarded outside the prison walls by market traders, he stared at the window and listened to the patter of raindrops peppering the outside of the building.

While the rest of the condemned prisoners spent their free time in the more welcoming environment of the press rooms, a narrow area replete with tables, benches and a fire, Pyke opted to remain in his cell, anxious that no one should look too carefully at his leg-irons and handcuffs.

He found himself thinking about Mary Johnson and Gerald McKeown – how grateful they had been when he had offered to put them up in a lodging house – and he imagined what torture they might have suffered as someone dragged them to a wild spot on Hounslow Heath, and strangled them. He also thought about Lizzie and whether she had known what was happening to her.

It was already dark by the time the Reverend Arthur Foote arrived, with Godfrey. Godfrey seemed nervous – both of them had been drinking and he stumbled as he entered the cell – but Pyke assumed that Foote was either too inebriated or excited by the prospect of eliciting a dramatic eleventh-hour confession from Pyke, which he could then 'sell' to Godfrey, thereby making a significant sum of money, to realise what was about to happen.

Pyke greeted them and said he was sorry that he could not offer them anything to drink. Foote produced a flask of what Pyke presumed was gin and said he had brought his own supplies. He took a swig, without offering it to either Godfrey or Pyke. He was wearing a long black cassock under a black robe, a white undershirt, a dog collar and a pair of black shoes, and was carrying a wide-brimmed hat.

Godfrey pulled the cell door closed and through the grated hole told the turnkeys that they would knock when they were ready to leave.

'So you've decided to confess, boy? Excellent, excellent. God loves repenting sinners as much as the rest of his flock. More, even.' Even in the candlelight, Pyke could see Foote's blackened teeth as he smiled. 'I like 'em too but for different reasons. Isn't that right, Godfrey? Those little sheets you publish can be quite profitable, I've heard, especially when the confession's been so eagerly awaited.' He peered down at Pyke through the gloom. 'You're looking queer, boy. Your skin is all mottled and blotchy.'

This was the effect of the rouge and charcoal. Pyke hadn't expected Foote to notice. It meant he didn't have much time.

'Your hair, it's shorter and greyer, too.' Foote appeared confused. 'And didn't you once have sideburns?'

Pyke had hacked them off with the razor, along with some of his hair, and had brushed it with flecks of chalk.

'Very queer indeed.' Foote's frown deepened. 'So how do you want to do this, boy?'

Pyke waited until Godfrey had positioned himself in front of the grated hole in the cell door.

'How about you sit next to me on the mat here and I'll begin my confession.'

'Sit on the floor?' Foote seemed unsure. 'I suppose, given the lack of amenities, I might be able to countenance such a plan. You say next to you, eh? I like that.' Grinning, Foote lifted up his cassock and planted himself awkwardly on the part of the mat Pyke had prepared for him.

Freeing himself from the handcuffs, Pyke struck Foote once, as hard as he could, with the full force of his clenched fist, and once Foote had collapsed on to him he jammed both thumbs firmly into the Ordinary's neck and pushed until he heard a gurgling sound.

For the turnkeys' sake, he proffered a few garbled sentiments about inner demons and breaking the Sabbath. Meanwhile, he went to work on Foote's body, stripping him of his hat and shoes, his dog collar and finally his cassock and undershirt. He dressed Foote in his own clothes and, in turn, put on the Ordinary's attire. The shoes were too small for his feet but he just about managed to squeeze into them. He laid Foote out on the hemp mat, his back facing the door, as though he were asleep, and secured the leg-irons and handcuffs in the appropriate places. He had a drink from Foote's flask and then pulled the black robe around his shoulders.

'Is Arthur going to live?' Godfrey whispered, looking down at Foote's unmoving body. His hands were trembling.

Pyke shrugged.

'Is he going to live, Pyke?'

'He'll live. Probably.' Pyke picked up the Ordinary's hat. 'Are the turnkeys outside the ones I've paid?'

Godfrey nodded. 'Two of them are, anyhow. There are three or four of 'em out there.'

This wasn't something Pyke had planned for, but he would have to take his chances and hope the two turnkeys earned their money and distracted the other two.

'Just take my arm and walk at a nice easy pace. Take my lead. Don't rush, whatever you do. Anyone tries to talk to us, we keep going. Tell 'em I'm drunk and can barely speak. I'll just mumble. I'll make it appear that if you weren't supporting me, I'd fall down. People here know Foote. It won't seem strange.'

Godfrey stared down at Foote's unmoving form and whispered, 'Christ, Pyke, did you have to hurt Arthur as badly as that?'

Pyke ignored him and pulled the hat down as far over his face as it would go. The dog collar felt tight and scratchy around his neck. He gathered up the items Godfrey had smuggled into the cell, so as not to implicate the turnkeys when the escape was discovered.

'Ready?'

Godfrey still seemed shaken but knocked on the door and said they were ready to leave. One of the turnkeys unbolted the door and pushed it open. The man peered into the gloomy cell and saw what he assumed to be Pyke lying on the floor. He asked whether Pyke had 'confessed his sins before God'. Godfrey answered in the affirmative and said the prisoner wanted to be left alone. He added that the confession had also exhausted Reverend Foote and winked. 'He needs his victuals.' The man laughed.

Godfrey led Pyke into the corridor. Two men were sitting around an overturned wooden cask playing cards. Neither of them even bothered to look up. The turnkey who had spoken to them had one final look in the cell before closing the door and sliding the heavy iron bolts into place.

'Be careful on the stairs. The stone gets mighty slippery when it rains.'

Godfrey said they would and led Pyke along the corridor towards the staircase. The man followed them, jangling some keys. He told them that unless he unlocked the condemned block's main door, they would be spending the night there. Pyke allowed his heartbeat to settle and took his uncle's lead. He tried to relax and put himself in the mind of a drunk. Mumbling something, he made a point of shuffling along rather than walking; he also swayed from side to side, trying not to appear too rigid, and just grunted when the guard asked him whether he was all right. The staircase between the floors was dark and narrow and Pyke walked down the steps at an appropriately modest pace, holding on to the stone walls as he did so. When they reached the bottom, the turnkey pushed in front of them and as he did so said, 'Well then, sirs, I'll bid you both goodnight,' and unlocked the main door and waited for them to step outside into the rain.

Pyke held on to his hat to stop it blowing off his head.

As they walked through the press yard, a confined area about ten feet wide and seventy feet long, bordered on either side by a high wall, Pyke whispered to Godfrey that he was doing well. 'Just keep your calm, we're almost there.' Pyke knew how much his uncle was risking to assist him; knew that Godfrey disliked physical exertion of any kind; knew how hard it must be for him.

Godfrey exhaled loudly. 'Easy for you to say, Pyke.'

Pyke knew, of course that they were *not* almost there; he knew that the most dangerous part of the escape still lay ahead of them – walking out through the prison's guarded and well-lit main entrance without arousing suspicion – but chose not to say anything, because he could feel his uncle trembling.

It took them a minute or so to shuffle across the press yard and perhaps another minute to pass through the male felons' quadrangle and the arcade under the chapel and approach the gatekeeper's house via a series of poorly lit passages. No one had stopped them or even asked them a question. Seeing the bedraggled figure of the Ordinary stumble through the prison must have seemed the most natural sight in the world.

By the time they reached the keeper's house, they had been ushered through three sets of locked doors by a succession of incurious turnkeys.

The keeper's house was little more than a dark passageway that housed a series of small rooms which belonged to him and which linked the prison's main door with a stone-floored entrance hall.

They had to pass through two sets of locked doors, but since there was no one attending the first door, Godfrey had to call out for assistance. A small, feral man with an unkempt beard appeared from one of the adjoining rooms and said, 'Ah, Reverend Foote, I was hoping it might be you, sir. The governor wanted a word about the condemned's sermon tomorrow. Told me to tell you to wait 'ere while I fetch 'im.'

Pyke mumbled something nonsensical and Godfrey barked, 'Perhaps it could wait until tomorrow morning. You can see for yourself that Reverend Foote is maybe not in the best state of mind to assist the governor.' Pyke, whose face was turned down towards his feet so that the keeper could see only the top of his hat, belched. Godfrey added, 'He just needs a good night's sleep.'

The keeper, who was standing the other side of the iron bars, shrugged and produced a set of keys from his jacket pocket. 'I don't suppose it would matter, though the governor was insistent that I fetched 'im when you was ready to leave, sir.' He inserted one of the keys into the lock, turned it and pulled open the first of two reinforced doors that blocked their path to the outside world.

As they shuffled past the keeper, Pyke heard him whisper, 'Good luck, Mr Pyke.' To Pyke's horror, Godfrey acknowledged the remark and said, 'Thanks,' as the keeper stepped back through the rectangular gap in the iron bars, swung the door closed and locked it from the other side.

Pyke heard the governor before he saw him. 'Gentlemen. I'm so pleased I managed to catch up with you before you disappeared.' Ahead of them, the main prison entrance was still locked. There was nowhere left to go. 'Please step away from the prisoner, Mr Bond.' Turning around for the first time, Pyke saw that the governor was surrounded by a group of turnkeys. The keeper was grinning. This had been Pyke's last opportunity to gain his freedom and his plan lay in tatters. His despair was palpable and the governor seemed to sense it. 'What a shame.' He strutted towards them, like a prize cockerel. 'To think you came so close . . .'

That evening, they removed the two other prisoners awaiting execution from the top floor of the condemned block
to cells on the first floor and turned it into a fortress. No
visitors were permitted to enter the block. Turnkeys
guarded the staircase. Shackled by leg-irons and handcuffs
and gagged by cloth, Pyke had been thrown into a different
cell. A turnkey sat with Pyke inside the cell. Additional
turnkeys guarded the cell from the outside. The governor
made regular visits throughout the night and the following
day, Sunday, to make certain that his keepers remained
vigilant; through the grated hole, he informed Pyke that
Foote's throat had been so badly damaged by the assault he
might never speak again. He explained that Godfrey had
been charged with assisting an escape attempt and would
be spending considerable time in prison. He said the two
turnkeys whom Pyke had bought off had been dismissed
and also charged with aiding and abetting. He told Pyke,
with some glee, that one of the turnkeys had been overheard in a nearby tavern boasting about his role in Pyke's
escape bid and the money he was to receive. He reminded
Pyke he would die the following morning, adding that
such was the interest in Pyke's execution – an interest that
had been further stoked by Pyke's 'cowardly' escape bid –
crowds had already started to gather in the street outside
Debtors' Door.

'If the hangman doesn't get you,' the governor said,
almost drooling, 'then the angry mob will.'

Inside the cell Pyke stared at the tarred wall and listened
to the lowing of cattle as they were driven into their stalls
and pens.

The bells tolled. Outside, beyond the walls of the prison, he
heard them baying for his blood; working people who had

been gathered since early in the morning drinking, laughing, shouting, singing and, above all, waiting for the greatest show on earth to begin. The scaffold outside Debtors' Door would now be finished, a single noose hanging from the wooden beam. Across the street, the King of Denmark would be crawling with moneyed flesh. Viewing spots on roofs and up lamp-posts would be taken. The procession of clergymen, sheriffs, visitors and, of course, Pyke began to make its way from the press room down a flight of stone steps into an underground passage.

He was walking down the aisle of St Paul's Cathedral with a younger woman dressed in white on his arm. Above him the grand dome was full of chirruping blackbirds.

Dead Man's Walk, they called it. His own father was reading from the scriptures. Emily was next to him. Then it was Foote who was reading, but just his disembodied head. Damnation and forgiveness. Pyke could still taste the sweetness of the wine on his parched lips.

They were walking up some steps and Pyke found himself in a small hall. They waited momentarily. Ahead of them lay Debtors' Door, and beyond that he could hear the crowd. He could smell them: their excitement, their fear, their hatred of him. Closing his eyes, he saw his own father fall, arms raised, under their stamping boots. He heard his father scream; heard the screams of animals being slaughtered.

Does anyone deserve to die? Do I deserve to die?

When he stepped out of the gloom of the prison into the foggy sunshine, followed by the Ordinary, the clergymen, the under-sheriffs and the visitors, he might have been forgiven for mistaking the squalid din of human noise that greeted him for approval, but almost at once the mood turned ugly: the gallows were pelted with food. The dignitaries held back and waited for the marshals to bring the mob to order. On the gallows, Pyke watched the hangman tug on the noose, to check it was properly attached to the beam. He was ushered towards the beam by Foote, who made a point of neither touching him nor looking at him. Foote waited for the crowd to settle before he turned to address Pyke. His vein-knotted hands shook ever so slightly while he read from the Bible. Standing on the gallows next to him was Sir Richard Fox.

'You have another moment between this and death, and as a condemned man I implore you in God's name to tell the truth.' Fox was staring at him. 'Have you got anything to repent?'

Edmonton guffawed. He ran his index finger across his bulbous throat.

Pyke said nothing. He felt detached even from himself. He tasted laudanum at the back of his throat. Folk in the crowd gathered below him, a faceless mass of people that stretched as far as he could see up Giltspur Street and along Old Bailey. The hangman was carrying a cloth sack. Pyke looked up and saw himself in the crowd: a scared, orphaned boy. He heard his own youthful sobs. The hangman pushed him towards the beam and put the sack over his head. He arranged the noose around his neck.

In his fitful dreams, he heard himself ask: *What kind of life have you led when no one mourns?*

'Hush,' one of the turnkeys said.

The 'new' Ordinary – Arthur Foote's replacement, a stern-looking man who seemed genuinely enthused by the prospect of Pyke's death – clapped his hands. Standing in his pulpit, dressed in ceremonial robes, he surveyed the chapel and its occupants with what appeared to be contempt.

'Let us sing to the praise and glory of God,' he said.

Everyone except Pyke stood.

The sheriffs and under-sheriffs in their gold chains and fur collars and their footmen sat on one side of the chapel. In the pews in the middle the general mass of the prison population took their seats. The schoolmaster and juvenile prisoners were arranged around the communion table opposite the pulpit. Pyke himself sat alone in a large dock-like construction in the centre of the chapel. It had been painted black. Pyke had been allowed to take his seat only once everyone else had taken their places. Shackled and gagged, he kept his head up and met no one's stare.

'This service is for the dead,' the Ordinary bellowed from the pulpit, once the hymn had been sung. 'The condemned man who is about to suffer the gravest penalty of the law *will* read from the prayer book and sing the lamentation of a wretched sinner.'

An elderly clerk shuffled across to the black pew and removed Pyke's gag. Pyke stared down at the prayer book opened in front of him. He closed his eyes. The Ordinary reiterated his demand; Pyke looked down at the words in front of him. When it was clear that Pyke would not do as he was asked, the Ordinary began his sermon and a hushed silence fell over the dour chapel. He painted a grim picture of Hell, insisting that the time for forgiveness had passed and judgement would soon be upon Pyke. He described the brutality of Pyke's crimes and reminded the congregation that Pyke had attacked a venerable man of the cloth.

Pyke looked around at the unfamiliar faces gathered in the galleries and pews around him.

It was six o'clock on Sunday evening. He would hang in a little more than twelve hours.

Pyke asked for food and porter but even as he did so it struck him as an odd tradition: eating in order to prepare for one's death. He was not hungry, nor did he want to dull his senses with alcohol.

The victuals arrived about an hour after he had been returned to his cell: stewed mutton with carrots and barley and a jug of porter. Food and drink were also brought for the turnkey in his cell. Pyke picked at the food for a while with his cuffed hands but did not eat anything. Instead he watched, without interest, as the young man scooped the mutton from the bowl in front of him and shovelled it into his mouth, gravy dripping down both sides of his chin. Outside the cell the mood seemed almost festive. Everyone, it appeared, was looking forward to the hanging. Pyke listened as the turnkeys talked excitedly about the vantage points they were going to occupy in relation to the scaffold. One of the turnkeys said there were already thirty thousand people gathered in the streets outside the prison. Another reckoned there would be close to a hundred thousand by the following morning.

The young turnkey had an unnaturally thin face, as though his head had somehow been deformed in childbirth. He had tried to compensate for this deformity by growing an excess of facial hair, which meant that scraps of food and drops of porter gathered in his beard.

Pyke heard footsteps, hard-soled shoes clicking against the stone floor. They came to a stop outside his cell. He listened to voices and heard a jangling of keys. From outside, one of the turnkeys inserted a key into the lock, twisted it, slid the iron bolts back and pulled open the heavy wooden door. Candlelight illuminated the gloomy cell. Pyke looked up. Another turnkey issued an instruction, telling whoever it was out there that they would be searched on the way in and the way out as well. 'Governor's orders.' The turnkey added, 'Remember what we agreed, madam. The door remains open at all times and young Jenkins stays in the cell with you. To make sure there ain't no funny stuff.'

Emily Blackwood stepped into the cell, removed her bonnet and looked at him. Her smile was warm but awkward.

'Mr Pyke. I'm sure it is unnecessary for me to ask how you are.' She stepped farther into the cell. 'But I did want to see you before . . .' The words died in her mouth.

Pyke stood up and bowed. He smelled her perfume. Her face was composed but alert.

'I have porter. I have food.' He pointed at the untouched plate. 'What more could a man ask for?'

'It is barbaric, what they are planning to do to you.'

'Is it?' Pyke wasn't absolutely sure but thought he saw her wink at him. 'The last time we were in Newgate together I said that we live and die according to the whims of chance. This is merely confirming the truthfulness of that sentiment.'

'But with chance perhaps comes hope?' Emily seemed suddenly unsteady on her feet.

Pyke asked whether she cared for a seat.

'No, I'm fine.' But she did not seem to be well. Again she wobbled a little and when, a few moments later, she fell forward, Pyke instinctively reached out to break her fall. As he did so, he felt her press something cold and hard into his open palm. Jenkins did not seem to know what to do, but from outside the cell Pyke heard one of the older turnkeys say, 'Step away from the visitor.' Ignoring his demand, Pyke carefully laid Emily on the bed. The turnkey reiterated his demand and hurried into the cell. Pyke held up his hands, as if to protest his innocence. He had already transferred what Emily had given him into his mouth.

On the bed, Emily was sighing and holding her forehead. The older turnkey looked at Pyke, unimpressed. He asked

Emily whether she felt better. Emily said yes, she did, but she couldn't explain what had happened. All of a sudden she had felt faint and hadn't been able to stop herself from falling. The turnkey nodded in a manner that suggested he did not believe her explanation.

'Well, you've seen the prisoner now and said your farewell. Jenkins, perhaps you could escort the lady back to the keeper's house.'

Gingerly Emily rose to her feet and took a deep breath. Turning to leave, she exhaled. 'Who knows, Mr Pyke. Perhaps the governor may yet opt for clemency.'

'I'm afraid the time has long passed.' He looked at her for some indication of what she might be referring to but saw little in her blank stare. 'And it is not in the governor's powers to grant such clemency. Only the Home Secretary's intervention will make a difference and I fear this will not be forthcoming.'

'But surely the governor's office is not entirely closed to you, even at this late stage?'

Pyke said that, unfortunately, it was. As he bade her farewell, he felt sickened by the idea that he might never see her again.

Once she had departed, the older turnkey folded his arms and said, 'What was all that about, then?'

Pyke said nothing. The small key was hidden under his tongue.

'Hands,' the turnkey barked. 'Show me your hands, prisoner.'

Pyke held out his palms.

'Turn out your pockets.'

Again Pyke did as he was asked.

The turnkey edged closer to him. 'Open your mouth.'

Pyke forced the small key as far back under his tongue as it would go.

'Open your fucking mouth.'

The turnkey peered gingerly into Pyke's open mouth but could not see much because of the poor light. He seemed reluctant to do more than this; doubtless the thought that Pyke might bite him had crossed his mind.

The cell door was bolted from the outside and the turnkey checked to see that Pyke's handcuffs and leg-irons were secure and then settled down on a chair inside the cell.

An hour or so later, the man was asleep. While he dozed, Pyke spat the key out into his cuffed hand. It took him a while to find a way of manoeuvring it into the lock of his handcuffs, but upon doing so he was astonished to discover that the key not only fitted the lock but also released the cuffs. Freeing his hands, he set to work on the leg-irons. It took him less than five minutes to unshackle himself. For a few moments, Pyke sat on the bed, staring at the sleeping turnkey and then at his unlocked handcuffs and leg-irons, thinking about something Emily had said: *But surely the governor's office is not entirely closed to you, even at this late stage?* What had she meant? Of course the governor's office was closed to him. But what if he *could* arrange an audience with Hunt in his office? Might there be some route of escape open to him from there?

The sheer granite walls that rose up fifty feet from the ground were impossible to scale, a task that was made even harder by a row of inward-facing iron spikes attached to the wall about three-quarters of the way up, and another row of even larger spikes that protected the top of the wall. But if he could drop down from the governor's quarters on to the top of the wall, there might be a chance.

Carefully Pyke secured the cuffs and leg-irons and pressed the key into the palm of his hand.

'Turnkey.' The shrillness of Pyke's tone startled the older man from his slumber.

'Eh?' He looked around the cell, still disoriented.

'I want you to take a message to Governor Hunt. Tell the governor that I am willing to divulge to him the exact nature of my business with the Home Secretary but, and this is my one demand, only if he grants me a private audience in his office.'

The turnkey seemed unconvinced. 'Why should I wake the governor at this time of night?'

'The governor will want to hear what I have to say to him.' Pyke shrugged. 'And if, at some later point, he hears that you failed to avail him of the opportunity to hear my revelations, I can promise you he will not be happy.'

The turnkey still looked unsure so Pyke said, 'If you pass on the message, and he refuses to see me, what have you lost?'

Later, when the old man had been replaced by another turnkey, all that was left for Pyke to do was wait.

'This is a most unusual situation,' the governor said, as he lightly tapped his fingers on his desk. His bald head glistened in the candlelight. 'But I cannot pretend that I am not a little intrigued by the nature of your business with the Home Secretary.'

Pyke was separated from the governor only by his mahogany desk. The turnkeys had brought him into the room and checked his handcuffs and leg-irons. He had also been searched, once in his cell and again before he entered the governor's office. The two of them were now alone. Pyke asked whether he might take a seat. The governor said that he did not see why not. With the desk to obscure Hunt's view of his hands, he set to work with the key.

Outside, the skies were beginning to lighten. He was due to hang in less than two hours.

'If I am honest, I am also curious about your motives for

sharing this information with me, since there is nothing I can offer you in return.'

Pyke nodded, as though he had been expecting this response. 'But you are no supporter of the Home Secretary, either.'

Hunt licked his lips. 'And you feel this information might be damaging to his prospects, eh?'

'Perhaps even more than damaging,' Pyke said, nodding.

'Is that so?' Hunt seemed both pained and excited by such an idea. 'You think it might even force Peel's resignation?'

'It might.'

'That's a grave assertion.' He seemed to be weighing up what he might gain from such a situation. 'But how can I attest to the information's authenticity?'

'Its authenticity would be legitimised by the reaction of the Home Secretary.' Pyke freed his handcuffs.

'I see,' the governor said, nodding carefully. 'Perhaps you might share this information with me now?'

Pyke looked around at the closed door and whispered, 'Are you certain that no one will be listening?'

'The turnkeys won't be interested in our conversation.'

'But the information is only valuable if it is wielded carefully and by the right people,' Pyke said carefully.

'So what do you suggest?'

'Since I cannot write while shackled,' Pyke said, holding up his handcuffs, 'perhaps I might venture a little closer, so that I can be sure we're not overheard.'

The governor considered his proposal. 'Your hands will remain shackled. But I can see no reason why you might not come closer, so long as you maintain a respectful distance.'

Pyke heaved himself up off the chair and shuffled around Hunt's desk in his leg-irons and advanced a few paces towards the governor, until the man held up his hand and said, 'That's far enough.' It was near enough too. Pyke let the metal handcuffs slip from his wrists and managed to catch them before they struck the floor by clutching the chain. In the same motion, he swung the chain upwards and directed the shackles at the governor's uncomprehending face. The iron cuffs struck Hunt squarely on the head and he slumped forward on to the desk. Preparing himself for an invasion of turnkeys alerted by the noise, Pyke turned to face the door. Silently he counted to ten. No one appeared. He exhaled slightly and used the key to release his leg-irons.

The governor's quarters occupied a separate building at the rear of the prison, set back from the main wards. The governor's office, located on the second floor, looked down over the enclosed press yard which separated the prison from the condemned block. Pyke tried to open the window behind the governor's desk; to his surprise, it was unlocked. Somehow, Emily had come through for him. He pulled up the sash and looked out into the misty dawn. Below was a sheer drop of fifty feet down to the yard. If he jumped, Pyke knew he would break both his legs, and would still have to scale a high wall protected by two rows of iron spikes in order to make it out of the prison. Better to climb upwards, on to the roof, if that were possible, and from there try to drop down on to the brick wall that ran the entire length of the press yard. The problem was that the wall was clearly visible from the governor's office. Even if he made it that far, Pyke would certainly be seen by one of the turnkeys.

He needed an alternative plan.

On the governor's desk he found a letter opener in the shape of a dagger. Taking the implement in his hand, and without giving it another thought, he thrust the sharp end into Hunt's neck and felt the metal slice through sinew and muscle. He had to step back so the blood that spilled from the wound did not cover his hands and feet.

Moments later, the turnkeys burst into the room. Before them they saw the governor's motionless body, slumped on his desk, surrounded by a thick pool of his own blood. The man's head, as usual, was hidden under his black hat. Behind him, the window was open. Pyke was nowhere to be seen. When one of the turnkeys raced to the window and looked down into the yard beneath him, he saw what he thought to be Pyke's unmoving body, splattered against the hard ground.

One of the turnkeys shouted, 'Prisoner escaped.'

The other, by the window, yelled, 'Prisoner fallen. Get someone down there. He looks to be dead.'

Another said, 'How in God's name did he do it? We searched him, didn't we?'

Still another said, 'I take it the governor's dead.'

'I ain't touching him.'

'Fetch a doctor.'

Another voice. 'Get the Ordinary, not a doctor. Too late for that.'

'Come on. Let's see whether Pyke's dead.'

Moments later, alone in the governor's office, Pyke removed the hat from his head and used it to wipe the governor's blood from his face and neck. He climbed out on to the narrow window ledge. Holding on to the stone arch that framed the window, he pulled himself up on to the building's roof and lay there for a moment, staring up into the dawn skies. In the distance, he could hear the mass of people beginning to gather outside the prison to witness a hanging that would not now take place. Then he was up on his feet and scurrying across the sloping roof. Then he lowered himself on to the wall and traversed the press yard.

Far below, he could see the outline of the governor's body, and he moved as quickly along the wall as its narrow width would allow. At the end of the wall, he dropped down into the garden of the Royal College of Physicians, as the first of the turnkeys reached the governor's body.

The last thing Pyke heard the man say was, 'It's not him. It isn't bleedin' him.' Then he shouted, '*Prisoner escaped.*'

PART II

*

Belfast, Ireland

JULY 1829

FOURTEEN

Pyke had no idea what type of dog it was, except that it was not a pure-bred. It possessed an unkempt coat and a deformed ear, and hauled itself along on three stubby legs, the fourth being entirely lame. It was no larger than a moderate-sized ferret, and was about as lovable, but for a reason Pyke could not explain the animal had developed a fierce loyalty to him in the short time since he had disembarked from the steamship. So much so that even when he retired to his room for the night, the dog would still be waiting for him the following morning. Finding this attachment irritating rather than endearing, Pyke had tried to shoo the dog away, to no avail. It did not seem to want his affection in any explicit manner, and Pyke was far too sensible to try to pet it. Rather, it simply followed him wherever he went in the town, happily trotting behind him on its three good legs. After a day or so of this, and when a firm kick to the dog's groin had not managed to drive it away, Pyke had relented a little and deigned to address the animal merely as 'dog'. It seemed content with the name.

The inn, if it could be called that, jostled for attention alongside the taverns, music halls and spirit shops of North Queen Street. The area also housed the town's main infantry barracks, which perhaps explained the large number of brothels located in the immediate vicinity. In fact, it had taken Pyke a few hours to work out that his own place of residence offered more than simply room and board. It was the kind of place in which you could die and not be discovered for days. For one thing, there was the odour: the corridors were not just damp and musty but smelt of something riper and more obscene, as though human flesh in an adjacent room had turned gangrenous. For another thing, he never actually saw any guests. He heard them, though; heard them beg for sexual relief through the paper-thin walls of his room, which was no bigger than a coffin and much less hospitable. If he'd had the money, he would have stayed in one of the hotels overlooking the Linen Hall, but his funds – effectively what he had retrieved from Godfrey's apartment in London – were running perilously low. Such a dilemma, unfortunately, necessitated prudence.

Pyke's search for Davy Magennis had led him to Ireland – he had been reliably informed that Magennis had long since fled London – but in Belfast he felt both anonymous and hopelessly visible. He sensed acutely the fact of being a stranger in a town where people seemed to be warily accustomed to each others' faces. The previous day, Pyke had gone out with the intention of asking for Davy Magennis in the public houses and terraces of Brown's Square, but had soon realised the futility and, indeed, the danger of such a mission. It was not that the pubs were any more menacing than those in St Giles in London, or that the district was any poorer, though it probably was. It was simply that, in Belfast, his reputation counted for nothing, and when he had walked into one particular pub, the Boot and Crown on the north side of Smithfield Square, the hostile silence he had provoked and the collection of brick-bats, swords and knives hanging up on the wall behind the counter had convinced him of the need for a subtler approach.

On his first morning in the town, Pyke was approached

by a scruffy adolescent. 'How'ye,' the lad said, nervously pushing past the dog. 'You here for the celebrations, mister?'

The dog growled and bared its teeth. The lad retreated a little.

'The celebrations?' Pyke said, uncomprehendingly, even though he had been asked the same question by others.

'You know, the parades.'

Pyke stared at him blankly. 'What parades?'

'To celebrate King Billy's victory.' The lad sounded breathless with excitement. 'You know, over the papists at the Boyne.'

'Oh, you mean the Dutchman's victory over the French king a hundred and fifty years ago?'

'Eh?' the lad said, stepping warily round the dog this time. 'There's gonna be a show of strength this year, so there is, whatever the lodge masters reckon. Ordinary Orange folk want to show nothing's changed, despite the Catholics gettin' emaciated.'

Pyke smiled, pushing the dog gently towards the lad. 'Aren't they eating enough, then?'

'Eh?' The lad seemed both confused by Pyke and intimidated by the small dog.

To its credit, the dog seemed to know what was expected of it and nipped at the boy's leg. The boy swore and said, 'Would ye away,' to the dog. The dog bit him harder, causing him to yowl with pain and fall to the ground clutching his ankle. Pyke heard himself say inadvertently, 'Good dog.' It wagged its runty tail even harder.

Pyke had been told that Belfast was a tidy, orderly town comprising stout, red-bricked edifices and broad, straight streets: a clean-living, industrious place, someone had said to him on the steamship, an Ulster–Liverpool, eminently preferable to Dublin's effete grandeur. Another man had commented on its enviable setting: a pleasant location at the mouth of a beautiful bay ringed by soaring gorse-clad mountains. What Pyke had discovered, however, was a squalid, industrial town spoiled by unedifying warehouses and monstrous cotton and linen mills – gargantuan structures that policed the town's skyline and belched plumes of black smoke through giant chimneys into overcast skies.

As in most industrial towns eager to show off their new-found wealth, there were a few buildings, such as the White Linen Hall on Donegall Square, which were palatable enough. There was also a smattering of attractively attired people going about their daily business. But on the whole, Pyke quickly concluded, Belfast was a drab town, inhabited by unattractive creatures, made even worse by the fact that it had been built on a bog. Accordingly, sanitation was non-existent, and at high tide the seawater rose up into the town's sewers and overflowed into the streets, turning them into noxious rivers of waste.

London faced similar problems, of course. But London had other attractions that tempered the bleakness. Here, everything seemed different, more depressing. For one thing, it was a fervently religious town; there were more meeting houses and churches than there were public houses. For another, the guttural accents, as much Scottish as Irish, reminded Pyke that, despite the Act of Union, he was in a foreign country. The green-clad mountains that ringed the town compounded this sense of difference, and while some may have regarded them with approval, Pyke found them oppressive.

From his less than desirable lodgings, it took him only five minutes to walk to the newly constructed mill on York Street. Pyke did not have to ask for directions. All he had to do was look upwards: it was possible to see the giant, six-floor edifice from most parts of the town. From the end of the street, the mill towered above the neighbouring houses, a sheer wall of red brick soaring vertically into the gloomy sky. There was something forbidding, even monstrous, about the building. Its giant chimney stack, its depressingly uniform symmetry and its long, angular windows reminded him of a prison. This impression was augmented both by the number of cripples in the immediate vicinity of the building – mostly women whose hands and feet had been deformed by operating the new machinery – and by his first impressions of the cavernous interior. Pyke wandered through the vast chamber and inspected the hundreds of thousands of whirring wheels, all connected to a giant steam engine, and feeding an army of individual machines. Slumped over each of these was a legion of women and children, some as young as ten, red-faced and blotchy from the stifling humidity. Their dull stares told of the deadening nature of the work.

Eventually Pyke found his way to the main office, where the mill owner, John Arnold, was waiting for him. Pyke had arranged the meeting by correspondence, prior to his departure from Liverpool. In his introductory letter, he had claimed to be the son of a Lancastrian mill owner who was to embark on a fact-finding tour of linen and cotton mills in Ulster and who was particularly interested in those mills that had recently been adapted to the wet-spinning of flax.

Arnold was a younger man than Pyke had been expecting, no more than forty years of age. He cut an ungainly figure, with large jug-like ears and a thick wall of black hair which had been cut into the shape of a pudding bowl. On first impression, he seemed like the kind of man who had once been bullied, but then Pyke noticed his cold, symmetrical face, his wax-like skin and his studied gaze, and understood that this was a man who was comfortable with violence. Pyke took against him immediately and reluctantly consented to a tour of the factory during which Arnold wasted no opportunity to laud his own achievements and business acumen.

Throughout this drawn-out introduction to the intricacies of wet-spinning flax, Pyke had thought about getting straight to the point and asking Arnold whether he knew where Davy Magennis was hiding, but he managed to bite his tongue and limit himself to an apparently innocuous question about the employment of Roman Catholics in the mill.

For a moment, it was as though he had unbuttoned his fly and urinated on the floor. Arnold's stare suggested incomprehension as well as revulsion.

'Are you a card player, Mr Hawkes?' This was the name Pyke had given himself.

Pyke shrugged.

'Perhaps we could continue this conversation later, in more . . . *relaxed* surroundings.' Arnold grinned, as though pleased with something he had said. 'There's a card game, takes place tomorrow night in a gentleman's club called the Royal on the south side of Smithfield.' He was about to dismiss Pyke but instead focused on his unprepossessing attire and started to frown. 'It's just a silly wee game, nothing fancy, you'll understand, but, if I were you, I'd think about wearing an outfit that better suited your rank and station.'

Without another word, he left Pyke to ponder the implications of his parting remark.

Entering his room, Pyke was greeted by the sight of a young woman standing over the bedside table, carefully inspecting his gold fob-watch. More surprising, for Pyke, was the fact that she displayed no embarrassment at being caught. When she finally turned to acknowledge him, still holding the fob-watch, he saw that she was quite attractive: mid-twenties, with a firm, almost plump figure, thick coal-black hair that flowed down her back practically as far as her waist, and the clearest blue eyes he had ever seen. She wore a simple white cotton dress and plain black shoes.

'Lookit,' she said, holding up the watch. 'Make no mistake, mister, you've been cheated.' Her accent was softer than many he had heard, but it still had a vaguely unappealing twang.

'And you were going to do me the favour of taking the watch away, I suppose?'

'Why in the Lord's name would I want a cheap old watch?' She studied him warily for a moment. 'Come to think of it, what are ye doing with a cheap old watch?'

'Maybe I like cheap old watches,' he said, amused now it was clear she wasn't a threat.

'What? Ye just playin' at bein' rich?' She paused for a moment and looked him over. 'That could be it, because ye don't look too comfortable in your new clothes. And if ye were rich, ye wouldn't be stayin' in a boggin' room like this.' She looked around the room, shaking her head.

'How do you know they're new?' He'd purchased shirt and jacket from a gentlemen's outfitters on Castle Place.

She shrugged, as though the answer was obvious. 'Why else would ye be scratchin' yourself under the collar like you got the fleas?'

'What are you doing here?'

'Cleaning the room, what does it look like?' She raised her eyebrows and then nodded, as though coming to some kind of realisation. 'I was thinkin' ye travelled awful light for a gentl'man. No clothes to speak of, no servants. Still, ye hide your money well. Friend of mine, works in the new bank in Castle Place, happened to mention a fellow fitting your description changed up twenty pound the other day.'

'Maybe I should go to the bank right now and have it out with your friend,' Pyke said, still sizing her up.

'And what would ye want to go and do a thing like that for? Getting poor hard-working folk into trouble,' she said, finally putting the watch back on the dresser. 'Now, back to what I was sayin'. Your money's not in the room which means you're carrying it around with ye.' She smiled, disarmingly. 'Am I right?'

'If you were, would I tell you?'

'Walkin' the streets with a whole pile of money? Tell me one gentl'man who'd be stupid enough to do that.' She laughed at her own joke. 'Then again, tell me one gentl'man who'd willingly stay in a dump like this.' Then she was offering him her hand. 'Name's Megan, nice to make your acquaintance.'

Pyke took it, surprised at the firmness of her shake, and said, 'Francis Hawkes.'

'So what brings ye to our fair town, Mr Hawkes? And don't be tellin' me you're here to see the marchin'.'

'I take it you don't approve,' he said, pointing at the red ribbon she wore on her cuff.

'Ye mean this?' She motioned at the ribbon and laughed.

'What's so amusing?'

'You heard of this fella Pastorini?' Pyke shook his head. Megan went on, 'Ribbonmen reckoned your man's prophesies said the Protestant faith would be destroyed under orders of the Lord Almighty on the twenty-first of November 1825.'

'What happened?'

'It rained.'

Pyke smiled. 'Is that why you wear the ribbon?'

Megan shrugged. 'Maybe I'm hopin' he just messed up the date.'

'Meanwhile it's still raining,' he said, brushing water from his coat.

'So you're *not* here for the marchin',' she said, cocking her head flirtatiously to one side.

Instinctively he decided to jettison part of his cover. 'To everyone else, I'm the eldest son of Robert Hawkes, owner of the Hawkes cotton mill in Lancashire.'

She seemed amused by this. 'And to me?'

'I'm just someone looking for a way to meet John Arnold.'

'Why didn't ye say that sooner?' she said, shaking her head mischievously.

This time, Pyke scrutinised her face carefully for signs of lying. 'You know him?'

'Of him.' She shrugged, as though it wasn't important. 'I worked for a while in the big house in Ballynafeigh, the family's grand new residence. I never cared for the place myself, ugly-looking building, pretendin' to be something it ain't. All its pretensions, mind, it didn't have running water, so it were my job to fetch and carry water from a well. It's how I came to get these manly-looking arms.' She flexed her muscles, only half joking, for him to see.

'Tell me about Arnold,' Pyke said, becoming impatient.

'What's to tell?'

'Well, for a start, what do you know about him?'

Megan held his gaze for a while. 'Well, there are these meetings in front of the Custom House. Every Sunday, after church, folk head there, like they're the best thing to happen in the whole week. Not the likes of me, you'll understand, but other folk. Protestant folk. Gather there dressed in their Sunday best and watch with gleaming eyes as men less respectable than Cooke scalp and burn effigies of the Pope. Arnold, in particular, likes to put on a performance.'

'A rabble-rouser *and* a businessman.' Pyke waited for a moment. 'As the latter, he seems canny enough.'

Megan looked away. 'Aye, he's a canny one, that's for sure.'

'Not to be underestimated?'

'What's your real business with him, Mr Hawkes?' This time her expression seemed graver.

'He's invited me to a card game tomorrow night.'

Megan nodded, as though she was aware of such an event. 'Aye, at the Royal.' She looked him up and down. 'Ye turn up lookin' like that, they'll eat you alive.'

Pyke assimilated this new information without giving anything away.

'Arnold is a fella who started out life with next to nothing. He likes to surround himself with tough labourin' types, to remind everyone else where he's come from, he's no pushover. He likes to hurt folk, too, or likes to watch as other folk do the hurtin'. There are those in the Royal who might take against a well-dressed Englishman.' Megan shrugged. 'Unless he's a friend a' ye, I'd say that Arnold is maybe countin' on that fact.'

Pyke took out his wallet and removed a five-pound note. 'You want to earn some money?'

'Thought you'd never ask,' she said, grinning.

'From what you've just told me, I'll need a pistol.' He already had a knife but it might not be sufficient.

'A pistol.' Her expression became serious. 'What ye plannin' to do?'

'It's for my own protection.'

'But ye know how to use one, I'd wager.' She came a little closer, and looked up at him, playfully holding his stare.

'I'd know which way to point it.'

She cocked her head to one side. 'How would the son of a mill owner know that?'

'Shooting workers who step out of line.'

That drew a giggle. 'An' what would ye do with me, if I were to step out of line?' She was now close enough so that he could smell the tobacco on her clothes.

He started to sigh. 'I just need a gun, Megan.'

'So?' She made no attempt to move away. 'What about what I might need?'

FIFTEEN

Outside smelled of rotting carcasses from the nearby tannery. Inside smelt of stale tobacco and turf. Pyke did not necessarily think the latter smell was any better than the former, but he was glad to get in from the driving rain.

As soon as he stepped into the taproom, Pyke became aware of the rancorous stares of those men – for they were, as he later realised, all men – who sat on wooden benches attached to the wall, clutching pots of black stout. To a man, they stopped whatever they had been doing and looked at him, silently assessing the threat that he posed. In the middle of the room, a man who had been playing the fiddle turned his instrument around and pointed it at Pyke's head, as though it were a rifle. His teeth were bloody at their roots. Pyke reached into his coat pocket and ran the tip of his index finger across the sharp point of his knife. On the far wall, the wooden handles of an axe and a machete had been decoratively arranged to form a make-shift cross. Next to it was a lurid painting of King Billy riding a white horse.

The absence of women, and the resultant lack of sexual tension, made the violence even more palpable.

When he asked about the card game, there was no response. He repeated the question. Finally someone said, 'Who wants 'a know?' Before he could answer, another voice had said, 'Where ye from, mister?' Pyke told him

Manchester. The same voice said, 'That's England, right?' A ripple of noise spread throughout the room.

Standing in the doorway, Pyke was approached by a young man who looked as if his face had been mauled by a savage dog. He swayed slightly from side to side, as though drunk. Up close, his face was a thatch of coarse skin and scar tissue. Without much conviction, he took a lazy swing at Pyke's chin and missed it by a good six inches, by which time Pyke had spun him around, twisted his arm, and was pressing the sharpened blade of his knife into the man's neck. Calmly, he repeated his question about the card game and added that he had been invited by John Arnold. At once, an older man said, 'You mighta said that earlier, steada stannin' there with a face on ye.'

In the far doorway, Arnold appeared and carefully surveyed the scene. Pyke released the young man from his grip. For some reason, Arnold seemed disappointed. 'I see you've met the welcoming party,' he said, without any warmth.

Pyke pocketed his knife. Arnold met him in the centre of the room and held out his hand. Pyke made to shake it but Arnold withdrew it slightly and said, 'The knife, if you don't mind.' Realising that he didn't have any option, Pyke gave up the knife. Arnold smiled. 'You come well armed for a businessman.' Without hesitating, he whipped his arm down and sent the knife cartwheeling through the air until it lodged in the frame of the door, narrowly missing the head of a nonplussed drinker. The sound reverberated around the otherwise silent room. Arnold motioned for someone to search Pyke for further weapons, 'just as a precaution'. Pyke acquiesced, if only because he had already lost his knife and Megan had not returned to the inn with the pistol he had requested. Stripped of his knife, he felt even more vulnerable. Arnold, though, seemed oblivious to his unease. Already out of the room, he said, 'You'll have to excuse our manners. I'm afraid we started without you.'

The card game was taking place in the cellar beneath the taproom. It was a stuffy, low-ceilinged room, and even though it was July, a turf fire smouldered in the grate. Above them, in the taproom itself, the fiddle-playing had started up and the resulting foot-stomping caused flecks of dust and plaster to rain down on the makeshift card table. On the floor was spread a generous layer of butcher's-shop sawdust. As he introduced the other two players, Archie Tait, a former pugilist who owned a small whisky distillery, and Bill Campbell, who taught moral philosophy at the Academical Institution, Arnold himself took no notice of the disturbance. Lining the walls around the cramped room were a motley assortment of hangers-on: shipyard builders and brick-field labourers in working clothes, with dirty fingernails, drinking Dublin stout from chipped pots, staring with silent envy at the small pile of money gathered on the table.

As he sat down on a wooden chair, Pyke glanced up at the shaking ceiling and said, 'Dancing without women.' No one reciprocated his smile.

'You'll excuse our unfamiliarity with your more sophisticated tastes,' Arnold said, pouring himself a fresh glass of whisky. 'We're hard-working folk, not necessarily inured to the effects of alcohol like the rest of Ireland. But you see, tomorrow is a holiday, a celebration to commemorate smashing the papists, and so we're giving our moral diligence a rest for the night.' With feigned sentiment, he held up his whisky glass. 'A toast to King Billy.' A murmur of approval rippled around the room, followed by a chink of ale pots. Pyke left his own glass on the table.

'Ye don't care to join us in a drink?' The ex-pugilist

stared at him fiercely. He was an ugly man made uglier by the visible scars of his former profession.

Pyke picked up his glass and poured its contents down his open throat. That seemed to satisfy the gathered crowd, if not the pugilist.

Campbell laughed nervously. He was unctuous but appeasing. 'So what do you think of our wee town, Mr Hawkes?'

Pyke told him that, so far, he'd found it cold, wet and dreary. Campbell smiled genially but Tait and Arnold met his flippancy with stony faces.

'It's a liberal Presbyterian town,' Campbell said, 'or at least it used to be, back when people read Paine and Franklin as avidly as they did Knox and Calvin. Of course, the Anglicans always held the purse-strings, still do' – he glanced nervously at Arnold – 'but for a while, at least, people were calling us the northern Athens, with their tongues only half in their cheek. These are darker times, though. The good Reverend Henry Cooke will soon have us dressing in sackcloth and reading nothing but the Good Book. Wouldn't that be a good thing for all of us, John?' His tone dripped with sarcasm.

Arnold shrugged and picked up the playing cards. 'As long as the mills continue to make a profit and the papists are kept on the rack, the Reverend Cooke can say or do what he likes.' He turned to Pyke and said, 'We were playing Primero. I'll presume ye have enough money to cover whatever debts you accrue.' He cracked his knuckles and began to deal the cards. 'As you might readily believe, things could turn ugly for folk who canna settle their debts.'

Pyke lost steadily over the course of the following hour but limited his losses to a few pounds by betting frugally and folding often. Quickly, the other players came to regard him as an irrelevance. Even Arnold seemed to relax his guard.

They talked in clipped sentences about people they knew in a way that was designed to exclude him. When it was his turn to deal, Pyke used the opportunity to slip himself an additional card, the six of clubs, which he dropped into his lap and, later, shunted up his sleeve. Even the onlookers had ceased to notice him.

Now slightly drunk, Arnold was rhapsodising about the prosperity his new mill would bring the town.

'I saw some of that prosperity on the streets surrounding the mill.'

'Did ye now?' Arnold eyed him cautiously.

'More cripples than you could shake a stick at.' He held the mill owner's stare.

Arnold smiled, not rising to the bait. 'I suppose your own labourers don't suffer from leg injuries or chest diseases, Mr Hawkes?'

This time Pyke returned the smile.

'Which part of Lancashire did you say you were from?' Campbell asked.

'Bury.' Pyke waited for a moment. 'The town that gave us our fine Home Secretary.' He fixed his gaze on Arnold.

'That would be a matter of personal opinion,' Arnold said, folding his arms.

'What? That Peel and myself share a common heritage?'

'That he's a fine man,' Arnold replied, through gritted teeth.

'Oh?' Pyke tried to sound appropriately bemused.

'He did a good enough job while he was here, I'll give him that.' Arnold filled up his whisky glass. 'Makes it harder to believe he could turn papist and live with himself.'

'You knew him when he was the Chief Secretary here?'

Arnold's eyes narrowed. 'Of him, aye.'

'Then you must have known a friend of mine who worked for him. Still does, I think.'

'And who might that be?'

'Fitzroy Tilling.'

But Arnold's stare gave nothing at all away. 'Aye, I know the man.'

'Well or not?'

'He's a friend a' yours, ye say?'

'We haven't spoken to one another in a while.'

'I never much warmed to the man myself.' Arnold took a sip of whisky and tossed a guinea into the pot. 'Any of you interested in playin' a game of cards?' he said, this time avoiding Pyke's stare.

Earlier in the day, Pyke had considered holding a knife to Arnold's throat and asking him about his relationship with Tilling. On reflection, though, he had ruled out such an idea. From experience, he knew that people didn't necessarily provide truthful answers when confronted with physical violence.

It had been his plan to see how Arnold reacted when Tilling's name was mentioned. Now, though, he felt confused and disappointed. At the very least, he had hoped that Arnold might be thrown off kilter, but the man had responded as though he barely knew him. Pyke took a moment to organise his thoughts. He knew that Tilling had once acted as Peel's eyes and ears in Ulster. He had been told by Mary Johnson, in London, that Davy Magennis had been drafted into the Royal Irish Constabulary because his father, Andrew, had asked Arnold to recommend him. Mary had insisted that, on the strength of this recommendation, someone had travelled to Armagh, in person, to offer Magennis a position in the new force. For some reason, perhaps because of Tilling's reaction to his mentioning Davy Magennis's name, Pyke had assumed that Tilling was the person who had travelled to Armagh. Now, though, he was not so sure. On the evidence of Arnold's tepid response, it didn't seem the two men were even on friendly terms.

Pyke wondered whether Tilling was as important to his investigation as he wanted to believe.

For the following two rounds, Pyke waited in vain for another six, to add to the one he had hidden up his sleeve. He betted moderately and lost unspectacularly. The game was a little under two hours old when Pyke dealt himself a hand that included the six of hearts and the six of diamonds. Together with the hidden card, it gave him a very strong hand. Seated to his left, Arnold opened the betting and pushed five guineas into the pot.

Meanwhile, Pyke had steered the conversation on to the subject of the marches.

'The rank and file will march tomorrow, in defiance of what the Grand Master has instructed them to do,' Campbell muttered, as though he did not approve.

Arnold shook his head vigorously. 'I'm giving my workers a holiday. Good luck to 'em if they decide to march. Fact is, I've told 'em that if they can walk, then they should bloody well march.' That drew an approving murmur from the gathering. Then Arnold added, mostly for Pyke's benefit, 'You'll see blood spilled tomorrow, that's for sure.'

Campbell winced. 'We're not a violent people, Mr Hawkes. But you must understand, we regard the Roman Catholic religion as little more than idolatry; they worship symbols, the crucifix, statues of the Virgin Mary, rosary beads, while we worship Christ himself. For us, it's about developing an interior relationship with God.'

'And if God happens to instruct you to beat a Catholic man nearly to death with your bare fists?'

Campbell appeared shocked by such a notion. Arnold smirked. 'That might happen in England . . .'

'But not here?'

'We're law-abiding people.'

Removing his wallet, Pyke took out a crisp ten-pound note and tossed it into the pot. 'Your five and another five.' Without missing a beat, he turned to Arnold. 'You're saying that kind of hate doesn't have a place here?'

'What? Around this table?' Arnold said, mocking. Laughter filled the small room.

Pyke's eyes narrowed. 'You know what I meant.'

'And things were fine here till Cromwell turned up and slaughtered folk in their thousands. Believe it or not, Mr Hawkes, we can sort out our problem without the *help* of the English.' He looked again at his hand. 'Another five, eh? Yes, I think I'll have some of that,' he said, throwing a pile of coins into the mounting pot.

'I'm out,' Tait said, folding his hand.

'A pugilist with no stomach for a fight,' Campbell chided. 'I'll see the both of you.'

Arnold wanted one fresh card, Campbell two. Pyke discarded a jack and a queen and dealt himself two new cards. Turning them over, he found himself staring at the six of spades and the ace of clubs. Together with the two sixes already in his hand and the six of clubs up his sleeve, it gave him an all but unbeatable hand.

He just needed to find a way of retrieving the hidden card and discarding the ace.

'I'm surprised you don't see Cromwell as something of a hero,' Pyke said, feeling for the card up his sleeve.

'How can an Englishman be a hero?' Arnold smirked. 'Anyway, the English have never understood what it's actually like, having to live with the papists.' He consulted his hand. 'Would anyone object if I were to raise the bet to fifty pound?'

The mood quickly intensified. The gathered crowd murmured excitedly. This was more money than any of them would earn in ten years. Briefly, Pyke wondered whether someone might lose their head and make a grab for the whole pot.

'Bet too rich for you, Bill?' Arnold said.

Campbell winced. 'Aye. Damn.' He folded his hand.

Arnold's stare returned to Pyke. 'Hawkes?'

'Fifty pounds, you say?' Pyke had another look at his hand. 'How about we raise the bet by a further hundred?'

'*Pounds*?' The word seemed to catch in Tait's throat. Campbell stared at him without emotion.

Arnold weighed up the offer. 'You've got the money to cover any losses, I presume?'

'You can presume.'

'On your person?'

Pyke raised his eyes to meet Arnold's gaze. 'You can check my wallet, if you don't believe me.' But he did not retrieve it from his jacket because he did not want Arnold to see how thin it was.

Arnold wiped his mouth with his sleeve. 'A hundred, you say? That's a powerful bet.' He allowed a smile to ripple across his lips.

Until now it had not entered Pyke's head that he might lose the hand. For Arnold to beat him, he would need to be holding four sevens. The odds of two such hands emerging from the same round were practically impossible. No, he decided, Arnold might be holding a strong hand, a flush perhaps, but nothing that would beat his four sixes. He glanced down at the pile of coins and banknotes on the table.

'Aye, I'll see your bet,' Arnold said, his hands trembling a little. 'Let's see what you're holdin'.'

Concealed by the table, Pyke let the ace slip out of his hand into his lap. He then placed the four cards face down on the table and turned them over one at a time. 'One six, two sixes, three sixes.' He waited for a moment before turning over the final card. 'Four sixes.' He permitted himself a smile and, as he did so, took a moment to slide the discarded ace up his sleeve.

'Good hand,' Campbell murmured, glancing nervously at Arnold.

'Aye,' Arnold said, staring drily at Pyke.

As casually as he could manage, he threw his hand down on the table, as though to concede defeat.

'Would ye away a' that.' It was only then he smiled. 'Four sevens.' He motioned at the cards. 'Check 'em if you don't believe me.' Now the grin had spread across his face. Addressing Pyke as though the others were not even in the room, he said, 'That's one hundred and fifty pound ye owe me.' An excited cheer erupted from the onlookers. 'Make no mistake, mister, I plan on collectin' the money, too.'

That Arnold might also have cheated was indicated by the man's general demeanour and the sheer mathematical improbability of two such strong hands appearing in the same round.

But since Pyke had not even considered the possibility he might lose, it was only once he *had* actually lost, and had been seen to lose, that the seriousness of his situation became apparent.

He had gambled unnecessarily, allowed his dislike of Arnold to cloud his judgement, and now, since he could not pay what he owed, his prospects were bleak. He estimated there were ten or twelve labouring men in the room, in addition to Arnold and the ex-pugilist, who would relish the opportunity to work him over with their bare fists. As a man with no acquaintances or allies, his life was marginally more valuable than that of the crippled dog that had followed him to the tavern. And any of those men would have killed that dog and given it less thought than whether to order an ale or a stout from the bar.

Briefly, Pyke considered his options, or lack of them. Without a weapon, he could not hope to fight his way out of the tavern. Nor could he simply bolt for the nearest exit. The only way out of the cellar was up the staircase and into the waiting arms, and brickbats, of the mob gathered in the taproom.

To compound his discomfort, it was now unbearably hot, because of the turf fire and the sheer number of bodies packed into the small room. Pyke's armpits were leaking sweat and his throat felt scratchy. Arnold wiped his brow with the sleeve of his jacket for the third time in as many minutes, before declaring that the time was right for Pyke to settle his debt.

Pyke took a breath, removed his jacket, making sure to retain his wallet, and asked whether it might be possible for him to visit the privy before he attended to the matter in hand. Initially Arnold baulked at such a suggestion but eventually relented, once it was agreed that the pugilist would accompany him as far as the privy door; this was as much of a plan as Pyke had formed.

The outdoor privy was much darker than Pyke had expected. In fact, it was so dark he had to place himself over the privy itself before he could relieve himself. The stench was vile. Outside, he heard Tait tap on the door and ask whether he was done, but he did not hear the movement *inside* the privy until it was too late; a shuffle of feet and then a click. Something hard and cold – the barrel of a pistol – was pressed into his head.

For a moment, he was stunned at the inappropriateness of it; that he should be killed in such a place, in such a pointless manner. It seemed almost comical. He braced himself for the shot.

'So how did ye do?'

Pyke heard Megan's voice but still could not see her in the darkness.

Outside, Tait rapped on the door. Pyke could hear other voices now, too.

'They tell me it's loaded but, to be sure, I didn't check,' Megan whispered.

'How did you know I . . .'

'I figured that sooner or later you'd need to visit the privy.'

Pyke was momentarily overwhelmed with gratitude. 'Why have you done this for me?' He tried to retrieve the pistol from Megan's hand but she was not about to give it up.

'What?' she said, sounding amused. 'Ye think I'd just give it to ye for nothing?'

'But I've already paid you for it.'

Tait banged on the door, harder this time. Thirty seconds and I'm breakin' the door down.'

'And now the price has suddenly gone up.'

'I don't have any more money.' He took out his wallet to show her.

Megan took what little he had left and said, 'Bet there's plenty more on the table you been usin' to play cards.'

'You want more, I'll get it for you,' he spat. 'But can I please have the pistol?'

'Here.' Megan handed it to him. 'But hear me, mister, I want whatever's on that table.'

One shot. That was all he had. One shot for ten or fifteen men in the cellar; another fifty or so upstairs in the taproom.

Pyke was alongside Arnold when he removed the pistol from his shirt and jabbed the end of the barrel into the man's left temple. For a moment, no one moved. No one even breathed. Pyke used the opportunity to position himself behind Arnold, to use him as a shield, all the while keeping the pistol aimed at his head. Arnold ordered the men in the cellar to remain calm. From behind him, Pyke explained what was going to happen; explained that if anyone tried to prevent him and Arnold from walking up the stairs and leaving via the rear door, or tried to warn people in the upstairs room, then he would pull the trigger and take his chances. As he spoke, and with one hand holding the pistol to Arnold's head, he gathered up the pile of coins and banknotes from the table with the other hand. The stares of those gathered in the room left Pyke in no doubt what they had planned for him.

Halfway up the staircase, Arnold said, 'Don't be thinkin' you'll walk away from this, Pyke.'

It was only once they were outside, moving quickly through the back yard and along a narrow passageway that ran between two rows of terraced houses, that Pyke realised what Arnold had said.

Ahead of them, at the end of the alley, Megan and the dog were waiting for him, but instead of joining them Pyke forced open a nearby back gate and pushed Arnold roughly through it and into the yard of a derelict house.

It was a cool, starless night. The ground under their feet was soggy and riddled with puddles. In the near distance, Pyke heard the angry shouts of men spilling out of the tavern. One said, 'Let's kill 'im.' Another said, 'No fuckin' mercy.'

Pyke prodded the pistol into Arnold's throat. 'How did you know my name?' In the darkness, he could see the whites of the man's eyes. '*Speak.*'

'After you escaped from prison, I received a letter from Tilling. The man warned me that you might try to contact me. I didn't think anything of it. Then when you mentioned Tilling's name, I suppose I knew. I should a' dealt with ye then but I wanted to have some fun. I figured – wrongly, it turns out – you weren't a threat.'

Pyke digested this news and wondered what it indicated. That Tilling wanted to conceal a trail of complicity that led back to him?

'You know the Magennis family of Loughgall? Yes or no?' Pyke jabbed the pistol into Arnold's Adam's apple.

'Andrew Magennis is the Grand Secretary for County Armagh.'

'A few years ago, he contacted you, asked if you could put in a good word for his son, Davy. You arranged for someone to visit Loughgall in person, to enlist Davy in the Royal Irish Constabulary.'

'If you say so.' Arnold's voice sounded as though it had been flattened with hammers.

'You went to see Tilling. Later, Tilling paid Davy Magennis a visit and recruited him into the new force.'

'You'd have to ask Tilling about that.'

At the far end of the alleyway, Pyke heard voices, a scuffle of footsteps. He had less time than he needed.

'There were three murders earlier this year in London. A man, a woman and a baby. I found the bodies. Magennis killed them. One of the victims was Magennis's brother. I saw the cut to his throat. It was so deep the man's head had practically been severed from his body. Magennis throttled the baby with his bare hands, *with his bare fucking hands*, and then dumped it into a metal piss-pot.' Pyke took a breath and tried to calm himself.

Arnold waited for a moment. 'You have a powerful way wi' words.' In the street, his brogue was stronger.

'Magennis is hiding somewhere in Ulster.'

'What's that got to do wi' me?'

'I think you know where he might be.' Pyke raised the pistol and aimed it at Arnold's forehead.

On the other side of the gate, two men hurried past. He heard one of them say, farther along the alley, 'Archie reckoned they must be around here somewhere.' Pyke pressed his finger to his lips. Seconds later, they had moved on.

'I've never met the man.'

'But you know where he might be hiding.'

'I know he's got family in the town. That's all.' Arnold seemed irritated enough to be telling the truth.

'Family? Where.'

'A house on Sandy Row.' Arnold let out a heavy sigh. 'You know, if you shoot me, they'll send the whole garrison after you.'

'Except they won't know where I've gone.' Pyke thought about it for a moment. 'And if I let you live, you'll send a warning to Andrew Magennis in Loughgall. Perhaps arrange for an ambush along the way.'

Pyke heard footsteps and saw the gate open. He felt something brush against his boot, heard a yap. The little dog brushed against his leg and wagged its tail.

'No one else knows who I am, do they?'

Arnold didn't speak but, for the first time, Pyke sensed his discomfort. He was a canny man and understood the precarious nature of his own situation: the garrison would be looking for a man called Hawkes, not Pyke.

'That was a mistake, telling me you knew who I was.'

Arnold seemed to shrink before him. His eyes darkened with fear.

That settled it: Pyke knew what he had to do.

Megan appeared, silhouetted against the frame of the gate. The dog was licking his boot. Pyke told her to wait for him at the far end of the alleyway. She said they had to move; that all the streets were crawling with armed vigilantes. Pyke heard a shout at the other end of the alleyway. He decided he could not wait any longer, so he raised the pistol and shot Arnold in the middle of his forehead. The blast was drowned by Megan's scream.

SIXTEEN

The first time it had happened, Pyke was not even certain whether he had killed the man or not. He had spotted him, a forger who had returned illegally from transportation, in a crowded pub in Clerkenwell and pursued him through labyrinthine back alleys and courtyards, across traffic-choked streets, through bustling warehouses and eventually up on to the roof of an abandoned lunatic asylum. Cornering the fugitive, Pyke had advanced slowly, hands in the air, to show that he was not carrying a weapon, and backed the terrified man towards the edge of the roof until he could go no farther. Afterwards, when it was finished and the man was dead, Pyke had not been able to tell, with any conviction, whether he had pushed the man or whether he had jumped, but in the end it did not seem to matter: the man was still dead. Later, he would become accomplished at constructing whatever moral justification his actions seemed to require, but in that moment, as he stared down from the roof of the building at that unmoving figure sprawled on the stone floor, Pyke had been struck both by the pointlessness of the man's death and by his own culpability in it.

Pyke had no time to explain his actions to Megan, who was looking at him, her hands covering her mouth. Taking her hand, he pulled her into the yard and, from there, into the derelict house. Others had heard the blast, of course, and were converging on where they thought it had come from. Safely inside the house, he took Megan in his hands and shook her, to stop her from wailing. 'I didn't plan to kill him, but in the end I didn't have a choice. I need you to understand. I also need your help. Do you live with your family?'

At his feet, the little dog was panting and wagging its runty tail. He reached down and patted the dog on its head.

'Megan?' He shook her shoulders harder this time.

'I got my own room,' she said, finally.

'Whereabouts.'

'The Pound.'

'Is it far?'

'Eh?' She seemed distant, still in shock.

'*Megan*. Is it far?'

He heard more voices, outside in the back alleyway. Pyke knew it was only a matter of time before they were discovered. They had to find a better place to hide. Through the broken windows at the front of the house, he looked out on to the main square. In the darkness, it made for a miserable view. There were four or five taverns, in addition to the Royal, which overlooked the square, and with the news of the shooting all of them had emptied and the square itself was now bustling with vigilantes.

'No, it's not far at all,' Megan said, in a quiet, almost childlike voice.

In the ebbing candlelight, Pyke sat down next to her and tried to say something that was appropriate to the situation.

Megan's room was located on the ground floor of a brick-built terraced house. It had a solitary window that looked out on to the street, and a pile of damp straw for a mattress.

'I was just a wee child when Mammy died.' She was still

223

shaking. 'To this day, I don't know what from. We all knew she was powerful sick but one morning, me da tol' us the fairies had come in the night and taken her away. Course, even then we knew the fairies were made up but it helped, in a way.'

Pyke touched her face, felt the wetness of her tears on her flesh. She flinched, though not enough to discourage him entirely.

'Wha' makes ye think ye can just kill a man and get away wi' it?' Her tone was flinty, even aggressive. 'Ye can't just shoot a man as powerful as Arnold and get away a' it.'

'Rich men bleed the same as poor men.' As soon as he said it, Pyke knew the remark was facile.

'Wha'? That's supposed to make everything all right?' She sounded angry. 'I got ye the pistol. As good as killed the man myself.'

'I'm sorry for involving you, Megan.' Pyke touched her gently on the cheek. 'You don't deserve this. I didn't plan on shooting him and I didn't take any pleasure from it. I did it because I had to. That makes me sound callous, I know. Perhaps I am. Perhaps I have to be.'

This time she turned to face him. 'Couldn't ye have shown him mercy?'

'And left him in a position to threaten or kill me later?'

Megan stared at him, uncomprehending.

'I'm a Bow Street Runner in London. Do you know what that is?'

Megan shrugged.

'Like one of the constables in green here.'

She looked at him. 'Ye think they'd shoot a man in cold blood?'

'Five or six years ago, I knew a man, not a wholly bad man, you understand, but troubled in his own way. He was a thief and would provide me with useful bits of information. He was a jealous man with a violent temper and he liked to drink. I would visit him in his lodgings, which he shared with his wife and three young boys. One night, I interrupted a terrible fight; or rather, he was inebriated and chasing after his wife and his three boys with a bottle in one hand and a leather belt in the other. He was accusing her of cuckolding him. The oldest boy couldn't have been more than three. It was a brutal scene. I broke things up and warned the man if he ever touched his wife or his boys again, I would find out and I'd track him down and kill him. I showed him mercy. Two months later, a Bow Street patrol was called to the lodgings. The woman had been beaten so badly that her face was no longer recognisable. I was told her eyeballs hung from their sockets. She was dead by the time the patrol arrived. The three young boys had been drowned in a metal tub.' Pyke stopped himself, not wanting to add to Megan's woe.

But in a hushed voice, she asked, 'What became of the man?'

Pyke turned away so she could not see his expression. 'It took me a year to find him but, when I eventually did, I wasn't as merciful.'

For a while, neither of them spoke. 'You know they'll come after ye with everything they got. Police, soldiers, everyone.'

Pyke nodded. 'I'm leaving tomorrow. I don't know whether I'll be back.'

'Oh, aye.' Something – anxiety, fear, pain – registered in her expression. 'Have ye got a woman a' home?' In her sadness, Pyke saw a reflection of his own unfulfilled desires. He thought of Lizzie's body, two stab wounds in her abdomen.

'I don't guess you'd allow anyone to get too close to ye.'

'I'm sorry I involved you in this.'

'Sure you are.' As she said it, some of her bitterness seemed to ebb away. 'Will you take me wi' ye, Mr . . . ?'

'My name's Pyke. There are people who'd pay a lot of money for this information.'

'Just Pyke?'

He nodded and for a while neither of them spoke. 'Well,' she said finally, 'will ye or not?' She stared at him, both angry and forlorn, as though she didn't require an answer.

Later, as Pyke wrapped his arms around Megan, he was vaguely aware he was using her in some undefined manner. But such was his own nocturnally magnified sense of melancholy that he couldn't help himself. As he pressed himself against her and kissed her ear lobe, he could not tell whether or not her murmurs were signs of grudging approval.

It was still raining the following morning. Billowing clouds clung to the peaks of the hills that ringed the town and dumped their rainwater on to an already saturated landscape. Still, the streets were choked with ordinary people going about their daily business and dead-eyed groups of males silently congregating on street corners carrying brickbats, knives and even swords. It was a Catholic district, Megan had told him, and some of the men there were fixing themselves up for a fight with the Orangemen who were planning their own twelfth of July celebrations. On one corner, men wearing red ribbons attached to their coats were gathering together piles of bolts and half-bricks. On another, someone was scribbling 'No Cooke' on the wall in chalk.

Barrack Street was thronging with uniformed soldiers and armed police dressed in dark green. It was also crowded with slow-moving traffic. The sound of horses and carts rattling over the uneven cobbles was drowned only by the excited chatter of a thousand conversations; shopkeepers told their customers in hushed tones about the shooting; road sweepers swapped embellished tales of murder with anyone who cared to listen. Everyone was nonplussed and excited by the news of Arnold's death. The question that most people seemed to be asking was: had the mill owner been killed by papists? If nothing else, the shooting promised to further spice up an occasion already made fraught by Catholic emancipation.

Disguised as a mill labourer, Pyke moved carefully but unhindered through the crowds. At his heel, the dog panted with excitement. Megan had left by the time he awoke. He found the clothes next to him. Briefly he wondered whether she would be angered by the money from the card game that he had left for her, and whether he had done so in order to appease his own guilt.

While he ate his breakfast, an undistinguished meat pie, he watched as an older man wrapped a leather grip around one end of a four-foot brickbat. Alongside him, soldiers, shopkeepers and ruffians mixed uneasily on the narrow pavements. The cobbled street was awash with manure. From hand-held barrows, vendors sold fruit and fresh fish.

At the end of Barrack Street, Pyke turned on to Durham Place and the neighbourhood deteriorated further. Pigs, sheep and goats roamed freely in and out of brick terraces, whose makeshift windows were constructed from hessian sacks. Underfoot, the track itself was flooded with human effluvia and water that had broken the banks of the nearby river. The whole area seemed to be ripe for a cholera epidemic. From gloomy doorways, men and women dressed in ragged clothes stared at him without smiling and talked to one another in hushed voices.

The previous night, Megan had told him Sandy Row was so called because, at one time, the tidal waters of the Lagan had met the fresh waters of the Blackstaff to form a small sandy cove where mill workers had once washed their clothes. In the cold light of day, however, it was hard to detect any such cove. The area surrounding the river was boggy: an unclaimed scrub of land between two warring communities. A few slovenly thatched cottages hovered in the shadows of the giant linen mill. Farther back along the road, a group of mill workers attacked an unarmed coal carrier. A soldier looked on without interest, making no effort to intervene, even when the coal carrier fell to the ground clutching his knife-wounded belly.

Ahead of him, on the other side of the bridge, he could see more terraced houses. A crowd had gathered outside one of the terraces and someone was addressing them from a first-floor window. Pyke could not hear what was being said, but many in the crowd were supporting orange banners, fringed with gold lace. He decided to hold back, to allow the mob to disperse or go about its business. Eventually, after much whooping and pistol-firing, the crowd began to shuffle off in the opposite direction. At his feet, even the small dog seemed chastened by the whiff of violence.

On the other side of the river, he stopped a woman and asked whether this was Sandy Row. 'Depends on who's askin',' she said, with ill-concealed suspicion. Pyke enquired whether she knew which one the Magennis house was, but she ignored the question and disappeared into her front room. Others were similarly obstructive. It was only when the dog befriended a young girl that his luck turned. While the girl patted the dog's head, and the dog wagged its little tail, she said, 'Second house on the right, before the road takes youse up to Grimshaw's mill.' Pyke thanked her and handed her a shilling coin.

The house the young girl had identified was typically

bleak. It was a small edifice with soiled walls. Its windows were sealed up with paper. The door was open and Pyke stepped into the hallway. 'Hello?' He dug into his pocket and felt the reassuring touch of the pistol. It took him a few moments to readjust to the darkness. In front of him, the staircase rose precariously to the upper floor; all the balustrades had been used for firewood. He entered the front room. There, a barefooted old woman tended to a young baby. In the back room, Pyke heard the clink of pots, and a voice shout, 'Who is it?' A younger woman, wearing a dirty cotton dress, joined them at the front door. She formed a protective barrier in front of the baby.

'I was looking for Davy.'

'An' who are ye?' the old woman said, staring at him through grizzled eyes. Her white hair was tied up in a bonnet. In her arms, the baby was crying.

'A friend,' he said, without conviction.

'Oh aye, sure ye are.'

Finding her voice, the young woman said, 'Aye, the big man's gone, mister.' She was a small woman with pale, freckled skin and curly red hair.

'*Ann*,' the older woman snapped.

'Wha'? We don't know where he's away to, Mam.'

'But he was here?'

'Aye,' the older woman said, still suspicious. 'Left about a week ago, so he did.'

'Why did he leave?'

The old woman studied him carefully. 'Ask a lot of questions, don't ye?'

'I think he might be in danger.'

The young woman shrugged. 'Big man just said something about the grim reaper comin' for him.' She looked across at her mother. 'Mind, he'd been in an odd way, the whole time he was stayin' here. Wouldn't sleep inside. Said he was happy with the yard out back. He didn't show much interest in food and no interest in going to work, even though da fixed him up with a job in the mill. See, my da and his are brothers. Didn't know what Davy did with his days until one of the lasses followed him to the church on Fisherwick Place.'

'A church? What was he doing in a church?' Pyke asked, certain now the women were telling the truth.

'Prayin',' the older woman said, staring at him. 'What else do ye do in a church?' When Pyke didn't answer, she continued, 'Davy done something wrong, then?'

'What makes you say that?'

'You're not here to shake him by the hand, are ye?'

'Davy say anything about his time in London?'

This time it was the older woman's turn to frown. 'The big man was in London?'

'He went there to find his brother, Stephen.'

Briefly the two women exchanged looks but neither of them said a word.

As he watched their reactions, he thought about the two brothers, Stephen and Davy, and the nature of their relationship. Was it possible that Davy could have killed his own brother? And how, if at all, did that profit Tilling, and therefore Peel?

Pyke felt he had overlooked something that might bring the whole affair into focus.

'We're just poor workin' folk, mister, but we're honest and God-fearing, so we are. The men are out there marchin' 'cos we're proud to be Protestant but none of us care much for violence, and that's the truth. It ain't our fault the papists want to drive us from our homes and run us off the island.'

Focusing his attention on the younger woman, Pyke asked, 'Was Stephen your cousin?'

Before her mother could intervene, the woman had nodded. She was shaking a little.

'You do know that Stephen was murdered? And that he had just had a baby himself? Look at your own baby. Could you imagine doing that? Throttling its tiny throat with your bare hands . . .'

The older woman stepped in between them, to shield her daughter from Pyke. 'I think you should be leavin'.'

'You know whereabouts Davy might have gone?'

The old woman crossed her arms and stared at him. 'Who shall I tell the menfolk was askin' after the big man?'

It was a clear night with a full moon and from his vantage point on the far side of the Ormeau bridge the town might have looked almost peaceful, silhouetted against the dark shadows of the hills, had it not been for the numerous fires, whose reflections shimmered brightly on the glassy surface of the river. He was too far removed from the town to hear the sound of clashing rioters but occasional gunpowder blasts and musket shots skimmed across the water and illuminated the night sky. Pyke was glad of the disturbances because they distracted soldiers and police from their search for him. That said, earlier in the day he had taken no satisfaction from what he had seen: a mob of young Catholic men carrying muskets and pitchforks, rampaging down a narrow residential street and sacking the houses, regardless of who was inside them, dragging mattresses out and setting light to them.

Behind him, in the opposite direction, he turned his attention back to the imposing, Tudor-style house in the far distance, with its faux-crenellated walls and grand spires, and then to the stables, which were much closer, a few hundred yards across well-maintained grounds.

Having locked the dog inside a disused building on the other side of the river, Pyke was now alone. He had been informed that the house, and especially the stables, which belonged to the marquess of Donegal, would furnish him with what he required.

Skirting around the lodge, which occupied a prominent place at the front of the stables, using the moonlight to guide him, Pyke negotiated his passage across a small courtyard and slipped into a much larger courtyard around which individual stables were arranged. He could, of course, have taken any of the horses at gunpoint but, more than anything else, he did not want to raise the alarm and be forced into a position where soldiers on horseback chased after him in direct pursuit. It was important the theft went unnoticed until at least the following morning.

The animal he finally selected did not appear to be too bothered by Pyke's presence in his stable. He was a large black horse with a long mane. Pyke approached the beast carefully, maintaining eye contact throughout, and went to pat its nose. He had done so countless times while he had served on the Bow Street horse patrol. The animal whinnied slightly but did not seem to mind his touch. Taking care not to make any sudden movements, Pyke set to work, fixing a saddle and reins, which he had discovered in a cupboard at the back of the room, on the seemingly pliant horse. He had almost completed this task when he heard what sounded like two men on the other side of the court-yard but apparently heading in his direction. There was no chance of making a break for it, which meant he would have to hide in the stables and wait for them to pass.

As he went to close the door, he felt something brush against his leg.

Instantly the horse was aroused. Pyke pulled on its reins, attempting to bring it under control, but the powerful beast broke free from his grip and reared upwards, baring its gums as it whinnied. Then he heard a timid yap and saw the dog, its deformed tail wagging with obvious delight. Letting go of the reins, Pyke fell on top of the dog and seized its small head with his arms and hands. Now sitting on the straw-covered ground, he clamped the dog's jaws closed with his hands and listened out for the two voices. The horse seemed placated and shook its head a few times, neighing without much animosity. In spite of its size, however, the small dog was a determined, muscular creature and squirmed almost uncontrollably in his vice-like grip. At one point, Pyke lost control of the dog's mouth and it issued forth a terrorised yap, though the sound was perhaps not loud enough to alert the two stable hands, who had come to a stop in the middle of the courtyard. Still, Pyke could no longer risk being exposed and made his decision. Holding the dog's snarling jaws tightly shut with one hand, he took the animal's neck with the other, clamping its body with his shoulders, and squeezed it as hard as he could. The little dog fought him in unadulterated terror for what seemed like minutes, squirming in his arms, but Pyke's hold on its neck did not relent and finally, with a sickening gurgle that seemed to emanate from the pit of the poor dog's stomach, its taut frame went limp and the struggle was over.

It was only then that the voices from outside began to recede into the distance. A little shocked, Pyke laid the dead animal on the ground and covered it in straw. It had defecated on him: a hopeless final act before dying.

Later, once Pyke had led the now amenable black horse from the stables and mounted it, using moonlight to guide his boots into the stirrups, he took a few moments to arrange himself in the saddle, and then kicked the heels of his boots into the horse's midriff and steadied himself as the beast surged forward, carrying him into the darkness of the marquess's estate.

He'd liked that little dog, Pyke thought without joy, as he took up the reins and steered the horse away from the main house.

SEVENTEEN

Though the sun had been up for almost three hours, the air was still cool – it smelt of burning wood and freshly cut hay – and the dew-covered ground shimmered like a dazzling carpet of precious cut stones. It was attractive country, Pyke thought, as he looked down on the tiny hamlet from his vantage point on ground that rose gently up from the Blackwater river. In one direction, four miles away through estate land and orchards and beyond sporadic dwellings linked by hedge-lined tracks, was the village of Loughgall. In the other direction, the hills fell away gradually towards an expansive lough. The small valley below him was dotted with beech, ash and sycamore trees.

He had ridden for three hours the previous night, stopping to rest only when the terrain had become too marshy to negotiate in the fading moonlight. Sleeping fitfully on the floor of an abandoned cottage, Pyke had resumed his journey at first light and it had taken him a further two hours of hard riding to reach Loughgall, and from there, following directions given to him by a passing farmer, another hour to find the hamlet where the Magennis family lived.

The hamlet itself, straddling a junction between two tracks, consisted of seven mud-walled cottages roofed with straw thatches. From what he had been told by the farmer, the Magennis family occupied the farthest dwelling from the crossroads. In the centre of the hamlet was old Dan Winters' pub. The farmer had said this as though he would know exactly who 'old Dan Winters' was.

Tying the horse to a tree on the slopes above the hamlet, Pyke made his way down the hill, using cover from the oak and beech trees to keep himself hidden, until he was less than fifty yards from the Magennis cottage. From there, concealed behind a hawthorn bush, he spent the next hour watching the various comings and goings. Shortly after settling, he witnessed an adolescent dressed in labourers' clothes emerge from the cottage and disappear along the track heading east out of the hamlet. Later, he was followed by a slightly older girl. Pyke had watched with interest when a much older man, wearing a cotton shirt tucked into coarse trousers, appeared in the doorway, stretched, looked around him and then disappeared back inside the cottage.

In that time, Pyke did not see any indication of Davy Magennis's presence, but he knew this was no guarantee that 'the big man' was not there.

From what he had been told about the father, Pyke did not imagine that the man would easily give up information about his family, nor did Pyke think he could be tricked or fooled into doing so.

Pyke pushed open the door and stepped over the threshold. In the middle of the orderly room was a fire with stumps of cut wood and turf glowing in the metal grate and, above, a hole in the roof for a chimney. Next to the fire, an older woman attended to a saucepan filled with milk and wilted green leaves. Nearby was a solid wood table surrounded by tree stumps for seats. On the table, next to a pool of dried candle wax, there was an open prayer book. Bedclothes were tossed carelessly around the earthen floor.

'Can I help you?' a male voice said, from behind him. The woman looked up at him, startled. Pyke turned around to face who he presumed was Andrew Magennis and saw at once that the old man had noticed his pistol. 'Aye,' he said, slowly, his eyes not leaving Pyke's. 'Will you leave us alone for a moment, Martha?'

He was a wiry man of about sixty, but his apparently slight build and taut frame belied his age. Aside from his paintbrush moustache, which was flecked with grey, the rest of his hair was still dark. His piercing, almost translucent eyes gave no intimation of what he was thinking.

Once Martha had left them, he said, 'I don't take kindly to strangers bringin' weapons into my family's home.'

Pyke allowed the man's hostility to subside before he said, 'Is Davy here?'

Magennis did not seem surprised by Pyke's mention of his son's name. 'No.'

'Mind if I look around?'

'I mind, sure I do, but I don't reckon I can stop you.'

Pyke conducted a very brief search of the small cottage but found no one.

'Has he been here recently?' They were standing on opposite sides of the wooden table.

'No.'

'How well do you know John Arnold?' Pyke asked, trying to throw the older man off balance with his questions.

'What's he got to do with anything?'

Pyke realised that Magennis had probably not heard the news.

'Would you say that the two of you are friends?'

'Not friends,' Magennis said, frowning. 'Him, the Grand Masters, they like givin' orders but none of 'em know what it's like, actually havin' to live alongside the papists.'

'When was the last time you saw Davy?'

'Davy? A year back, maybe more.' Magennis shrugged.

'Where was that?'

That drew a determined sigh. 'Mind telling me why you're interested in Davy?'

'A year back, you say?' Pyke said, ignoring the question. 'This was just after he'd been thrown out of the police? For beating a Catholic man to within an inch of his life during a riot in Monaghan?'

Magennis did not seem to be impressed by his knowledge. 'What do you need from me? You have all the answers.'

'So let me tell you what else I know,' Pyke said. 'I know Davy wasn't prosecuted for that particular crime. I know he got that job in the first place because Arnold arranged it. I know that a man called Fitzroy Tilling came to this house in person, as a favour to Arnold, to sign Davy up. Do you want me to continue? I know your other son Stephen fell in love with a Catholic girl, ran away to London and had a child. I also know that Stephen, Clare and the baby were murdered in their lodging room in London. The baby was strangled and discarded in a piss-filled metal pail. I know Davy was seen in London around the same time. I don't know but I can only guess that Davy hated Stephen for running off with a Catholic and siring a half-Catholic child. All of you did, no doubt. Except Davy took your pronouncements of hate literally, didn't he? I can imagine Davy sitting here in this room listening to you telling stories of Catholic rapists and whores. I can make other deductions, too, but I'm sure you don't need me to tell you what those might be.'

This time Pyke kept his anger in check, guessing it would have no effect on the older man's attitude. Pyke wanted answers but he also needed proof of Davy Magennis's involvement. If Pyke could nail Magennis, he could implicate Tilling – and therefore Peel.

Magennis took a while to prepare his response. 'You

know a lot, but then again, you know nothing.' He pulled out a stump to sit down on, and motioned for Pyke to do the same. 'For example, do you know where you are right now?'

'A hamlet near Loughgall.'

Magennis nodded. 'You talk of our hate as though it's something other-worldly, monstrous even. But what about the hate that's been turned against us, for no other reason than we're proud, God-fearin' Orangemen? If you know so much, why don't you tell me about the time when, two hundred years back, Irish papists led by Phelim O'Neill marched into Market Hill, a few miles from here, and started gleefully killin' all the good Protestant men, women and children they could lay their hands on, ended up murderin' thirty thousand, three-quarters of all the Protestants in Ireland.'

His voice was trembling a little. Pyke decided to let him finish.

'Let me tell you the story of this wee place. We call it the Diamond. Twenty-four years back, I was a strapping lad, like you, just startin' off in the world, a new wife and child to protect. Thing was, we'd suffered terrible losses to the papist Defenders over the previous few months. One fellow on the Jackson estate, he'd had his tongue ripped out, his fingers cut off one by one. They'd sliced his wife's breasts clean off her chest. Mutilated his wee boy. Things were gettin' mighty tense, to be sure. Both sides started to gather themselves, the Defenders, looking to run us off our land, and our boys, Orange boys and the Peep o' Days, skirmishin' a little, just tryin' to hold the line. The Defenders massed yonder at Tartarghan an' we gathered up on that whinny hill on the other side of the river. One of their lot was killed and when the magistrates heard of it, they joined together with three Catholic priests, to try an' make

239

the peace. Some agreement was reached but the papists were itchin' for a scrap and they started to move into the fort up on yonder hill. Later, they ran down the hill and attacked Dan Winters' pub, tried to set it alight. But we were ready for 'em, we were stronger than 'em, too. We fought 'em hand to hand, and killed maybe thirty of 'em before they finally saw sense, and retreated to lick their wounds.'

At some point during the telling of the tale, it was transformed from a story of hate and recriminations to one of unfettered masculine glory.

Pyke allowed his stare to drift over the man's shoulder. 'And thirty-year-old tales of bravado and killing are somehow more important than your own flesh and blood?'

' "You are a chosen race, a royal priesthood, a holy nation, a people He claims for His own to proclaim the glorious works of One who has called you from darkness into light." First book of Peter, chapter two, verse nine.'

'Do those sentiments help you to deal with the death of your son?'

Magennis stared at him through narrowing eyes. 'Stephen was lost to us long before he died.'

Pyke slammed his fist down on the table so hard the prayer book jumped. 'He didn't *die*, he was *murdered*. Killed. Stabbed. Don't you understand? Your grandchild, too.'

Just for a moment, the words seem to dry up in the old man's throat.

'Did Davy kill his own brother?'

'No,' Magennis said, with little conviction.

'Did he kill the baby?'

'He's impressionable but he's not a monster, the big lad,' Magennis said, less sure, trembling more acutely.

Pyke had to resist reaching out and grabbing hold of him. 'Can you imagine what it must have been like? How delicate a newborn is?' He waited until Magennis looked up at him before adding, '*Your* flesh and blood.'

'What is it you want from me?'

'I want to speak to Davy.'

'And who, exactly, are you?'

Pyke ignored the question. 'Whereabouts did Davy go, after he'd been dismissed from the constabulary?'

The old man stared at him with steely eyes. 'I don't know.'

'Did he stay in Ireland?'

Magennis just shrugged.

Pyke thought about Davy Magennis, hiding out in the yard of a Sandy Row terraced house. Alone and afraid.

'I think he might need your help.'

The old man's eyes narrowed. 'Need my help? How would you know that?'

'Is there a particular church that he liked to frequent?'

'A church, you say? Davy never was one for prayin'.'

'Your family in Belfast tell a different story. Reckon Davy spent most of his time in a church praying.'

'You been to Sandy Row?' The old man sounded alarmed.

'Davy was stopping there until very recently. He left in a hurry, I was told. I think he might be in trouble.' Pyke felt himself sigh. 'All I want to do is ask Davy a few questions.'

'That right?' The old man stared at him with suspicion. 'I suppose that's why you've got the pistol.'

'Look, I'm not the one who got Davy into the mess he's in.'

Pyke could feel the old man's animosity but there was something else in his stare, too. Fear, perhaps. Sadness?

'You were askin' about a church,' the old man said, after about half a minute's silence.

Pyke nodded.

'I don't know about any church in particular but you could have a look for him in the vicinity of Market Hill.'

'Does he have family or friends there?'

Andrew Magennis crossed his arms and said nothing.

'Is that where he went after he was thrown out of the constabulary?'

Magennis stared at him without emotion.

'Why might Davy have gone there?'

The old man's expression remained resolute, intent on concealing whatever feelings Pyke's questions had provoked.

But Pyke did not find Davy Magennis in any of the churches or meeting rooms in Market Hill. Nor did anyone in the town admit to knowing him. When he asked about churches in the outlying area, he was told of one about two miles north of the town, on the road to Hamilton's Bawn.

It had turned into a warm, sunny day. A cooling breeze blew gently off the lough and a few clouds drifted harmlessly across an otherwise unbroken vista of blue. The air felt light, even balmy, as Pyke led his black horse up to the perimeter of the old church. It was the kind of day that should have made him feel lucky to be alive, but Pyke was bothered by something he could not quite fathom.

As soon as he stepped into the draughty old church, which was pleasantly cool out of the sun, he saw a young man kneeling down at the altar at the front of the building. It was a dour place, with clear rather than stained-glass windows and an unusually low ceiling.

Pyke did not make any attempt to conceal his presence. He walked down the aisle and came to a halt only a few yards away from the place where the priest was kneeling. The man looked up at him, startled.

He stood up, rearranged his cloak and dog collar, and smiled. 'Simon Hunter.' He held out his hand. 'Pleased to make your acquaintance, sir.' He spoke in a crisp English accent.

'Pyke.' He shook the priest's hand, not seeing any reason to conceal his identity.

The priest continued to smile. 'Well, Mr Pyke, what brings you to Mullabrack?'

'I'm looking for a big man called Davy Magennis.'

The priest's good humour vanished. Lines of concern appeared on his brow. 'Davy, you say?'

'Big man. At least six and a half feet tall.'

The priest continued to look at him, unsure what to say.

'You know him?'

Very slowly, the priest nodded his head.

'Do you know where I can find him?'

Again, the young priest nodded.

'Well, can I speak to him?'

'I'm afraid that would be impossible.'

Pyke looked deep into the man's concerned face and imagined the sheltered, comfortable upbringing that had produced it. 'You might not believe it, but I think he might need my help.'

'A few days ago, I would have agreed with you.'

The priest ran his fingers through his wavy hair. He seemed upset, as though Pyke's request had put him in a difficult position. Neither of them spoke for a while. Finally the priest told Pyke to follow him. Outside, the yard was dotted with graves. It was cool in the shade provided by giant oak trees. They came to a halt next to what appeared to be a recently filled grave. Pyke understood what the priest had been trying to tell him. He felt angry and cheated but managed to ask what had happened.

'Davy showed up here about a week ago. He wouldn't

tell me his surname.' The priest wiped sweat from his brow. 'He didn't make a great deal of sense. I could see he was deeply troubled by something. I let him stay in the church. I wouldn't usually make such an allowance but he was insistent. He assured me he didn't feel safe anywhere else.' The priest looked away, faltering. He tried to gather himself. 'The following morning, I came to see if he was still here, and ask if he wanted any food or drink, and, well, I found him . . .' Pyke could see tears building up behind the young man's eyes. 'I found him lying on the floor at the front of the church surrounded by his own blood. There was a knife on the floor next to his hand. He had cut his own throat, or so they reckoned. Two officers from the constabulary and the magistrate were here by midday. They asked me who he was. I told them what I told you, that I only knew him by the name Davy. None of them recognised him. In the end, they decided it was most likely a suicide and since there wasn't any way of identifying him, the magistrate said it was probably best that we give him a Christian burial, even if what he had done was a mortal sin in the eyes of God.'

Later, in the front room of a village tavern, the priest took a sip of ale and said, 'Back in the church, you told me you were a friend of Davy's?'

'In a manner of speaking.' Pyke had the feeling the man wanted to tell him something important.

'I'm afraid I wasn't entirely honest with the magistrate and the constables. I wasn't thinking straight at the time. I'm not certain I'm thinking straight even now.'

'Finding a dead body can be a terrible shock,' Pyke said.

'Yes, it was.' For a moment, the priest shuddered and looked down into his half-empty glass.

'Davy told you something, didn't he?'

Still unable to meet Pyke's stare, the young priest simply nodded his head.

'He told you what he had done. Confessed his sins?'

When the priest looked up, his eyes were clear. 'Yes.'

'But you can't tell me what he told you.' Pyke waited for a moment, before he added, 'Or can you?'

'I'm not a Catholic minister, if that's what you mean. I'm an Anglican. We're not bound by the confessional oath.' That drew a frown. 'But that's not to say I don't have a moral obligation to safeguard what has been told to me in the strictest confidence.'

'Of course. I understand.' Pyke tried to keep his tone as neutral as possible. 'But what if I already knew what Davy had done? What he confessed to you?'

'How would you know?'

'When I told you I was a friend of Davy's I was lying. I'm a Bow Street Runner. Does that mean anything to you?'

The young priest stared down at his trembling hands. 'That's like a London policeman, isn't it?'

Pyke nodded. 'I was the one who found the bodies.'

'Oh God.' The priest's face whitened. For a moment, it looked as if he might pass out.

'I understand that, first and foremost, you serve God,' Pyke said, as gently as he could, 'but you also have an obligation to see justice served in this world.'

'I suppose.'

'How about I tell you what I already know or think I know and, if I make a mistake, then you can perhaps point me in the right direction?' Pyke smiled easily. 'Does that sound acceptable to you or not?'

The priest nodded and took a long draught of ale.

'I want to talk about the man who Davy went to work for, after he'd been dismissed from the police.' As he pointed his pistol at Andrew Magennis's eye, Pyke cocked the trigger, as though about to fire. He had found the old man sitting alone at the table, staring into space.

'What do you want to know?' This time the old man's expression seemed placid.

'His name, for a start.'

'I can't remember. I'm not sure I even found that out.'

Pyke brought the pistol closer to the old man's eye. 'The priest either didn't know or wouldn't give me his name.'

'What priest?'

'The one Davy confessed to,' Pyke said. 'He told me Davy's former employer owns a few acres of land on the Armagh road just outside Market Hill.'

'That sounds about right.'

'I went looking for the house today. I think I found it. It's been boarded up. No one's living there.'

'Wha's that got to do wi' me?'

'I asked in the town. No one wanted to talk to me about him.'

'Folk in this part of the world don't much care for loose talk with strangers.'

'I'm not a stranger to you.'

Andrew Magennis shrugged.

Pyke nodded. He had expected to be stonewalled. 'Davy's dead. He cut his own throat. They buried him in an unmarked grave outside a church in Mullabrack.'

This was sufficient to break the old man's resolve. 'The big lad's dead?' His lip quivered. 'My Davy?' Tears welled up behind his glassy stare.

'The man who Davy went to work for . . .'

A solitary tear rolled down the old man's face.

'Let me assure you of one thing,' Pyke continued. 'He was no friend to Davy.'

Beaten now, the old man just nodded. His eyes were dark with exhaustion, his hair matted with sweat.

'You met him, didn't you?'

'Once, about two years back,' Magennis said, slowly. 'I paid Davy a visit, when he was still workin' there.'

Pyke took his time. 'I just need you to answer one question for me.'

'Then you'll leave us to grieve?' The old man stared at him through bloodshot eyes.

'Did this man have a brown mole on his chin?'

Magennis seemed momentarily nonplussed.

'Did he have a large brown mole on his chin?'

'Jimmy Swift,' Magennis said, nodding his head. 'How did ye know?'

Pyke closed his eyes. It was as though an anvil had fallen on his skull from a great height. He felt sickened. *How did he know?* God, the real question was: how could he have been so blind?

PART III

*

London, England

SEPTEMBER 1829

EIGHTEEN

It started when a curmudgeonly black bear, with fur shaved from its head to make it appear more human, broke free from its shackles outside the Old Cock tavern in Holborn. Perhaps wanting retribution for years of humiliation and ill-treatment, the bear lumbered up the creaking staircase at the back of the building and forced its way into the crowded upper room where red-faced market vendors were screaming their support for a seven-foot man wearing full military uniform to resemble the duke of Wellington. The outfit would have been too small on a man half his size. The giant had placed a dwarf, dressed as Napoleon, in a headlock, and was squeezing his neck with such intensity that the little man's eyeballs seemed as though they might pop out of their sockets.

Pyke could not hear the dwarf's chokes over the de-lighted cheers of the crowd, at least eight deep around every side of the gas-lit ring. That was until the bewildered bear paused briefly in the doorway to the upper room and surveyed the surroundings. It would have been a familiar sight: the tavern owner, Ned Villums, put the beast to work twice a week in that same ring, performing a version of *Little Red Riding Hood*, taking the part of the wolf. The crowd did not pay half a shilling each to watch the bear growl his few lines, though. They came for the ratting, bare-knuckle fights or a bout of wrestling. The bear sniffed the fetid air, saturated with the combined stench of cheap gin and unwashed clothes. The crowd gathered on the bear's side of the room visibly parted and shrank into the room's darker recesses, affording the bear a clear view of the ring.

Without giving it a second thought, the bear shuffled on all fours, ignoring the silent and evidently petrified crowd, and hauled itself over the ring's waist-high wooden wall, with more aplomb than might have been expected from a beast that weighed fifty stone. By that time, the giant's grip around the dwarf's neck had slackened enough for some of the dwarf's colour to return to his cheeks. For a few seconds, the bear and the giant wrestler stood rooted to their positions, no more than ten feet apart, each silently contemplating the other. Later, Pyke was not sure how it had started: whether the bear had attacked without provocation, or someone from the audience had thrown an object at the animal, but the result was the same. Ignoring the dwarf, who was slumped on the ground gulping for air, the bear launched itself at the stricken giant, who, in an instant, was transformed into a taller version of the dwarf he had just been strangling.

Almost at once, someone from the crowd cheered, either mistaking what was happening for part of the fight or simply enjoying the sight of the helpless giant being mauled by the powerful bear. These cheers produced a counter-response, this time in support of the giant, either out of patriotic duty, because the giant was dressed as the duke of Wellington, or because they had money staked on the outcome of the fight. Soon, there was bedlam. Villums himself was trapped by the baying mob on the far side of the room and was screaming at Pyke to take action — more to protect his tavern's already dubious reputation than to save the giant. The bear was tearing flesh from the giant's flayed torso when Pyke returned from Villums's garret carrying a flintock blunderbuss with a long brass cannon barrel loaded with powder and ball shot.

From a distance of fifteen yards, Pyke rested the butt of the blunderbuss against his shoulder and took aim at the bear, but before he could pull the trigger someone knocked him from behind and the projectile exploded out of the barrel of the blunderbuss; instead of hitting the bear as planned, it struck the recovering dwarf squarely in the belly, lifting him clean off his feet and almost cutting him in two. People tried to flee the room, but Pyke took his time and reloaded the weapon. The first shot hit the bear in the chest; the second shot blew off the entire right side of its head. Bone, cartilage, tissue, blood, chunks of fur and even an eyeball splattered those who had not managed to leave the room. The bear seemed not to have been affected by the double blast at first, aside from the obvious loss of body parts. On all fours, it surveyed the carnage: the mauled giant, the dwarf's twitching corpse and the vast carpet of blood and intestines that covered the floor of the ring. It tried to open its mouth but, as it did so, its will to live finally leaked from its gargantuan frame, and it collapsed on to the floor with a thud. The remaining audience, such as it was, turned and watched the gruesome spectacle. As soon as the bear had stopped moving, one of them broke into applause. Others joined in. No one seemed to know whether the applause was for the bear, the dwarf or the giant, but since the giant was the only one of them left alive, he presumed it must be for him and hauled himself to his feet to receive the accolades. A flap of skin the size of a large book hung down from his bleeding neck.

Once he had put the blunderbuss down, no one seemed to be interested in Pyke, just as no one appeared to have recognised him. But without his unkempt hair and bushy sideburns, this was to be expected.

'I dunno whether to thank you or strangle you,' Villums said later, while Pyke inspected his new outfit in the mirror. He had discarded his labourer's clothes and changed into formal attire. 'You don't think it was too much of a risk, coming back to your old haunts?'

In addition to running a sizeable gambling operation in the Old Cock tavern, Villums fenced stolen property. Pyke had employed his services in this latter capacity on more than a few occasions. He would not have described him as a friend but he trusted Villums as much as he did anyone, and he was paying handsomely for the garret that Villums provided for him.

'Perhaps, but then again, I don't have a choice.' Pyke shrugged. He knew as well as anyone that he was only one step, or mishap, away from being recognised and arrested. 'And I can blend in here just as well as anywhere.'

'Can I ask you a question, Pyke?'

They were in Villums's parlour, drinking gin from pewter tankards. Pyke was preparing to go out for the evening.

'In all the time I've known you, I've never seen you act like you're scared or express any kind of remorse or nothing.' Villums looked puzzled. 'Don't you feel bad for the dwarf?'

'I feel worse for the bear,' Pyke said, allowing his gaze to settle on Villums. 'Are you trying to tell me the dwarf would have been spared if the bear hadn't interrupted the fight?'

Villums shrugged. 'The magistrates will have to investigate, write a report. They'll want paying, too. Then there's the dwarf's family. They'll certainly want something.'

Pyke gulped back his gin. 'I'll need a loan, as well.'

'How much?' Villums stared at him, suspiciously.

'Twenty or thirty ought to cover it.' Pyke gazed at Villums, waiting.

'Pounds?' The older man had to loosen the collar around

his bulbous neck. 'You're dressed up like a toff, to go to the opera, and you want to borrow money off a poor man like me? Look at these rags.' He tugged at his tatty frock-coat.

'You know I'm good for the money.'

'Yeah, I know.' Villums sighed. 'But you'll have to make yourself scarce tonight. The place'll be crawling with police. Don't worry. No one'll say a word to 'em and I'll tell 'em I fired the blunderbuss.'

'Thank you,' Pyke said. 'I suppose there's no word about Godfrey?'

'Didn't you hear the news? He's out. They let him go about a week ago. Dropped the charges.' Villums scratched his vein-riddled nose and wiped his cheeks. 'Very coincidental, I know. You don't reckon someone knows you're back in London?'

The thought had already crossed Pyke's mind. 'If so, they'll be watching Godfrey's shop and apartment.'

'Since they were sworn in at Coram's Foundling Hospital, they're fuckin' everywhere, Peel's blue devils. Everywhere that's poor, anyway.'

'There's a reward, you know, for my capture. Quite a generous one, I believe.' Pyke watched Villums's reaction.

'A hundred pounds, I'm told. But as poor and desperate as people are, no one will dare collect the reward till they've seen you swing.'

'How reassuring,' Pyke said, without smiling. 'Maybe you could pass word to Godfrey that I'm staying here.'

'You sure that's a wise idea?'

Pyke shrugged and thought about what Villums had said about not feeling remorse. 'Do people think I'm a monster?'

'You really give a damn what people think?' Villums asked. 'Back there in the gaming room, you didn't stand to gain a thing by killing the bear. If you were as self-interested as men sometimes claim you are, then why didn't you sit back, do nothing and watch the bear maul the duke?'

From his seat in the fifth row of the stalls, Pyke looked through a pair of hired binoculars at the figures in the grandest box of the Theatre Royal. The bell had just sounded and a man appeared on stage announcing that the performance of Rossini's *Il Barbiere di Siviglia* would commence shortly. Along with the rest of the audience, he watched as Emily Blackwood glided elegantly into the box and arranged herself before carefully taking her seat. She wore a delicate pale-pink crêpe dress with thin gauze sleeves that showed just enough of her slender arms; her hair was elaborately tied up, drawing attention to the diamond necklace that was just visible, silhouetted against the milky whiteness of her skin.

It thrilled him to see that she was so obviously trading on her looks for the purposes of the evening – a charity event from which all the money collected during the interval would be donated to her society of women. On their first meeting, he had made the mistake of assuming that her reputation as a do-gooder and her exquisite skills as a pianist marked her as a particular type of woman. Now, as he watched her greet others in the box and noticed the effect she was having on them, especially the men, he felt a pang of jealousy and admiration for the way that she was using her beauty.

For three days since he had arrived back in the city, Pyke had followed Emily at a discreet distance, as she had gone about her business. He had been surprised by the scope and extent of her work; not merely time spent in her organisation's offices on the Strand but also visits to both prisons and asylums. In one such establishment, a crumbling former nunnery in the village of Stoke Newington, curiosity had compelled him to bear even closer witness to her actions. As far as he understood it, her work involved inspecting premises and living conditions and writing reports in order to lobby for change; he had not expected her to spend time with the Bedlamites, or to be so openly affectionate with them. As Pyke had watched Emily perch on the edge of an elderly woman's bed and stroke her bony visage, he had thought about her deceased mother and how much, if anything, Emily knew about her fall from sanity and Edmonton's role in orchestrating her removal to an asylum. Even from a distance, her warmth of character was impossible not to notice, but her good intentions carried a hidden cost. In an alley next to the asylum, she had produced a small flask from under her shawl and, unseen by everyone, except for Pyke, pressed it to her lips and drunk. Startled by the sudden arrival of her carriage, Emily had discarded the flask in a nearby bush. Later, Pyke retrieved it and discovered its content to be gin: something that surprised and pleased him. She was as flawed and vulnerable as everyone else.

Pyke surveyed the charities that were to benefit from the event and the list of people who would be attending the function on their behalf in the performance notes. Emily Blackwood was described as Lord Edmonton's daughter, reminding him of Emily's association with the aristocrat. He wondered how much she knew.

Ten minutes after the performance had started, Pyke vacated his seat in the stalls and ascended the theatre's main staircase from the lobby to the circle. He found a bored attendant and instructed him to deliver an urgent note to a lady seated in one of the boxes. He described Emily and handed him the note, together with a guinea coin.

He felt out of place in such a setting, as though it was as clear to everyone else as it was to him that he did not belong there. He had been more comfortable firing blunderbuss ball shot into a crowded tavern surrounded by some of the city's most violent criminals than he did in such esteemed surroundings.

It was fifteen minutes before he heard footsteps glide across the carpet over the muffled sounds of soprano and tenor voices reverberating throughout the theatre. As Emily walked towards him, her hips moved gracefully under her dress. When he stepped out of the shadows and approached her, she jumped slightly, as though she had not actually expected it to be him, and it took her a few moments to recover her composure. Pyke took her hand and led her to the female cloakroom.

Alone, in the dimness of the room, they contemplated each other without speaking. He felt his jaw tighten as he took in the whiteness of her neck, her sculpted cheekbones, her gloved hands and smoky eyes. Pyke was about to say something when she reached out and pressed her index finger lightly against his lips. He felt his throat tighten in anticipation but it was she, rather than he, who stepped forward into the space between them and raised her neck to meet his stare, their lips practically touching.

'All of your lovely hair . . .' She brushed her fingertips across his freshly shaven head.

Pyke shrugged. He had cut it with a razor even before he had left for Ireland. 'I had to see you.'

'We cannot talk here,' she whispered, her eyes never once leaving his.

'If not here, then where?' He did not want her to visit him in a place as sordid as the Old Cock tavern.

Her eyes filled. 'I thought you might be dead.'

Gently, he took her hand. She made no effort to resist his overture. 'I wondered if I would see you again.'

'Where are you staying?' Her fingers coiled around his thumb.

Pyke opened his palm and allowed her to trace a line down it with her little finger. He told her about his garret.

'My father owns a town house in Islington. On rare occasions, he permits me to use it, if I have to attend social occasions late in the evening.' She gave him the address. 'Will you meet me there after ten? There's a gate at the side. Come around to the back door and knock twice.'

The desire to kiss her was now so intense that Pyke could barely restrain himself, but Emily acted before he had the opportunity and withdrew; nor would her stare meet his. Later, as he thought about what had happened, he was struck by competing sentiments: on the one hand, the intimacy that they had generated had seemed, to him at least, utterly authentic; on the other hand, he could not help but feel that her attempts to keep him at arm's length were motivated by more than a respect for social convention.

Edmonton's Islington residence was a three-storey town house on Cloudsley Terrace, a row of new houses looking out over an attractive expanse of common land, ten minutes' walk from the junction of New Road and High Street in Islington. Although the house was beyond his own financial means, Pyke was disappointed by its size and scale. It was more than adequate for ambitious office clerks who worked in the City, but it seemed far too modest for a titled aristocrat. This impression was reinforced when he was escorted by Emily's servant to the drawing room on the first floor.

It was a well-appointed and tastefully decorated room, with a Turkey carpet covering most of the wooden floor, a high ceiling adorned by intricate cornice-work, a large bay window at the front of the room and a series of easy chairs and a cream sofa arranged around a grand piano. But as he settled down on the sofa and waited for Emily to appear, it struck him that, aside from the marble fireplace, there was nothing extravagant about its decor. On closer inspection, the sofa and chairs seemed threadbare, and apart from two small but intriguing drawings that hung on one of the walls, the overall impression was one of modesty and even thrift. Again he wondered about Godfrey's comments about the perilous state of Edmonton's finances.

Emily had changed into a pale-grey cotton dress with a high-cut empire waist. Alone in the room, there was a palpable awkwardness between them, as though neither of them knew how to greet the other or what to say.

Perhaps to strip away some of this politeness, Pyke told her as much of the truth about what had happened to him as he felt was necessary. He intimated, though only obliquely, that her father was involved in the blood-letting that had taken place, mostly because he did not want to deceive her about his own intentions towards the man. Perhaps he told her too much, because when he had finished her expression seemed to indicate a mixture of bemusement and fear.

Emily was not as brittle as he had first supposed, but he did not yet know whether she was as robust as she pretended to be. Nor, despite her apparently self-evident loathing of her father, did he know where her loyalties ultimately lay. Therefore telling her even a little of the truth had been a calculated risk.

Emily looked at him with an impenetrable expression. 'One night, shortly before you showed up at Hambledon, I overheard my father talking about an incident in which you had tricked him into paying for the return of goods that you'd stolen from him. He called you a scoundrel but sounded a little impressed too.' She looked away and shrugged. 'He's not a man who's easily impressed.'

Pyke weighed up this information.

'I knew my father had something planned for you but I didn't know what.' Her expression softened. 'I should have said something to you.'

'You have done more than enough to assist me and I will for ever be in your debt.' He hesitated for a moment, to collect his thoughts.

Blushing slightly, she said, 'But you still seem bothered by something.'

'I am not so much bothered as . . .'

'Yes?'

'Don't think for a moment I am not eternally grateful for what you did for me but I am struck that your actions carried very grave risks for you.'

'What? In terms of upsetting my father?' This time Emily laughed. 'As you may have noticed, ours is not a warm or even a close relationship.'

'But he is still your father.' He studied her reaction carefully. The light from the candle accentuated the shape of her cheekbones.

Emily took her time to respond. 'When we last talked outside Newgate, you intimated that you were cognisant of certain aspects of my mother's demise.' She shook her head. 'When she finally passed away, he did not even permit me to attend her funeral.' Pyke waited for her to continue but she seemed to want some kind of acknowledgement, so he just nodded. 'I hate him. I know that's a terrible thing to say but I can't help it . . .'

'I would imagine he's not an easy man to like.'

She nodded forlornly.

Pyke decided to push a little further. 'But you are perhaps beholden to him in other ways?'

'As are all children of wealthy parents.' Emily seemed amused by his boldness. 'It would not surprise me, given your prowess as an investigator, if you already knew something about my own situation.'

'I've heard rumours, that's all.'

'About?'

To the effect that your financial well-being is not *wholly* tied to your father's generosity. Or lack of.'

Emily had a way of staring at him that he found deeply unnerving. 'As a result of my mother's foresight, I have a very modest independent income.'

Pyke thought about the information he had received from Godfrey and Townsend. 'In which case, taking my side against your father reveals much about your courage.'

'It reveals much, but not about my courageousness.' Her tone was playful.

'Oh?'

'As you suggested to me on our visit to Newgate, altruism isn't always divorced from self-interest.'

'And coming to my rescue was an act of altruism?'

Emily licked her lips. 'I liked the fact that you weren't overawed by him. You mocked him without him realising it. Some people find him quite intimidating.'

Pyke bowed his head. 'Then I accept the compliment.'

For a moment, neither of them spoke. 'But there is still something you want to ask me, isn't there?' she added.

'You would make a good investigator.' His laugh ebbed away as he contemplated the subject of his question. 'There's a man who might be employed, in some capacity, by your father. I was led to believe that he worked as a security adviser for one of your uncle's banks. He was the man who led me to the corpses in St Giles. Subsequently I discovered he's Anglo-Irish and owns a small plot of land in County Armagh. Jimmy Swift. He's got sandy-coloured hair and a distinctive mole on his chin. Do you know him?'

Emily furrowed her brow. 'No, I don't think I've come

across such a person.' She shrugged, apologetically. 'You see, my father has business with so many people . . .'

'I understand.'

'Then perhaps I could ask you a question.'

'I can't very well say no, can I?'

'No, you can't,' she told him firmly. 'You come here and tell me these terrible things about my father, what he might have done, what he might be mixed up in, and I don't challenge or correct you, or stand up for his honour. Then you question me about this man who may or may not work for my father, as though I'm some kind of suspect, or that I'm deliberately concealing something from you.'

'I certainly didn't mean to imply—'

'Ssshhh, for a moment.' She pressed her finger to her lips. 'I'd say . . .' She paused. 'I'd say you're not an easy man to get to know.'

Pyke pondered her statement. 'I'm not sure anyone can truly know anyone else, if that's what you mean.'

This drew a forced laugh. 'Spoken like a man.' But Emily was not finished with him. 'In your world, I would imagine people have to *prove* themselves to you, in order to earn your trust.'

'If I told you I've never wholly trusted *anyone*, would you think me a kind of machine?'

'Perhaps not a machine but . . .' Concern was etched on her face. 'It must be a lonely existence.'

'It is an existence. Or at least I am still . . . *here*.'

'I think you're missing the point,' she chided him, gently. 'It is I who am asking for a little of your trust.' She seemed puzzled. 'I would hope I've already proved myself to some extent.'

Suddenly Pyke felt foolish and self-interested. 'You must think me unpardonably rude,' he told her, not sure what else to say.

'I wouldn't imagine a man of your *abilities* cares to be in someone else's debt.'

Pyke shrugged. 'It would depend upon whose debt I was in.'

'In which case, I should confess that my motivations for visiting your cell were not entirely selfless.' Emily was smiling now.

'Oh?'

'Of course, I had to be assured you were innocent of those terrible things the police and the court claimed you had done.'

He bowed his head, to acknowledge her confidence, but said nothing.

Emily laughed nervously. 'It's a terrible habit. I'm sorry. I must stop prying.'

Pyke wondered whether his discomfort at having to discuss personal matters was as obvious as Emily made it seem.

An awkward silence followed. 'Did you know that most people believe an unmarried woman in her early thirties has failed to reach her potential?' Emily seemed to be saying it as a challenge.

'What potential might that be?'

'To sire my future husband's children, I suppose.' It seemed to amuse her.

'And to provide your father with an heir.'

'You, too, are very perceptive.' The humour left her expression. 'My father has lined up a suitor and told me I'm to marry him before the year's out. He said it's high time, as you put it, that I provided him with an heir.'

'Have you met this man?' Pyke asked quickly.

'I am led to believe he has certain political ambitions but I have refused even to learn his name.' She seemed genuinely aggrieved. 'I think it's absurd that a woman in my position should even consider getting married, given the hopelessly inequitable laws of this country. You know that a married woman cannot own property, or retain control of her own earnings? She has the legal status of a minor and can't divorce her husband, even if he beats her and even though he can divorce her for no good reason.' She grew more serious. 'Most of the men I meet are either rich and stupid or poor and desperate and see me as their ticket to a life of wealth and glamour.'

Pyke pulled her into his stare. 'I am certainly not rich and I would hope I'm not stupid.'

'I would not characterise you as poor or desperate, either.'

'Where does that leave me, then?'

'I don't know.' She laughed gently. 'Somewhere in the middle.'

'Is that a good place to be?'

'I would say so.'

Pyke edged closer to her. 'Here might be an even better place to be.' He wanted to touch her cheekbones, run his finger down to her lips . . .

'Perhaps, but . . .' Emily stood up and turned to face him. 'But it is late and I am aware that in my keenness to solicit your company, I must have kept you from other engagements.'

'None as pressing as this one, I can assure you.' Pyke noticed she was blushing ever so slightly. 'But I am certain I have detained you far too long.'

'It is surely I who have detained you . . .'

'Then I have thoroughly enjoyed being detained.' He stood up and prepared to leave. 'Perhaps you might detain me again on some future occasion?'

This time her gaze was cool. 'You make me sound like a Newgate gaoler.'

He laughed heartily. 'You have seen such figures in person, as I have, and should be in little doubt that their poise, sophistication and elegance are something mere mortals such as ourselves cannot hope to aspire to.'

Emily flashed him a wicked stare. 'What? You don't think I'd like to lock you up and throw away the key?'

'In the condemned block at Newgate?'

Her eyes glistened in the candlelight. 'Actually, I was thinking of more comfortable surroundings.'

NINETEEN

'What a perfectly delightful place this is,' Godfrey said, pushing open the door to Pyke's garret in the Old Cock tavern. 'First, I had the good fortune to interrupt a young couple rutting in the alley outside and then, when I had to relieve myself, I discovered what appeared to be a pool of blood on the floor.' Godfrey had put on some weight in prison and waddled around the small bed to greet him.

Clasping Pyke's shoulders, he looked at him and said, 'It's wonderful to see you, dear boy. Veritably, I did not imagine I would get this opportunity. You look different. Leaner. And the hair, or the absence of hair . . .' He ran his hands across Pyke's head. 'Very becoming.'

'And it's good to see you, too.' Pyke meant it. He *was* glad to see his uncle. 'When did you get out?'

'Last week, dear boy. It was unexpected, I have to say. Geoffrey Quince, the lawyer whose services you so miserably failed to retain, claims to be quite baffled as to why they decided to drop the charges against me.' Godfrey ran his stubby hands through his mane of white hair and looked expectantly around the tiny room.

'Did Quince tell you I had need of his services?'

'You saw Quince?' Godfrey stared through his bushy eyebrows.

Pyke produced a sheaf of papers from the table next to

his bed. 'I had him draw up a contract. I've signed the gin palace over to you.'

'To *me*?' Godfrey's brow wrinkled with bewilderment. 'What on earth will I do with it?'

'Isn't that akin to asking a lion what he intends to do with a bloodied carcass?'

'I am no rapacious businessman.'

'But you are a rapacious drinker.'

'Ah, indeed.' Godfrey's expression lightened. 'But why sign it over to me?'

'Call it penance on my part. Or part-payment for time served.' Pyke handed him the papers.

'Very decent of you.' Godfrey nodded. 'It would seem churlish or ungrateful of me to mention another agreement we had . . .'

'It would.'

'Quite.' His expression became pensive. 'Of course, you would not have heard.'

'Heard what?'

'After your escape from Newgate, a lynch mob set upon your gin palace. The staff did what they could to defend it but there were too many of them. The place was stoned and set on fire.' Godfrey held up the contract and shrugged. 'I'm sure the lease is still worth a great deal . . .'

Pyke took his time digesting this news.

Downstairs in the gaming room, a ratting contest was taking place. All traces of human and bear matter had been removed from the pit and a sizeable crowd had amassed around the ring. Some carried stop-watches; others ale pots and slips of paper. The betting was furious. In the ring itself, a determined bull terrier had pulled a solitary sewer rat from a larger pile of rats and was biting into its wriggling body. Specks of blood peppered the dog's snarling mouth. Pyke and Godfrey passed through the room unnoticed and settled in the parlour on the ground floor. Unlike Pyke's gin palace, this was an older tavern without a counter. They were served at their table by a pot boy who brought their drinks from a bar room in the middle of the building.

Pyke poured a few drops of laudanum into his gin. Godfrey watched him carefully but said nothing. The room was empty, but Pyke wore his black cap low over his face, nonetheless. It was difficult, becoming accustomed to his status as prey. Each time he left his garret it felt as though a phalanx of police constables might be waiting around the next corner to ambush him. But he also knew that the real threat to his liberty came not from the police but from snitches who might hear of his return and happen upon him by chance.

'Don't worry, m'boy. After the last time, I made certain that I wasn't followed,' Godfrey said, glancing nervously at the door.

'You think that's why they released you?'

'Perhaps they heard you were back in the vicinity.' Godfrey shrugged. 'I know for a fact there's two of 'em watching the shop and two outside my apartment. I'd say it's a safe bet that someone in a position of authority would like to see you swing from the scaffold.'

Pyke wondered whether these men were police constables and whether they'd been dispatched by Peel.

'No one knows I'm here. Apart from Villums.' Pyke had also told Emily but did not mention her.

'And you trust him?'

'Not really. But I'm paying him well. Too well. And he hasn't seen a penny of it, as yet.'

'I won't ask what your plans are, but just be careful, will you?' A glint appeared in Godfrey's eyes. 'I don't want to have to rescue you from Newgate for a second time.'

Pyke was about to speak when he noticed someone he

recognised on the other side of the room. His first instinct was to bolt. Godfrey noticed his reaction and turned around, saying, 'What is it?' He sounded breathless and afraid. Standing on the threshold of the parlour room, wearing a simple brown dress and white bonnet, was Emily Blackwood. Despite her efforts to dress in a manner appropriate to her surroundings, she looked as out of place as a peacock in a pit full of snakes.

Her anxiety seemed to lift as soon as she saw them; she gathered up her dress and hurried across the room to greet Pyke. He introduced her to his uncle, who was delighted to make her acquaintance, and when the pot boy came to take her drinks order, she surprised both of them by asking for a pint of porter. This delighted Godfrey even more. For a while they talked about his imprisonment.

'I was in Coldbath Fields rather than Newgate, my dear, but generally I found everything to be most agreeable. The food, which was brought to me from a bakeshop, was quite acceptable, under the circumstances, and the pot boy kept me in plentiful supplies of ale and claret.'

Emily had sufficient good sense not to try to patronise Godfrey or act in a deliberately pious manner, but Pyke could tell she was bothered by some of the stories he was telling.

'Perhaps if you were poorer or without connections your stay might not have been as agreeable?'

'On the contrary, my dear. The common lags seemed to be having a whale of a time. On occasion, it was hard to tell the difference between the ward and a tavern.'

'I think the question Emily is seeking to ask is whether it is *appropriate* for convicts to behave in such a manner.'

Emily glared at him. 'I can speak perfectly well for myself, thank you.' Then her smile returned as she turned to Godfrey. 'Isn't it desirable that the prison is run well enough to ensure that prisoners' clothes are occasionally fumigated, that the genuinely sick have the chance to consult a doctor, and that the child thief is separated from the adult murderer?'

Godfrey clapped his hands together. 'Well said, my dear. Well said, indeed. What have you to say to that, eh?' He looked across at Pyke and grinned.

'I would simply point out that in the new Millbank prison, where everyone has their own cell, suicides have tripled, scurvy and dysentery are rife and that, very recently, prisoners rioted, and even hung the warder's pet cat, just so they could be transferred to one of the hulks.'

'A good point,' Godfrey said, scratching his chin in mock contemplation. 'My dear?'

'You could perhaps inform your nephew that all the evidence indicates individual cells arrest the moral infection of the young by the old.'

'Moral infection?' Godfrey said, frowning. 'Sounds like something that I might be responsible for spreading.'

'I've heard it can make you go blind,' Pyke said.

'Now you're both mocking me.' She looked at them, with a smile on her face.

'Not at all, my dear. I think the point you make is an excellent one.'

Pyke stared at her, waiting. It was true that he enjoyed their verbal sparring and that they both had sufficient intelligence to discuss highfalutin subjects, but he also wanted to fuck her with an urgency and intensity that even he found surprising. 'In the end, I think we do what we do because we want to. Whether that's robbing a blind man or helping him across the street.'

Emily thought about this for a moment. 'And what would you do? Rob the blind man or assist him?'

'You really need to ask?'

271

She regarded him across the table with an amused stare. 'It's funny, Pyke. For all your cynicism, you have a peculiarly romanticised vision of yourself.'

'I am a romantic now?'

'You see yourself as a dying breed. There's a certain romanticism in that.'

'Wonderful,' Godfrey said, raising his empty glass in mock celebration. 'She's as sharp as a tack.' He turned to Emily. 'Pyke is, indeed, a dying breed. I'm sure he hasn't told you of the time when he, single-handedly, pursued a rogue kidnapper who had snatched the young daughter of a landed aristocrat across open country for two days and two nights.'

'That was a long time ago.'

Emily seemed at once amused and intrigued. 'If such bravery and selflessness were ever made public, your reputation would be ruined.'

Pyke shrugged. 'I was well paid.'

Emily studied his reaction. 'What became of the daughter?'

'Oh, she was shaken up but came through the ordeal with flying colours.' Godfrey scratched his chin. 'If I'm not mistaken, I heard the other day she's due to marry a man who will one day inherit the earl of Norfolk's title and estate.'

'And the kidnapper?'

Godfrey's expression darkened. Briefly he shared a look with Pyke. Neither of them said a word.

Later, when Godfrey had disappeared to talk to an acquaintance in another room, Emily said, 'I'm sorry if I sounded too serious in front of your uncle. But you talk about my work as though it were both frivolous and pointless.' She seemed bewildered. 'Is it wrong I care about something other than myself?'

At the table next to them, three blackguards had taken note of Emily and were eyeing her, and whispering to one another, in a manner that made Pyke uncomfortable.

'On the contrary, it is admirable,' he said, keeping an eye on the men. 'But am I to assume that the opposite applies to me?'

'If it did,' Emily said, gently, 'then it would seem odd that you have occupied your time in the last six months in the manner you have done.'

He stared into her languid brown eyes and felt a flush of sexual anxiety spill through him.

One of the ruffians at a nearby table stood up and brushed against Emily; the other two sniggered into their ale pots. Emily did her best to ignore them.

'You seem concerned,' she said, reaching out to touch his hand. 'Is it my presence *here* that's upsetting you?'

'Why should it upset me?' He glanced across at the three men, who were making lewd gestures to one another and laughing.

'What? You can mix freely in my world, but I'm to be barred from entering yours?'

Pyke said nothing but again looked across at the three men.

'Do you think I am bothered by their uncouth behaviour?'

'And when they feel sufficiently confident from the ale to approach you directly, am I supposed to step aside and permit them to speak to you?'

This seemed to amuse her. 'You do not strike me as the kind of man who would easily step aside in any situation.'

'Perhaps not,' he said, unable to conceal his annoyance. 'But such action, in my current circumstances, would open both of us to very great risks.'

A shadow fell across her face. 'I did not think . . .'

She was interrupted when one of the men stood up, all of a sudden, and stumbled towards them, barging past Pyke as he did so. The other two also got to their feet in preparation for a fight. Their crossed arms and mean stares told Pyke what he needed to know. The man nearest to them, flabby-faced with whiskers, stammered something incoherently to Emily. She recoiled from him.

'Leave her alone.' Pyke was on his feet. He spoke in a calm, measured tone.

The whiskered man turned to square up to him. He had a scar that zigzagged down the right side of his face. 'Sit down if you don't want to be hurt. Let that be your final warning, boy.'

Feeling hopelessly exposed, Pyke pulled down the cap in an effort to conceal his face. Proceedings in the room had come to a halt as the gathered few looked expectantly in their direction.

'You want to fuck?' the whiskered ruffian said, staring cross-eyed at Emily. He was unsteady on his feet.

The first hammer blow was the decisive one. It came out of nowhere and landed the uncomprehending man squarely on his backside with a dull thump. Pyke cracked his bruised knuckles and turned to face his two friends. One of them launched himself at Pyke and barrelled into his midriff, sending them both sprawling on to the floor and knocking his cap off in the process. Pyke, though, recovered quickest and manoeuvred his startled assailant into a headlock. Pulling him to his feet, Pyke used the man's torso as a shield against his friend's assault, pushing them both backwards with sufficient force to topple them on to a nearby table. He followed this up with a kick to the groin of the taller man. The other man picked himself up and circled around Pyke with his fists raised; his expression was guarded and fearful. But when Pyke attacked he was too slow and too drunk to parry the blow. Those watching the spectacle took a sharp collective breath as Pyke landed the decisive punch on the bridge of the man's nose; it snapped with an audible pop before blood exploded from his nostrils.

Pyke took Emily's hand and was halfway across the room and walking briskly towards the door when someone shouted, 'That's Pyke.' Another murmured something in agreement. No one seemed to know what to do, whether to block his path or let him leave. Pyke knew that their indecision, and fear, represented his best and only chance of escape.

Outside, he told Emily to run. Behind them, drinkers from the Old Cock spilled out on to the street. Angry shouts filled the eerie silence. *'That's Pyke . . . someone stop him . . . get him . . . lynch the bastard.'* At the end of the street, they turned into a side alley and from there into a small courtyard. For a moment, they waited and listened over the noise of their beating hearts as their pursuers raced past. A half-open door beckoned. Silently, Pyke led Emily into the darkened interior of what seemed to be someone's kitchen. The room was deserted. A pair of boots hung over the grate. He closed the door behind them and turned to face Emily, whose face glistened with excitement.

Her hair, damp from the rain, clung to her smooth, angular face and brushed against her delicate shoulder blades. Without speaking, Pyke ran his fingers gently through her locks and stared into her wide-open eyes. Her lips parted before she embraced him, an urgent, smouldering kiss that seemed to envelop them and, for the briefest of moments, turn their thoughts from the events of the evening. When she looked at him again, through her long, wispy lashes, she was grinning.

'Why are you smiling?'

Her eyes glistened with anticipation.

'What is it?'

'Thank you.'

'For what?'

Emily's knowing smile revealed the whiteness of her teeth.

'The real reason I came to find you today,' she said, waiting for a moment. 'I wanted to tell you about a transfer of money that's due to take place between the Bank of England here in London and two of my uncle's banks in Norfolk.' She seemed to read his mind because almost at once she added, 'This time, I believe, it is a genuine one.'

Pyke pulled back from their intimate embrace to study her expression. 'Tell me more.'

Still whispering, Emily proceeded to describe what she had overheard at her father's house. She explained that at harvest times the eastern counties were swamped with itinerant workers, but that the banks did not carry sufficient funds in reserve to cover the farmers' costs. In order to ensure that the Blackwood banks had enough money to pay these wages, funds had to be physically transferred from a vault in the Bank of England to the various banks in Norfolk.

'So why are you telling me this?' he asked, eventually.

'It is not in your nature to make things easy for me, is it?' But her wounded expression seemed a little feigned.

'I'm not sure what you mean.'

This time, she looked directly at him. 'Why do you imagine that I am here?'

For once, Pyke did not have an answer.

She stepped forward into the space between them and kissed him on the mouth. 'Is it so hard for you to accept that my loyalties may lie somewhere other than at Hambledon?'

'It is hard but not *that* hard.' This time he reciprocated the embrace. A hot spike of desire swelled up within him. 'Of course, if this information fell into the wrong hands, it could cause your father significant harm.'

Emily nodded. 'There would certainly be no money available to the farmers to pay my father's rents.'

'Would that cause him difficulties?'

'At present?' Emily shrugged. 'I would think so.'

Pyke nodded. 'Such an undertaking could be highly dangerous.'

'It shouldn't be undertaken lightly, that is certain.' Emily reached out and ran her fingers across his cheek. 'Nor might such action be suitable for the faint-hearted.'

'One would have to be of a particular constitution, I agree.'

'One would have to be bold,' Emily said, nodding.

Pyke nodded, playing along. 'Strong as well as bold.'

'That goes without saying.' Emily broke into a wide smile.

'Strong enough to chase down a stagecoach on horse-back?'

'I would say so.'

'Strong enough to fire a pistol?'

That drew a slight frown. 'Would that be necessary?'

Pyke waited until she was looking at him. 'Strong enough to stand up to your father?' His remark registered and he wondered why he found her disconcertion as sexually gratifying as her more obvious attempts to appeal to him. But when he tried to kiss her again she pulled away from him and gathered herself to leave, as though unaware that his ardour could not as easily be put aside.

The air in the crowded taproom was musty and the floors were caked in mud. The room itself was heaving with red-faced milliners and seamstresses dressed in tatty shawls and bonnets, carousing with drunken hop-pickers, flush with the earnings of their labours in Kent. Urged on by the melodious strains of a fiddle, they may have looked like a good-natured lot, dancing ankle-deep in butcher's sawdust that still carried the stink of rancid meat, but Pyke knew that every one of them would have crawled over their loved ones' corpses for the chance to earn the reward that had been offered for information leading to his arrest.

Along with Townsend, Goddard was an acquaintance from Bow Street. Though younger and more immature than his partner, Goddard was, perversely, the one with a family. His wife had just given birth to twin daughters. He had a thin face, with sunken cheeks that accentuated the dark patches around his eyes. Pyke listened while he explained that the Runners were effectively being dismantled, despite Fox's best efforts to sabotage the new dispensation for law enforcement.

'Sir Richard's even got us ingratiating ourselves in radical circles, Hunt's lot, to try and stir up some trouble,' Townsend added. 'To see if he can't overstretch the new force and show Peel the Runners are still needed.'

'He's losing his fuckin' mind, more like,' Goddard said.

'Peel's having none of it,' Townsend added, ignoring that last remark. 'And he won't let any Runner join the new force. Says he wants a clean start.'

Pyke had already told them about his plans to rob Blackwood's armoured carriage and both had willingly consented to help him. Townsend needed no persuasion – any opportunity to upset Edmonton's affairs was to be welcomed – and Goddard was attracted by the monetary incentive. For Pyke, such a venture carried certain risks, not least because it would draw Edmonton's attention to his presence in the capital. But the potential benefits outweighed the risks. The money, which would be divided equally between them, would be extremely welcome. But the real reason Pyke was willing to pursue such a venture was because it would undermine Edmonton's financial stability and perhaps draw Jimmy Swift from his hiding place.

In hushed voices, they discussed the best place to stage the attack and contemplated the most appropriate course of action. They had agreed upon a plan and Goddard excused himself. A few moments later, Townsend turned to Pyke and said, 'Before you went away, you asked about the mother.'

Pyke frowned. 'Whose mother?'

'The daughter's. Edmonton's wife.'

Pyke strained to conceal his interest. 'Apparently she died, while incarcerated in an asylum.'

'That was the commonly held assumption.'

'What are you suggesting?'

Townsend seemed to be enjoying himself, 'Do you know of anyone who attended the funeral?'

'The daughter wasn't permitted to.'

'But she believes her mother to be dead?'

'Are you saying that she's still alive?'

Townsend took a swig of ale. 'I managed to track down one of the old servants. She didn't want to talk to me at first – it seems that even former employees are terrified of Edmonton's vindictiveness – but she remembered my brother and eventually opened up to me.'

'I am interested.' Pyke shrugged. 'I can't pretend otherwise.'

Townsend leaned closer and whispered, 'The old woman was adamant. The mother is by no means dead.'

'Does she know where I might be able to find her?'

'Perhaps.' Townsend wiped his mouth with the sleeve of his coat.

'But this information is going to cost me,' Pyke said, nodding his head.

Townsend shrugged.

'What if I were to offer you half of my share of the robbery proceeds?'

Townsend whistled and raised his eyebrows. 'She must be important to you.'

'You mean the mother?'

'Or the daughter.'

When Pyke looked up, he saw Emily's servant, Jo, enter the taproom. Compared to the dressmakers and shop workers who frequented the tavern, she stood out in the surroundings almost as sorely as her mistress. Pyke excused himself and went to join her. They exchanged formal pleasantries and he suggested that the relative quiet of his garret might be a more convivial place to talk. As they ascended the staircase, he wondered why Emily had not come herself.

'My mistress has asked me to pass on a message. She assured me you would know what it meant.'

With a buxom figure and a round, rosy-cheeked face that, above all, intimated a sense of ripeness, Jo seemed nervous and fidgeted as she stood in the doorway, unwilling to enter his room. Not for the first time, he was struck by the thought that he had come across her before.

'I would be able to respond to that sentiment if I knew more about the message itself,' he said, with a smile.

'Of course.' She seemed flustered. Pyke wondered whether it had been wise to bring an unaccompanied young woman – Emily's servant, no less – up to his garret.

'Tomorrow, at six in the morning.' Jo looked at him. 'She said you would know what it meant.' Jo had painted her eyelashes and Pyke wondered whether this was usual for a servant.

It was the time that the armoured carriage was due to depart from the Bank of England. Again he wondered why Emily had opted to send her servant with such an important message. Since he could not ask Jo such a direct question, he enquired after Emily's health. Jo informed him that her mistress was perfectly well.

Despite her apparent nerves, Jo did not seem to be in any hurry to leave. Instead, she removed her bonnet and started to rearrange her hair. Without it, he was able to admire her smooth round face, her flawless pale skin and her extraordinary red hair.

'I made sure no one followed me,' she said, still unwilling to meet his stare. Her accent indicated a certain level of education. 'Don't worry, I'll be gone in a minute.'

'Please, take all the time you need.' Pyke watched as she bent forward to attend to her boots. He found himself wondering what her relationship with Emily was like and whether there was any kind of ulterior motive to her presence in his room. He also didn't know what she knew about him and whether he could trust her.

'There.' Jo stood up and smiled. 'Done.'

She went to retrieve her bonnet but Pyke had already picked it up. He handed it to her. 'This may sound like an immodest question, but are you aware of who I am?'

Jo stared down at her feet. 'My mistress felt it was necessary to inform me of certain things.'

'Such as?' He raised his eyebrows, half-aware that he might be flirting with her.

'That, unless crossed, you were not a dangerous man. That you didn't tolerate fools. That your bark was worse than your bite.' She looked away and blushed slightly. 'She also warned me you were . . . rather dashing.'

'She said that?'

'Well, she actually said exceedingly dashing but I thought I'd appeal to your modesty.' Jo laughed nervously. She seemed more confident of herself now and even allowed her gaze to meet his.

'And why do you think Emily furnished you with this information?' Pyke watched her carefully. She was remarkably attractive. He wondered whether she was aware of this fact.

'I don't know. To warn me, perhaps.'

'Warn you to be on your guard?' Pyke could not help but smile at this prospect. Clearly Emily did not trust him, but did he trust her? And could he be certain that her loyalties did not, as she put it, lie at Hambledon?

'Have we met somewhere before?' He studied her features closely.

'Aside from when you first visited my mistress in Islington . . .'

'Your face seems familiar,' he said, absent-mindedly. 'It's a pretty face, of course . . .'

Jo blushed again and edged towards the door. Impulsively, he moved into the space between them, leaned forward and kissed her on the mouth. She did not resist but nor did she make any attempt to reciprocate. Unthinkingly, he tried to pull her closer, smelling perfume on her clothes, but this time she baulked and, instinctively perhaps, her entire body recoiled backwards. For a brief moment, they stared at one another, opaquely, neither certain what the other was thinking. Finally, without saying a word, Jo turned to depart, leaving Pyke angry at himself that he had done such an utterly stupid thing and wondering whether Jo would tell her mistress.

It was only later that it struck him where he had seen her before. It was not her face that he recognised but her voice – the voice that had warned him in the Blue Dog. He could not be absolutely certain of this but, if it was the case, it meant that Emily's servant had been keeping an eye on him even before he had first visited Hambledon Hall.

TWENTY

In thick early-morning fog that made it all but impossible to see for more than a few yards ahead, the armoured carriage departed from the Bank of England on Threadneedle Street shortly after six o'clock, just as Emily had predicted. It had rained heavily during the night and the streets, though empty of traffic, were muddy and treacherous. The occasional gas light illuminated the otherwise gloomy route. Pyke followed the carriage at a respectful distance, riding a clapped-out nag Townsend had procured from a band of gypsies on Hampstead Heath. The carriage was a converted stagecoach: iron bars protected the doors and windows. Alongside the driver were two heavy-set figures dressed in black cloaks and hats. Pyke presumed them to be security men and supposed they were armed. The coach itself was pulled by four sturdy horses. The newly macadamised turnpike beyond would be more heavily patrolled and, on such ground, the carriage would be able to outrun them without difficulty, which was why they had opted to attack it in the city. Such a tactic also meant they would be able to lose themselves in the vastness of the metropolis before any alarm could be raised.

The thickness of the fog made it hard for Pyke to keep the armoured carriage in sight but he did not mind the inconvenience because the poor visibility would assist them in the robbery.

It was still too early for traders to be setting up their stalls – it was barely light and in this part of the world commerce did not properly commence until eight or nine in the morning – but the streets were not entirely clear of carts and barrows. As they rattled along Bishopsgate Street they passed the occasional street sweeper and beggar pushing a makeshift cart, scouring the roadside for scraps of food. Sewer rats as large as dogs scuttled down deserted alleyways, startled by the clip-clopping of iron hoofs on stone cobbles.

The laudanum Pyke had ingested earlier had calmed him slightly, but as they reached the outskirts of Shoreditch he felt his nerves jangle and the muscles in his stomach tighten. Reaching down, he made sure that the two pistols and length of iron pipe were safely tucked into his belt. Nearing the spot where the attack was due to take place, Pyke kicked his boots into his horse's midriff and urged it on. The beast responded, though less willingly than he would have liked. Evidently concerned by Pyke's presence, the driver of the armoured carriage conferred with the two guards and proceeded to lash his whip against the horses' backs to quicken their pace. Pyke stepped up his pursuit. Ahead of him, the carriage bounced more vigorously as it raced across the uneven surface of the road. The guards were shouting at each other and, as far as Pyke could make out in the fog, had turned to look at him, rather than focus on the road ahead.

It meant they would not see the wire that Goddard and Townsend had pulled taut across the entire width of the road and fixed to gas lamps on either side of the street.

Ahead were the rising spires of St Leonard's church. Pyke prepared himself for the attack. The carriage was now speeding across the uneven cobbles at such a velocity that when it passed under the wire – for it had been set at such a height to ensure that the carriage and horses would pass under it without any problems – the three figures sitting on top were pulled from their seats and dumped on the road.

Pyke heard them land on the cobbles with a dull thump but did not have time to determine the exact nature of their injuries, though he was relieved to see that there had been nothing as calamitous as a beheading. This had been Townsend's fear: that the wire, if placed at the wrong height, might slice clean through their necks and behead the driver and guards. Rather than concerning himself with these matters, Pyke took care to duck underneath the wire himself and pursue the now driverless carriage as it careened onwards, zigzagging across the road and narrowly avoiding a fruit seller who was hauling his barrow up on to the pavement. It had been his plan to overtake the carriage, if this was possible, and somehow bring the horses under control, but such was their speed, or his own nag's weariness, that the best he could do was pull alongside the back wheel of the now out-of-control carriage and thrust the length of lead piping into the wheel's spokes. The effect was instantaneous. Pyke pulled back behind the carriage as the wheel splintered and disintegrated; the carriage teetered momentarily on its one good rear wheel before toppling sideways and crashing into the pavement, where a chestnut seller was setting up his stall. The carriage obliterated the wooden stand and narrowly missed the man himself, who just managed to take evasive action. The impact of the crash snapped one side of the yoke and freed two of the horses, but the other side of the yoke somehow held together, and the petrified beasts continued to surge forward, dragging the stranded carriage on its side through mud and puddles, producing a grim, ear-splitting noise.

Eventually, the effort of having to drag a heavy object on

its side through thick mud took its toll and the two horses slowed to a trot and then a complete stop, and neighed to show their unease. As Pyke dismounted, he saw that Goddard and Townsend were rattling towards him on their horse and cart. All of them had pulled black handkerchiefs up over the lower part of their faces.

Afterwards Pyke could not remember exactly what had happened next, though he knew, for obvious reasons, that it was Goddard who had first approached the rear door of the prostrate carriage. Later, Townsend told him Goddard was attempting to rip off the damaged rear door when a shot, fired from inside the carriage, struck him squarely in the chest. He died before either of them reached him.

While the guard who had fired the shot attempted to reload his pistol, Townsend tore open the door, hauled the trembling man out and kicked him into an unrecognisable mess of quivering, bloody flesh.

Pyke attended to the contents of the carriage. A small crowd had gathered, albeit at a distance, around the crash site, and he knew they did not have much time. He had expected the carriage to be empty of everything except its cargo, but as he peered into the darkened recesses of the coach, through fog and gunpowder smoke, he came upon the dazed face of William Blackwood. Edmonton's brother had scrambled on top of a metal trunk. His expression was a mixture of fear, veneration and defiance. Somehow, during the crash, he had managed to retain his pistol, which he held in trembling hands.

Pyke pulled the handkerchief from his face and watched Blackwood's fortitude dissolve as easily as the carriage's wheel.

Once Pyke and Townsend had, between them, carried the trunk to the waiting horse and cart, Pyke returned to Blackwood; the banker had started to weep.

'They'll get you for this, you know, Mr Pyke. Edmonton won't rest till you're hanging from a scaffold.'

'I look forward to a day of reckoning with your brother,' Pyke said, pointing his pistol at Blackwood's face. 'But I do have a question for you.' He smiled easily. 'That first time we met, at Hambledon Hall, when your brother employed my services to investigate an alleged bank robbery . . .'

'I remember.' Blackwood's hands were still trembling.

'Am I right in thinking that no such robberies took place?' Pyke asked. 'That's why you were so outraged at the disparaging remarks that your brother made about your business acumen.' He glanced behind him, to see what was happening outside the carriage.

A thin smile passed across Blackwood's lips. 'And you walked happily into his trap.'

'We were both used by your brother.' Pyke met the man's baleful stare and said, 'Tell him I'll be coming for him next.'

Townsend was attempting to haul Goddard's bloodied corpse on to the back of the cart when Pyke joined him. The rear axle was already buckling under the weight of the trunk. In the distance, he could hear the sound of hoofs thundering against the square-set stones of the road.

'We have to go.' He shook Townsend's arm. Townsend tried to push him away. Pyke saw that he was crying. 'We have to leave him. There might be a horse patrol on its way.'

'Leave him?' Townsend stared through bloodshot eyes. 'I've known him since he was a lad.'

Pyke pulled his arm, harder this time. 'We can't take him *and* the money.'

'He'll lead them straight back to me,' Townsend shouted.

Pyke took his pistol and fired a shot into Goddard's face. 'Not if they can't identify him.'

Townsend stared at him, uncomprehending. Pyke turned the pistol on him and said, 'I'll shoot you, too, unless you get up on the cart right now.'

The haul, when they counted it half an hour later, in an abandoned house, came to just under seven thousand pounds. Pyke said he would take a thousand of it, and Townsend could have the rest. He could keep it or give it to Goddard's family or do what he wanted with it.

'We agreed a three-way split. That works out as two thousand three hundred pounds each. I'll give Goddard's share to his wife.'

'I promised you half of my split, if you told me where I might be able to locate the mother.' Pyke's expression hardened. 'He was dead and the cavalry was coming. Even if we'd been able to balance him on the cart, do you think we would have been able to outrun them?'

Townsend shook his head, pushing some of the money away. 'I don't want your blood money.'

Pyke waited, hands on hips, for the moment to pass.

'You can take the rest of my share and offer it as a reward for information about a man called Jimmy Swift.' Pyke gave a brief description. 'I also want you to get in touch with these radical types you were telling me about. I want to talk with anyone who might be interested in stirring up trouble on Edmonton's estate.'

'You forget I don't work for you.'

'But even now you hate Edmonton more than you hate me.'

The hotness of Townsend's anger seemed to dissipate.

Pyke picked up the disputed money and thrust it at Townsend. 'Take it. Do what you want with it.' He stared into the other man's sullen face. 'I didn't kill Goddard. I'm sorry he's dead. I'm sorry for his wife and his young girls.

I'm sorry for leaving him behind. I didn't think we had a choice. But, for me at least, this doesn't end here. Maybe it does for you. If so, I accept. We'll shake hands and go our separate ways.' He shrugged. 'But I need to know where the mother is.'

Townsend stared at Pyke for a moment, contemplating what he had said. 'I was told she's been locked up in an asylum in Portsmouth for the last fifteen years.' He hesitated. 'But if she wasn't insane when she was *placed* there, I'm assured she is now.'

'You're suggesting she won't be of use to me?'

'I'm saying she won't be in a position to furnish you with whatever information you're looking for.'

Pyke picked up the satchel that contained his share of the money. 'Who says I want information?'

'Then why do you want to talk to her?'

'I don't want to talk to her,' Pyke said, heading for the door.

'Pyke?'

Something in Townsend's voice made him turn around. 'Yes?'

Townsend looked at him for a while and then sighed. 'Do you need my help?'

'This is highly irregular and most perturbing.' Mr Ezra Kennett, who was not only the chief physician but also the administrator and general handyman of the establishment, waddled to keep up with Pyke, his round face and ruddy cheeks puffing with indignation. Dressed in a dark jacket, fitted trousers, black cloak and Wellington boots, Pyke had pushed past him into the entrance hall of the crumbling building, a row of terraces near the docks which had been haphazardly converted into an asylum. Interior walls had been knocked down to create space for a communal ward, but the construction work itself had been of poor quality and, even to an untrained eye, it was easy to see that the edifice was on the verge of collapse: walls were buckling, ceilings sagged and the unmistakable stench of rising damp saturated the air. In this higgledy-piggledy room no larger than a parlour, Pyke counted ten iron-framed beds, pressed so tightly together that even a skinny man would have struggled to navigate between them. In each, a pitiful specimen of humanity, little more than an amalgam of hair, skin and bones, was chained to the frame with hand- and leg-cuffs. The wails and cries emanating from their mouths collectively constituted a din that was so unpleasant Pyke was compelled to seek out Kennett's private quarters. Townsend, who was dressed in the attire of a hospital porter, thrust a copy of the *Chronicle* into Kennett's chubby hand as they walked, and pointed to an article, describing the work of Thomas Southwood Smith at the London Fever Hospital and drawing attention to a new treatise on fever he was about to publish. Pyke had come across the article the previous afternoon and formulated his plan accordingly.

'A ship docked in the port last week from the East Indies,' Pyke said, having barged his way into what he presumed was Kennett's office, though the damp seemed even riper here than in the rest of the building. He placed his hat down on the table and tapped his cane against the stone floor, as though to chivvy a response from the physician.

Kennett seemed both befuddled and concerned by their unsolicited intrusion. He ran a private asylum that, Pyke supposed, had been financed by public money. The lunatics housed in the ward they had just passed through would not have come from poor backgrounds. Rather, wealthy patrons such as Edmonton would have paid handsomely for Kennett to take unwanted relatives off their hands and would not have concerned themselves with the conditions of care. Pyke was certain Kennett turned a considerable profit from the enterprise.

'I was alerted to the possible manifestation of Asiatic cholera in one of the crew.' Pyke wore a monocle and removed it to properly inspect Kennett. 'Are you aware of this condition?'

The rotund physician wiped sweat from his brow. 'I have heard stories of its relentless march across whole continents.'

Pyke nodded briskly. 'It is a monstrous disease. The man in question was suffering from chronic diarrhoea and vomiting, severe dehydration and acute pain in the stomach and limbs. These are, indeed, the symptoms of Asiatic cholera. In addition, his ravaged skin had assumed a ghastly blue-grey complexion. But even more terrifying is its contagiousness; the speed with which it can spread across entire neighbourhoods. Entire cities.' He sniffed the air.

'You do not think . . .' Kennett was not able to complete his sentence, perhaps fearing that his concerns might actually be borne out if he spoke their name.

'The docks, as you know, are within a half-mile radius of your establishment. I have been instructed to visit all such premises, in order to determine the precise nature of any risk posed to those living in the vicinity.' Pyke replaced the monocle and looked at Kennett. 'Are you aware of my work on fever?'

The physician reddened. 'This is a modest practice and in my capacity as—'

Pyke interrupted. 'It is my belief that diseases such as typhus or indeed cholera thrive on account of particular atmospheric and environmental conditions. The laws of diffusion mean that anyone within a certain distance of an infected person is vulnerable to the disease. But the likelihood of the disease spreading is greatly enhanced by poor sanitary conditions: damp and filthy interiors, proximity to open sewers, use of dirty water, inadequate food preparation.' He trained his stare on the rattled physician. 'Only a fool or a blind man would say that these conditions do not exist here. Allow me to be blunt: this place is a disgrace and, in the current circumstances, I could have the premises vacated within the day and the establishment closed down.'

Kennett did not seem to know whether to be chastened or outraged.

Pyke continued, 'I am not a vindictive man and I can tell from your response that concern for your own well-being, if not your patients, is evident. I am prepared, at this stage, to monitor the situation rather than advocate more drastic action. But I will need to examine the patients for early signs of the disease . . .'

The chance that Pyke might leave him alone produced a change in the physician's demeanour. 'Of course, I would welcome your opinion and would be greatly honoured if you would permit me to accompany you and to assist your work in every way that I can.'

Pyke wondered whether he should lift up his boots so the man could lick them. He checked his fob-watch. Earlier, Townsend had visited the kitchen and bribed the cook to mix a plant extract Pyke had procured from a London botanist with Sarah Blackwood's gruel. It would, the botanist promised him, temporarily induce sickness once the extract had been properly digested. The cook had also helped to identify which one of the fifteen patients was Emily's mother. Not that the cook knew her name or any of their names; but having served under Kennett for as long as the asylum had been running, she was quite certain there was only one patient who had been there for as long as fifteen years.

Back in the ward, Pyke wandered along the row of tightly arranged beds and eventually came to a halt at the foot of one occupied by the figure identified by the cook. For a while, he studied her withered, bony face but saw nothing that connected her to Emily. What was left of her hair was parted in the middle to reveal a wrinkled scalp, and the bones in her arms and legs seemed so brittle that Pyke wondered how it might be possible to move her. Her stare was hollow and the stink of faeces and camphor emanating from her made him want to gag. Pyke could see that her whole side was covered in bed sores. A spool of vomit had congealed down the front of her gown.

Stepping forward, he inspected her in greater detail. This was largely for Kennett's benefit, but Pyke also wanted some reassurance that this elderly woman was, indeed, Emily's mother.

'This patient will have to be isolated immediately,' he said, without equivocation.

'But I don't have such facilities,' Kennett stammered weakly.

'Then we shall have to remove her from these premises forthwith.' He turned to face the physician. 'What's her name?'

Kennett seemed panicked. 'I can't . . .'

'Her name, dammit.' Pyke turned to Townsend and ordered him to fetch the trolley.

'I can't release her without the permission of her guardian.'

Pyke turned on him. 'Have you any idea how quickly the disease can spread in these situations?'

'I . . . I . . .'

'Stop stuttering, man.' Pyke shouted after Townsend. 'Quickly, man. We haven't got a moment to lose.'

At this point, the old woman whom Pyke presumed and hoped was Emily's mother groaned and from her mouth came a blast of frothy vomit. That seemed to put an end to the physician's resistance.

'Take the old bitch,' he muttered, defeated.

Pyke had to rein in his desire to assault the pudgy doctor with every sinew in his body.

In the carriage that he had commandeered for the purpose of transporting the elderly patient back to London, Pyke arranged the stretcher carrying Emily's mother in order to make the journey as painless as possible, but the turnpike was not smooth and the suspension on the carriage had been worn down. Each jolt and bump produced an exclamation of discomfort, and after each Pyke leaned forward, stroked the old woman's face and offered words of reassurance. Townsend looked on, perhaps bewildered by Pyke's attempts at tenderness. The woman had said nothing since leaving the asylum. It was a cool, overcast day but the interior of the carriage was not so gloomy that Pyke couldn't make out the woman's features. But it was only when she fully opened her eyes, after he had said Emily's name, that he saw what he had been looking for: for the briefest of moments, she gave him a lucid stare. Emily had inherited her mother's eyes.

Quietly, Townsend said, 'She won't be able to tell you whatever it is you want to know.'

Without looking up, Pyke continued to stroke the old woman's head.

'What do you plan on doing with her when we get to London?'

'Do you mean where do I plan to take her?'

'Yes.'

'I have made arrangements. She will be well looked after.'

Townsend nodded. 'But what did we go through all of this rigmarole *for*?'

'You mean how do I intend to profit from this action?' This time, Pyke looked at his old acquaintance.

'Exactly.'

Pyke glanced down at the old woman. 'I don't.'

Townsend stared at him as though he didn't believe or couldn't comprehend what Pyke had told him. 'You mean you don't know?'

'I mean I don't have any such plans.'

Edmonton had gone to work with impressive but, from Pyke's point of view, alarming haste to propagate his own version of the robbery. By the following evening, the story had colonised the front page of the *London Chronicle*. The luridly written account announced that twenty thousand pounds had been stolen at gunpoint from a stagecoach transporting money to the provinces. It did not mention which bank the money belonged to. The report claimed that one of the robbers had been shot and killed but two accomplices had escaped and were currently being pursued by the new police. It identified Pyke as one of the suspects and announced that an unknown benefactor had posted a reward of five hundred pounds for information leading to Pyke's capture and the return of the stolen money. Pyke was described in the report as an armed and highly dangerous convicted murderer who had stabbed and killed his own mistress and who should be approached with extreme caution. The report concluded with an inaccurate account of his criminal exploits and listed a number of addresses where he might be hiding.

Pyke was under no illusions about the magnitude of the task he now faced. It would be hard, if not impossible, to move anonymously through a city where every police constable and every man and woman – every coiner, dock worker, scavenger, canal digger, harvest worker, river pirate, embezzler, dustman, chimney sweep, butcher, swindler, publican, pickpocket, ballad singer and dog stealer – would be looking to collect the five hundred pounds reward.

Certainly he had not counted on Edmonton's response being decisive, and he now wondered about the wisdom of revealing his identity to the brother. He had wanted the fat lord to know that he had taken his money, if only to engage his accomplice – Jimmy Swift – in a more direct confrontation. Now, though, he would have to contend with half the city as he did so.

Having arrived back in London and established Emily's mother in a private apartment with her own nurse, Pyke travelled across the city under the blanket of darkness and was met at the gate at the bottom of the garden by Jo and ushered into the back of the Islington town house. Thankfully Jo did not try to engage him in conversation or discuss her recent visit to his garret, nor did he confront her with his own suspicions about her. These would have to wait for another occasion.

But something had changed.

In the upstairs drawing room, Emily did not embrace him, nor could she bring herself to look at him. Pyke stole a glance at Jo and wondered what the girl had told Emily about their encounter in his garret, once again kicking himself for his stupidity, and for having ruined his chances with Emily over what had amounted to the mildest of flirtations. He listened, chastened, as Emily described how news of the robbery had sent her father into the most violent rage she had ever witnessed.

Already, he had spoken with the new Metropolitan Police commissioners and had taken the step of employing his own private operatives.

'I heard him and my uncle talking. My father is convinced that someone currently working in the bank supplied you with information about the transfer of money.'

'Do you think that he suspects you?' Pyke asked, wondering now whether Emily did, in fact, know about his indiscretion with Jo.

'I am certain he has no idea about the extent of our . . . *liaison*.' Her mood seemed to darken. 'But I had to fight him to allow me to stay here even for one night.'

On the table in the large bay window was the same evening-newspaper report that he had consulted. 'Contrary to what the report claimed, there wasn't anything like twenty thousand pounds.' He removed a sealed envelope from his pocket. 'That's a small contribution for your charity.'

Emily stared at the envelope, as though it were a dagger. He thrust it into her trembling hands. 'Here. Take it.'

'I can't.' She allowed the envelope to drop on to the Turkey carpet.

'Can't or won't?'

She exhaled loudly. 'A man was killed. Two others, a guard and the driver, are grievously injured. The driver may never walk again.' She looked up at him. Her eyes were dry. 'Was he a friend of yours?'

'The man who was killed?' Pyke didn't know whether to be relieved that she didn't seem to know about his foolishness with Jo or concerned that something new had come between them.

Emily nodded.

'He understood the risks. It was a robbery.'

'Did the driver of the coach understand the risks, too?'

Pyke allowed a little of his frustration to show. 'What do you want me to say? That I regret what happened to him? That I'm sorry for what we did?'

'Perhaps,' Emily said, staring down at the envelope on the carpet.

'If I felt that way, then we shouldn't have undertaken the robbery in the first place.' It was as though he had punched her in the stomach.

For a while, the only sound in the room was the ticking of the grandfather clock. 'Does it fill you with satisfaction,' she asked, finally, 'that I've now been initiated into your world?' There was weariness rather than bitterness in her tone.

'My world? And what exactly is *my* world? If you are referring to a place where one has to take hard decisions that, in turn, have unedifying consequences, then it *does* fill me with satisfaction.'

His remarks stung her, as they were meant to. 'Do you really think the work I do is straightforward and doesn't require having to make hard choices?'

'Perhaps not, but surely this experience has softened your attitude to other people's failings?'

'When people are powerless and cannot help themselves, I am more than sympathetic to their plight,' she snapped.

Pyke waited for some of her anger to cool. 'Then you should understand that decisions, taken in rushed circumstances, sometimes lead to unpleasant outcomes.'

This didn't entirely placate her. She laughed bitterly. 'And in the end, one cannot tell right from wrong.'

'Perhaps right and wrong are not the absolute markers you imagine them to be.'

Emily's gaze betrayed her disappointment. 'Is it right that children as young as six have to work for fifteen hours a day in windowless rooms for only a few shillings a week?'

'Or that an aristocrat arranges the slaughter of innocent people for no other reason than to satisfy his own bigotry?'

Emily stared with consternation but she did not know how to answer him.

'What if punishing this person could not be achieved without hurting other people?'

'You're asking me to sanction the loss of innocent lives as a way of legitimising this feud between you and my father?' She sounded weary.

'I'm not asking for your sanction.' Pyke walked across to the bay window. The curtains were drawn. 'I'm asking for your understanding.' He turned to face her. 'You make it sound as though my reasons for hating him are entirely selfish.'

'So you *do* hate him?'

'Don't you?'

Emily shrugged. 'I have my reasons.'

Pyke peeked through the curtains and looked down at the empty street below him. He thought about Emily's mother and wondered how she was settling into her new living arrangements.

Emily had followed him across to the window and when he turned around she was standing so close to him that he could count the freckles on her nose. He reached out and touched her face. Her smile was a sad one.

'What is it that you want from me?' he said, finally. His fingertip brushed across the top of her lip.

'Who says I *want* anything from you?'

'I seem to disappoint you.' He shrugged.

That drew a puzzled expression. 'I'm not disappointed by you.'

'But?'

'You paint me as this saintly prig.'

'Because you're always talking about your work.' He waited for a moment. 'Not about what *you* want, what *you* desire . . .'

Outside on the street, a coach came to halt.

'You don't think I desire you?' Emily said, in part distracted by the sound of someone approaching the front door.

Moments later, they were interrupted by a knock on the door. Jo peered into the room. She said that Lord Edmonton's coachman was downstairs in the hall, demanding that Emily, on her father's explicit orders, accompany him back to Hambledon.

'But it's so late . . .' Emily looked at Pyke, frowning.

'The coachman is quite insistent. Apparently your father is demanding your presence,' Jo said, with a shrug. 'Perhaps you could talk to him yourself?'

'Of course.' As Emily gathered her shawl and bonnet, she turned to Pyke and said, 'I shall have to travel to Hambledon tonight. If I refused, it would cause more trouble than it's worth.' She shrugged apologetically.

'Do you think it might have something to do with the robbery?'

'It might.' She began to tie her bonnet. 'But my father is notorious for his temperamental behaviour. I am guessing he just wants someone to listen to his rants.'

She picked up her gloves and turned to face him. Her smile was forced. 'I'm sorry I have to leave . . .'

'And I am sorry for some of my intemperate remarks.' He hesitated. 'It's just . . .'

'Yes?' Her eyes lit up with hope.

But he could not bring himself to say what he imagined that she wanted to hear. 'It's nothing.'

'Oh.' She seemed disappointed but sought to conceal this by pulling her shawl tightly around her shoulders. 'You shall stay here tonight, of course. There is a bed on the upper floor but you might find it more hospitable on the sofa.'

'When will I see you again?'

From the doorway, she turned around. 'I'm afraid I don't know.' Her tone was formal, perhaps because Jo was waiting for her on the landing.

'Emily . . .'

Her expression seemed both annoyed and expectant. 'Yes?'

Pyke swallowed his disconcertion. 'I hope that your father doesn't suspect you.'

'I hope so too.' And she was gone.

Pyke watched her leave from the drawing-room window and settled down on the sofa. Jo had already laid out a blanket and a pillow for him. He had not planned to stay the night in Edmonton's house – in spite of Emily's insistence, he did not think it was entirely safe for him to do so – but the long trip to Portsmouth and the exertions of the robbery had taken their toll, and as soon as he laid his head on one of the pillows and pulled the blanket over him, tiredness overcame him. He remembered thinking that he should rouse Jo and ask her whether she had indeed followed him to the Blue Dog tavern and warned him of Flynn's presence, but as his face burrowed down into the soft pillow, such thoughts ebbed away and, before he knew it, he had slipped into a deep, dreamless sleep.

TWENTY-ONE

The following afternoon, Pyke met Townsend at the Red Lion inn in Highgate and there they hired a private coach and driver to take them around a collection of villages located within Edmonton's two-thousand-acre estate, just to the north of the outer fringes of the metropolis. It was only late September but already there was an autumnal chill in the air; the leaves had turned from green to gold and many had already fallen on to muddy ground. The overcast skies did little to lift the melancholy air that seemed to hang over the villages they visited, places made up of little more than a few shacks, a church and a solitary public house. They had passed through the suburbs and were now deep in the countryside. The fields were busy with labourers bringing in the last of the harvest, the rickyards and barns were brimming with flax, and the narrow tracks were choked with wagons and carts.

Townsend had arranged for them to be accompanied by James Canning, a shoemaker, and Jack Saville, a straw-plait merchant from Bedfordshire. Both men had made a name for themselves in radical circles and both were known, or known of, by at least someone in the different village inns. In each place, they heard a variation of the same story: Edmonton was a corrupt landlord who charged his tenant farmers an exorbitant rent, which meant that the farmers had no choice but to squeeze as much work as possible from their labourers, for an insulting wage that did not even cover their basic subsistence.

Townsend had informed Canning and Saville that Pyke was an acquaintance of Hunt and was exploring the possibilities of forming links between metropolitan and rural political activists.

The villagers were hostile to outsiders, and spoke to them only because they knew, or had heard of, Canning and Saville. Ale lubricated their tongues, though, and most willingly and bitterly complained of Edmonton's high-handed manner and greedy ways. Once they had finished with him, they started in on other targets: the combination of low wages and a reduction in their Poor Law allowances, which meant that most could not afford to feed their children; the increased use of threshing machines rather than their own labour to break corn in the quiet winter months; the terrible harvest and the bleak prospect for the upcoming winter; the poor weather; and the business of tithing, which meant that a tenth of their meagre income went directly to the Anglican Church.

In one village, Pyke listened while an elderly cabinet-maker told him about the untimely death of the local Member of Parliament.

'Means Lord Edm'nton will 'ave to choose himself a new man.' He wiped his nose on the sleeve of his jacket. 'This is the rottenest borough of the lot. Folk 'ere can only vote what got a chimney and an 'arth, and Lord Edm'nton owns all of the cottages with chimneys and 'arths. 'Less you vote the way he says, he throws you out.'

Another said, 'He'll sell the seat to the 'ighest bidder.'

Still another said, 'I 'eard he's already found his man. I also 'eard the other chap's death may not have been an accident.'

'Poppycock,' the cabinetmaker said. 'I 'eard he died of an 'eart attack.'

'Drowned, he did.'

They talked this way for a further half-hour without openly condemning Edmonton, and Pyke found his patience beginning to wane.

It was only in the last place they called into that something happened to elicit Pyke's attention.

Pyke thought himself to be immune to stories of other people's suffering, but there was something about the old man's broken-down manner, his hobbling gait, weather-beaten hands and watery eyes, which he could not dismiss.

The old man had, until very recently, lived with his heavily pregnant daughter and son-in-law in a small thatched cottage built on common land which had subsequently been appropriated by Edmonton. His family had lived in the cottage for two hundred years, or so the old man reckoned, but since they did not own the land, they weren't entitled to any compensation when Edmonton decided that he needed the cottage for other purposes. At the previous election, the old man hadn't bothered to vote, in spite of the fact that, since he resided in a property that boasted a hearth, he was one of the few who was entitled to do so. With another election looming, Edmonton's emissary had informed the old man that his master required someone more reliable in the property. The old man and his family had been evicted a month before his daughter was due to give birth. Two days later, the daughter had gone into premature labour. Both mother and child had perished. A week later, the son-in-law had taken his own life.

With each sentence, the old man had to pause and collect himself, as if the memories were so painful to him he could hardly bear to relive them.

'There was a time when rich folk liked to frighten poor

folk with the idea that Boney and the French were coming and used fear to steal all the land.' The old man grabbed Pyke's sleeve. 'Tell me that time's gone, mister.'

Outside, a wagon passed by and Pyke heard the flattened chink of milk cans.

Without missing a beat, the old man fixed his stare on Pyke. 'You'll make him pay, won't you?'

Pyke removed his sleeve from the old man's surprisingly firm grip. 'I'll do my best,' he said, eventually.

The old man nodded sadly, as though he understood what Pyke was telling him. 'You don't, I'll kill 'im myself.'

Later that night, Pyke and Townsend visited ten farms on Edmonton's estate. Carrying burning torches with them on horseback, they rode along narrow tracks using the moonlight to guide them, and set light to rickyards, barns and outhouses brimming with recently harvested crops. As they did so, Pyke thought about the old man's determination to see that Edmonton was properly punished. Part of him wanted to believe that destroying property on land owned by Edmonton constituted some kind of payback for the grievances suffered by the old man, but he knew that his affinity with such people had long since passed and that his actions, then as now, were motivated by less selfless inclinations.

Still, the damage looked impressive and briefly Pyke wondered whether the old man might hear of, or even witness, the fires and think that his plea for action had somehow been answered. For if anyone had thought to position themselves at the epicentre of the paths they had taken between the various farms, they would have witnessed a night sky that shone so fiercely under the orange glare of burning hay that they might have believed themselves transported to Hell.

*

The following night Pyke made arrangements to sleep in a draughty old church in Saffron Hill. Godfrey knew the rector and, without indicating who Pyke was or what he had done, had persuaded him to allow Pyke to make a bed out of one of the pews. In the light of the attention that was still being paid to him in the newspapers and the extent of the reward being offered for information leading to his arrest, it was now far too dangerous for him to return to the Old Cock tavern.

When Godfrey arrived, a little after ten o'clock, carrying blankets and a bottle of gin, he was out of breath and sweating. After assuring Pyke that he had not been followed, Godfrey recounted that there had been alleged sightings of Pyke right across the city from the Ratcliffe highway in the east to Battersea Fields in the west. He explained that a man who apparently resembled Pyke had been lynched outside the Plough inn, around the corner from his own gin palace. Godfrey told him the gin palace had been further ransacked by fortune hunters who had heard a rumour that Pyke may have been hiding there.

'Did you bring my laudanum?' Pyke asked, while digesting these developments.

Reluctantly, Godfrey produced the small bottle from his coat pocket.

'Are you sure you know what you're getting yourself into?' His uncle's expression suggested both concern and discomfort. 'You do know the farmers lost everything. Barns, equipment, the entire harvest. I fancy this was the point. I mean, they won't be able to pay Edmonton what they owe him in rent.'

'Is that my problem?' Pyke stood up and walked to the end of the pew.

'What of the ordinary men and women who'll go hungry this winter because there isn't enough food to go around?'

It was dark inside the church, but not so dark that Pyke could not see the expression on Godfrey's face.

'People are starving right now because Edmonton is squeezing every last penny from them.' Pyke dug his hands into his pockets to keep them warm.

'And he'll continue to squeeze and eventually someone will bite back and then he'll squeeze even harder, and more and more people will be hurt in the process.' Godfrey seemed puzzled. 'Is that what you want?'

Pyke did not meet his stare. 'Did I ask you to find out whatever you could about a man called Jimmy Swift?'

'Three times. You described him for me, too.' Godfrey shook his head and waited for a moment. 'I don't know what to say . . . I just . . .' He stared at Pyke awkwardly. 'I'm just worried about you, that's all.'

Pyke reached down and picked up the bottle of gin. He opened it and took a swig. 'Thank you for bringing this and the blankets.'

The serrated edge of the blade cut into Polly Masters' leathery throat and drew a few droplets of blood. Standing behind her, Pyke locked his left arm around her neck.

It was a dank, windowless room. The walls had been stained black with coal dust and on the ceiling there were large circular smudges from where candles had been left to burn. Close-up, Polly Masters' skin smelled of camphor and rancid mutton. Barely twitching, she muttered, 'That you, Pyke?'

'Who else did you tell about Mary Johnson?' He repeated the question he had just asked.

'I don't ever show my feelings, Pyke, but when I heard they was gonna kill you, I did a little jig,' she whispered hoarsely.

'Someone tracked Mary and her boyfriend Gerald down

to an inn in Isleworth. This person strangled them and dumped the bodies on Hounslow Heath.'

'I din't tell no one 'bout Mary.'

Pyke pressed the blade deeper into her neck. More blood bubbled up from the wound. 'No one else, apart from you, knew where they were hiding.'

'I swear, I din't tell a soul.' Her tone remained defiant.

'Mary Johnson was a nice girl who didn't deserve to die. I don't care whether you liked or hated her. I know you're a greedy woman and you would have sold her out in the blink of an eye. But I want to hear it from you. I want to know who you told about Mary's whereabouts. I want a name or I want a description.'

Polly Masters tried to wriggle free from his armlock but couldn't manage it. Eventually she exhaled loudly and croaked, 'You're a marked man, Pyke. Downstairs, there must be close to a hundred men who'd kill each other for the chance to pummel you with their bare knuckles and collect the reward what's been offered. There's men givin' out handbills with your likeness across the whole city. All I have to do is scream . . .'

'And I'd slit your throat and leave you to bleed to death on the floor like a slaughtered pig,' Pyke said, jabbing the knife even deeper into her flesh. 'Like you said, I'm a marked man. I don't have anything left to lose.'

Her bruised lip quivered with anticipation.

'Tell me the truth this time,' he said, slowly. 'Did someone come here asking about Mary Johnson?'

'No.'

'Polly, I want the truth. Did a man with a brown mole on his chin come here asking for Mary?'

'*No.*'

'One last time. Did you tell anyone where Mary Johnson was hiding?'

'Fuck you, Pyke.' Polly Masters was crying now. 'You're a monster. Fuck you, fuck you and fuck you again.'

Later, as Pyke wandered through the mud-crusted alleyways and cobbled streets around Covent Garden, comfortable in his disguise, he thought about Polly's defiance and decided she had probably been telling him the truth. But just because Swift had not found out about Mary Johnson from Polly Masters did not mean he hadn't strangled her. No one else apart from Pyke had known which guest house she had been staying at.

So how had they found her? How had *Swift* found her? Pyke sensed that the answer was staring him in the face but he still couldn't work it out.

It was raining and mud clung to his boots, weighing them down as he walked. Ignoring the outstretched hands of a sooty-faced beggar and walking past an old man who was chewing on a bar of soap in order to simulate having a fit, he tried to arrange his thoughts.

Pyke liked the grimy anonymity the city afforded him but knew he belonged neither to the world that Polly Masters inhabited – that grubby, hand-to-mouth existence he'd known for much of his early life – nor to Emily's comfortable world, where propriety and social mores determined what was and wasn't permissible. Pyke wasn't naive or rich enough to romanticise the poverty he had once known, but nor was he blind to the suffocating aspect of privilege that seemed to characterise Emily's circle of acquaintances. It was a curse and a blessing, being able to move between different worlds without feeling a sense of belonging. This adaptability was an advantage, but in his darker moments he wondered whether the loneliness he often felt would be a permanent condition.

Emily came from aristocratic stock and it was folly to contemplate a different life with her. Nonetheless, he felt drawn to her in a way that assumed, perhaps foolishly, that such desires were reciprocal. Part of him wanted to give in to his yearnings, but he was also aware of the dangers this course of action posed. Like it or not, he couldn't get Emily out of his mind. In his pocket, he ran his fingers over the bottle of laudanum to check it was still there.

'Hello, Sir Richard.' Pyke stepped into the light being emitted from candles resting on the mantelpiece. Above the fireplace, on the wall, was a portrait of Sir Henry Fielding.

Fox stopped writing a letter, and looked up at Pyke, suddenly ashen-faced. The quill fell from his trembling ink-stained fingers. He started to say something but the words wouldn't form on his tongue. '*My God*,' he finally managed. 'It *is* you.' He looked older and frailer than Pyke remembered. He had lost some weight, too, and the skin seemed to hang off his face and neck. Fox stood up, grimaced a little, pulled down his frock-coat, and shuffled around his desk to greet him. Pyke wasn't sure whether the old man wanted to hug him or shake his hand. In the end, they managed an awkward mix of the two. 'You *are* alive,' Fox said, not wanting to let go of his arm.

Pyke disentangled himself from Fox's embrace. 'So it would seem.'

'I had given up hope,' Fox said, guardedly.

'I wasn't aware you were hopeful.' He stared at the old man. 'But I see you've been keeping up with recent developments.' He pointed at the newspapers laid out on Fox's desk.

'I heard you were in the capital, of course, but I didn't know whether to believe the stories or not.' Fox's expression was polite and opaque. 'Was that you? The robbery?'

'I came back to take care of some unfinished business.'

'Not with me I hope,' Fox said, with a chuckle.

Pyke raised his eyebrows and folded his arms.

'There was nothing I could have done, Pyke. Nothing at all. Peel wanted you dead. There was no way of overturning the sentence.'

Pyke thought about this for a while. 'Did you even try?'

'You might not have noticed, Pyke, but my authority, such as it is, has been much curtailed these days.' He sounded both aggrieved and irritated.

'I see the new police everywhere.' Pyke walked over to the window and looked out at the Brown Bear tavern on the other side of the street.

'Bodies on the street only matter in times of civil unrest. What this city needs, what I have always hoped that Bow Street might become, is a central clearing house for information regarding crime and criminals. Prevention without detection is as worthless as a pistol without powder.' Fox looked up balefully at the portrait of Sir Henry Fielding. 'But Peel's having none of it. In ten years' time, nothing of the old ways will remain.' He shook his head. 'Listen to me. I sound like a Tory.'

Pyke turned from the window and said, 'I want two things from you. Then I'll never bother you again.'

'What things?' Fox looked at him suspiciously. His eyes narrowed to pale grey slits.

'I want you to provide me with two home addresses. That's all.'

'Addresses?'

'Fitzroy Tilling and Brownlow Vines.'

'What do you want with Brownlow?'

'That's my business, not yours.'

'I don't have Tilling's home address.'

'But you can get it, can't you?'

Fox waited for a moment, pondering Pyke's request. 'I might be able to.'

'What about Vines?'

'Brownlow?' Fox laughed nervously. 'I'm afraid he's out of town at the moment.'

'Where's he gone?'

'I'm not entirely sure. Scotland, I think. For a family wedding.'

Pyke digested this information. 'When will he be back?'

'Another week, perhaps.'

'What's his address, anyway?'

'Can't you tell me what this is all about, Pyke?'

'His address.'

'He lives in Bloomsbury somewhere. I can't remember offhand which street it is. Gerrard would know.' He smiled apologetically.

'Tomorrow, then. I'll come for both addresses at the same time.'

'Of course.' Fox fiddled with his moustache, as he did whenever he was nervous. 'But tell me where I can contact you. I'll send someone with the information.'

Pyke thought about this for a moment. 'No, I think I'll contact you.'

'Really, Pyke, all this cloak-and-dagger stuff . . .'

Pyke cut him off and turned to leave. As he did so, the old man called out his name. Pyke spun around just as Fox was saying, 'You're much . . .'

'Much what?'

'You were never a warm person. I fancy the same could be said about me. Maybe that's why we were able to work together. But even compared to that, you're colder somehow, colder and harder . . .'

Fox's eyes glowed like hot coals behind amber glass, as

though his righteous sense of disappointment were beyond Pyke's comprehension.

The stout physician peered down at Sarah Blackwood's wizened frame and gently tapped his hand against her chest. Throughout his examination, the old woman said nothing; nor did she appear to know where she was, or even that she had been moved from the asylum in Portsmouth. From the threshold of the small room, Pyke watched the proceedings with interest. Behind him, in the adjoining kitchen, the nurse he had hired was preparing dinner. The apartment was situated on the south bank of the river within a stone's throw of Blackfriars Bridge. He had paid three months' rent in advance. The nurse had cost him an additional ten guineas a week.

'You say she has been housed in an asylum for the past fifteen years?' the physician asked, once he had completed his examination.

'As far as I am aware.'

'And you do not know of the circumstances that led to this state of affairs in the first place?'

'I have been told her malady, if indeed she was ill at all, was not a serious one.'

The physician nodded. 'She displays no signs of active cogitation. She doesn't seem to be cognisant of the outside world.'

'In your opinion,' Pyke asked, 'is she mad?'

That drew a short chuckle. 'It would depend on what you mean by mad, sir.' He went to retrieve his hat and coat. 'But if she was not affected by any illness when she first entered this asylum fifteen years ago, your mother is by no means a well or sane woman today.'

Pyke let the remark about 'his' mother pass. 'Is her condition likely to change?'

'You mean is it likely to improve or worsen?'

Pyke nodded.

'In my opinion, your mother's malady is so deep rooted that she will never be roused from her torpor.'

After the physician had left and the nurse had retired for the night, Pyke sat with Emily's mother in the dark and held her bony hand in his own.

TWENTY-TWO

The stone-clad exterior of Newgate prison, long since blackened by smoke and filth, did an acceptable job of concealing what lay inside: the dirty wards, the cold, barren cells and the stink of despair. To the uninitiated, it may have seemed like an ordinary building, but to those who lived in the nearby maze of streets and alleyways, the prison's imposing walls and brooding Palladian architecture cast a dark shadow over the entire neighbourhood. Even the name conjured up dread. Bare-footed children who scampered alongside cabs and the new omnibuses, begging for coins, did not seem to notice its horrible pall. But others, like the group of labouring men gathered outside the Fortune of War tavern, or the hunchbacked man selling Yarmouth herring from an old wicker basket, or the drunken ballad singer who visibly swayed from side to side as he regaled whoever would stop and listen with songs, seemed to be visibly affected by their proximity to the prison.

Fifty years earlier a Protestant mob had rampaged through the streets around the prison and, armed with crowbars and pitchforks, had attacked it in order to free fellow rioters who had been imprisoned within its walls. Some three hundred prisoners had escaped, but at least as many had died in the resulting fire. It had taken the army a number of days to restore calm to the streets of the capital, and the recriminations had been as brutal as the disturbances; more than fifty rioters had been hanged on different scaffolds across the city.

Despite attempts to rebuild and modernise the prison, it remained a dirty, overcrowded, dark and stinking place. As he waited on Old Bailey, Pyke stared up at the fortress-like walls and wondered whether the prison, which had outlived baying mobs, would soon fall victim to reformist zeal, and whether such an eventuality was to be welcomed or mourned.

Of more immediate concern was the presence of two police constables wearing their familiar dark-blue uniform. The constables were fifty yards away, walking towards him on the same side of the street, when Emily emerged from the prison and looked up and down, perhaps for her carriage. It was Thursday afternoon, the allocated time for her weekly prison visit, and whatever problems or difficulties she may have been facing at Hambledon, she would not miss this appointment. Taking her gently by the arm, he led her down one of the alleyways that ran into Old Bailey. Emily was both agitated and pleased to see him. He took off his cap and wiped soot from his face.

'We can't be seen together,' Emily whispered. At the other end of the alleyway, two figures, one male and one female, lurked in the shadows. 'I am to be met outside the prison and taken back to Hambledon.' Her eyes darted nervously back to the street.

'The other night,' Pyke said. 'What did he want?'

Emily laughed bitterly. 'Oh, the usual. Someone to rant at.'

Pyke studied her expression. 'He did not suspect you with regard to the robbery?'

'If he did, he did not say so.' Emily looked at him. She

seemed nervous and a little distant as well. At the far end of the alley, the two figures were slowly moving towards them.

'Is something the matter?' he asked, trying to keep one eye on the man and the woman.

Emily wetted her lips. 'I'm soon to be married.' She sounded both upset and resigned to this prospect. 'As soon as my father can make arrangements.'

'*Married?* That's why he wanted to see you the other night?'

Emily nodded. 'To tell me.' She shrugged apologetically. 'This time, he is insistent.'

He looked at her calmly, waiting. 'I take it you flatly refused him.'

'He said if I didn't marry, then he would disinherit me.'

'He would do that?' As soon as he had asked the question, Pyke realised how stupid it sounded. The question of what Edmonton *wouldn't* do was more pertinent.

Emily confirmed the stupidity of his question with a look of exasperation.

'But you can't marry someone simply because your father tells you to.'

'The money that was settled on me by trust is only a very modest sum.' She refused to look at him. 'If I agree to this marriage, my father has promised to quadruple the amount.'

Pyke thought about Emily's mother and the bleak assessment of the physician.

'And money is that important to you?'

'To my work it is. There are many worthy causes it could be put towards.'

'But you would actually consider marrying some stranger, only for material gain?'

'You make me sound like some kind of courtesan.'

'A stranger selected by Edmonton,' Pyke continued,

regardless of whether he hurt her or not. 'What kind of man might that be?'

'I don't know.' Emily looked down at the ground. Her hands were shaking. 'I haven't met him yet.'

'But you plan to?'

'I don't seem to have a choice.' Emily shrugged. 'I'm told his name is James Sloan. He's a solicitor by profession but has political ambitions. He has just been elected as Member of Parliament to represent a constituency near Hambledon. Perhaps you've heard of him?'

Pyke thought about the farm labourers and their talk about the suspicious death of their sitting parliamentarian.

'I've heard your father bullies people into voting for whichever candidate he has put up.'

Emily looked towards the main street and then down at her pocket watch. 'I can't delay any longer. Perhaps I could visit you later?'

In the other direction, the two figures, a prostitute and her pimp perhaps, were now strolling towards them with purpose.

'You can't marry this man,' Pyke said bluntly.

Emily adjusted her bonnet. 'Tell me where you're staying and we can talk about this later. I'll find an excuse to get out of Hambledon.'

Pyke told her about the church. 'What about everything you said to me the other night about not wanting to marry *at all*?'

'I know.' Her expression was pained. 'It's just not that straightforward.'

The prostitute and the pimp were only ten or fifteen yards away when the two police constables stopped at the end of the alley and looked towards them. Instinctively, Pyke pulled Emily towards him and pressed his lips against hers. It was an awkward kiss. The two police constables called out, either to them or to the pimp and the prostitute, and proceeded to walk briskly down the alleyway towards them. Pyke pulled Emily into an even closer embrace. Beyond them, the couple ran back down the alley in the opposite direction. The police constables passed them without comment.

Long after Emily had gathered up her skirt and hurried to her waiting carriage, Pyke could taste both the lingering sweetness of her kiss and her fear and reticence.

Later that afternoon, Pyke met Townsend in a country inn on the outskirts of Enfield. It was a bare room with whitewashed walls and sanded floors. Farm labourers dressed in smock-frocks sat around a large wooden table exchanging stories. A lurcher lay in front of the open fire. When they first entered the inn, conversations paused and heads turned towards them, but they were soon ignored. A pot boy brought them porter in pewter tankards from the adjoining taproom. Pyke asked about Goddard's wife and how she had reacted to news of his death.

Townsend muttered that it had been terrible, having to inform her, but did not elaborate on this. As they drank, Pyke found himself wondering how much he could trust Townsend and whether he might be tempted to claim the reward that was being offered for Pyke's capture in order to avenge Goddard's death.

Townsend told him that a private militia acting under Edmonton's orders had ransacked and closed down three village inns used regularly by the protesters. This had, in turn, provoked a series of counteractions. In one instance, a mob had attacked the village priest and dragged him through a duck pond. In another, a group of workers had used sledgehammers to destroy a threshing machine on a farm near Waltham Abbey. In the meantime, Canning and

Saville had produced a clutch of handbills advertising a protest meeting and distributed them in the affected villages. The meeting was due to take place that evening on the land of a farmer who had long resented Edmonton's exorbitant rents.

'What about any news of this man Jimmy Swift?' Pyke asked.

'I'm afraid there's nothing at all. No one seems to have heard of him or know anything about him.'

'In spite of the reward?' Pyke was incredulous. It was almost impossible for someone to disappear without trace.

'There are people who claim they know where he is, of course, because of the reward, but as yet no one's actually managed to identify him.'

Townsend gave him one of the handbills. It announced the date, time and place of the meeting and listed a series of grievances and unspectacular demands. At the bottom of the handbill was a quote: 'The laws passed within the last fifty years present an unbroken and unparalleled series of endeavours to enrich and increase the power of the aristocracy and to impoverish the labouring people.'

If nothing else, such a quote would get under Edmonton's skin.

'And Edmonton's likely to hear about this?'

'Almost certainly,' Townsend said, warily. 'Given the number of handbills we've distributed.'

'Edmonton won't let an opportunity like this pass.'

'It doesn't seem likely,' Townsend said, staring down into his tankard.

Pyke waited for a moment. 'If you have a problem with what I'm doing, then say so.'

'A lot of ordinary men and women are going to be caught in the middle and some might get hurt.' Townsend shrugged. 'That's all.'

'But we're not forcing anyone to come to the meeting who doesn't want to.'

'No, we're not.'

'And the fact that these people have been driven to near-breaking point isn't our doing, is it?'

'No, it's not,' Townsend said, still refusing to meet Pyke's stare. 'But there'll be a lot of anger in that barn.'

'I'm sure there will be.'

'And when Edmonton's militia turns up?'

'There'll probably be some fighting,' Pyke said, trying not to think about what might happen.

This time Townsend looked up at him. 'And what are we supposed to do, when this fighting breaks out?'

Pyke stared at him. He had nothing to say that would alleviate Townsend's righteous sense of guilt.

They arrived in twos and threes. Some walked, others came on horse-drawn carts, others rode donkeys. They trudged into the barn in their coats, frocks, pantaloons, breeches, boots and shoes, young and old men alike, some with whiskers and others who were cleanly shaven. By seven o'clock, as dusk settled over the freshly harvested fields and gently rolling hills, there were fifty or sixty people crowded into the small barn. Inside, Saville and Canning were addressing the gathering. Meanwhile, Pyke had positioned himself behind an oak tree, some fifty yards from the barn's entrance. It was a cold night, almost cold enough for a frost, but the skies were clear and, though it was not dark enough to see the stars, a half-moon was visible above the farmhouse.

Pyke heard them before he saw them: the sound of hoofs moving in unison, vibrating against the hard ground.

They turned on to the track that led up to the farm, at least ten of them, all riding horses and holding torches.

They rode slowly but with purpose along the flinty track and came to a halt about a hundred yards from where Pyke was standing. In the light of their torches, he scanned their faces and was disappointed not to see Swift among them.

As they gathered together in a circle, all on horseback, one of their rank, their leader perhaps, addressed them in hushed tones. Pyke tried to determine who this man was, but his view was blocked by another rider. In the barn, a raucous cheer erupted from the gathered crowd which seemed to get the raiding party's attention. Pyke could not hear what they were saying to each other, but they were clearly preparing themselves to attack; they lined up in formation alongside one another, their torches held aloft. From somewhere behind them, their leader gave the signal and the men roused their horses into action. It did not take them long to pick up speed, and once they had done so, and were bearing in on their target, they started to shout: angry, blood-curdling cries whose sole purpose was to terrorise those inside the barn. As the horses thundered past him, Pyke scanned their faces again, but saw no one he recognised.

Just as the first figures stumbled out of the barn, the raiders were upon them, scything them down and using their torches to set the rickety wooden building alight. Moments later, the trickle of men emerging from the barn became a deluge. As they spilled out into the darkness, the raiders were waiting for them and attacked without mercy; some were trampled under hoofs, others were beaten with sticks and set alight.

It was a bloody sight and Pyke bore his own responsibility for initiating the conflict heavily. He tried to close his eyes to the horror of what was happening but the cruelty of the raiders and the helplessness of the protesters elicited a feeling of self-disgust.

As he scanned the faces of the mob, he saw the familiar gait of the old man who had lost his daughter and grand-child. He was trying to hobble to safety when one of the men on horseback flew past him and struck him on the head with what looked like a makeshift hammer. The old man went down. The rider pulled up the horse, turned around and without another thought rode the horse over the old man's prostrate figure. The man quivered for a moment and then stopped moving.

But Pyke's attention was distracted by one of the raiding party who had kept himself back from the fray and was watching the unfolding mayhem from a safe distance. Without pausing to determine whether this was Swift or not, he scurried across the track that led to the farm, concealing himself in the shadows of the grassy verge. Ten yards away, he paused to take aim with the pistol; his plan was to shoot the horse and take Swift alive.

He steadied himself and cocked the pistol.

But in the instant before Pyke fired, something alerted the horse to his presence and the animal reared upwards; the shot whistled harmlessly past its head.

In these circumstances, most riders would have fallen off. But Swift – if indeed that was who it was – was a skilled horseman and remained upright, even as the horse reared up. Before Pyke could further unsettle the animal, or reload the pistol, the rider had managed to calm the horse down and goad it into action. With the man clinging to its back, the animal bolted off along the track, leaving Pyke on the ground staring upwards into a cloud of dust. But just before the galloping horse turned the corner at the end of the hedge-lined track, the rider pulled up and, turning around to face him, waited for a few moments and waved.

*

'I have come with a message from my mistress.' Jo's timid voice echoed around the draughty church. She removed her bonnet and approached the pew where Pyke was sitting, with obvious caution.

Sensing her unease, Pyke invited her to take a seat, but she ignored his offer and opted to remain where she was. 'I was under the impression that Emily planned to visit herself.' He watched as she brushed the rain from her short red hair.

Jo looked down at her feet. 'She instructed me to tell you that Edmonton will not permit her to leave Hambledon.'

'I see.'

For a while, neither of them seemed to know what to say. 'Mr Pyke . . .'

'Please,' he said, gently, 'Pyke will do.' He tried to smile. 'I'm not used to being addressed in such a formal manner.'

This drew a pained expression. 'Miss Blackwood has been so good to me, and I don't want to lose my job . . .'

'Please don't blame yourself,' Pyke said, raising his hand. 'It was not your fault. I shouldn't have . . .' He hesitated, not sure what else to say.

But this seemed enough to put her at ease. 'She's so unhappy. She didn't tell me to say that to you, but I thought I should say something anyway.'

Pyke stood up and rubbed his hands together to keep them warm. 'Is it your impression she intends to go ahead with this marriage?'

'I know such a thought appals her.'

'But she's at least willing to contemplate it as a possibility?'

'It is not a question of being willing, I think.' This time Jo raised her eyes to meet his stare.

'But she *is* on the verge of succumbing to her father's bullying?'

'I wouldn't know about that, but . . .' Jo hesitated, as though unsure about whether she should continue. She pulled her woollen shawl tighter around her shoulders.

'Go on.'

'I know she's to meet this man the day after tomorrow. He's sending a carriage for her.'

Pyke studied her expression. 'Did Emily instruct you to inform me of this meeting?'

'Not in so many words.' Jo stared up at the ceiling of the church. 'But I know how unhappy she is at the prospect of it.'

Pyke assessed her seemingly well-intentioned concern. 'Perhaps I may ask another question?'

Jo gave him an unsettled look.

'Have you heard of Edmonton's threats to disinherit her? Or, indeed, to quadruple her allowance, should she agree to marry this man?'

'I have not heard such a conversation for myself but my mistress has informed me of certain matters.'

'And you think this is why Emily is considering the claims of this suitor?'

'In part.'

'Only in part?'

'Mr . . .' Jo hesitated. 'Sorry . . . *Pyke.*' She looked at him and smiled. 'I overheard a conversation at Hambledon between Lord Edmonton and his lawyer. I haven't yet told my mistress what I learned but I presume that she is aware of what they talked about.'

Pyke nodded at her to continue.

'As far as I understand it, Lord Edmonton has not simply threatened to disinherit my mistress, should she refuse to countenance this marriage. He has also instructed his lawyer to draw up a codicil to his will. From what I could gather from their conversation, the codicil states that if, at any point following Lord Edmonton's death and the death of any of my mistress's future husbands, she should marry you, then she would forfeit any claim to her inheritance and the family estate.'

'I am to be personally named in this new document?'

'As I understand it.' Her manner was almost apologetic.

So it was a choice between him and the money, Pyke thought bitterly. The fat lord was indeed a formidable adversary.

'And how can I contact Emily, should I need to,' Pyke asked, 'if she's to be kept locked up in her quarters?'

Jo told him Emily would make arrangements to contact him.

'Where? Here?'

Jo shrugged and said she did not know.

'Here,' he said, scribbling his uncle's address down on a scrap of paper. 'Should Emily need to get in touch.' Pyke waited for a moment. 'Thank you for making the journey from Hambledon.'

This time, Jo could not bring herself to look at him. 'I just want what is best for my mistress.' She fidgeted, shifting her body weight awkwardly from foot to foot.

'But I have yet another reason to be grateful to *you* in particular.'

This time Jo neither answered him nor even looked at him. He approached her, smiling.

'Do you know what I'm referring to?'

'No.'

'The occasion you warned me about the assault in the Blue Dog tavern.' As Jo tried to leave, he grabbed her wrist. 'Well?'

She stared at him like a trapped rabbit but managed to mutter, 'I don't know what you mean.'

'You shouted my name. I presume to warn me.' He

tightened his hold on her wrist. 'But I cannot for the life of me work out why you might have been following me in the first place.'

'I have never even been to that place.' She grimaced, struggling in vain to free herself from Pyke's grip.

'You concealed your face well under the bonnet. But it was your voice that gave you away.'

'I'm afraid you're mistaken, sir.'

'Am I?' Pyke let go of her wrist, aware that he had perhaps bruised her, and watched as she gathered up her skirt and hurried from the church.

TWENTY-THREE

Sir Richard Fox disembarked from his private carriage and was hurrying towards the entrance to number five Bow Street when Pyke caught up with him. Pyke was dressed as a beggar and Fox did not recognise him until he said, 'Don't look at me, Sir Richard. Just keep on walking, as though you have somewhere else to go.'

Rigid as a washboard, Fox did as he was told. Though Pyke could not be certain, it struck him that Fox may have been frightened.

Thirty yards past the Bow Street offices, they came to a halt. Pyke looked around, to make sure that no one had followed them. The street was thronging with the usual traffic of carriages, carts and traders.

'The addresses,' he said, not bothering with any formalities.

Fox looked around him, as though searching for assistance. 'I told you yesterday, Pyke. Vines is away at the moment.'

'His address.'

'It's somewhere in the office, if you want to come in with me and wait . . .' He smoothed his moustache.

'Tilling's, then.'

'Ah, yes, I managed to find that one for you.' He reached into his jacket, pulled out his wallet, removed a scrap of paper and thrust it into Pyke's outstretched hand.

Pyke read what was on the scrap, stuffed it into his own pocket and said, 'I'll be back for Vines's address.'

Pyke was already five yards along the street, disappearing into the crowd, when he heard Fox shout, '*Pyke.*'

It was an innocent mistake, or so Pyke believed — uttering the name of an old friend or acquaintance, as one might do under normal circumstances. But its consequences were startling. At first, other passers-by seemed not to have heard Fox's mistake, or at least did not outwardly respond to it. Pyke pulled the cap down over his face and walked briskly in the direction of Covent Garden market, trying not to draw attention to himself. But after a few moments, the impact of this public utterance of his name percolated into the minds of those who had heard it, a few looked at him and finally one shouted, '*That's Pyke.*' The effect of these words was astonishing. Perhaps it was simply the reward money: five hundred pounds was a monumental, almost unheard-of, sum, and suddenly everyone on Bow Street could taste a share of it. Another voice shouted, '*That's Pyke, that is.*' Still another, '*Someone stop 'im.*' It was possible his name electrified those who heard it for different reasons: some may have been afraid, others wanted to see him hang. In the end, the effect was the same: suddenly he was a marked man and others joined the hunt. 'Is that 'im?' one asked. Another said, 'He's got a pistol.' Still another said, 'Just kill him. They'll pay up for a corpse too.'

Pyke darted into a side street and broke into a run. Doing so may have been a mistake: it unnecessarily drew attention to him. But he could not help it. He needed to put as much distance between himself and his pursuers as possible. That was his ambition, but alerted to his presence by shouts from behind, others were spilling out of dilapidated buildings almost at the same moment as he was passing them.

Turning into an even smaller alleyway, he pushed his way past a newsboy. From behind, someone tried to grab his shoulder; he pulled himself free and ducked into a dingy entrance. Shouts followed. It was a pawnshop: there were racks of shawls, petticoats, skirts, stays, gowns, shirt-fronts, handkerchiefs and trousers. Ignoring the owner, he barged his way through the shop, knocking over piles of clothes as he did so. He kicked down the back door, and found himself in a small courtyard, surrounded by buildings. A fighting dog, chained to its kennel, sprang to its feet and growled at him through bared teeth. Pyke took no notice of it and forced his way into another building on the other side of the court. He could still hear voices behind him. This time he found himself in the kitchen of a lodging house: a fire was blazing in the grate, rashers of bacon suspended before it. Around a table sat seven or eight men dressed in working clothes. No one made any effort to block his path. As he left the lodging house, this time by the front entrance, he could not see any sign of his pursuers. Across the alley-way, he entered another lodging house, this one more run down, and pushed his way through to the back of the building, where he found himself in an identical courtyard. This time, however, he hesitated for a moment and looked behind him.

No one seemed to have followed him.

It was dark and quiet in the yard. Above him rain fell lightly out of a desolate sky. Pyke kept moving deeper and deeper into the rookery. If he had stopped to think about it, he might have likened himself to a hunted animal, but such was his fear, and his desire to evade capture, that he did not once pause to consider his predicament. Perhaps his nerves were dulled by the laudanum. In any case, he felt oddly calm by the time he finally came to a halt, in an empty skittle yard attached to a beer shop. At first he just chuckled, but very soon this had mutated into a deep belly-laugh and finally into uncontrolled hysteria. He laughed because he was not yet dead.

From the bay window in Fitzroy Tilling's front room, the view took in Hampstead Heath and extended far beyond to the sprawling metropolis, which spilled out in every direction. A blanket of fog clung to the city's smoke-blackened buildings, and the sun was barely visible through the murkiness.

From a cursory inspection, Pyke concluded that it was a masculine environment and, as such, was appropriately anonymous. There were no personal effects in the rooms and few decorative features. The ground floor comprised a front and a back room, in addition to the small – and from what Pyke could tell unused – kitchen in the basement. The rooms were furnished with dingy Turkey carpets and an assortment of old-fashioned tables and chairs. Above the fireplace in the front room sat two old-fashioned silver candlesticks, but otherwise the furnishings were sparse and utilitarian.

Pyke had inserted a thin metal instrument between the sash windows at the back of the house and undone the catch.

While he waited for Tilling to return, he perused the books lining the walls of the back room. He was surprised at the overlap with his own interests, but whereas he was self-educated and could read the works of Machiavelli or Descartes only in translation, Tilling had their original works in Italian and French.

Tilling finally arrived home shortly after seven in the evening. He was dressed in the same jacket and trousers as he had worn the previous time they had met in the basement of Whitehall. Beneath the jacket, his white linen shirt glowed against dark skin. His gaze swept the room, his bug-like eyes pulled close together with worry, as though he sensed that something was amiss even before he spotted Pyke sitting on one of his horsehair chairs in the front room.

Tilling did not seem unduly concerned or surprised by Pyke's presence in his home, though on closer inspection his tar-black hair, which had seemed greasy at first, was slick with perspiration.

'I fancied it would only be a matter of time before you tried to make contact,' Tilling said, entering the small front room. Walking towards a cupboard at the back of the room, he asked Pyke whether he wanted a drink.

Tilling poured them both a brandy. At the last minute, Pyke took the glass Tilling was about to drink from.

Tilling smiled at the switch. 'After all that's happened, I can understand why you might be nervous.' His smile became a smirk. 'That's quite a trail of destruction you have left behind. Governor Hunt *and* John Arnold. And now I read about arson attacks and rioting on land owned by Edmonton. You're a veritable one-man Armageddon.' He held up his glass and said, 'To your health.' He looked at Pyke and smiled. 'So tell me something. Have you got a particular problem with authority figures or do you just like killing them?'

'It would depend on the authority figure in question.' He regarded Tilling with a dispassionate stare. 'Why is Peel nervous?' He felt tired and washed out from the laudanum he had taken the previous night, and bloated from the pastries and sweet cakes he'd consumed that morning.

'Should he be?'

'That's what I'm here to find out.'

'Holding a gun to the Home Secretary's head with half of

London looking for you.' Tilling raised his bushy eyebrows. 'I'm a little impressed.'

'Only a little?'

'I'm impressed you haven't been captured.' Tilling smiled. 'You're the most wanted man in the country.'

Pyke took a sip of brandy. 'I didn't get the impression you were on particularly friendly terms with John Arnold.' The fiery liquid did little to settle his stomach.

'I wasn't.' Tilling shrugged. 'I couldn't stand any of the Orange Order. Neither could Peel, despite the nickname O'Connell gave him. Still, aside from his bluster, Arnold wasn't the worst of them.'

Pyke watched his expression carefully. 'You're sorry to see him dead?'

'Not really.' Tilling shrugged.

'But when you were stationed in Ulster, you agreed to assist the man, didn't you? On his request, you rode to Armagh and recruited a brawny Protestant thug into the Irish Constabulary.'

'It's the way political business is conducted, Pyke. As I remember, Peel required the order's assistance in some matter.'

'So you went to Loughgall and told Davy Magennis the new Irish Constabulary needed good strong Protestant men like him.'

'I can't remember exactly *what* I said to him.'

'But you washed your hands of him quick enough, when he nearly beat a Catholic man to death in front of a thousand witnesses.'

'No, in fact I was keen to prosecute him, but I was told such a practice wasn't conducive to the long-term stability of the Union. As it was explained to me, how could I punish a young lad from an upstanding Orange family for simply doing what came naturally to him?'

Tilling shrugged and looked down, as a ginger cat with white paws strolled into the room and jumped up on to his lap. He shrugged. 'The cat must have got in through the window you left open.' He patted the purring animal on his head. 'He sometimes comes to visit me.' Tilling looked at him. 'We did what we could. We dismissed him from the force.'

Pyke allowed himself a weak smile. 'I'm gratified to know that your conscience is clear.'

'And it makes *me* feel a whole lot better to know that you approve.'

Pyke ignored his sarcasm. 'And this was the last you heard of him?'

Tilling nodded. 'Until you came to see me in March and dangled his name in front of me.'

'You did a reasonable job of hiding your concern.'

'But not good enough.' Tilling's eyebrows were arched in amusement.

'Your reaction revealed you knew Magennis. At the time, I was also fairly sure Magennis had killed those people. It didn't seem possible it was an innocent coincidence. Quite reasonably, I assumed that if you knew Magennis, and Magennis had killed those people, then you must have been involved in the murders, too.'

Tilling's expression revealed little. 'But I didn't stand to gain anything from slaughtering innocent people. Neither did Peel.'

'On the contrary,' Pyke said, taking another sip of brandy. 'The murders strengthened the case for police reform. Afterwards, people were falling over themselves to demand a better police force.'

Tilling shook his head, angry for the first time. 'The case for a new police force had already been made. Peel had won the argument through skill and hard work. We didn't need to kill anyone, let alone a young family, to make our case.' Tilling looked at him coolly. 'And in case you have forgotten, the government wanted to push through two pieces of legislation: the police bill *and* Catholic emancipation. By the time those people were butchered in St Giles, Peel had already thrown his weight behind Catholic emancipation. And those murders made it a hundred times harder to force the legislation through both Houses.'

'I know.' Pyke exhaled loudly. 'In the end, I reached the same conclusion. I knew, or I believed, you were involved because of your link with Davy Magennis, but I couldn't see what you or Peel had to gain.'

Tilling cut in. 'We had nothing to gain and everything to lose.'

'But that notion only struck me much later. Before I went to Ireland, I was so obsessed with the idea of implicating you and Peel I didn't see what was right in front of me.'

'Which was?'

'I'd been set up from the outset.'

'By Edmonton?' Tilling asked, as though he didn't already know the answer.

'I think Edmonton planned for me to discover the bodies.'

'How did he manage to do that?'

Pyke chose to ignore the question. 'When I first glanced down into that metal pail, I thought it was an animal of some kind.'

'And you believed Peel himself might have sanctioned such a heinous act?'

'I see you're a widely read man. Sometimes moral absolutes can be as harmful as acts of kindness. People have committed terrible crimes in the name of some greater good.'

Tilling paused, rubbing his eyes. 'Peel might be prickly and arrogant but he's not a killer.'

'But he presided over a murder investigation that wilfully identified, pursued and, in the end, executed a wholly innocent man.'

Tilling was visibly shaken by this accusation. 'In that particular instance, the circumstantial evidence seemed to be compelling.' He wiped his forehead with the sleeve of his jacket.

'As compelling as the existence of a family member who had good reason to hate his brother and who had been seen in the vicinity of the lodging house on the same day as the murders?'

'You're right that such a claim should have been investigated more thoroughly.' Tilling seemed downcast.

'But to do so would have been to acknowledge, and lay bare, your own connection to the chief suspect.'

Still unsettled, Tilling gently lifted the cat down on to the floor. It yawned and stretched a little. 'It is a folly of mine, but I like to give the cat a saucer of milk. Excuse me for a moment.' He disappeared into the kitchen and the cat followed jauntily. When he returned, Pyke said, 'Meanwhile, an innocent man gets put to death for something he didn't do.'

Tilling stared at him coldly. 'Do you have unequivocal proof that Magennis committed those murders?'

Pyke thought about what he had learned from the priest in Ireland.

'I know Edmonton meant me to find Magennis or at least find out about him. Whatever else I am, I'm a good investigator. Edmonton knew this, too.' Pyke shrugged. 'Edmonton also knew that Hume's attempts to threaten me and close down my investigation would spur me on.'

'That was the whole point, wasn't it?' Tilling looked at

him carefully, waiting. 'Once you had decided that Magennis was the killer, and then witnessed Peel's investigation go after the wrong suspect, and then discovered the connection between Magennis and myself, what other conclusion could you have drawn?'

'You mean that Peel was implicated in the murders?'

'Of course.'

'And Edmonton gets what he wants; the events stir up a hornet's nest of anti-Catholic sentiment and threaten the smooth passage of the Catholic Emancipation Bill. By getting me to expose Peel's alleged culpability in the murders . . .'

'Edmonton might have been able to bring down the whole administration and ruin Peel's political career in the process.' He regarded Pyke with a quizzical stare. 'I suppose we should be grateful to you – now that Edmonton's plans have been foiled and he's taken it upon himself to destroy you.'

'I am glad to be of service.' Pyke couldn't help but smile. 'But I'm not naive enough to think that such a notion will persuade the Home Secretary to come to my assistance.'

Tilling's gaze slid away from Pyke's face. 'Assuming that Edmonton did manage to set this whole thing up, I still don't understand how he found Davy Magennis in the first place and made the connection back to me.'

Pyke thought about what he had discovered in Ireland but said nothing to Tilling; he wanted to keep all knowledge of Swift to himself.

'Perhaps we might go for a walk on the heath. Get some fresh air and continue our talk outside.' Tilling must have noticed Pyke's reaction because almost at once he laughed and said, 'What? You don't trust me? You don't think I could have had you arrested already?' He shook his head jovially. 'When I returned home, I noticed the gate at the side of the house had been tampered with. I thought initially it might have been house burglars but then I remembered you.' He picked up his brandy glass and drained it. 'Come on, Pyke. Accompany me on a walk.'

It was a pleasant evening and some of the smog had cleared, affording them an arresting view of the city.

'Sometimes I wonder what it would be like to live in another town or in the country perhaps, but then I come out here on an evening like this, the sun just about to set and everything looking so peaceful, and I can't imagine living anywhere else.'

Pyke paused for a moment, to take in the view. 'There,' he said, pointing towards the giant dome of St Paul's. 'Just to the right, you can see the Sessions House and, next to it, Newgate prison.'

They had walked almost to the top of the hill. Tilling turned to face him, hands in pockets. 'I take your point.'

'Do you?' This time Pyke allowed himself to show his anger. 'Can you imagine what it was like, being locked up in that God-forsaken place, knowing I was to be executed for something I hadn't done?'

Tilling started to walk again. 'You might not believe me, but Peel liked you. He wanted to help you, Pyke, but given what happened at your trial, the manner in which you ran your own defence and the fact the jury found you guilty, there was nothing at all he could have done.'

'I think Peel had done quite enough already.'

That seemed to confuse Tilling.

Pyke laughed bitterly. 'Once you realised I had found out about Magennis, you moved quickly.'

This time Tilling touched him on the arm. 'You think that business with your mistress was *our* doing?'

'That business? Let's call it by its proper name, Tilling.

Murdering Lizzie in cold blood and then making it look like I had killed her.'

Tilling stared at him, incredulous. 'My God, you actually think Peel and I planned all that?' He sounded upset.

'Well, it couldn't have been Edmonton. I mean, he didn't want me locked up or executed. It didn't suit his plans. Think about it. He wanted me out there, stirring up trouble and making the connection between Magennis and you public. You see, the moment I was arrested his plan failed. The whole conspiracy was finished. In the end, nothing about the link between Peel and Magennis was ever made public. And Peel, the administration, all of you, emerged unscathed.'

That seemed to placate Tilling. 'So all along, you've been working from the premise that Peel arranged to have your mistress killed and then you framed for the murder.' He still sounded shocked.

'Maybe I still am. For a start, there was the timing. I happened to mention Davy Magennis to you and two days later Lizzie is murdered and I'm in prison. What am I meant to think?' Tilling stood there, with a puzzled look on his face. 'Then there's the business with Brownlow Vines,' Pyke added.

'What business with Vines?' Tilling's confusion seemed to be genuine. 'What's he got to do with this?'

Pyke told him what had happened on the night of Lizzie's murder.

Tilling stared at him, aghast. 'None of this came out in the trial.'

'What was the point? I assumed the verdict had already been determined before the trial had even started.'

'And you believed that Vines was dispatched by Peel in order to drug you?'

'It made sense at the time.' Pyke stared out across the

city. It was almost dark. 'There's no doubt in my mind Vines administered the drug. I just assumed he had cut a deal with Peel. A top job in the new police force or something like that.'

Tilling seemed to find such a notion amusing.

'I'm glad you find my predicament funny.' But Pyke felt confused more than anything.

Since his return from Ireland, he had known that his initial suspicions regarding Peel's involvement in the St Giles murders were unfounded. Nonetheless, he had still been convinced of Peel's complicity in Lizzie's murder. It was not that he believed Peel to be a heartless monster. Rather, he had assumed Peel had taken the decision to kill Lizzie and frame him for pragmatic reasons. Now, though, Tilling's forceful denial had deflated that theory, and Pyke had to face up to the unappealing truth that he had no idea who had butchered Lizzie.

In the gloom, Tilling's expression darkened. 'I was only laughing because, as I said earlier, I find the idea Peel might have involved himself in such a base plot to be, quite frankly, ridiculous. I have worked with him for twenty years. He might be self-interested, arrogant and aloof but he is not a cold-blooded murderer.'

'I'm almost persuaded by your testimony.'

'Almost?'

'You didn't see the note Peel sent me while in prison.'

'Ah, the note.' Tilling smiled. '*We can say cruelty is used well when it is employed once and for all, and one's safety depends on it and then it is not persisted in but as far as possible turned to the good of one's subjects.*'

Pyke remembered the volumes in Tilling's library. 'Peel gave me the impression *he* was the admirer of Machiavelli.'

'He has read *The Prince*. But Peel is a politician, not a philosopher or an intellectual. What do you expect?'

Tilling shrugged. 'I'd wager you and I are the amoral pragmatists.'

Suddenly Pyke felt foolish for having suspected the Home Secretary.

'However much he might have wanted to, Peel was not in a position to grant you a pardon,' Tilling said, matter-of-factly. 'That was all the note was supposed to indicate.'

'And Vines?' Pyke said, hollowly. He had been so sure of Peel's hand in Lizzie's murder and his own imprisonment that he had not even contemplated an alternative scenario. Now, he had no idea how he would avenge her death.

Tilling shrugged. 'We *did* approach Vines and consulted him about the police bill in order to determine where his loyalties lay.'

'And?'

'As far as we could tell, they remained squarely aligned with Sir Richard.'

Pyke nodded, trying to digest this information. 'I'll need a private audience with him.'

'Who, Vines?' Tilling asked.

'No, Peel.'

'Out of the question,' Tilling said, shaking his head.

'Away from Whitehall. Somewhere like your house, for example.'

'Perhaps if you had come to us with all this before the trial, he might have been able to grant you a pardon. I presume that's what you want? But not after everything you have done, everything that has happened.'

Pyke had expected such a response and was not put off by it. 'Tell Peel that it will be in his own interest to make the appointment. Point out I'm not a man to be underestimated.'

'Oh, believe me, Peel is well aware of that fact.'

'So you'll arrange a meeting? Tomorrow evening. At your house.'

'I'll see what I can do.' Tilling waited for a moment. 'But I can tell you one thing. Peel won't tolerate any more of this carry-on with Edmonton. The situation's spiralling out of control. He's going to dispatch the Seventh Dragoons to the area to quell any further unrest.'

'Edmonton has made his own bed,' Pyke said, coldly.

'That may be, but Peel will want a line drawn under *everything*.'

Pyke thought about this for a moment. There was still so much he didn't know or couldn't work out. 'And Edmonton?'

'What about Edmonton?'

'What am I supposed to do with him?'

'That's your business, Pyke, not mine.'

Tilling touched his arm and told Pyke he would try to arrange the meeting for the following day. As he turned to leave, he paused and said, almost as an afterthought, 'Do what you need to do but do it *quickly*.'

Pyke stood there and watched Tilling stroll down the hill, and did not move until he was a faint speck in the distance.

TWENTY-FOUR

When Pyke visited Hambledon Hall for the second time, the conditions were just as foul as they had been on the first occasion. It was not quite as cold, for it was October rather than February, but a fierce easterly wind drove billowing clouds across the flat, unprotected valley with such intensity that rain fell horizontally rather than vertically. Still, the inclement weather suited his mood and, anyway, Pyke could not have imagined the ugly monstrosity of Hambledon Hall bathed in warm sunlight. The hall had been constructed on marshy terrain and the relentless uniformity of the landscape gave the setting a menacing feel, as though the land had been cursed.

This time Pyke had not been invited to the hall, nor did he make any attempt to enter its grounds. Rather, he tied up his horse well out of sight of the track leading up to the hall, positioned himself across from the main gate behind a large holly bush and prepared for a long wait. About an hour later, a carriage pulled by two horses skidded through the gate; Pyke could not see its occupants but supposed that the carriage belonged to James Sloan. As he waited for it to reappear, he wondered what kind of man Sloan was.

If he had struck some kind of deal with Edmonton, he could not be honest or virtuous or, for that matter, *nice*, but what if he was handsome or intelligent or attractively roguish? What if Emily found herself liking him? Pyke found this thought as unlikely as it was distasteful, but was it beyond the bounds of possibility? He knew Emily didn't have to *like* this man. In order to safeguard her income and inheritance, all she had to do was tolerate him. And, of course, Sloan would want to come across as generous and courteous. A lot was at stake for him.

Pyke wondered whether he might be jealous. It was certainly an odd sentiment, as irrational as it was consuming. Old prejudices towards privilege surfaced: what had this man done to merit Emily? He had, no doubt, led a sheltered, comfortable existence. Perhaps he had been set up in business by his father. He would have a sizeable private income, in order to satisfy Edmonton that he was an appropriate match for his daughter and in order to pay for the parliamentary seat Edmonton had given him.

It felt strange, spying on Emily. As he did so, he wondered whether she had instructed Jo to tell him about this meeting. Was he there at Emily's implicit behest? If so, for what purpose had he been summoned? What did he plan to do with the knowledge he hoped to gain from this particular outing? What might Emily want him to do? Again the thought struck him that she might be ambivalent about rather than hostile to the prospect of an arranged marriage: Emily was by no means materialistic, but she was passionately committed to her charity work and, if she saw this marriage as a way of securing a much-needed source of income for the work, then what was to say she wouldn't accept this man's proposal?

An hour later, he watched as the same carriage journeyed up the well-maintained drive from the hall and swept through the gate; he caught a brief glimpse of Emily through one of the windows but could not see whether she was alone or had company.

*

345

When the carriage finally pulled up outside a smart-looking terraced residence in a pleasant, leafy street that adjoined Russell Square, the footman climbed down from the roof and waited until a servant appeared from inside the house holding an umbrella before pulling down the steps and opening the door. The servant held open the umbrella and escorted Emily up the steps to the Doric porch. Pyke watched as they disappeared into the entrance hall; the brightly painted front door closed behind them.

As he waited on the far side of the street, watching a sweeper move through the traffic collecting coins from passing cabs and carts, Pyke wondered how long Emily would remain in the house. What would be an appropriate amount of time? Would an hour be too long? What if she stayed there for the entire morning? What might this indicate in terms of future intentions?

He was so occupied with these thoughts that he almost didn't notice Emily scampering down the steps in front of the house after only a few minutes and hailing a passing cab.

His first inclination was to go after her, to find out what had taken place and to make sure that she was all right. But he could not be certain she would appreciate such a gesture, especially if she hadn't actually instructed Jo to tell him about this meeting. She might resent him for spying on her and say nothing of what had happened in the house.

Instead, Pyke watched the cab turn into Russell Square and found himself standing in front of the man's residence.

Pyke's curiosity had been sufficiently piqued to risk approaching the front door. He didn't know what he might say to Sloan, but if Sloan represented Edmonton's parliamentary interests there might be some advantage in confronting him. If he seemed to be virtuous, Pyke could take this opportunity to further besmirch Edmonton's reputation. And if he seemed to be a rogue, Pyke could make his accusations and see how he responded.

It did not cross Pyke's mind that the man himself might open the door, particularly given his earlier sighting of at least one servant. That said, even before the door was opened, he heard the man mutter angrily, 'I wondered if you might reconsider,' as though he believed the visitor to be Emily.

Up close, the mole on his chin was purple rather than brown.

'You're a formidable man, Pyke. Formidable indeed,' Peel said, without bothering to stand up or shake his hand.

Tilling had ushered Pyke into his front room and pointed to one of the horsehair chairs. Pyke assured him that he was more comfortable standing.

Peel was much as he remembered: tall, elegantly dressed, with a long angular face and reddish hair.

'I think Fitzroy has already told you of my regrets at not being able to do more for you. It was with a heavy heart that I permitted your execution to proceed.'

'What about the man who was hanged for the St Giles murders? Was it with a heavy heart that you permitted *his* execution to proceed?'

For a moment, Peel seemed flummoxed. Then irritation and anger appeared to take over. He stared at Pyke and asked, 'Do you think I am immoral?'

'I think you are a politician. The two are perhaps not unrelated.' Pyke sighed, not really wanting to further provoke the man.

This seemed to irritate Peel. 'Servants of the state who are responsible for enforcing the law are justified in taking certain actions only if, *as a whole*, they result in greater freedom and happiness for the state's citizens.'

'I'm sure the top brass who dispatched troops to quell the working poor at Peterloo said much the same thing as they quaffed their cognac.'

Peel was outraged. Springing to his feet, he spluttered, 'Take that remark back, sir.'

'Perhaps it was just tea they quaffed.'

Tilling shot him a hard stare. 'I'm sure Pyke didn't mean his flippancy to cause serious offence.'

Peel sat down, a little sheepish at his outburst. 'Well.'

'What I'm suggesting is that when virtue is defined by its consequences, it is possible good intentions can be hijacked for other purposes.' Pyke shrugged, as though the matter were of no consequence.

Peel nodded, calmer now. 'Nonetheless we have to make decisions – difficult decisions, sometimes – because we feel that they are in the best interests of the majority.' He paused. 'I'm sure you have been compelled to make such decisions too.'

'But if the innocent are slaughtered and the guilty go unpunished only because it better serves the greater good, is that morally acceptable?' Pyke said, surprised he had proposed this argument.

'But morality and real politics are sometimes strange bedfellows.' Peel shook his head. 'As a follower of Machiavelli, I would have thought you might be sympathetic to this dilemma.'

Pyke nodded amiably. 'I am well aware that people such as yourself have to make difficult decisions at every turn, but my point is simply that the very nature of those decisions makes it difficult for you to be wholly good.'

'Are you suggesting that I am somehow *not* good?' This time, Peel seemed puzzled more than angry.

'Neither good nor bad,' Pyke smiled. 'Like me.'

'I would hope and pray I am nothing like you,' Peel said coldly.

'No.' Pyke was suddenly weary of the sound of his own voice. 'You are much more powerful.'

'And now you want me to use my power to grant you clemency?'

'Yes,' Pyke said, folding his arms.

The ginger cat strolled into the room and curled itself around Peel's leg. Tilling went to shoo the cat from the room but Peel shoved it away with the end of his boot. The cat scurried over to where Pyke was standing. Pyke bent over to stroke it. The cat arched itself around his leg and began to purr.

'I know what you intend to ask me but I am afraid nothing can be done in this instance.' Peel's smile had no warmth. 'Given the extent of your own lawlessness and the rather odd and disrespectful manner in which you conducted yourself at your trial, I am not in a position to grant you a pardon.'

'I'm sorry about that, because it will force me to place the contents of this document in the public domain.' He reached into his jacket pocket and produced an envelope.

Peel's eyes narrowed. 'And what, pray, is this document?'

Pyke removed the first page from the envelope. 'It's an affidavit sworn by Andrew Magennis, the father of Davy Magennis, before a solicitor in Armagh.' He passed it to Peel. 'In it, he describes how Tilling rode to Armagh in person in order to recruit Davy into the Irish Constabulary.'

'So?'

Pyke felt the coldness of Peel's stare. 'On subsequent pages, he recounts a confession Davy made to him shortly before he took his own life. Davy admits to having murdered his brother, his brother's mistress and baby.'

'May I see the rest of it?'

'Not at this juncture. What would be the point? I have no promise of goodwill on your part.'

Peel glanced nervously at Tilling. 'If it could be proven this man was responsible for the murders . . .'

Pyke nodded, as though giving this notion serious consideration. 'I'm still not minded to let you see the rest of the affidavit. I would, though, like to make you aware of a man called Simon Hunter, a rector from a church in Mullabrack, County Armagh. Hunter also heard Davy's confession and said that, if he was instructed to give evidence in court and was placed under oath, then he would corroborate this assertion.'

'That Magennis committed the St Giles murders?' Tilling sounded sceptical.

Pyke nodded.

'Then why not let us see the rest of this affidavit?'

'I might do, but not before I have received an official pardon from the Home Office.' This time he looked at Peel.

'You will not receive any such pardon without revealing the contents of that document.'

Pyke shrugged. 'Then I shall take my chances with the press.'

'This is most vexing. Most vexing indeed.' Peel was scowling. His face had reddened. 'It is even more vexing in the light of the robbery and unwanted disturbances on land owned by Lord Edmonton.'

'I had no hand in the Shoreditch robbery,' Pyke said.

'For some reason, I find that difficult to believe,' Tilling responded.

Pyke shrugged. 'If someone were to steal the crown jewels from the Tower, I would no doubt be blamed for that, too.' Pyke walked over to the bay window and looked out at the view over Hampstead Heath. 'But the disturbances on Edmonton's land are a different matter. What if I could arrange for them to cease?'

'And how could you manage that?' Peel demanded.

'The point surely is, *if* I could manage it, and in light of the damage I could potentially cause you by revealing that you knowingly executed the wrong man for the St Giles murders, then wouldn't it seem *appropriate* to come to some kind of arrangement with me?'

Peel still seemed unconvinced. 'You have the ear of this particular mob?'

'I think it is fair to assume that Pyke has played some role in fermenting and channelling their unhappiness,' Tilling said, arching his eyebrows.

'I don't have any control over their righteous anger, but at present their grievances are limited in scope. I could perhaps broker an agreement to ensure fairer conditions of service and a slightly improved wage.'

A long time ago, Pyke might have comforted himself with the notion that he was not, nor had ever been, part of the system of rule and law enforcement that he occasionally served, but his belief in his own independence had long since been eroded.

Peel frowned. 'But surely that would mean having to negotiate a deal with Edmonton, wouldn't it? And from what I hear, you would be unlikely to elicit a favourable response from him.'

'Leave Edmonton to me,' Pyke said, walking over to the fireplace. 'But if I can placate the mob, with or without Edmonton's assistance, would I be right to think that we have an agreement?'

Peel glanced at Tilling. 'I have given no such assurance.'

'But you will.' Pyke smiled amiably. 'Because you don't have a choice.'

Tilling looked at Peel, and then at Pyke, and shrugged. 'Pyke would seem to be holding a strong hand.'

Peel's face reddened further.

'So we have an agreement?'

In the end, Peel gave him a grudging nod. But he did not stand or offer to shake Pyke's hand.

Later, as Tilling followed Pyke to the front door, he patted him on the shoulder. He was smiling. 'You handled yourself well.'

Pyke accepted the compliment. 'But you'll make sure Peel's true to his word?'

'You still don't understand, do you? Peel is not your enemy here.' Tilling started to shake his head.

'Can I ask you a question?' Pyke said, buttoning up his jacket.

'Of course.'

'The last time we met, you said something about Vines and Sir Richard Fox, the two of them being closer than I thought.'

'So, ask *them* about it. Not me.'

'I can't ask Vines. Apparently he's in Scotland at a family wedding.'

The interest in Tilling's face faded. 'Scotland? I saw him the other day walking down the street.'

They shook hands and Pyke wandered down the steps towards the heath. It was only then that the implication of Vines being in London finally struck him.

It was after midnight when Pyke made it back to the Old Cock tavern in Holborn. He entered the building through the back door and went straight down to the cellar. He lit a candle, jammed it into a tin sconce and carried the flickering light carefully through to the room where Villums had built a cage for the creatures used in the ratting contests. Villums paid sewer hunters sixpence per rat; the hunters themselves worked in pairs, for if they worked alone they ran the risk of being overwhelmed by their venomous prey. Villums preferred sewer to water-ditch rats because he reckoned they were meaner and hence posed more of a challenge to the dogs. They were certainly ravenous; the three hundred or so creatures that currently occupied the wooden cage had stripped the fifty-stone carcass of the dead bear in less than five minutes.

Earlier, Pyke had bound Swift's wrists and ankles to the outside of the cage with rope; below Swift's tethered form was a seething carpet of sinew, wet black fur, whiskers, beady eyes, pincer teeth and ribbed tails the size of horsewhips.

In the end, it had simply been a matter of who had responded quickest. Since Pyke's reactions had been sharper than Swift's and Pyke had reached for his knife before Swift could decide what course of action to take, it was Pyke who had triumphed in their skirmish. Pyke had forced the blade of his knife deep into the flesh of Swift's thigh and immobilised him. He had then transported Swift from Russell Square to the tavern in Swift's carriage.

Lifting the candle up in order to throw some light on Swift's unmoving body, Pyke inspected his adversary for a while. He was nearer forty-five than thirty-five, Pyke decided, with bushy, sandy-coloured hair and a gaunt, almost oblong face. He was by no means an attractive man, but there was something arresting about his features; his taut, weathered skin, his slate-grey eyes, his pursed lips and his almost translucent eyebrows gave the impression of someone who had been mummified. But it was his mole that attracted one's attention; it was an ugly purple mark, almost as large as a half-shilling coin, located in the middle of his chin.

Swift seemed barely alive so Pyke opened a bottle of gin and sloshed it liberally into his eyes. When that did not rouse the man, Pyke took out his knife, heated the metal blade over the flame of the candle for a few moments, steadied himself, sliced the mole from Swift's chin and then daubed the open wound with gin.

For an instant, Pyke was worried the man's agonised screams might have attracted the attention of those upstairs in the tavern.

He tossed the remains of the mole into the cage and watched as the long-tailed rats fought one another for the fleshy morsel. Blood poured from the wound and dripped into the cage, sending the rats into an even more heightened state of anticipation.

Pyke rested the candle on top of the cage, next to Swift's head, and unbound his gag. Swift's mouth sagged open; his stare was uncomprehending, as though he had not yet adjusted to his new fate.

'Jimmy Swift. Or should I call you James Sloan?' Pyke spoke in a soft whisper.

Swift stared at Pyke for a while.

'Well?'

'Sloan was my mother's name. I adopted it when I left Ireland and came to London. Funny, I didn't want my past catching up with me. The very last thing I did as Jimmy Swift was lead you to St Giles.' He spoke in a gentle, nasal tone. 'You walked straight into that one.'

Pyke nodded, 'I visited your old house in Hamilton's Bawn. It's comfortable but a little run down perhaps. Nothing compared to your Russell Square residence. Or Hambledon Hall.'

Pyke's taunt registered in Swift's eyes but he said nothing.

'A seat in Parliament. The daughter's hand in marriage.

And the prospect of one day inheriting a country estate. That's quite a reward, particularly from someone as ungenerous as Lord Edmonton.'

For a moment, Swift was distracted by the sound of the rats. He was tied to the cage in such a way that he couldn't see them, but he could hear them.

'You're going to kill me anyway, so why should I tell you what you want to know?' His face betrayed some of the dread that he was, doubtless, feeling.

Pyke took out his pistol and fired a shot into the sea of rats. He must have wounded or most probably killed one of them because the others began to swarm around its twitching form and feed on its carcass.

'You hear that sound?' he said to Swift. 'There are three hundred rats in the cage, three hundred sets of pincer-like teeth. Can you even imagine what short work that many teeth would make of your flesh? You would be dead in a matter of seconds, of course, but imagine those final moments of your life, rats crawling on your face, chewing out your eyes.' He aimed the barrel of his pistol at Swift's head. 'But if I felt you were telling the truth, I might consider simply shooting you.'

Swift watched him carefully but said nothing. He was listening to the rats beneath him.

'Perhaps I might outline what I think took place,' Pyke said. 'You can interrupt me if I have made a mistake or if I require your assistance.' Again Swift did not respond.

Pyke began by indicating how he believed Swift's relationship with Edmonton had started. He said they had probably met through the Orange Order and the Brunswick Club and corresponded regularly over issues of mutual concern. The unappealing prospect of Catholic emancipation had certainly been one such issue, and Edmonton had asked Swift to be vigilant for anything they might use to thwart or disrupt the smooth passage of the Catholic Emancipation Bill through Parliament. This had taken place some time in October or even November of the previous year. Six months earlier, Swift had employed the services of Davy Magennis to tend his small plot of land. Magennis had been dismissed from the Irish Constabulary for violent misconduct but had been recommended to Swift by someone in the order. Swift had never particularly liked Magennis but his interest in the big man was piqued by a story he told about his brother, Stephen, who had fallen in love with a Catholic girl and had absconded to London. Magennis had spoken about his brother's betrayal with an anger that bordered on mania. When Magennis had also revealed that he had once been personally recruited into the constabulary by Tilling, Peel's emissary in Ulster, Swift had seen an opportunity that was too good to pass up, especially as Peel was openly talking about changing his position on the Catholic question and throwing his support behind the push for emancipation.

But Swift had had to move quickly. He had contacted Edmonton in London and explained what he had discovered and how this information might be used in such a way as to further their cause. Edmonton had been delighted by the idea: that Swift would accompany Davy Magennis to London and talk him into, if any talk were required, killing his brother. For their plan to work, any subsequent investigation would have to establish a connection between Peel and Magennis. They could then claim that Peel had staged the murder in order to bolster support for the police bill that he was attempting to push through Parliament at the same time as Catholic emancipation. In any case, if it could be leaked to the newspapers that a Protestant man from Ulster had been murdered, seemingly by a Catholic, then such news would, no doubt, spark a wave of anti-Catholic protests that might end up blowing Peel's plans out of the water. Edmonton had assumed responsibility for planning events in the capital. He had paid someone to track down Stephen Magennis and his mistress and given some consideration to how he might ensure that the subsequent investigation into the murders would unearth the connection between Davy Magennis and Peel.

This was the moment when Edmonton had struck upon the notion of using Pyke. He had known, for a fact, that Pyke was a formidable investigator. If it could somehow be arranged that Pyke discovered the dead bodies, he would have to be a part of any investigation, and given his tenacity and contrariness, he might begin to suspect some kind of conspiracy. If not, he could always be pushed in such a direction once the investigation had commenced. In any case, Pyke could be used and then discarded once his purpose had been served.

Pyke paused for a moment. Swift seemed to be more preoccupied by the sound of rats. Pyke continued with his narrative.

Swift was, by no means, a papist sympathiser. After all, he had grown up in the Orange Order and had been initiated into a way of thinking that saw Catholics as both a threat and a menace. Nonetheless, he was not a rabid Catholic-hating extremist like Edmonton. For him, there had to be prospect of significant personal and material advancement to compensate him for the dangers he would have to face in actually executing the plan. Hence Edmonton's generous offer of a parliamentary seat, his own daughter's hand in marriage and the prospect of one day inheriting the family estate. The unpredictable element had been Davy Magennis. For the plan to work, Swift would have to prime his anger and transform the big man's violent threats into something tangible.

'But you weren't aware that Clare, Stephen's mistress, had just given birth, were you?' Pyke said.

Swift looked at him with growing contempt.

'And when Davy saw the baby, the whole plan fell apart.' Pyke ran his knife across the open wound on Swift's chin and saw him wince. 'Suddenly, he couldn't go through with it. Davy didn't kill them. Did he?'

Swift shrugged, as though the issue were a trifling one.

'So it was down to you. Either go through with the murders yourself or risk losing everything you'd been promised by Edmonton.' Pyke watched his sullen reaction. 'You made Magennis stay, initially at least. You made him help you tie up Stephen and Clare, and then you slit their throats with a razor.' Pyke did not need to close his eyes to recall the sight of their severed throats. 'But what I don't know, what I still can't work out, is why you had to kill the baby as well.'

Swift licked his blood-caked lips. 'It wouldn't stop crying.'

Pyke stared at him. He felt his innards tighten. 'Is that it?'

'The other two were dead. Magennis was blubbering. He wanted to leave. Then we heard a sound at the door. I'd forgotten to lock it behind us. It was the cousin, Mary. She saw Davy, who she obviously knew, and saw the blood on the floor and screamed. Magennis ran after her. I told him to. I thought he would know what to do. Later, I realised that he wasn't coming back and that, perhaps, he hadn't taken care of the girl as I'd hoped. At the time, I was left in that God-forsaken room with the crying baby. I picked it up. I hadn't thought about killing it until it started to bawl even louder, and I couldn't bear it. I shook it a few times but it wouldn't stop. So I shook it again, much harder this time, but the screams still wouldn't stop. That was when I decided I'd had enough. I throttled it and dumped it in the pail.' He looked up at Pyke and shrugged. 'That's it. That's everything.'

It was as though he had described throwing away a pot of boiled meat bones.

There it was. Pyke could not help but feel a little deflated by Swift's revelations, as though they made all his own efforts to conceive of Swift's crimes as degenerate and monstrous seem wholly misplaced. His moment of vindication had somehow floundered on the banality of Swift's evil. In particular, Pyke felt foolish for having imagined a gruesome scenario in which the killer had deliberately tortured the parents by forcing them to watch their baby's murder. Through such acts of imagination and fantasies of revenge, Pyke had given the murders a status that far exceeded their squalid reality. Swift had killed the baby simply because it would not stop crying. Pyke did not know whether the mundanity of this explanation was less upsetting than the macabre constructions of his own imagination, but, in the end, it didn't really matter. For six months, he had pursued phantoms inside and outside his head, and now that those phantoms had been rendered visible, given recognisable shape and form, in the figure of Swift, he felt only drained and soiled as a consequence. Somehow, too, this made his revenge seem less legitimate than it had been, at least in his own mind. More than anything else, Pyke just wanted Swift to be dead. Swift saw this, too, and any lingering hope evaporated in his eyes.

'Just one more question,' Pyke said, lifting the hatch next to Swift's bound form. 'How did you know where to find the cousin, Mary Johnson? I mean, I presume it was you who strangled her and her boyfriend?'

Swift tugged at the bindings around his wrists and ankles and strained to look beneath him at the rats that covered every inch of floor and wall space at the bottom of the cage.

'How did you find her?'

'I can't remember,' Swift said, sounding panicky. 'I don't know. Edmonton must have told me.'

Pyke took his knife and cut through Swift's hand bonds. He gouged his thumb into the wound on Swift's chin. Swift gurgled and momentarily passed out. Pyke cut the bonds around his ankles and shunted Swift's prostrate body across towards the open hatch. Beneath him, the carpet of rats seemed to move as one.

He waited until Swift came round. His hands were gripping Swift's ankles. The rest of his body was dangling upside down inside the cage. The rats could almost touch his scalp. He was screaming now, screaming and pleading with Pyke for pity and for mercy. Pyke held him there for as long as he was able to. Finally, however, his grip weakened; he let go of Swift's ankles and watched as he fell into the mass of rats, at least six or seven deep, watched as Swift's body – first his legs and then his arms, torso and, finally, his neck and mouth – seemed to disappear as the rats swarmed over him. He watched – fascinated and sickened – as a body of wet, black fur and long, twitching tails engulfed Swift's disintegrating form, and he listened as the almost unbearable carnivorous screeches finally drowned out the stomach-churning gurgles emerging from Swift's body. Eventually, the only sound in the cellar was the unmistakable noise of ten thousand teeth tearing into bloodied flesh. Pyke would remember that terrible sound for as long as he lived.

TWENTY-FIVE

'My God, you look terrible, m'boy. Come in.' Godfrey looked up and down the street outside his apartment. It seemed quiet enough. Certainly there was no sign of the men who had been stationed there but it was late, after two in the morning. Still, Pyke had taken great care to slip into the building unnoticed.

He had not been able to face the prospect of another long, cold night in the church and had walked the three miles from Holborn to his uncle's apartment in Camden Town.

In the front room, Godfrey poured him a large brandy and threw some more coal on to the fire. The room was as untidy as Pyke remembered it: piles of books, pamphlets and papers covered every inch of floor space. It had been a while since he was last there, perhaps as much as a year. Pyke felt himself begin to relax. This had been as much a home for him as he had ever known: even the vaguely musty smell was reassuringly familiar.

'So you gave Emily my address, then?' Godfrey was wearing his silk dressing gown.

'How did you know?'

'I know because she's here. She turned up on my doorstep a few hours ago in quite a state. Told me she'd tried to find you in the church but you weren't there. Thought you might have been arrested. Or worse.'

Pyke found Emily, half-asleep, curled up in his old bed. For a few moments, she stared at him, as though she did not know where she was, but her anxiety soon gave way to relief; she threw her arms around his neck and pulled him into an embrace.

'I thought you were dead,' she said, wiping tears from her eyes. 'I really thought you were dead.'

As he rubbed the tears from her cheeks, he wondered whether she could smell the pungent vermin odour on him.

'I can't do it any more,' Emily said, once the relief at seeing him had worn off.

'Can't do what any more?'

'It's such a mess.' Emily sighed. 'The man my father expects me to marry . . .'

'He's dead.'

'Dead?' Emily stared at him, bewildered.

'James Sloan, otherwise known as Jimmy Swift, is dead.'

Briefly, a look of relief registered on her face. Emily had identified Sloan as Swift from Pyke's earlier description. This was the reason she had fled from his home.

'Dead how?' she mouthed.

'He's dead,' Pyke said. 'That's all you need to know.'

'When?'

Pyke stood up and looked around his old bedroom, expecting more of a reaction, but he felt neither validated nor unsettled by the feelings and memories that surfaced.

'I presume it's a naive question, but did you . . . *kill* him?'

'No.'

She screwed up her face and gave him a quizzical stare. 'But he's dead,' she repeated.

He waited for a few moments. 'Will you marry me?' There. He had asked the question.

'Pardon?' She did not seem to have understood what he had asked her.

Pyke exhaled loudly. In the silence, he could hear his own heart beating. He wanted to tell her how he felt but his willingness to do so was foundering on her apparent indifference.

'You just asked me to marry you, didn't you?' she exclaimed, as though the notion were an absurd one.

'It's perhaps a stupid question, but do you . . .' He couldn't bring himself to say it.

'Do I love you?' Her expression softened. She even smiled a little. 'Of course I do.' The way she said it sounded so pained, so heartfelt, so doomed, he couldn't help but reach out to her.

'Perhaps I could talk to him.' He threaded his fingers through hers.

'Who? My father?' She laughed in a derisive manner.

'I can be quite persuasive.'

'He won't countenance it.' She shrugged. 'He would never relent. He *detests* you.'

He pretended to ponder this notion for a while. 'But can he stop you?'

'No, but he can disinherit me,' she said, as though this put an end to the discussion.

Pyke nodded, as though he appreciated the problem. 'But what if I were to confront him?'

'For what purpose?' Emily seemed almost irritated by such a suggestion. 'Anyway, he's holed up in Hambledon, protected by his own private militia. You wouldn't get as far as the main gates.'

'But it's a large house. There must be other ways of getting in.'

'There are, I suppose. But what would you say to him?'

'I would ask him for your hand in marriage.'

That drew an incredulous laugh. 'And you think he would readily agree to such an arrangement?'

'Let me ask you a question. If it was not for the terms of your father's will, would you marry me then?'

'But that's a hypothetical question, isn't it?'

'A hypothetical question?' He tried not to appear annoyed by her answer. 'What's hypothetical about it?'

Emily just shrugged.

'Then perhaps we should address the dilemma from a legal perspective.'

Emily looked at him, frowning. 'What do you mean?'

'Perhaps I should talk to your father's lawyer instead.'

'You think he'd divulge anything to you?'

'You know him, then?'

Emily shrugged. 'We've met on occasions. Gerald Atkins. He's as mean as my father.'

Pyke wondered whether he had already said too much. Emily's brown eyes were unreadable.

'I don't know,' she said, shaking her head. 'It all seems so hopeless.' They stared at one another for a while.

'Hopeless,' he repeated listlessly.

'But you know, it means a lot to me, that you even asked,' she said, smiling belatedly, as though the subject were no longer worth discussing. She kissed him gently on the mouth.

Pyke wanted so badly to reciprocate, to give in to the kiss, but he managed to pull back from her embrace. In the ebbing candlelight, he could tell from her puzzled reaction that she did not know what he was thinking.

'What is it?' Her voice was taut with expectation.

Pyke waited for a moment. Outside on the street, a man and woman were shouting at each other. 'But if it's all so hopeless,' he said, no longer trying to hide his frustration, 'I don't understand why you came here tonight.'

It was Emily's turn to look confused.

'I understand that you want what is owed to you . . .'

'What was stolen from my mother,' Emily said, this time with real anger in her voice.

'Not simply for yourself but perhaps for your work,' he agreed.

She nodded gently.

'It is certainly hard to explain our inclinations and actions in straightforward ways.' He hesitated and took a deep breath; he knew that now was the time to tell Emily about her mother, but at the very last moment he could not bring himself to do so. It had been his plan to tell her what he had done in order to elicit some kind of favourable response. She would want him because of what he had done. Now, though, he wanted her to want him *without* knowing what he had done. Perhaps it was stubbornness but dangling her mother in front of Emily seemed, all of a sudden, like a cheap bribe.

'But?'

'In the end we all have to make choices.' Pyke could not bring himself to look at her. 'And with choices come consequences.'

'You're saying I have to make a choice between you and my rightful inheritance?' She sounded pained.

'No,' he said, as softly as he could. 'That's what *you* seem to be saying.'

Emily turned away from him and stared at the wall.

'Just now, when I said choices bring consequences . . .'

'Yes?' But she did not turn around.

'One might be that when I walk out of this door, we never see one another again.'

He saw that her whole body quivered but still she did not turn to face him.

*

365

Later, when Pyke could not sleep, he returned to the living room and found Godfrey sitting up in his easy chair, a blanket wrapped around his legs. His uncle put his book down. 'You couldn't sleep either?'

'Afraid not.'

Godfrey nodded. 'She's a lovely girl. And she seems devoted to you.'

'You think?' He laughed bitterly.

'Have to be blind not to see it,' Godfrey said, reaching for his brandy glass.

'Perhaps I am.'

'What? Blind?'

Pyke just shrugged. His whole body felt listless.

Godfrey laughed. 'Since I rarely find you in such a confessional mood, can I ask you a question?'

'So long as it has nothing to do with this damned book you want me to write.'

'No, it's not that,' Godfrey said, shaking his head. 'But don't think I've forgotten about your promise.'

'What is it, then?'

'In all the time I've known you, you haven't once asked me about your father; or, for that matter, about your mother.'

Pyke felt his chest tighten. 'So?'

'Don't you want to know what kind of a man he was?'

'Why should I?'

'Because he was your father, for a start,' Godfrey said, exasperated.

'You were more of a father to me than he was.' Pyke looked away, uncomfortable with this subject.

'It's kind of you, my boy, and I'm gratified to hear you say it, but your father *produced* you.'

'Let me ask you a question, then. What good would it do me, to hear what a great man or, alternatively, what a fool he was?'

'I just thought you might be interested,' Godfrey said, sounding disappointed. 'That's all.'

Pyke took a piece of paper from his trouser pocket, unfolded it and handed it to his uncle. 'I'll be gone tomorrow by the time Emily rises. Could you possibly take her to this address for me?'

Godfrey stared at the address for a few moments and frowned. 'Can you tell me what this is about?'

Pyke shook his head.

'Will Emily know?'

'She won't at first,' Pyke said, choosing his words carefully. 'At first, it'll be a terrible shock. If she can't guess, tell her I visited an asylum in Portsmouth . . .'

'An asylum?' Godfrey screwed up his face. 'Really, Pyke, what is this about?'

Pyke stared at the fire but didn't give his uncle an answer.

Brownlow Vines was dining alone at Simpson's on the Strand. He was eating boiled mutton and washing it down with a bottle of claret. Dressed in a stylish black frock-coat, fitted trousers, polished leather boots and a starched white cravat, he looked every inch the dandy. His foppish sideburns and tousled hair completed the look. Pyke waited until he had finished his meal before he appeared. He took a seat opposite him without being invited. Vines stared at him, open-mouthed.

'Pyke, my God. This is a . . . surprise.' Vines glanced around the crowded restaurant for assistance.

'You have to answer for what you did,' Pyke said, taking his time. He was not in any hurry.

Vines picked up his glass and finished what was in it. 'Listen, man . . .' His voice was hoarse. He took off his frock-coat, and Pyke noticed a large sweat stain underneath each armpit.

Pyke leaned forward across the small table and whispered, 'At any moment, you will start to experience stomach cramps. These will get progressively more painful. Eventually, you will not be able to breathe. The poison you have just ingested' – Pyke motioned at the empty plate in front of him – 'is quite deadly but, unlike cyanide or arsenic, it is not a fast-acting agent. I'm afraid you will experience a fair amount of pain. You'll vomit. You might lose your sight. Eventually you won't be able to move. I'm told that's the first indication you're close to death. Once paralysis sets in, you might have another five or ten minutes of life.'

Vines stared at him for a while, unable to fathom what he had just been told. 'But I didn't kill her,' he said, eventually, quivering with indignation. 'It wasn't anything to do with me.'

Pyke stood up, pulled his jacket down and shrugged. 'I know.' As he turned to leave, he saw Vines clutch his stomach.

Pyke had one final stop to make before he started out on the journey to Hambledon Hall for the last time.

Fox was a difficult man to fathom and it was hard to warm to him: he was cold, often aloof and possessed an air of his own superiority that was the product of perceived intellectual prowess rather than breeding. Perhaps it was this intellectual snobbery that drew him to Pyke, and vice versa, or perhaps Fox was frightened of him or, rather, had needed him to perform tasks that other Runners were unable or unwilling to do. Whatever it was, there was a bond between them that went beyond familiarity. Fox may have been vain and high-handed but he was also fair and scrupulous. He had risked censure and ridicule for treating those who exhibited some remorse for their crimes and whose recidivism could be explained by social circumstances with compassion. He also turned a blind eye to many of Pyke's moral lapses, and did so without demanding any of the proceeds from his illicit activities.

'I fancy I can guess why you're here,' Fox said, wearily, as though he were indifferent to the whole matter. He offered Pyke a cadaverous smile.

Pyke pulled back his jacket to reveal the pistol that he had tucked into his belt. 'Vines is dead. So is Swift.'

Fox nodded, as though he had expected as much. 'For what it's worth, Brownlow was simply following orders.' He smiled weakly. 'I was going to ask you to spare him for old times' sake, but you were never much of a sentimentalist, were you?'

'I never much liked him, either.' Pyke looked away. He didn't want Fox to see his own sadness.

'No, quite.' Fox ran his finger across his moustache. After an awkward silence he asked in a feathery voice, 'How did you find out?'

'You mean aside from your pathetic attempt to have me lynched the other day, outside your office?'

'I was desperate.' Fox's eyes were dark with exhaustion.

Pyke waited for a moment, to organise his thoughts, and then explained that he had been bothered by two separate incidents. He had not been able to work out how Swift had known where to find the cousin, Mary Johnson, and her boyfriend, Gerry McKeown. And he had not known who had sanctioned Lizzie's killing, especially after his initial assumption concerning Peel's involvement had turned out to be wildly wrong.

'And this led you to me?'

'Not exactly.' Pyke permitted himself a small sigh. 'For a start, I talked to Tilling. He told me that Vines had not been of any help to Peel over the issue of police reform. He told me Vines's loyalty, and I quote, "lay squarely with Sir Richard". That's when I realised what I had missed all along. Apart from me, the one other person who knew where Mary and Gerry had been staying was your coachman. He had taken us to an inn in Isleworth. I suppose I didn't think about him because I didn't remotely suspect you.'

Fox shrugged, almost apologetically. 'She had to die, I'm afraid. You *do* know she'd actually interrupted the murders?' He shook his head. 'Poor girl.'

Sickened, Pyke couldn't bring himself to look at his mentor. 'It explains why you were so keen to locate her.'

'Quite.' Fox's laugh was without humour or warmth. 'I'm afraid Edmonton was blackmailing me by then. I had no choice but to tell him what I knew.'

'That's how he found out about Flynn?'

Fox nodded.

'But once upon a time the two of you *were* partners, so to speak.'

'I suppose so.' Fox smiled weakly. 'I had already signed my own Faustian pact.' He looked up at the portrait of Sir Henry Fielding above the fireplace. 'But it was Edmonton who approached me initially, rather than the other way around.'

'He had heard about your disagreements with Peel over the whole business of police reform.'

Fox shrugged. 'He didn't need to tell me that he'd fallen out with the Home Secretary himself. That much was common knowledge.'

'Both of you united by your hatred of Peel.'

Fox looked at him, clear-eyed. 'Is that so hard to believe? That I might hate someone who was seeking to pull down everything that I believed in? Everything I'd spent my life building up?'

'You knew Peel was determined to bring Bow Street under the auspices of the Home Office . . .'

'And in effect kill off the Runners.' A little colour returned to Fox's cheeks. 'I thought that if Peel could be persuaded, if not by logic then by blackmail, to go back on his plans . . .'

'Then the Runners might be saved.'

Fox nodded appreciatively. 'Exactly.'

Pyke appeared to digest this information. 'And your job, once the bodies had been discovered in St Giles, was simply to make sure that any subsequent murder investigation would implicate Davy Magennis, and eventually uncover his link to Tilling and hence Peel.'

'Except that you did most of that work for me,' Fox said, matter-of-factly.

'All I had to do was lead you to Mary Johnson.'

Fox shrugged. 'For what it's worth, I took no pleasure in deceiving you.'

'What about murdering an innocent young couple and their newborn baby? Did you take any pleasure in that?'

Fox seemed aghast. 'I didn't *kill* those people.'

'But you as good as murdered them.'

'I wasn't told about the plan in detail. Of course, I was told there would have to be a murder. But I didn't know a baby might be killed. I was as appalled by that as you were.'

'You were so appalled that you carried on as though you were wholly innocent.'

'None of this was easy for me, Pyke. I did what I did because I thought it would be in the best interests of the Runners.'

Pyke had not expected to lose his temper, nor to react to what he learned from Fox in a violent manner, but as he listened to the old man's callow, pathetic self-justifications, he felt a heat rising up through his chest, a knotted ball of anger that had been kept in check throughout the previous months but was now billowing up inside him like a squall of wind, clearing the emotional debris from its path.

Reaching Fox's cowering figure in a few steps and paying no attention to the difference in their respective size or strength, he hauled him to his feet and swung at his face. His fist connected with Fox's chin and lifted him up off his feet. As Fox crumpled on to his desk, a blast of fetid breath escaped from his mouth.

'And did you *have* to kill Lizzie, too?' Pyke said, wiping saliva from his mouth with his sleeve.

'*Lizzie?*' Fox still seemed to be dazed from the blow.

'Why did you kill her?'

Fox pretended to be confused.

This time Pyke slapped the old man around the face, but the threat of further violence was enough to loosen his memory and tongue.

'I didn't mean to.' His face had assumed a ghastly pale complexion. His hands were trembling as well. 'I'm sorry. I didn't intend it to happen.'

'Didn't intend what to happen?' It was as though Pyke had swallowed shards of broken glass.

Fox stared down disconsolately at the floor. 'By that stage, it was too late, at least for me. The police bill was set to breeze through both Houses. I'd failed miserably. But Edmonton was cock-a-hoop. He not only believed he could destroy the whole Catholic Emancipation Bill but also felt he could ruin Peel's career in the process. Meanwhile, Protestant vigilante groups were butchering Catholics right across the city. I just wanted it all to be over. I wanted to ruin Edmonton's plans without exposing my own culpability. And I knew that, sooner rather than later, you would discover the truth and come after me. So I decided to protect myself from such a fate. I knew if you were no longer around, then the investigation into the St Giles murders would die a natural death and things could return to how they were. And I also knew that if you were dead, Edmonton would not be able to exploit what you would inevitably find out.'

It made some kind of perverted sense. 'So you dispatched Vines to Lizzie's place? To drug me?'

'You mustn't hold it against Brownlow. He had no idea what I was planning to do. He didn't know about any of this.'

Pyke was sickened by all of it. He was sickened by Fox, Edmonton, Peel, Swift and even by himself.

Fox crawled off his desk and sat down on the chair, smoothing his moustache with the palms of his hands. 'I knew you preferred to sleep alone. You had mentioned it to me once or twice before. But Vines, or whoever it was that carried you up the stairs, put you in Lizzie's room. Later, after everyone had gone, I crept up the stairs. I had one of your knives in my hand. I went to your room, initially, and found it was empty. So I tiptoed across the landing to Lizzie's room. It was dark. I stood next to your motionless body for what seemed like hours. I had the knife in my hand but I could not bring myself to do it. In the end, my nerve failed me. I'm not going to give a dramatic speech about the closeness of our relationship but, in the end, I could not kill you. I was about to leave when Lizzie woke up. Of course, she recognised me. I tried to placate her, but I had no way of explaining my presence in her bedroom. I suppose she must have seen the knife and then screamed for help, because the next thing I remember, I was trying to grab her, to stop the screaming. That's when it must have happened. I didn't mean to, I swear to God. I just remember standing there, staring horrified at the blood oozing from her stomach.'

For a while, neither of them spoke. Pyke thought about the last time he had seen Lizzie alive; the time they had kissed in front of Vines. On that and other occasions he had used her, but he still mourned her death. And he would grieve for her when this was done.

'But you didn't just flee the scene, did you?'

Fox looked up at him and sniffed. 'What do you mean?'

'You watched Lizzie die. You waited until she was dead and you laid her next to me and you planted the knife that you'd used on the floor by my bed.' His throat felt arid. 'It was how the constables you dispatched the next morning were supposed to find me.'

Fox didn't disagree. He sat there, unmoving, staring blankly at the wall behind Pyke.

Pyke took his pistol and placed it carefully on the desk. Fox looked at it and then up at Pyke. 'I was good to you once, wasn't I?' But there was no pleading or desperation in his tone.

'You tolerated me because I was a good investigator.'

'And you looked up to me,' Fox said, almost dreamily.

'I was young and naive.' Pyke pushed the pistol across the desk towards him. 'Take it. It's loaded.' It did not matter what the old man said; it still felt like a betrayal.

Fox stared at the pistol as though it were a poisonous snake. 'It's too late for apologies, Pyke, but for what it's worth, I am sorry.'

As he closed the office door behind him, Pyke heard the deafening blast of the pistol, and felt nothing at all; not anger, nor regret, nor even some kind of perverse satisfaction. More than anything else, he wanted it to be over. He wanted the killing to be over.

Townsend was as good as his word. When Pyke rode up to the entrance of Hambledon Hall, he was greeted by the sight of a hundred or more men, carrying torches and pitchforks. Saville and Canning were among the gathered mob, though neither appeared to recognise him. The mood of the crowd was ugly. Townsend had already told him of continuing reprisals being carried out by Edmonton's militia against certain villages. Three inns had been ransacked and set on fire. As a response, more threshing machines had been destroyed. Earlier, in a nearby inn, Townsend had paid for as much ale as the men could imbibe and many in the assembled crowd were drunk, and talking openly of violent retribution.

Ahead of them, on the other side of the main gates, Edmonton's militia were lined up seven or eight deep down the tree-lined avenue that led up to the hall; they would be armed with muskets and rifles, Pyke realised, and would not be afraid to use them. Pyke was not concerned whether the irate mob stormed the front gates and attacked the hall, whether there was a pitched battle or simply a tense stand-off. That was their business. He just required them as a distraction, in order that he might slip unnoticed into the grounds.

He had warned Townsend that Edmonton's militia would be armed. The rest was up to them.

Pyke was not an impetuous man but when he finally laid eyes on Edmonton, sprawled out on his four-poster Queen Anne bed, he had to resist an urge to attack him without further ceremony. Edmonton seemed both unsettled and gratified by Pyke's intrusion, fumbling to retrieve something he had hidden under the many pillows and bolsters that were propping him up. The bedroom itself was a plush, elaborately decorated affair. Lit up by candles that sat on top of the marble mantelpiece and the mahogany dresser, the gilt-striped wallpaper seemed to glisten in the light.

Edmonton finally produced a flintlock pistol, and waved it triumphantly at Pyke, nearly knocking over a decanter filled with port that adorned his bedside table.

'I see that you have availed yourself of the view,' Pyke said, not bothered by the pistol, as he walked across the room to the window that overlooked the main gate. 'Maybe the mob will storm the defences, ransack the hall and cut off your head.'

'This is England, not the Continent.' Edmonton laughed. 'And the mob will never get in here. I've offered the men outside a bonus of ten guineas for every peasant they shoot dead.' He was holding the pistol as though his life depended on it.

'I had no problem getting in here.'

That elicited a fatuous smile. 'The past few months have demonstrated that I am more than capable of taking care of you.'

'I'll admit I had no proper understanding of the extent of your depravity.'

'Ah, excellent. A lesson in ethics from a common thief and convicted murderer. I bow to your superior wisdom.'

'Better a common thief than a moral simpleton with innocent blood smeared over his fat hands.'

'In what way am I a moral simpleton?' Edmonton seemed amused rather than annoyed. 'Tell me this. Do you really want a country full of papist spies running amok in every department of state, passing our secrets to the foul Roman Church? Conspiring to replace our goodly Anglican brethren with depraved, child-molesting Catholic priests? In God's name, don't you understand what's been happening? One day soon, papist traitors like O'Connell will be able to stand up in the House and vote on matters concerning the true Church. What if I was to stand back and do *nothing*? We would soon have rosary beads adorning every mantelpiece, incense burning in every home, and lust-driven monks roaming the streets preying on our innocent Protestant children.'

Pyke had come to Hambledon in the expectation that he might find something that explained the terrible scene that he had witnessed in that lodging room. Now, though, as he stared into Edmonton's reptilian eyes, it was hard not to conceive of his pathetic ranting as a form of madness, and as such he felt less outrage than he had expected to; less outrage but no pity.

Pyke supposed it was relatively easy for Edmonton to despise Catholics: to see them somehow as subhuman and not deserving of life. For him, it was simply a matter of personal preference, an opinion that could be strongly held precisely because it did not impinge on his life in any way, except in abstract terms. Catholics were akin to demons; monstrous figures that existed only in his imagination. For Andrew Magennis, or his son Davy, or even for Jimmy Swift, it was different. At least their hatred, malignant and debilitating as it was, had a history; it made some kind of perverse sense in the context of two hundred years of religious animosity and upheaval. It made sense because they had lived among and fought with people who, in the process, had become their bitterest enemies. For Edmonton, though, Catholics were faceless and anonymous – barbarians amassing at the gate to sack Protestant civilisation – and therefore could be subjected to any degree of inhumanity in the name of a nobler cause. Closeted in his English home, and buoyed by a formless hatred, Edmonton had overseen a chain of events that had led to many deaths. But it was pointless to expect him to feel guilt for what he had done.

'But you failed, Edmonton. Catholic emancipation passed through both Houses. Peel remains in office. Swift is dead. And I'm still here.' Pyke walked across the room towards the four-poster bed. 'And it will be my very great pleasure to take away everything you have left.'

'How delightfully naive,' Edmonton said, still waving the pistol. But he was perspiring like a hog.

'I'm here to ask for your daughter's hand in marriage.'

'You're here to *ask* me?' Edmonton started to laugh. 'That's rich. Rather wonderful, actually. You're quite the brigand, aren't you?' His feigned laughter subsided. 'But did you actually imagine I would give you my *blessing*?'

'Is that a yes or a no?'

'By God, you're certainly a man to admire, that's for certain. A cad and a brigand. Obstinate. Quite obstinate.' Edmonton's rosy cheeks glowed in the candlelight.

Pyke nodded, as though Edmonton had given him the answer he had been expecting. 'By the way, that pistol is quite useless. While you were preparing for bed, I found it under one of the pillows and disarmed it.'

Edmonton looked down at the pistol, then up at Pyke, cocked the trigger and fired it. Nothing happened.

'Let me rephrase the question. I'm going to marry your daughter. There. No longer a question, was it?' He smiled easily.

'The two of you can do whatever you damn well like, but you won't ever see a penny of my money.' His eyes narrowed.

'Not even when you're *dead*?'

This drew a leering grin. 'Especially when I'm dead.'

'Oh?' Pyke said, happy to play along with him for the moment.

'If she should marry *unwisely*, she loses everything. The estate would pass to a distant cousin in America.'

'Really? And how is this business of an "unwise marriage" characterised in your will?'

'It's not in my original will,' Edmonton said, beginning

to enjoy himself. 'But I had the foresight to draw up a codicil.'

'A codicil?'

'An amendment to my original will which names you in person. It means that if she were ever to marry you, then she would lose the estate and any claim to it.'

'Is that legal?'

'Perfectly.' Edmonton was grinning. 'She also loses the estate if she uses any income accrued from it or from the sale of land to benefit that damn charity of hers.'

'That will hurt her,' Pyke said, digesting this news.

'It will, won't it?'

'You put that in this codicil, too?'

'I did indeed.' Edmonton appeared relaxed. 'At heart, my daughter is as self-interested as you or I. She won't want to give up her inheritance either for you or her damn charity. So you see, this proposed marriage is nonsense.'

Pyke nodded amiably. 'I discussed this with your lawyer earlier this afternoon.'

'My lawyer?'

'On Chancery Lane,' Pyke said, nodding.

'What business did you have with my lawyer?'

'Well, I knew for a start you did not keep certain important documents here at the hall.'

'Who told you that?'

Pyke shrugged as though it was not important.

'Dammit, what did you say to my lawyer?'

'I put a pistol to his head and told him that if he didn't produce your will from inside his safe, I would blow his brains out.'

Edmonton stared at him, open-mouthed. 'And did he?'

'The will *and* the codicil. I looked at both. I told him to hold on to the will. I kept the codicil for myself.'

He produced the document from his pocket and tossed

it on to the bed so Edmonton could see that it was the genuine article.

'I'll destroy it after I have killed you, of course,' Pyke said, calmly.

'But if you shoot me, there'll be an investigation. My lawyer will talk. In which case, you will never get your hands on my money.' There was a rushed, panicky tone in his voice.

Pyke picked up one of Edmonton's pillows and plumped it with his fist. 'But let's just imagine for a minute that you were to die peacefully. From a heart attack. The stress of having to watch all those angry people gathered outside your gates.' Pyke shrugged. 'You're no longer a young man and, I have to say, you're not in the best physical condition. Do you think anyone would really find it so surprising?'

Edmonton cowered as Pyke stood over him, holding the pillow with both hands. 'There won't even be an investigation.'

'Now really, Pyke, be a good chap. I'm sure that we can come to some kind of . . . manly accommodation.'

'Swift is dead. So is Fox. It's time to answer for what you have done.' Pyke stood over him, waiting. 'I found your wife in an asylum in Portsmouth. Very soon, she'll be back here at Hambledon where she belongs.'

The shock in Edmonton's eyes was as palpable as his disbelief. But before he had the opportunity to register it in words, Pyke pressed the pillow down on his face. As he did so, he said, 'Before you die I want you to be aware of what is going to happen. Your daughter will inherit your estate. I will marry your daughter. If or when Emily produces a son, then he will inherit your title. *My son* will inherit your title.'

Edmonton struggled, of course, but he was no match for Pyke's superior physical strength. All in all, it did not take more than a few minutes. Once it was finished Pyke placed the pillow down on the bed, wiped the saliva from his mouth, and arranged Edmonton's corpse to make it seem as if he had passed away in his sleep.

Pyke should have felt elated, but as he contemplated the previous days and months – and thought about his own complicity in what had happened – he felt no satisfaction. Instead, as he wandered across to the window and looked down at the protesters who were gathering outside the main gates, he felt a gnawing sense of guilt and loneliness that would not be easily put to rest.

Outside, he heard a rifle shot.

Lord Edmonton's funeral was a solemn but elaborate affair. His giant coffin, covered with a pall embroidered with the family's coat of arms, was carried into St Paul's Cathedral by eight heavy-set pall-bearers, preceded by two feathermen carrying trays of black plumes, a man holding a staff with a black ribbon tied around it, countless pages and attendants and, of course, the mourners themselves. The roll-call of those who attended the funeral read like a 'who's who' of London society. There was an impressive turnout from the Tory party grandees. Lord Eldon attended in a wheelchair. The duke of Cumberland arrived wearing the uniform of a Hanoverian general and wept bitterly throughout the long service. The duke of Wellington – the Prime Minister himself – represented the government and studiously avoided, among others, Lord Winchelsea, with whom he had recently conducted an aborted duel over the issue of the duke's apparent 'about-turn' over the Catholic question. During the service, Sir Edward Knatchbull was heard to utter to his friend Lord Newcastle that Edmonton's death marked 'the end of an era'. Peel did not attend but sent a garland. The men were indistinguishable in their black coats, black trousers, black cloaks and tall black hats. A few of the hats had weepers tied around them.

As Edmonton's surviving child and heiress to his estate, Emily wore a black scarf and hood over a black dress. As she followed the coffin up the aisle at the end of the service, Pyke, who had watched the proceedings from a concealed position in the cathedral's gallery, studied her reaction carefully. Her face was a mask of composure.

Earlier in the week, Pyke had asked his uncle how Emily had reacted when she had first laid eyes on her mother. Godfrey chuckled and said, 'After the shock had subsided?' He waited a moment and added, 'She burst into tears.'

'And then?'

'She hugged her, wouldn't let go. The poor old woman didn't know what had happened to her.'

'And then?'

'You mean did she say anything about your role in the business?'

'Well?'

'She wanted to know how you'd found out . . .'

'But was she . . .'

'Grateful? Indebted? Happy?'

Pyke shrugged, not knowing what to say.

Godfrey smiled knowingly. 'You'll have to ask her yourself.'

EPILOGUE

The marriage was not announced in any newspaper, nor did news of their nuptials appear in any gossip magazine or society column. Given the proximity of the ceremony to Edmonton's funeral service, Emily felt it would be prudent to delay any announcement until at least after Christmas. As it was, Pyke's pardon elicited much attention and controversy. Newspaper journalists and columnists pursued him relentlessly, even after he had resigned his position as a Bow Street Runner. They wanted to know how someone who had been fairly tried for murdering his mistress and who had sensationally escaped from Newgate prison, having killed the prison's governor in the process, could be deserving of a Home Office pardon. For a while, one or two of the more committed journalists sought to make a connection between Pyke's pardon and the St Giles murders, but none of them ever got close to determining what had taken place.

To escape this unwanted attention, Pyke and Emily retired to the Hambledon estate, together with Emily's mother, who had not recovered her mental faculties but was nonetheless doted on by her daughter. Emily had decided against making her mother's 'return from the dead' public because she did not want to draw further attention to her family's affairs.

Meanwhile, in order to address the problem of

disturbances on the Hambledon estate, Pyke lowered the exorbitant rents that were charged to farmers on the proviso that they agreed to pay their labourers more and offer better terms of employment. He also scrapped the unsavoury practice of tithing. In a stormy meeting with outraged local church leaders, he informed them they would have to earn or deserve any money that was paid to them in the future. But he could do nothing to prevent the arrest of fifteen protesters, including Saville and Canning, and when they were tried and found guilty of criminal damage and inciting revolution, it took another meeting with Tilling to persuade the Home Secretary to commute their sentences. They were transported to an Australian penal colony rather than hanged.

The following year saw the outbreak of agricultural rioting across many of the southern counties, but Hambledon remained largely untouched by the trouble.

In the end, Edmonton's will was uncontroversial and uncontested. The estate passed to Emily, as his only direct descendant. By the same token, Godfrey, who had 'inherited' Pyke's gin palace, having tried initially to return it to its former 'glory', signed the establishment over to an acquaintance after a particularly nasty brawl had left two men dead and another wounded.

On the night of their wedding, surrounded by the clothes that they had discarded, Pyke had watched the shadow of Emily's lean body flicker against the white wall of their bedroom in the ebbing candlelight. He remembered being surprised by the potency of his own feelings; the air around them was cool and reassuring and he had run his trembling fingers through her hair, kissed her mouth and pulled her down gently on to him. She hadn't seemed at all nervous. He remembered the way she had smiled at him, confident, in control. Aside from this, her look had been unreadable.

Later, she had dug her fingernails into the small of his back and whispered that she loved him, as though the notion surprised even her; and he had felt a tidal wave of euphoria sweep through him and, before he could stop it, he had finished in a series of painful spasms.

Afterwards, as they lay still, wrapped in each other's limp arms, she'd asked him what his first name was.

'Isn't it strange that we're now married and I still don't know what to call you?' Her tone was affectionate.

'What's the problem? Just call me Pyke,' he said, gently running his fingers across her bare shoulder.

'The same as everyone else.'

'You'll never be the same as anyone else.'

'Fine words.' She punched him playfully on the arm.

A little later, Pyke decided to ask her a question that had been bothering him for a long time. 'The second or third time I met you, after you'd given me a tour of Newgate, you said to me, "People aren't who you imagine them to be," and then added, "That applies to you as well as me." '

He felt her stiffen a little in his arms. 'You have a good memory.'

'What did you mean?' He hesitated, 'Why did you say it?'

Emily laughed, unconvincingly. 'I don't remember now.'

Pyke, though, wasn't ready to let the subject go. 'In what way were *you* not the person I might have imagined?'

'How can I possibly answer that, Pyke?' She sounded irritated. 'I don't know how you imagined me, do I?'

'Oh, I imagined you to be virtuous, honest, generous, open.'

For a while, they were both silent. 'And you don't think I am those things now?' She wouldn't look at him.

'I didn't say that.'

Emily wriggled free from his grasp and sat up. 'So what are you saying, then?'

'I was watching you talk to Jo today. I noticed how *close* the two of you seem to be.'

'What's this all about, Pyke? Am I being accused of inappropriate interactions with my servant?' Her tone and body language suggested she was tired but Pyke knew she was rattled, too.

'I'm not accusing you of anything.' Pyke waited for a moment. 'But if I asked what business your servant Jo had following me even before I had first visited Hambledon, what would you say?'

In the darkness, he could not make out Emily's expression. 'I don't understand, Pyke.'

He told Emily about his sighting of Jo in the Blue Dog tavern and said Jo's intervention had possibly saved his life.

'But why might Jo have been following you?'

'Perhaps she was assessing me.'

'Assessing you? For what purpose?' Something in Emily's voice struck an odd note.

'Or for what role?' Pyke waited for a moment. 'And I was also wondering what if Jo knew more than she let on, the time she came and visited me in the church.'

'You're talking in riddles.'

'She told me about your proposed meeting with James Sloan. She also happened to mention she'd overheard your father in conversation with his lawyer, something about a codicil to his will.'

'A codicil?' Emily's voice was quieter, her tone less combative.

'Did you know that your father had drawn up a codicil to his will?'

For a while, Emily didn't answer. The atmosphere between them grew strained, even tense. 'If I said that I'm happy now, happier than I could ever have imagined, and that you're the reason for my happiness, would that be a sufficient answer?'

'I'd be flattered, of course.'

'What you did for me, finding and rescuing my mother, and taking such good care of her, was the kindest, noblest thing anyone has ever done for me.' Now his eyes had adjusted to the darkness, he saw tears streaking her cheek.

'I did it because I wanted to.'

'But you're still not *reassured*?'

'In this codicil, your father stipulated that, after his death, not a penny of his money was to go to charitable causes.'

'I see.' Emily's expression was troubled. 'Don't you think some questions are best left unanswered?'

'Like whether you actually believe your father died of a heart attack?'

That drew a sigh of indignation, possibly even anger. 'What is it you want from me?'

But Pyke knew he already had everything he wanted. In the back of his mind, he had known all along that Emily had wanted something from him, and perhaps had selected him for a role that he himself had been happy enough to fulfil. It made it sound so calculating, so cold. Perhaps it was. Perhaps he had willingly allowed himself to be used. Perhaps he had used Emily himself, for he now had everything *he* had ever wanted. Edmonton's estate was in a rotten condition – it had long been mismanaged and, in spite of his greedy, high-handed ways, the cost of maintenance still outstripped rents – but the land itself was worth more money than Pyke had ever dreamt of, and he had married a woman he loved. But did it matter? Pyke thought about something he'd said to Peel. Virtue was defined by its consequences. What were the consequences, then? Emily had sufficient money to fund her charitable works. Edmonton was dead. But so were Lizzie, Mary

Johnson, Gerald McKeown, Stephen and Davy Magennis, Clare and her baby. And despite it all, Pyke was happy, or as happy as a man of his cautious disposition knew how to be. So did it matter that Emily had used him in some still-undefined way?

As Pyke pondered this question, Emily turned her back on him, the white cotton sheet draped across her shoulders. Even in the semi-darkness, he could admire her slim figure, her shapely, defined arms, the thickness of her hair. Instinctively, he reached out and gently touched the small of her back. She neither flinched nor moved in any way. In the end, Emily had done what she had needed to do, what *he* would have done. He could perhaps admire her even more, if that were possible, for her fortitude and cunning. It was true she had not been entirely honest with him, but he had never rated honesty as an important virtue; better to get what you wanted than be virtuous or honest. Momentarily taken aback by the strength of his feelings, he thought of what might become of them – intoxicating scenarios involving devotion, fun, passionate sex, maybe even children; and morbid ones, involving disease, loneliness and slow, painful death – and could no longer restrain himself. But this time, Emily was prepared for his touch and, in that moment, any niggling doubts dissipated before they had the chance to take root.

'Pyke?'

'It doesn't matter,' he whispered gently in her ear.

'What doesn't matter?'

'What we were just talking about.'

'How do you *know* that it doesn't matter?' But her expression was not accusatory.

Pyke kissed her gently on the forehead because he could not think of an appropriate answer.

A while later, she said, 'Do you think something good can come from something terrible?'

'The idea that virtue begets virtue is the least truthful of all the untruthful Christian doctrines.' But he didn't want to know what Emily thought to be terrible.

'So do you think that we might be . . . *happy*?'

He pulled away from her slightly, only to be able to see her expression; eyes that were warm and moist.

'*Might* be happy?'

'All right. Do you think we *will* be happy?'

'Do you?'

'Of course,' she said, laughing nervously. In the darkness, her skin was smoother than alabaster. 'What about you?' She bit her lip and tilted her head slightly to one side.

Briefly Pyke thought about the baby, strangled and discarded in a metal pail for no other reason than it had been crying. Shivering, he pulled Emily towards him, felt her warmth envelop him, and even before he had opened his mouth, he knew he was going to lie.

ACKNOWLEDGEMENTS

Thanks to Paul Cobley, Roger Cottrell, David Dwan, Adrian Street, Caroline Sumpter and Dave Torrens for either reading the manuscript and offering invaluable feedback or helping me to think more clearly about the subjects informing the novel in general. Thanks also to my agent, Luigi Bonomi, who persevered with me from start to finish and offered judicious advice and encouragement throughout and to Helen Garnons-Williams whose editorial insights and suggestions for revision significantly improved the finished manuscript. Above all, thanks to Debbie Lisle for sticking with me on this, offering unflagging enthusiasm and love, reading endless drafts and always providing incisive, supportive advice. This novel is dedicated to her.

While not making any great claims to historical accuracy, I have at least tried to evoke something of this fascinating historical period and, to this end, I am greatly indebted to the following and, by no means exhaustive, list of references: Peter Ackroyd, *London*; J. C. Becket et al., *Belfast*; Douglas Gordon Brown, *The Rise of Scotland Yard*; Patricia Craig, ed., *The Belfast Anthology*; Norman Gash, *Mr Secretary Peel*; Arthur Griffiths, *The Chronicles of Newgate*; Kevin Haddick-Flynn, *A Short History of Orangeism*; Eric Hollingsworth, *The Newgate Novel*; Fergus Linanne, *London's Underworld*; Donald Low, *The Regency Underworld*; Henry Mayhew, *London's Underworld*; John Marriot, ed., *Unknown London*; Edward Pearce, *Reform!*; Elaine Reynolds,

Before the Bobbies; Donald Thomas, *The Victorian Underworld*; E. P. Thompson, *The Making of the English Working Class*; George Theodore Wilkinson, ed., *The Newgate Calendar*; Sarah Wise, *The Italian Boy*. It goes without saying that the mistakes, and I am sure there are many of them, are all mine.